THE FAR FIELD

Praise for *The Far Field*

"Consuming . . . Vijay's command of storytelling is so supple that it's easy to discount the stealth with which she constructs her tale, shifting time frames with seamless ease and juggling a wealth of characters who cling to the heart. The show-stealer is Shalini's mercurial mother, an 'outrageous queen' of capricious gestures. Vijay smartly resists psychoanalyzing her, implying that the china-shop bulls in our families can be survived but never entirely explained away."

—*New York Times Book Review*

"Ambitious . . . Vijay's descriptions of the mountains, the people and their everyday lives are beautiful, and that makes the hidden ugliness all the more disturbing; this is a seriously impressive debut."

—*The Times* (UK)

"A beautifully nuanced tale in these times of no nuance . . . A febrile tension pulsates on each page of this coming-of-age story. *The Far Field* is an accomplished debut."

—*The Hindu*

"A masterful piece of fiction. Vijay writes with an assurance surprising in a first-time novelist, and is a delight to read. And while this is an in-depth expansion on the history and people of Jammu and Kashmir (humane but never sentimental), it is her protagonist who compels most, as Shalini watches her certainties gradually taken away from her and then returned laden with nuance and complexity."

—*Observer*

"Vijay probes grand themes—tribalism, despotism, betrayal, death, resurrection—in exquisite but unflowery prose, and with sincere sentiment but little sentimentality . . . Kashmir itself emerges in vivid details: the taste of salted chai, the 'dark rise of the mountains, freckled with their hundreds of glittering homes.'"

—*New Yorker*

"*The Far Field* is most poignant when it exposes the unintentional havoc of good intentions . . . For the vast majority of us, who hear of the troubles in Kashmir only as a faint strain in the general din of world tragedies, *The Far Field* offers something essential: a chance to glimpse the lives of distant people captured in prose gorgeous enough to make them indelible—and honest enough to make them real."

—*Washington Post*

"Ms. Vijay is an effortlessly assured prose writer . . . The book's length led me to expect something slow and atmospheric, but to my surprise I snapped it up in two sittings . . . *The Far Field* is illuminating about the persecutions in Kashmir, but at its heart it is about the ironclad laws of class by which all India is ruled."

—*Wall Street Journal*

"What makes this compelling book so page-turning is not the larger political situation but the drama of small, fraught human interactions . . . Vijay's mastery of traditional narrative skills wouldn't be out of place in a classic 19th-century novel . . . *The Far Field* is an impressive performance. It will be fascinating to see what Vijay does next."

—*Sunday Times*

"A courageous, insightful and affecting debut novel."

—*The Economist*

"Madhuri Vijay's supremely accomplished debut novel . . . is an expansive and wonderfully immersive work . . . [It] gives us a brilliant outsider's view of an exotic, off-the-beaten-track realm and a compelling portrayal of a character gradually unraveling due to forces beyond her control. This is a stunning novel that skillfully grapples with the complexities of human relationships. Madhuri Vijay's career looks very bright indeed."

—*Minneapolis Star Tribune*

"Luminous in outlining a young woman's struggle to shape her own life . . . One of Vijay's gifts is that she can make us feel for a protagonist who knows so little, yet yearns so deeply for something beyond her cushioned life . . . [A] remarkable story, and Vijay is likely to be a talent to watch."

—*Financial Times*

"Stunning . . . *The Far Field* chafes against the useless pity of outsiders and instead encourages a much more difficult solution: cross-cultural empathy."

—*Paris Review*

"*The Far Field* is a book about big ideas . . . It's a lot to ask of a novel, but Vijay knows exactly what she's doing. Precise, restrained and possessing a lightness of touch that eludes most writers, *The Far Field* is most thrilling in its heralding of a voice that is completely assured, and conveys a rare emotional wisdom while sidestepping any hints of the mawkish."

—*Indian Express*

"Loss can make a detective out of anyone . . . It can also, as Madhuri Vijay so thornily illustrates in her debut novel, *The Far Field,* blind us from all that's around us . . . *The Far Field* becomes a layered examination of pressing Indian political conflicts . . . Here is a singular story of mother and daughter—a loving, broken bond so strong it touches, changes, and hurts countless lives beyond theirs."

—*Entertainment Weekly*

"Arresting . . . captures Kashmir's everyday horror with exhilarating, puissant prose . . . *The Far Field* stands as an important reminder that all privilege is, in the end, political."

—*Bomb Magazine*

"Vijay is an astute chronicler of the everyday emotions that roil seemingly calm lives, whether in Bengaluru or in Kashmir. She is also a sharp observer of the myriad ways in which the Indian aspirational classes gloss over the state violence in Kashmir."

—*India Today*

"History, class prejudice, Indian politics, grief, guilt and the limits of compassion intertwine in this enthralling debut."

—*Newsweek*

"Hauntingly beautiful . . . *The Far Field* is rich in poignancy, in story and characters."

—*Hindustan Times*

"In Madhuri Vijay's exquisite debut novel, *The Far Field,* grief propels a young woman to northern India, where she seeks answers about her mother's past. She meets people and communities constantly on the brink of political violence, upending her assumptions about herself and her country."

—*Elle*

"The book's first and final chapters end with the same direct phrase: 'I am thirty years old and that is nothing.' Between the first and second time the reader sees these words, a story exploring the passage of time and the repercussions of one's actions sets out to ask the charged question of what it is that we spend our lives searching for."

—*Vanity Fair*

"Deals with big questions—Indian politics, class, history and sexuality—through beautiful prose."

—*Huffington Post* (India)

"Vijay is brilliant in capturing the anomie born of deep loneliness and repressed, raw emotions . . . *The Far Field*, while tracing a difficult narrative of vast political, cultural, and humanitarian import, does not offer easy, totalising, and predictable resolutions."

—*Scroll* (India)

"Go read this absorbing and remarkable first book. And look out for future writing from Madhuri Vijay."

—*Deccan Herald*

"Vijay intertwines her story's threads with dazzling skill. Dense, layered, impossible to pin—or put—down, her first novel is an engrossing tale of love and grief, politics and morality. Combining up-close character studies with finely plotted drama, this is a triumphant, transporting debut."

—*Booklist* (starred)

"[R]emarkable . . . an engrossing narrative of individual angst played out against political turmoil . . . Shalini's misguided attempts at love, fulfillment, and friendship are poignant. Vijay's stunning debut novel expertly intertwines the personal and political to pick apart the history of Jammu and Kashmir."

—*Publishers Weekly* (starred)

"Dazzling . . . Vijay's prose is exquisite, florid and descriptive at times, spare and pared back at others. The story keeps twisting unexpectedly until the end, keeping emotions fraught, questions percolating. [*The Far Field* is] a scintillating novel from a truly gifted writer."

—*Bookpage* (starred)

"Narrating Shalini's journey in chapters that alternate between past and present and utilizing strong characterizations throughout, Vijay has crafted an engaging, suspenseful, and impressive debut."

—*Library Journal*

"Vivid . . . [E]legant, calm prose and intense evocations of people and places . . . A striking debut."

—*Kirkus Reviews*

"[N]ot only is it an exceptional novel ... it also tells a story that the world would do well to read at the moment."

—Somak Ghoshal, *Livemint*

"*The Far Field* stands out as a debut novel because it displays two acts of courage: one, at just about 450 pages, it has heft . . . Vijay is not afraid to tell a long and complex story on a large canvas . . . Her second act of courage is presenting her reader people that are not easy to like—almost every one of her characters is deeply flawed, motivated by a constellation of impulses that are not always noble. This is a mature book, even when it wears its political heart on its sleeve."

—Arshia Sattar, *Explocity Bangalore*

"*The Far Field* is an irresistible blend of moral subtlety and intellectual precision. Ingeniously conceived and elegantly written, it is a first novel of startling accomplishment."

—Pankaj Mishra, author of *Age of Anger*

"A strikingly unusual book full of beauty and surprise."

—Sonia Faleiro, author of *Beautiful Thing*

"Vijay's characters are compelling and beguiling, and she superbly balances the complexity of her narrator against the conflict in Kashmir without allowing the latter to be reduced to a mere backdrop. *The Far Field* is incisive and utterly enthralling."

—Siddhartha Deb, author of *The Beautiful and the Damned*

"*The Far Field* is remarkable, a novel at once politically timely and morally timeless. Madhuri Vijay traces the fault lines of history, love, and obligation running through a fractured family and country. Few novels generate enough power to transform their characters, fewer still their readers. *The Far Field* does both."

—Anthony Marra, author of *The Tsar of Love and Techno*

"I loved this novel. Shalini is an utterly convincing narrator, particularly in her naïveté, which might very well serve as a metaphor for her country's refusal to see what it has wrought in Kashmir. Madhuri Vijay has written a brilliant and important book."

—Liaquat Ahamed, author of *Lords of Finance*

"I am in awe of Madhuri Vijay. With poised and measured grace, *The Far Field* tells a story as immediate and urgent as life beyond the page. I will think of these characters—tender and complex, mysterious and flawed, remarkably real to me—for years to come, as though I have lived alongside them."

—Anna Noyes, author of *Goodnight, Beautiful Women*

"I had to remind myself while reading *The Far Field* that this is the work of a debut novelist, and not a mid-career book by a master writer at the height of her powers

. . . Only the very best novels are *experienced,* as opposed to merely *read,* and this is one of those rare and brilliant novels."

—Ben Fountain, author of *Beautiful Country, Burn Again*

"This riveting and utterly unique book faces the most troubling and insoluble questions with a bold, keen clarity that has no patience for anything less than the most complete truth . . . The fierce and wonderful undertow of Vijay's flawless prose masterfully propels this story about loyalty, about how we create and sustain and protect and inevitably break down our bonds with other people."

—Merritt Tierce, author of *Love Me Back*

"Utterly immersive and vividly realized, *The Far Field* is that rare gem of a novel which effortlessly transports the reader into distant, unfamiliar terrain through the force of a story deeply anchored in the humanity of its characters. Madhuri Vijay's debut marks the arrival of an astonishing new talent."

—Elliot Ackerman, author of *Waiting for Eden*

"Stunning in its artistry, in its engagement with the world and the personal, this is a profound and monumental achievement composed with rage, vulnerability, humor, grief, and mystery. How dangerous this novel is, in the very best of ways, and how grateful I am for this writer and for her creation."

—Paul Yoon, author of *The Mountain*

"*The Far Field* is an impressively ambitious novel of stunning emotional and psychological acuity. This deeply introspective story, located in troubled Kashmir, is also a panoramic exploration of our ideas and assumptions about nationhood. Rendered in visually evocative, lucid prose, and driven by a fragile but compelling narrator-protagonist, this tragic novel teems with unforgettable characters. We are proud to celebrate the arrival of a luminous new talent in Indian literature."

—The JCB Prize for Literature 2019 Jury

"From Bangalore to Kishtwar and from Kishtwar to a remote mountain village in Kashmir, this is a story which traverses far even as its protagonist Shalini tries to unravel sides to her mother's life that she had shown little interest in when the mother was alive. A very personal story, firmly rooted in the realist tradition, it shows what happens when well-intentioned but ignorant do-gooders stray into territories and histories that they know little or nothing about."

—The DSC Prize for South Asian Literature 2019 Jury

THE FAR FIELD

A NOVEL

MADHURI VIJAY

FOURTH ESTATE • *New Delhi*

First published in the United States of America and Canada in 2019 by Grove Atlantic Inc.
First published in Great Britain in 2019 by Grove Press UK,
an imprint of Grove Atlantic Inc.

First published in India in 2019 by Fourth Estate
An imprint of HarperCollins *Publishers*

HarperCollins Publishers India, Cyber City, Building 10-A, Gurugram,
Haryana-122002, India
www.harpercollins.co.in

This edition published in India in 2020 by Fourth Estate

2 4 6 8 10 9 7 5 3 1

P-ISBN: 978-93-5357-793-3
E-ISBN: 978-93-5357-096-5

Printed and bound at
MicroPrints India, New Delhi

MIX
Paper
FSC FSC® C218906

This product is made of FSC®-certified and other controlled material.

HarperCollins Publishers, Macken House, 39/40 Mayor Street
Upper, Dublin 1, D01 C9W8, Ireland

For MBK, who loved to read

and

for X, who makes this island seem a world, and the world seem our island

Something else is yet to happen, only where and what?
Someone will head toward them, only when and who,
in how many shapes and with what intentions?
Given a choice,
maybe he will choose not to be the enemy and
leave them with some kind of life.

Wisława Szymborska, "Some People"

I

1

I AM THIRTY YEARS old and that is nothing.

I know what this sounds like, and I hesitate to begin with something so obvious, but let me say it anyway, at the risk of sounding naïve. And let it stand alongside this: six years ago, a man I knew vanished from his home in the mountains. He vanished in part because of me, because of certain things I said, but also things I did not have, until now, the courage to say. So, you see, there is nothing to be gained by pretending to a wisdom I do not possess. What I am, what I was, and what I have done—all of these will become clear soon enough.

This country, already ancient when I was born in 1982, has changed every instant I've been alive. Titanic events have ripped it apart year after year, each time rearranging it along slightly different seams and I have been touched by none of it: prime ministers assassinated, peasant-guerrillas waging war in emerald jungles, fields cracking under the iron heel of a drought, nuclear bombs cratering the wide desert floor, lethal gases blasting from pipes and into ten thousand lungs, mobs crashing against mobs and always coming away bloody. Consider this: even now, at this very moment, there are people huddled in a room somewhere, waiting to die. This is what I have told myself for the last six years, each time I have had the urge to speak. *It will make no difference in the end.*

But lately the urge has turned into something else, something with sharper edges, which sticks under the ribs and makes it dangerous to breathe.

So let me be clear, here at the start.

If I do speak, if I do tell what happened six years ago in that village in the mountains, a village so small it appears only on military maps, it will not be for reasons of nobility. The chance for nobility is over. Even this, story or confession or whatever it turns out to be, is too late.

My mother asleep. The summer afternoon, the sun an open wound, the air outside straining with heat and noise. But here, in our living room, the curtains are drawn; there is a dim and deadly silence. My mother lies on the sofa, cheek pressed to the armrest, asleep.

The bell rings. She doesn't open her eyes right away, but there is movement behind her lids, the long return from wherever she has been. She stands, walks to the door.

Hello, madam, hello, hello, I am selling some very nice pens—

Good afternoon, madam, please listen to this offer, if you subscribe to one magazine, you get fifty percent—

A long-lashed boy with a laminated sign: *I am from Deaf and Dumb Society—*

"Oh, get lost," my mother says. And shuts the door.

Somebody once described my mother as "a strong woman." From the speaker's tone, I knew it was not intended as a compliment. This was, after all, the woman who cut off all contact with her own father after he repeatedly ignored his wife's chronic lower back pain, which turned out to be the last stages of pancreatic cancer; the woman who once broke a flickering lightbulb by flinging a scalding hot vessel of rice at it; the woman whose mere approach made shopkeepers hurry into the back, praying for invisibility; the woman who sometimes didn't sleep for three nights in a row; the woman who nodded sympathetically through our neighbor's fond complaints about the naughtiness of her five-year-old son, then said, with every appearance of sincerity, "He sounds awful. Shall I slit his throat for you and get it over with?"

This was the woman whose daughter I am. Was. Am. All else flows from that.

When she died, I was twenty-one, in my last year of college. When I got the call, I took an overnight bus back to Bangalore, carrying nothing but a fistful of change from the ticket. Eleven people came to her funeral, including my father, me, and Stella, our maid, who brought her youngest son. We stood near the doorway, wedged between the blazing mouth of the electric crematorium and the March heat. The only breeze came from Stella's son, who kept spinning the red rotors of a toy helicopter.

The evening after the funeral, after everybody had gone, my father shut himself into his bedroom, and I left the house and walked. Between the two of us, we had finished several pegs of rum and a quarter bottle of whiskey. I found myself standing on a busy main road with no recollection of having arrived there. People flowed around me, shops and bars glittered and trembled, and I tried to think of the future. In a few days, I would return to college; my final-year exams were just weeks away. After that? I would pack up my things and return to Bangalore. After that? Nothing.

A bus rattled past, mostly empty, only a few tired heads lolling in the windows. A waiter in a dirty banian dumped a bucket of chalky water onto the road in front of a restaurant. Earlier that day, while a gangly priest droned on and on, my father had overturned my mother's ashes into a scummy green concrete tank, and then he had continued, somewhat helplessly, to hold on to the clay urn. Without thinking, I snatched it from his hand and dropped it onto a rubbish pile. It was something my mother herself might have done. The look on the vadhyar's face was of shock and faintly delighted disgust. I waited for my father to bring it up later, but he didn't.

I stood in the same spot until the waiter, now with two other men, emerged from the restaurant. They were dressed to go out, in close-fitting shirts lustrous as fish scales. They passed right before me. I heard a scrap of their laughter and tensed, ready for a fight, waiting for the leer, the catcall, the line from a love song. But instead they crossed the road and were gone.

Though he insisted on all the right rituals for my mother, my father claimed to have shed god and Brahminism long ago, in his own youth, finding a substitute in engineering, Simon and Garfunkel, *The Wealth of Nations*, and long-haired college companions who drank late into the night, filling the room with Wills smoke and boozy rants about politics, both of which eddied and went nowhere. Three years of a master's degree at Columbia left him with a fondness for America, especially her jazz, her confidence, and her coffee, which, he liked to say happily, was the worst he'd ever tasted. When he returned to India, he worked for a few years; then my grandfather, as had always been the plan, provided him with the capital to start a factory manufacturing construction equipment, and, when that foundered and fell apart, more capital for a second factory, which flourished.

My father, in those years, liked to speak of rationality and pragmatism as though they were personal friends of his, yet it was he who inevitably rose to his feet at the end of our dinner parties, who raised his glass and declared, blinking away tears, "To you, my dear friends, and to this rarest of nights." He had the intelligent man's faith in the weight of his own ideas, and the emotional man's impatience with anyone who did not share them. As he grew older and more successful, his confidence did not change; it merely settled and became wider, a well-fed confidence.

Only my mother could make him falter. She had, apparently, made him falter the day he arrived on a brand-new motorcycle to inspect as a potential bride the youngest daughter of a mid-level Indian Railways employee. He saw a woman standing barefoot on the street, wearing a shabby cotton sari. He asked if he was in the right place, and my mother replied, "Certainly, if what you're here to do is look ridiculous." My father used to love to tell this story, and also to tell how she had rejected suitor after suitor before him, one for asking about her family's dental and medical history, one for inquiring whether the dowry would be paid in gold or cash, one simply for smiling too much. I have no way of knowing if any of this is true, since my mother never told stories, least of all about herself, but I've heard they went on a walk, during which my father outlined his plans for his life: grow the company for a couple of years, have a child in three, maybe another child the year after. At the end, he paused for my mother's reaction. "Well, you *do* talk a lot," she said thoughtfully. "But if you're going to be working all day, I suppose I won't have to listen to most of it."

My mother, with her lightning tongue and her small collection of idols on a shelf in the kitchen. My mother, with her stubborn refusal to admit the existence of meat or other faiths, who crossed the street when we passed a halal butcher with his row of skinned goats, their flanks pink and shiny as burn scars. My father did not eat meat either, but he was quick to add that it was personal preference; according to him, there was "no logic-based argument against the consumption of meat." I myself had sampled bites of chicken and mutton, even beef, from friends' lunch boxes, and, apart from an initial queasiness, I liked them all. The one time I made the mistake of telling my mother, she held out her arm and said, "Still hungry, little beast?"

She could be vicious, and yet there were times, especially in a crowd, when she was pure energy, drawing the world to herself. She was already tall, but at these times, she became immense. Her mouth would fall open, and her crooked incisor, which looked like a single note held on a piano, acquired an oblique seductiveness. Men approached her, even when I was present. During a function at my father's factory one year, his floor manager tried to flatter her. "That's a beautiful sari," he said, his eyes on her breasts. The floor manager was an energetic stub of a man, who had been with my father since the beginning, had slept on the factory floor so they could save on a watchman. I had attended his son's birthday parties. Now he was looking at my mother's breasts. She was eating a samosa from a silver-foil plate, and there were crumbs on her cheek. Without pausing in her chewing, she said, "The conference room is empty. Shall we go?" The floor manager swallowed hard then glanced at me, as if I, a child, might tell him what to do. He sputtered something about getting her another samosa, and almost tripped on his flight to the buffet table. My mother shot me a quick, arch look before walking away.

It was only when she prayed in front of her idols that she shrank, became a person with ordinary dimensions. Every morning, she tucked flowers around their brass necks and lit the blackened lamp and stood for a minute without bending or moving her lips. My father wisely refrained from making his usual speech about the irrationality of organized religion, and she, in turn, chose not to point out that his beloved college LP collection, carefully dusted and alphabetized, was as good as a shrine. Likewise, my mother never insisted that I prostrate myself or learn the names of her gods, though I sometimes wish she had. She never forbade me from joining either, but it was implicit. And in that lay the fundamental irony of our relationship, and the clearest evidence of how she saw the world: my mother considered me, her only child, a suitable accomplice for the greatest secret of her life, but when she prayed, she wanted to be alone.

Here is another story my father once loved to tell: When I was about two, I went through a phase where I belonged, body and soul, to him.

I screamed bloody murder if he was in the room and not holding me, bloodier still when my mother tried to take me from him. I tolerated her while he was at work, but barely. One afternoon, seeing I was in a rare, calm mood, she hustled me out to go grocery shopping with her. It was a mistake. While she swiftly chose flour and oil, biscuits and tea, I'd started to whimper. By the time she was ready to pay, I'd launched into a full-blown tirade, howling, hitting her on the side of the head, clinging to any stranger that passed by. My mother was finally forced to ask the shopkeeper if she could use his phone. She called my father and explained, and thirty minutes later, he burst in with outstretched arms. He carried me home, a shameless, grinning trophy, while my mother trailed behind us, lugging the groceries.

I don't know when my allegiance shifted, when I went from being his to being hers. All I know are the facts: I was my father's daughter first, and then I became, gradually and irrevocably, my mother's. It's hard not to wonder how much might have been prevented if only I had loved him more, or, perhaps, loved her a little less. But that is useless thinking, and perilous. Better to let things stand as they were: she, my incandescent mother, and I, her little beast.

2

After the funeral and its gritty, exhausting aftermath, I went back to college for my final-year exams, which I barely passed. Without waiting for the inane graduation celebrations, I packed up my things and returned to Bangalore. Apart from my mother's absence, nothing had changed. My father still woke early and drove to the gym, sweatband around his wrist, towel over his shoulder. Stella still came in the late mornings, after my father left for the factory. She let herself in with her own key, and, over the next few hours, she scrubbed the vessels, ran the washing machine, swabbed the floors, ironed our clothes, dusted the bookshelves, watered the plants, and cooked enough food for a family of five. It was only I, it seemed, who had nothing to do.

So I began to go out. I agreed to everything. People I hardly knew invited me to clubs to hear their DJ friends play, and later to someone's flat, where the music was always too loud, the floor gluey with spilled beer, and the inevitable poster of Bob Marley grinned down from the wall like some affable, white-toothed deity. I remember faces floating from unlit corners to ask me questions to which my answer was always the same. *Yes,* I said when someone asked if I wanted another drink. *Yes,* I said when someone's hot breath whispered into my neck, *Does this feel good?* I lived by the word, kept it ready under my tongue. *Yes,* I said when they asked if I would be all right.

Thinking about it now, it seems I wasted the better part of the two years after my mother's death, but that isn't exactly true. For about five months, I volunteered as an assistant teacher—a title vastly out of proportion with my actual role—at a government-run school for children with cerebral palsy. I don't recall anymore how it came about, but for a few hours each day I helped a group of bright-eyed eight-year-olds build tottering colorful towers of plastic blocks, supposedly to improve their fine motor skills, while their mothers, usually tired domestic workers or anxious housewives, hovered in the corridor outside. I think I was probably happier there than I knew, and I might have stayed but for a little girl named Suneyna. From the beginning, I adored Suneyna for her shy smile and her habit of unconsciously reaching out to touch me whenever we were working together. Her little hand would wander out and graze some part of my face, my chin or nose, and then she would go on as before, busily choosing blocks, unaware that she had shaken me deeply. Her mother was a beautiful woman of tiny build, who had four other children and whose loud, lemon-sour voice could be heard as soon as she entered the school premises. She was always complaining, within earshot of the classroom, about how Suneyna seemed unimproved and how the school was wasting everyone's time. One afternoon, while the children were practicing their gestures for food, drink, and the desire to go to the toilet, her strident voice floated to us: "Every day this girl Suneyna comes home and does soo-soo all over the floor. I really don't know why I spend all this time bringing her to this useless school. In the end, let me tell you, all that works is a tight slap and a few hours in a room by herself. After that, she behaves like an angel." I remember standing, blocks tumbling to the ground. I remember going into the corridor and addressing Suneyna's diminutive mother for minutes together. I have no recollection of what I said, but by the end there was absolute silence in the school. Then I came back into the classroom. The teacher, as I recall, had some trouble meeting my eye. As for Suneyna, she continued building her tower, but she did not reach out once to touch my face for the rest of the day. That afternoon, I got into my car, drove home and never went back.

In the end, when it finally became clear to my father that I had no intention of helping myself, he got me a position with the daughter of one of his business associates, who had recently founded a tiny non-profit environmental agency in Bangalore. I was to manage accounts for them, a job that, as far as I could see, consisted almost exclusively of telling them what they couldn't do. "I'm sorry," I would say in a firm, regretful tone, "the numbers won't support that." The agency, ironically enough, was located in a building overlooking an open sewer, and though I didn't tell anybody, I thought the sludge rather beautiful, with its slow black currents that flashed green and gold during the hottest parts of the afternoon. Even the smell, ripe with rot, didn't bother me.

The projects the agency tried to implement were small and mostly wishful. Money in the agency was like the sewage beneath it, creeping in with sluggish reluctance, and I, for one, celebrated its immobility. It meant I had less to do. Days, then months, passed as I stared out of my window, while on my computer screen, the numbers stayed in their slots, fixed and comfortingly final.

About a year after I began at the agency, I wandered into my parents' bedroom one evening after work, as I did from time to time. Their cupboards faced each other in an alcove in the corner. As a child, I used to open the far door of each cupboard and hide inside, cradled by their odors: my father's leather belts and ironed shirts and aftershave, my mother's soap and perfume. I suddenly longed for her smell again so I opened her cupboard, only to receive a shock; it had been swept nearly clean. My father must have, at some point, quietly given her things away. Which shouldn't have surprised me, really. We had never been nostalgic people. Growing up, my drawings did not find a place on the fridge, my parents did not lovingly preserve my old report cards. Clothes, outgrown, were given away or ripped up for kitchen rags. Books were promptly donated to the library. We kept pace with the present, discarding as we went.

So it took me aback for a moment, the loss I felt at the sight of those bare shelves. Where had her things gone? Stella might have taken a sari or two, the rest likely given to a charity. Her jewelry was probably locked in the safe-deposit box at the bank. Her talcum powder, her Pond's cream, her jumble of safety pins, her comb, all of those were gone too. Only a few objects remained—a stack of stretched, discolored underwear, a snarled ball of drawstrings, and a peeling laminated photograph of the two idols in her ancestral village, which Stella, with her tidy gold cross, would have had no use for, but at the same time would not have had the heart to throw away.

I ran my hand across the knotted drawstrings and the photograph, and lightly touched the folded underwear, which slumped over. I was just about to close the cupboard when I caught sight of something small and pale peeking from behind the fallen stack. And even before I really saw it, I knew, by some dormant instinct, what I was seeing. I reached out and seized it, clenching hard, then, in a single motion, opened my fist and looked down.

In my palm sat the crude wooden figure of a beast, with stubby limbs and a featureless head. The wood was mottled and shiny with age, but the knife scar I remembered still showed clear across the belly, as if the animal had been injured in a fight. I had not seen it in years, not since I was a child. I'd thought it lost, in fact. I recalled how distraught I'd been when the wooden animal vanished from my room, the hours I'd spent on my hands and knees, scouring the house.

Had it been in my mother's cupboard this whole time? How had it come to be here?

For a long moment, I thought nothing. Then, very gradually, as if I might hurt myself by going too fast, I understood. The animal had not come to be here by accident. My mother had known it was here. No, not known. She had stolen it from my room and *hidden* it here.

A few months before she died, my mother called me at college. She had taken to calling at odd hours, at midnight or very early in the morning. This time it was just as I was dropping off to sleep, having studied late for a test the next day. I was tired and irritable, and, to make things worse, she didn't seem to have much to say. As a way to get her off the phone, I told her, "Why don't you go out tomorrow? Go shopping or something."

"Shopping?" I could hear the slow, mocking smile in her voice.

"Or visit friends."

"A quaint idea. Except that you seem to forget I've never had any."

"That's not true," I said without thinking.

"Oh?" Her sarcasm, always deadliest when it was softest. "Enlighten me then."

I paused before speaking his name. "What about Bashir Ahmed? Wasn't he a friend?"

There was silence on her end. I waited for her to answer, already regretting having mentioned his name. Then she said, "You know, I'd forgotten all about him."

"It's been a while," I agreed carefully. "Where do you think he is now?"

"Oh, who knows. Probably went back to that village he was always going on about."

She hung up soon after that. To tell the truth, I'd been relieved that she hadn't seemed all that interested in Bashir Ahmed. It had been seven years, after all, since the last time we'd seen him, and seven years were ample time for forgetting. But now, with the wooden creature balanced on my sweating palm, I understood that she had, ever so gently, lied to me. She had forgotten nothing.

I carried the creature back to my room, and stood it on my bedside table, the very spot from which my mother had stolen it all those years ago. For the rest of the evening, as I drifted through the rooms of our house, as I paged unseeingly through books, as I sat across from my father, eating the meal Stella had cooked earlier that day, the melancholic strains of Miles Davis's trumpet floating in from the living room, I thought only of the wooden beast, sitting beside my pillow, and, out of nowhere, a huge, unbearable joy exploded in me. Just like that, the secret I'd once shared with my mother was alive again. Looking back, I think that must have been when I decided to find him.

I was six the first time he came, and I still remember it. How my mother had not ceased moving, even for a second, all week. How she had decided the previous morning that her lantana bushes were sick, somehow infected, and had spent three hours pulling them up, only to abruptly abandon them, leaving the garden looking like a war zone. How she had surges of intense laughter at nothing. How she cooked, a pile of vessels growing dangerously high in the sink, but how, at the same time, she claimed never to be hungry. How she seemed to have endless energy for play, devising elaborate games that soon wore me out but left her unaffected.

When the bell rang that afternoon, I was in the living room. I moved to answer, but all of a sudden she was behind me, one hand gripping my shoulder hard. With her other hand, she threw the door open. And there he was: a dark-haired man wearing a green kurta and white skullcap, carrying over his shoulder a distended yellow bundle twice the width of his torso. His thick hair fell over his forehead, which was the color of unpolished rosewood, and his eyes were a light, stunning green. For a second, he stood there (perhaps wondering about the wrecked garden); then, in a deep, resonant voice that would become as recognizable to me as my own, he said to my mother in simple, polite Urdu, "Madam, would you wish to buy these beautiful clothes from Kashmir?"

"Sure," my mother answered, not missing a beat. "But if I do, what will *you* wear?"

The stranger laughed. Unhesitating, glad, as though he not only had been expecting her humor, but had traveled a long way just to hear it. My mother's grip on my shoulder tightened, though I couldn't tell whether it upset or pleased her. She was used to people being disconcerted by the things she said; this laughter was something new.

"Come in," she said in a slightly milder tone. "Let me see what you have."

And here I must ask the unavoidable question. Why him? Of all the people who came to our house over the years, to sell, to work, to visit, why should *he* have been the one she fixed her mind upon? It had to do with her mood that day, of course, the glittering in her eyes that had been there all week, but what else? The fact that he was handsome, in a style utterly foreign to our southern city? Those green eyes, which I'd never seen before, except in actors on TV? Had these things been enough, at least to start with?

He stepped inside with a ceremonial satisfaction, which I would come to think of as his trademark, as if our house were a dazzling place he'd been told of long ago. He hauled the bundle into our living room and tugged it open with an elegant motion, and there were clothes everywhere, spreading like a bright, choppy sea. My mother took a seat on the sofa across from him. I sat in between them. I did not know it then, but these would become our fixed places, our fixed roles: Bashir Ahmed speaking, my mother listening, and me watching them both.

He was riffling through the clothes, speaking rapidly but plainly in Urdu, a speech he'd obviously given many times before. ". . . six months for one piece, and everything is handmade. What shall I show you first, madam? You tell me. Kurtas? Shawls? Saris? Everything is guaranteed, one hundred percent, pure Kashmiri."

"One hundred percent pure Kashmiri," she echoed in a tone that could have just as easily been mockery as admiration. Then she waved her hand. "All of it. Show me all of it."

He began with the shawls. Ruby with pink paisley, white with mint paisley, each edged by a row of soft tassels, sinking one after the other in soft layers across his lap. It was a performance, practiced until flawless. The whole time he did not stop talking, his green eyes moving between my mother's face and the shawls. My mother watched their soundless descent, rapt, and even I, with my tomboy's revulsion for all things feminine, had to admit they were beautiful. When he had shown her all the shawls, she blinked. "Anything else?"

He launched into the same routine with his kurtas, all of which had panels of delicate embroidery down the front. This time he looked deeper into her face, and spoke in a lower, more confidential voice, but she remained still except for her eyes, which stayed riveted to the rise and fall of his hands, as though they might contain some vital code. When he came to the end of the kurtas, he started in with the saris, translucent jewel-tone chiffon with chain-stitched pansies along the borders. And when those too were rejected, he sat back on his heels, surveying the disorder around him, biting his lip, trying to hide his exasperation.

"Hm," my mother murmured, "now where are those beautiful clothes I was told about?"

His frown vanished in an instant. "Madam," he said, shaking his head sorrowfully, "I must be honest with you. I am feeling very bad right now. If I had known about you before coming here, I would have brought my friend with me."

She smiled. "Your friend?"

"Yes. My friend, he sells spectacles, you see. Maybe with the right pair you would have been able to see my clothes properly, and you wouldn't have embarrassed yourself like this."

I'd never heard anybody speak this way to my mother, with such liberty, such daring. She stared at him a moment then threw her head back and laughed and laughed. I imagined he would shrink at that wild, uncontrolled sound. But he didn't. He just looked at her with his head tilted to one side, smiling. Then, as if he'd suddenly remembered, he turned his large head to me. "What about beti here?" he asked her. "Would you like to see something for beti?"

"Yes," my mother said before I could speak. The man dug around in the pile and came up with a white cotton blouse, sprays of delicate pink roses edging the neckline and both sleeves. He shook it out then held it up to his own chest without a trace of self-consciousness. "It is so beautiful," he declared, "it even looks good on an ugly fool like me."

It sounds strange, but he was right. Not that he was ugly or a fool—he wasn't either—but he *did* look startlingly beautiful in that girl's blouse, with his dark hair falling over his forehead and his weathered throat rising so naturally from the pale, flimsy material. I glanced at my mother to find a strange expression on her face, a grimace that seemed to indicate real pain.

"Shalini," she said, and if nothing until then had made me sit up and take notice, that would have. She almost never used my name. "What do you think? Do you like it?"

And even though the blouse was nothing I would have dreamed of choosing for myself, I nodded. It seemed like the only thing to do. Some aspect of her mood had communicated itself to me, but, more than that, I had sensed an unfamiliar thing in the room, a flash of new color for which I had no name. I was rewarded when she reached out and squeezed my hand.

"It seems we'll be taking it," she said.

"It makes me very happy to know that at least *one* of you isn't blind," the man said, and then he, too, smiled at me. I flushed under the weight of their combined attention, one set of eyes green, the other deepest brown.

The man coughed discreetly into his fist and named a price, and, oddly enough, my mother, who ordinarily never lost a chance to haggle, agreed. He smiled, a figure of modest triumph, and began to pack up his wares. For a few seconds, she stared at his hands, which were busy folding and smoothing; then she said, in a rush, "When will you come back?"

He glanced up, startled. He raked his hair back with his fingers, nudging the skullcap askew.

"Ah. I'm not sure. I think—I'm expecting some new items in two or three months." He glanced quickly at her. "Should I—what I mean is, do you want me to—?"

He broke off, because she had started to scowl.

I braced myself. *Now,* I thought. *Now she will destroy him. Now she will cut him down.*

But, to my surprise, all she said was, "Yes. Please."

Then she jumped up and walked away from both of us. I gazed after her in astonishment, but the man only laughed again, a little softer this time, and kept folding.

I stayed with him until he had knotted the bundle three times and heaved it onto his shoulder, and then I followed him out. I wasn't sure why. As much as I liked him, I think I wanted to make sure he really left. He paused with his hand on the gate and gazed for a moment back at the house then down at me.

"I want you to tell her," he said, "that I will not forget. Tell her I will come again soon."

He spoke to me not as I was, a child of six, but as if I were an adult, his equal. That, combined with my mother's erratic behavior, created in me a desire to match his posture, his dignity.

I placed my hand on the gate in imitation of his. "I will tell her," I said.

I watched him walk up the road, the yellow bundle receding like a tiny sun. I kept watching until he turned left and disappeared.

Back inside, I found my mother upstairs in her bedroom, her head deep inside my father's cupboard. "Go put on your new blouse," she said, her voice muted by his fragrant shirts.

When she spoke like that, with that electric charge, that authority, I never disobeyed. I ran downstairs, threw off my T-shirt, and pulled the white blouse down over my shorts. It was so light I barely sensed it on my skin, but this only added to the prevailing atmosphere of unreality, and I took the stairs two at a time. Just as I reached her, my mother let out a muffled cry of triumph, emerging from the cupboard clutching my father's old, treasured Nikon.

She marched me out of the house, her hand on my shoulder. "Now pose," she commanded.

"What shall I do?"

She smiled, and a flash went off in my eyes. "Anything you want, little beast."

How can I explain what it was to be around her at those times? It was like being sealed within an invisible, protective, soundproof chamber. I saw and heard and smelled nothing but her. She photographed me in the wreckage of our garden, out on the street, pretending to climb our neighbors' gate while their ridiculous Pomeranian yipped itself into a frenzy. She photographed me in imaginary flight from the Pomeranian. Two young men were gaping at us, so she photographed them too. They fled, and that made her laugh so hard it seemed she would fly apart.

She photographed me until the roll in the camera ran out.

I don't know what happened to those photographs. I never saw them. Within a week, I more or less forgot about the man with his green eyes and his yellow bundle, the strange, unfamiliar thing I'd so briefly sensed. The white blouse lost its magic. I had no further intention of wearing it, so I stuffed it into the very back of my cupboard, along with the clothes I'd outgrown.

Finding the wooden animal in my mother's cupboard loosened something in me, to be sure, but not right away. For weeks afterward, life continued unchanged. My father went to the gym and to work. Stella came to clean and to cook. I went to the agency and out in the evenings. On the weekends, I would find myself wedged in a car between strangers, driving out of the city to somebody's "farmhouse," which usually meant a tasteless candy-pink monstrosity looming over some tiny, dusty village, whose impoverished residents we utterly ignored except when we took it into our heads to buy some of their cheap, home-brewed hooch. On the last of these excursions, I stayed awake drinking after the others had gone to sleep. It had been my twenty-fourth birthday, a fact I'd mentioned to nobody. At 3:00 a.m. I received a message from my father, wishing me a happy birthday from Tokyo. Just before dawn, I slipped out of the farmhouse and walked up the dark country road. Light was just limning the horizon, and the air smelled of woodsmoke. The first hut in the village had a thatched shed attached to the side. Deep groans of pain floated from the shed, so I approached. A pregnant cow lay on her side, the calf's face and forelegs protruding, filmed in milky white. The farmer sat on his haunches nearby, his lungi pulled up over his knees. He looked up when I came in, and his eyes widened, but he did not speak. We watched as the calf pushed out, its small body slick, and the gray afterbirth slithered and dropped. When the cow turned and started to lick her offspring, the farmer rose to his feet and led me around the shed, where I sat on a wooden bench facing the horizon, and a woman I took to be his wife brought me a tumbler of fresh, steaming milk. I tried to refuse, but she offered it again. So I accepted and she stepped back to watch me drink it. Right then, the sun suddenly burst into view, spilling light everywhere. And I? Well, I started to cry. The woman watched me, a drunk, weeping girl in rum-stained jeans, with a lack of sympathy that, if I had been older, I would have known to be grateful for. But the truth was, at that moment, I wasn't thinking of the woman at all. I was thinking, scared and lonely kid that I was: *I have just witnessed something true.*

At around the same time as I was weeping over calves, my father set about expanding his company, a project he pursued with such single-mindedness that even I could not fail to recognize it as his way of distancing himself from grief. Suddenly, he was always traveling. He went on business trips to Moscow and Tel Aviv. He flew to Houston, where he bought me a beer mug shaped like a snorting bull. He gave me our old Esteem and bought himself a sleek new BMW , and every Sunday night, he drove us in it to the same five-star restaurant, where he summoned the waiter with a subtle crook of his index finger—when exactly had he begun to do that?—and chatted easily with the head chef, who never failed to drop by our table to greet him.

It sounds obvious, I know, but it took me a while to see that my father, too, was changing in the wake of my mother's death. Now he wore crisp linen shirts tucked into Levi's, and his shoes, purchased in Milan, were of soft brown suede. Gone were his cracked Bata sandals, his old black rayon trousers, his faded T-shirts with yellow stains under the arms. He had turned into a reserved, polished version of the man I'd known all my life, and it was during those dinners that I saw him most clearly as others must have done: a handsome, tall, somber businessman of fifty-three, his hair not yet gray, leaning back in his chair, at ease with the world and his position in it. And I felt at these times a troubled wonder, the kind I imagine a parent feels for a grown child: pride, combined with the bittersweet notion that I had somehow, without noticing, without meaning to, lost him.

3

At work, I killed midges. They floated up from the sewer in soft clouds, and I slammed them into my desk with a register I kept exclusively for the purpose. Otherwise I attended meetings, presided over by the agency's founder, Ritu Shah. Ritu was tough and smart and had an MBA from Yale, where, she liked to keep reminding us lest we think her soft and privileged, she had been mugged four times, once at gunpoint. She drank oolong tea from a stained mug and was married to a World Bank man. The agency employed three other people, two bellicose women and a wilting boy. They were the ones who talked during meetings, vying with each other to offer ideas that Ritu listened to with her head cocked, rubbing her mug of oolong tea between her hands.

About a month after my twenty-fourth birthday and the calf, Ritu stopped by my desk to inform me of a meeting in ten minutes. "I'll be there," I said.

Gathering up some papers and a large file I'd never opened, I slunk into her room and sat at the back. The others were already there. Ritu clapped her hands. "Right. Let's get started, people."

The meeting turned out to about a new initiative to get roadside vendors—the ubiquitous stalls that sold tea or dosas or sugarcane juice—to stop dropping garbage on the pavement. Ritu rattled off numbers—thirty thousand vendors in the city center alone, dropping on average three kilograms of garbage per hour—and glanced at me, as if to verify the tragedy on a numerical level. I arranged my expression into one of grave despair. Ritu gave me a prolonged look then turned back to the others. "Got it?" she said briskly. "Now let's brainstorm."

One of the women thrust out a pugnacious chin and suggested marshaling a core group of vendors, who would form the nucleus of a proud cleanliness brigade. "Not bad," Ritu said.

The other woman, not to be outdone, suggested that vendors be rewarded with stickers that proclaimed their commitment to hygiene. Ritu thoughtfully rubbed her mug of oolong for a while. "Yes, I see where you're coming from," she said at last, and the woman beamed.

Then the wilting boy, in the tone of someone announcing a coup, leaned forward and proposed that the vendors form an alliance with a group of artists, who would use the discarded garbage to create massive public art installations that would raise awareness. He did not specify whose awareness would be so favored but fell back in his chair, as if exhausted.

Then Ritu turned to me.

"What about you, Shalini?" she said.

"Me?" I looked down at the papers on my lap. "I'll check the numbers."

"No," she said slowly. "I mean, do you have any ideas. Comments? Suggestions?"

"Oh," I said. "No."

"I see," she said and that was all. The meeting ended, and I forgot all about the exchange. So when Ritu appeared beside my desk at the end of the day, I was idiotic enough to be surprised. She set her mug on the edge of my desk and coughed.

"I want to ask you," she said, "if you're happy here."

"Yes," I said.

"The reason I'm asking," she continued, "is because you don't seem, how shall I say, fully *engaged*." Her voice changed, became, of all things, tender. "I know you've had a tough time since your mother died," she said, as if she'd felt the toughness inside me like some kind of rock. And, before I knew it, I was sobbing at my desk. I dropped my head, mortified and shaken.

I heard her cough. Her hand brushed the top of my head, a touch like a breeze.

"I think," Ritu said, "that you need some time off. Why don't you treat yourself to a holiday? Then, once you feel ready, we can talk about where you fit in with the agency."

It took a moment for her words to sink in. "You're firing me?"

She picked up her mug and stepped back, surveying me and my midge-stained desk. When she spoke, it was with boundless pity. "Go home, sweetheart," she said. "Go home."

Twenty minutes later, I stood in the middle of our living room, my eyes adjusting to the dimness. I'd driven too fast; I could still feel the tingle of speed in my palms. From the kitchen came the sound of a knife thudding against a board—Stella.

"It's me," I called.

She came out of the kitchen. Compact, with oiled hair pulled back into a perfect bun, her gold cross lying on top of her crisp red sari, she looked impeccable, even after hours of housework.

"What happened? Are you sick?" she demanded in Tamil.

"No."

She eyed me skeptically. "You look sick."

Stella had begun working for us half a decade before my mother died, and I still knew only a handful of things about her. She had three children who could do no wrong. Her husband, a part-time salesman, part-time drunk, could do no right. She was devoted to the Virgin

Mary and took her family on at least two church pilgrimages a year, for which she regularly requested money from my father, who gave it to her, but not before a lengthy lecture on the follies and perils of blind faith. She would hear him impassively to the end, then tuck the money into her blouse and proceed to do exactly as she pleased. But in her work, she was constant in all the ways my mother had been erratic. Even when my mother had been alive, it was Stella who remembered to buy the vegetables we needed, Stella who could recall when the gas cylinder had last been changed, Stella who knew which medicines were running low in the medicine cabinet.

Now I had the urge to follow her into the kitchen and tell her what had happened, but something prevented me. The idea, perhaps, that she was put out by my early return, that even though the house was ours, she might count on having these afternoons to herself, a spell of quiet before being sucked back into the clamor and claims of her own family life. I went up to my room and sat on the bed. Inch by inch, I slumped back until I was looking at the ceiling. I stayed that way until I heard Stella leave, and still I didn't move. It was only when it grew dark that I dragged myself up. The house felt forsaken. There was a message on my cell phone from my father, saying he was with an out-of-town client and would be back late; I should go ahead and eat without him.

Stella had left our dinner on the table: four bowls covered with steel plates. Beside them, a strip of ibuprofen. I stared at all of it for a long time. Then I walked from room to room, flicking on every single light and fan. I turned on the TV and raised the volume as high as it would go.

Then I got into my car and drove off, leaving the house ablaze.

I drove, inevitably, to Hari Dinakaran's. Hari was twenty-one and a photographer. I'd met him at a Japanese Buddhist ceremony a few months after my mother died. Someone, I've now forgotten who, had cajoled me into attending. The ceremony was in a bland one-story flat in

Whitefield. In the main room a shrine had been set up, draped in a red velvet cloth fringed with gold tassels, a large Buddha in the center. We were greeted by a trim, elderly Japanese woman, the only real Buddhist there. The rest of us were merely young, wealthy, and quite obviously adrift. She took me to a back room and gave me a form to fill out. Someone else was already in the room, filling out a similar form. His whole lanky body seemed to be one nervous tic: his knees bounced, his shoulders shook, his toes curled. But his hand, I noticed, rested quietly on the bulky, complicated-looking camera beside him, as if it were an infant that drew comfort from his touch.

During the ceremony, the women were ordered to kneel in a row, the men behind them. As the trim Japanese woman moved amongst us, saying, "This is the seat of the soul in the body," I was acutely aware of his constant shifting and fidgeting. When it was over, he jumped up and started photographing the Japanese woman beside her shrine. I watched for a while; then I went up to him. Looking straight into his eyes, I asked to see more of his work. He actually blushed.

Hari lived in a tiny rented room on the terrace of some family's bungalow in Ulsoor. As soon as I saw it, I fell in love with that terrace. There was a warped, sun-faded ladder in one corner, which led up to a ledge with a black water tank, and many times I climbed up there when I was too drunk or high to remember how to come back down. I would sit with my back against the tank, my feet scraping air, while Hari sat below, editing photos on his laptop, the worm of a joint glowing in his fingers, glancing up now and then at me, his face, small and worried, lit up by the screen.

The saddest thing, I see now, was that Hari never understood what I wanted from him. I barely understood it myself then. We would get high, the two of us lying on his mattress, and eventually his hand would float up to rest on my breast the way it had rested on the camera, and I would let it build, let him lift my shirt, and then, when I couldn't stand it anymore, I would push him away and sit up. He would look wretched but never protest. And maybe that was it, the sum of us and everything I'm grateful to him for: Hari allowed me the simple luxury of resistance. He allowed me to push back—in a way that was small and mean and unworthy, yes, but nevertheless to push back—against a world that had shown me it could beat me down whenever it wanted.

Now I parked and climbed the outer cement stairs that hugged the building and led directly up to the terrace, pausing before the final one. This was the moment I cherished most: stepping onto the barren red tiles, the black sky opening above, and the lighted room like a beacon at the far end. Inside, I found Hari on his mattress, wearing one of his three *Free Tibet* T-shirts, surrounded by squares of rolling papers and a giant box of weed. He smiled as I entered then returned to his task.

There was no furniture in Hari's room apart from the mattress and a low table, which was black with cigarette burns and ash. A small collection of books was stacked on a hot plate that he never used. *The Motorcycle Diaries*. A biography of the Dalai Lama. *Old Path White Clouds: Walking in the Footsteps of the Buddha.* It was a bohemian setup, but there was no truth to it. Like me, Hari received a generous allowance from his parents, graduates of AIIMS and Harvard Medical School. They would have gladly bought him a spacious two-bedroom flat if he'd asked, but Hari took his role as poor, struggling artist seriously and accepted only the cash. Likewise, his photographs focused on the plight of the poor, of whom Hari, with no irony whatsoever, considered himself a part. He thoughtfully shot toothless old women huddled next to stray dogs on broken pavements; hijra prostitutes applying makeup in rooms that were closer to dungeons; malnourished toddlers chasing each other in gray construction sites while their parents carried backbreaking loads of concrete just outside the frame. The more picturesque the poverty, the more he loved to shoot it. But if I'd said this to him, he would have been crushed, so I never had. In retrospect, that was my only act of consideration as far as Hari was concerned.

I sat down on the mattress and waited. Eventually, he produced a pale, bloated joint, which he held up to the light. "Hopeless, man," he sighed. Hari called everyone man, including his mother.

As we smoked, the night slowed to a crawl. At some point, I found myself lying with my head on Hari's lap, half listening to him go on and on about a virtuoso Finnish drummer who was coming to play in Bangalore next month, "a total mindfuck, I'm telling you, man, you can't even imagine." His fingers tapped the ashy table without pause, and, at that moment, I was seized with the sensation of falling. I squeezed my eyes shut, but it only made the falling worse, so I opened them again. I still felt Ritu's hand heavy on my head. *Once you feel ready, we can talk about where you fit in.* I knew I should stand up and leave, but I thought of our glowing, vacant house, and right then something cracked open within me.

Without knowing what I was doing, I reached out and began to fumble with the button of Hari's jeans. My fingertips were freezing, the denim as pliable as rock. Hari gave me no help. He just sat there, weirdly still. I managed to get the button open, then awkwardly tugged down his jeans, along with his underwear. His cock lay across his thigh, half erect.

I got to my knees, running my tongue in vain over my dry, aching teeth. Hari's eyes were fixed on the wall, a distant look on his face.

"Condom," I croaked.

He didn't move.

"Hari! Condom!" I couldn't believe the harshness in my own voice.

Startled into movement, Hari got to his feet. He pulled up his underwear then his jeans. He zipped them up. Smoothed down his *Free Tibet* T-shirt. Stubbed the joint out on the table with an odd tenderness. "You can't keep doing this, man," he said finally.

"Doing what?"

He shook his head. "You know."

"No. I don't."

"Yes," he said wearily. "You do." He looked away and said something I didn't catch.

"What? What was that?" I demanded.

He shook his head. "Nothing."

"Just *say* it, Hari."

He sighed and turned back to face me. "Sometimes you scare the shit out of me."

I don't remember driving back home. I do remember the house being completely dark when I pulled up, my father's closed bedroom door. I remember banging my shin against my bedside table so hard the wooden animal clattered to the floor. I remember the pitching of my bed, the storm-tossed violence of it. I remember drowning, then surfacing, then drowning again.

I continued to leave the house in the mornings. Because I had nowhere else to go, I went to the club where as a child I'd learned how to swim, and where, for a few heady years, I'd even believed I might become a professional swimmer. In those years, I'd known each one the coaches, attendants, guards, and cleaners by name, but now they'd been replaced by strangers. I sat at one of the wrought-iron tables beside the pool and watched the new coach, a man with dark, bedraggled hair and a beautiful, tapering torso, as he conveyed nervous wives in frilly swimsuits across the shallow end, one hand under their stomachs, the other behind his back, like a careful waiter bearing a series of expensive trays. Later in the day, groups of children arrived, practicing their freestyle strokes on a long bench, then holding on to foam boards and kicking the water white, while at the tables around me, their mothers talked and laughed with each other.

When I first started swimming, the same year Bashir Ahmed came into our lives, my mother had sat at these very wrought-iron tables, ankles in the sun, the rest of her in the shade of a sagging umbrella, while I practiced pointing my toes as I kicked. The other mothers sat clustered together, but mine sat splendidly alone. For weeks, she talked to nobody. Then one evening, I saw her stand and walk casually over to them. By the time practice ended, twenty minutes later, she had them all in her thrall. "Oh my *god*," I heard her drawl in a simpering accent that was not hers, "when I saw what her husband looked like, I'm not lying to you, my darlings, I *fainted*." Fanning herself with her hand while the rest of the women giggled, titillated by whatever wicked, untrue story she had spun for their benefit. But when we climbed into an auto to go home—my mother had never learned to drive—she dropped the accent and caught me hard by the wrist. "Promise me," she cried, her nails digging into my skin, hurting me, "promise me, Shalini, that if I *ever* become like one of those brainless, fat cows, you'll take a knife and stab me. Promise!" I could see she was becoming agitated, her voice rising in pitch. "Yes," I said, "I promise," and only then did she let go of me.

I stayed at the pool for as many hours as I could, but once the children left, the joy drained from the place, and I went home. Stella never asked why I was coming home early, and I knew she wouldn't mention it to my father. I wasn't sure why I was hiding it from him, other than that it gave me something to do, forced me to be wily and alert, at least until dinner was over. It was no great feat. His factory had recently run into union troubles, and he was distracted. As a belated birthday gift, he'd flown us the previous weekend to a resort in Bali, our first trip without my mother. The night we landed, he fell asleep early, and I drank at the beachfront bar with a sallow English journalist, while the bartender, a tired-looking, dark-skinned man my father's age, looked out at the ocean.

The week after we returned from Bali, my father flew to Seoul for a manufacturing exhibition. Grateful to abandon the sad charade of going to work, I stayed in bed every day, slinking downstairs only when I was nauseated from hunger. When Stella came, she tried my door, but I'd locked it. "Fine," I heard her say. "You want to live in a gutter?" The murmur of her broom faded, and I slept.

When the bell rang, I ignored it. Stella's voice floated through my window, then a man's voice, speaking, or so I thought, in Hindi or Urdu. I could not hear the words, but what reached me was some lilt, some familiar cadence, and suddenly I was scrambling out of bed, fighting with the locked door, and flying down the stairs to find Stella dusting the tables in the living room.

"Who was that?" I panted.

She shrugged. "Some fellow selling something."

"Selling what?"

"I didn't ask. Don't I have better things to do than ask a hundred questions to everybody who rings the bell?"

"What did he look like?"

She gave me a keen glance, which also held a gleam of what I suspected was pity. "What did he look like?" she repeated slowly. "Why do you ask that?"

And then I saw myself as I was, unwashed, hair matted, clothes crumpled and stinking after three days of continuous wear. I looked at her crisp, starched cotton sari.

"It doesn't matter," I said. "I was just asking."

"Those selling fellows," Stella said, and gave the table a last, decisive flick with her rag, "they're all the same anyway. Useless, every single one of them."

The second time Bashir Ahmed came to our house, it was the monsoon and I was recovering from chicken pox. I'd stayed home from school for weeks with a fever, covered in itchy scabs that drove me mad. I remember my mother gently bending my fingers back whenever she caught me scratching, gazing into my eyes as she did so, the flicker of pain I bore without flinching. The elongated days, the thick ropes of rain, the goggle-eyed lizards that plopped from the bathroom ceilings. The house felt stuffy, sealed, as though a cold fog had laid itself over every inch of it. Once my fever broke, I came downstairs and lay on the sofa for hours, watching my mother come and go. She seemed, I noticed, to live deep inside the fog, or it lived within her. I could see it in her slowed hands as she touched her brass idols, her diminished voice. Sometimes I had the feeling it was swallowing her, that soon she would vanish altogether.

The fog was disturbed, though not dispelled, only when my father came home, bringing with him all the energy and disorder of the world. Clicking on the TV, prying off his shoes, peeling off his black socks and tossing them carelessly onto the floor. Attacking me with his stubble, making me squirm, forcing a laugh from my weary body. Flopping down onto the sofa with a long sigh of contentment. "That's my girl. You sound better. Back to school on Monday, I think."

My mother had come out of the kitchen in time to hear this. Her eyes fixed first on the socks my father had left on the floor. For a while she was silent. Then she drew herself up to her full height, folded her thin arms, and said quietly, "She isn't ready to go back to school yet."

"Nonsense." My father didn't even glance in her direction. "Look at her. She's fine. No point in her sitting around at home. She's going to fall behind."

"Fall behind?" My mother's voice was thick, drawling. "Oh, I'm *so* sorry. Forgive me. I had *no* idea our six-year-old was getting her PhD. How stupid of me."

He bristled, as he always did, when she adopted that tone. "Maybe if you bothered to look at her books even once, you'd see that some of what she's learning isn't all that easy. " He turned to stare at the TV. "But I know this academic stuff doesn't really interest you," he muttered.

I did not dare look at either of them. It was no secret that my mother had not studied beyond the tenth standard. As I understand it, the calculations had been brutally simple: Her father had three children and earned a government employee's salary. My mother was the youngest and the only daughter. Her two brothers went to college. She did not.

My mother had gone rigid, and I knew it was the fog, moving up her body, curling itself around her brain, freezing her voice. Without speaking, she turned and went back into the kitchen. A tense moment later, my father stomped upstairs to change. The socks stayed on the floor all night.

The next day, Bashir Ahmed came.

My father had left earlier than usual for the factory. I remember my mother picking up the socks, one in each fist, as if not quite sure what they were. Then the bell rang, and when she saw him, something went out of her body with such force it was almost audible.

He smiled at her. "See? I told you I wouldn't forget."

She nodded. She appeared dazed. "Come in," she said.

He entered with the same satisfied expression as before. It had been raining that afternoon, and the shoulders of his green kurta were damp, which somehow made his eyes seem even brighter. He put the bundle down and ran both hands through his hair.

"Beti," he said to me, "three months since I saw you, and you've become so tall."

"Will you drink something?" my mother said. She was still, I realized, holding a black sock in each fist. "Tea? Coffee?"

"Thank you," he said, "but no."

"Why?" she demanded roughly. "Are you on a diet?"

"Okay, okay." He laughed and waved his arms like someone warding off an attack. "To you, how can I say no? I will have some tea, thank you very much."

She nodded, but I knew she was pleased. Once she'd gone into the kitchen, he turned back to me with an expectant smile, as if he was waiting for me to resume a conversation we'd been having. I found that I wanted to say something clever, to make him laugh the way she did.

"Where did you go?" I asked in Hindi. "When you left here the last time?"

"Everywhere, beti. I went everywhere."

"The whole world?"

He wrinkled his nose enigmatically. "Perhaps."

"America?"

"Psh, America," he said. "Who wants to go there?" He was rummaging in his kurta pockets. "Now, before I forget, beti, give me your hand. I have brought you something."

I held out my hand, and he dropped into it a hard, round shell, mud brown and smooth to the touch. A thick seam ran up the middle like the one on a leather cricket ball.

"What is it?" I asked.

"Akhrot. I won't tell you what it's called in English. You'll have to ask your mother." He grinned. "She has the answers to everything."

When my mother came out with a cup of tea, I held it up to her. "Walnut," she told me crisply in English. "You have to get it out of its shell."

"How do I get it out?"

"Good question," she said. "Try asking it nicely."

She sat down opposite him, and I sat between them, turning the walnut over in my fingers.

"Well, madam," he said. He had already begun working the knots of the bundle. "As I told you the last time, I have many, many beautiful new items. Even *you* won't be able to deny their beauty. Nobody in Bangalore is selling items like these, believe me. You can ask around, if you want. Shawls and kurtas and—"

"I don't want to see them."

His fingers froze. "Madam?"

"I don't want to see them." She leaned forward. "Tell me, what is your name?"

"Bashir Ahmed."

"Right then, Mr. Bashir Ahmed, there's one thing you should understand straightaway about me." It sounded as if she were dredging up the words from wet soil. They had a thick, labored feeling. "I am not one of those bored housewives you see every day, who keeps on buying new things because she doesn't know what else to do with herself. And if you think I am one of them then, well, you're not as intelligent as you seem."

There was silence after she'd spoken.

Then Bashir Ahmed started to laugh.

"Well," he said, shaking his head, "I had to try."

And when she too started laughing, I felt relief balloon in my chest. Bashir Ahmed deftly reknotted the bundle and nudged it away with his foot. That was the last time he ever tried to sell her anything. Looking back, I can see that something powerful occurred in that moment, and it still astonishes me all these years later: Bashir Ahmed understood in about five minutes what took my father decades. And me? What did I understand back then? Nothing, except that when my mother laughed like that, it made me want a million things at once. I wanted to run until I dropped; I wanted to roll on the ground; I wanted to climb into her lap and stay there forever.

"Where do you live?" she asked him.

"Me? I have a room near Russell Market."

"No, I meant originally. In Kashmir. That's where you're from, isn't it?"

"Oh, a small village. In the mountains. You wouldn't have heard of it." He grinned wickedly. "You people in India, you think Kashmir begins and ends with Srinagar."

"Is it beautiful there?"

"In my village? Why don't you come and see for yourself? Oh, but I forget," and he pointed mischievously to his green eyes, "you're a little blind. How sad. Actually, it's probably better if you don't come. You will look at the Himalayas and say, 'But where are the mountains?'"

"Maybe I *will* come," my mother declared, shaking her finger at him. "One of these days, you'll open the door and I'll be standing there. Then what will you do, Mr. Bashir Ahmed?"

"I will ask, 'Do you want tea or coffee, madam, or are you on a diet?'"

They laughed. I found that I was also grinning, though I didn't fully grasp the joke. All I knew was that there was a lovely hysteria in the air, and I wanted to inhale it deep, deep into my lungs. The fog that had obscured my mother for days suddenly seemed thinner. I could see her more clearly, hear the clarity and confidence in her voice.

"And what about you, beti?" Bashir Ahmed turned to me, smiling. "Are you coming too?"

"Yes," I answered promptly. "I am."

"Good!" he said, slapping his thigh with a large palm. "My son will enjoy meeting you."

At that, my mother's smile flickered. He noticed it right away and his own mouth became a tight line. In the few seconds of silence that followed, I heard the loud ticking of the clock on top of the TV. I looked from one to the other. Then Bashir Ahmed cleared his throat.

"Beti," he said quickly, "would you like to hear a story?"

I glanced at my mother, but she was unreachable now, offering no clue. It was the single most devastating habit she had, to withdraw, to take back the thrilling gift of her joy as casually as she bestowed it. I'd always believed that I was the only one in the world who saw it as clearly as I did, her lightning switch from one self to another. But one look at this stranger's face told me he understood it, too, and it gave me an odd and unexpected comfort.

"Yes," I said. "I would."

"All right," Bashir Ahmed said, nodding. "Then listen." His chin dropped so low it nearly touched his chest, and he took several deep breaths. His eyelids fluttered almost closed. His hands came to rest in his lap. Over the years, I would become familiar with his tactics: the long pause at the beginning, the swift rise of his deep voice followed by the precipitous drop, his trick of repeating innocuous phrases until they turned ominous.

"In Kashmir, a long time ago," he said, "there lived an old man. Because he had come from the city of Baghdad, in Iraq, people called him Shah Baghdadi. This old man, he was a pir. Do you know what that is, beti? A pir?"

I shook my head.

"A wise man," Bashir Ahmed said solemnly. "This Shah Baghdadi had read many books, and he knew a lot about the world. He could even perform magic. People who were sick would go to him, and he would heal them. But he was very careful with his powers, you see, because he knew that they were gifts from Allah."

From the corner of my eye, I could see my mother's head turn slightly.

"Now what I forgot to tell you, beti," Bashir Ahmed went on slowly, "was that Shah Baghdadi had a son. A son," he said again, and I felt a chill run up my arms. "A son who was born when Shah Baghdadi was already old, and whose mother had died. His father loved him very much, but from the beginning, the boy only knew how to break his heart. And, to make things worse, it became clear that he also had his father's powers. Shah Baghdadi tried to make him study, begged his son to understand that such powers should not be taken lightly, but the boy did not listen. When he was ten years old, he asked for a horse. Shah Baghdadi refused, so the boy became angry. He jumped up onto a wall, turned the wall into a beautiful black horse, and rode away."

My mother was listening, leaning forward now, but Bashir Ahmed's eyes did not so much as flicker in her direction. He spoke to me, as though everyone but the two of us had ceased to exist.

"This boy did these things as if they were nothing. And no matter how much his father tried to stop him, he kept doing them. Then something very sad happened. Shah Baghdadi's son had a best friend, a little Hindu boy. The two of them were supposed to meet one evening and finish playing one of their games. But the Hindu boy never arrived. Eventually, Shah Baghdadi's son found his best friend lying on a flat stone. A stone," Bashir Ahmed repeated. "The poor boy had been bitten by a snake. He was dead."

I longed to glance at my mother, but I did not dare to take my eyes off his face.

"The Hindu boy's mother and father were crying and beating their heads," Bashir Ahmed said, "but Shah Baghdadi's son was thinking only of himself. Now he wouldn't be able to finish his game. Then he had an idea. He said a prayer, and his friend opened his eyes. Shah Baghdadi's son laughed and pulled him to his feet and the two of them ran off to play.

"When the old Baghdadi heard about this, he knew that his son had finally gone too far. He was faced with a terrible decision, but he knew what he had to do. When his son came home, he called him to his side. With his own hands, he fed the boy a bowl of milk. As soon as his son had finished the milk, he closed his eyes and died." Bashir Ahmed's voice dropped to a whisper on these last words. "Shah Baghdadi had put poison in the milk, beti. He had killed his own son."

This was too much for me. I burst out, "That doesn't make any *sense!* Why would he—"

But then I stopped, because Bashir Ahmed was no longer looking at me. His green eyes were on my mother, whose own eyes, I saw, were bright. She smiled at him, a sad, radiant smile, and I saw that he had done what I believed nobody knew how to do, save for me. He had coaxed her back.

As before, I accompanied him out to the gate. I was bursting with questions about the story but restrained myself, sensing he wished to be quiet. But then he said absently, as he pushed the gate open, "I've seen it, you know. The stone where the boy died and was brought back to life."

"You have?" I asked. "How did you see it?"

Bashir Ahmed glanced back at the house, but my mother was no longer in the living room. "My wife's whole family is from there. The place where it happened," he told me, and his voice sounded, for a moment, very distant.

Then he left, and though he didn't ask me to tell my mother this time, I knew he would return soon. Later that day, I went out to get my towel from the clothesline and found my father's socks hanging out, washed and shriveled and limp.

4

MY FATHER FLEW HOME from Seoul on a Friday, and we went out to dinner as usual on Sunday night. He was restless; he kept picking up the small vase with a white rose that stood on our table. I, on the other hand, was exhausted. Three weeks had gone by since Ritu had fired me, and everything had begun to grate: the long, pointless hours at the club, the evening cheer I put on for my father. I hadn't talked to Hari after the night he said I frightened him. Part of me wanted to tell him I knew what he meant. He had merely seen the thing, loose and rattling and dangerous, that I had felt in myself. But the few times he'd called, I hadn't answered.

"The usual?" my father asked. I nodded. He ordered our drinks, whiskey for me, rum for him, and then he absently picked up the vase with the rose again.

"It doesn't look real," he murmured. "It's so perfect it could be plastic. Isn't that odd?"

I was already on edge, and his sudden lapse into sentimentality irritated me. "Look at this place," I snapped. "Does it seem like the kind of place that would use plastic roses?"

His eyebrows went up, but he didn't take the bait. He didn't launch into an analysis of how much the restaurant might have saved by using plastic flowers, or give me a lecture on how small frugalities kept giant businesses afloat. Instead he said, "How's work?"

"Fine."

"Still liking it?"

I made a vaguely assenting noise. The drinks came and we raised our glasses.

"Cheers," my father said. If my mother had been with us, she would have been drinking a lime soda. For all her extremism, she had a prim view on alcohol. My father would have turned to her and raised his glass, and, depending on her mood, she might have returned the gesture with a flourish. Or she might have stared at the tablecloth until he flushed. But my mother wasn't here, and my father set his glass down with a thud that startled me out of my dull absorption.

"Look at me, Shalini," my father said firmly.

I dragged my eyes up. I was twenty-four years old and felt ninety.

"It's been three years since Amma passed away," he said. "And I can see that you are making the mistake you were making when it first happened. You are stopping your life."

When my father spoke, it was with his complete mind. This was a man used to meeting with industry heads and crooked contractors, with recalcitrant employees and irate union leaders. He forgot himself, his surroundings, and became entirely immersed in what he was saying.

"I thought you would eventually find a way out, which is why I didn't say anything for a long time. I regret that, but enough is enough. Listen to me, Shalini. When something big happens—"

"By 'big,'" I said loudly, "do you mean your wife dying?" I knew it was childish, but I couldn't help myself. I *felt* like a child.

"When something big happens," he repeated firmly, ignoring me, "whatever it is, I understand that a person's first tendency is to freeze, to go numb and wait for something else, equally big, to come along and cancel out the first thing. Believe me, I understand. And I know that's what you're doing. But that's the mistake, don't you see? It's faulty, wishful logic. There *is* no second thing. At least, not externally. There is, however, action. Action is the second thing. Without action, there is only waiting for death."

The waiter came up then; we ordered and handed back our menus. Then my father looked at me again. "Do you understand what I'm saying, Shalini? You cannot stand around waiting for things to change, because chances are they won't. You must do something. You must act."

"What about you?" I snapped peevishly. "What are *you* doing? How are *you* acting?"

He smiled, as though he had been waiting for me to ask precisely this question. "I like to think I'm trying. I'm working harder than I've ever worked, for one. And there's something else, which I've been wanting to discuss with you." Until now, he'd been looking at me, but now he looked down and took a long sip of rum. For some reason, I found myself sitting straighter.

"I'm thinking of getting married again," he said. Then he hastily added, "Not right away. Not even soon, but I wanted to bring it up with you. To see what you thought."

I stared at his hands, wrapped around his glass. I'd inherited those same hands, the long, strong fingers, the broad palms, perfect for the swimmer I once thought I'd be.

"To whom?" I asked.

"I have no idea."

"How are you going to do it then?"

He smiled. "What am I, a dinosaur? There are all those websites."

I looked at my father, who was only fifty-three years old, and imagined him tapping out a description of himself on a matrimonial site. Adding a photograph, choosing *Widower* in the drop-down menu. Checking to see if there were any messages for him, patiently sorting through profiles for someone he liked, someone who struck him as—what, exactly?

Then the exchange of messages, the cautious expression of interest, followed by a phone call, a meeting, and, finally, talk of a marriage, a wedding. I waited for myself to grow resentful, but instead I grew sad.

"Well?" he asked, and I couldn't miss the pleading in his voice.

"I think it's nice," I said softly.

He leaned forward to look at my eyes, and when he saw I was being sincere, he smiled. "Thank you," he said. "It's important to me what you think."

"Now you know."

"In that case," he said, leaning forward, "I'll ask again. What about you?"

I looked up. "Me?"

"What do you plan to do?" he pressed. "You asked me how I'm acting, and I told you. Now you need to make a similar decision. I don't mean marriage, obviously, but it has to be *something*."

"Like what?"

"How should I know?" Now there was an edge of impatience to his voice. "I can't live your life for you, Shalini. You have to decide how you want to live, the way I did. It's as simple as that."

The sad glow I'd been feeling vanished, replaced by anger. He looked so smug and sure of himself, sitting there in his white linen shirt, the glass of rum like a crystal ball between his palms, so pleased with his announcement of the future and my approval of it. As if he had somehow done me a favor, and now he couldn't understand why I wasn't falling over myself thanking him. I had never made a scene in a restaurant before, but I saw myself screaming obscenities, knocking my drink over, the other diners staring then quickly averting their eyes.

"I *have* decided, " I said finally. "And my life is fine, thank you."

He said nothing, but the look on his face was enough to provoke me.

"Anyway," I said breezily. "I'm going on a trip soon."

That took us both by surprise. We were quiet; then my father asked, "Where?"

I paused, weighing the next words before I spoke them. How long had this idea been in my mind, half-formed and asleep? I thought of the wooden beast waiting beside my bed, and what I felt then was not fear, but the pure, blazing exhilaration of certainty.

"To the north," I said. "Jammu and Kashmir."

I sat there, watching him frown, waiting for his reaction. If he'd spoken Bashir Ahmed's name right then, I would have almost certainly lost my nerve. To this day, I don't know why he didn't say it. He just sat there staring at the table until I gathered my wits enough to say, "It's for work. A project Ritu wants to do up there. Something about rivers, I think."

"Is it safe to travel there these days?"

"Ritu wouldn't want to do it otherwise," I lied.

He still looked doubtful. "How long will you be gone?" he asked.

"I'm not sure."

After another pause, even longer this time, he said, "Do you need any money?"

"No."

"I'll give you some anyway."

I said nothing.

"Well," my father said heavily, "Been quite the evening of announcements, hasn't it?"

And then I thought of him, returning night after night to an empty house. I thought of him driving alone to this restaurant on Sundays, sitting at this table, reading the menu he already knew by heart, waiting in silence for his food. And, because I'm trying to evade nothing here, I don't think I ever loved him more than I did at that moment, when I pitied him most.

* * *

I woke early and refreshed the next morning. The first thing I did was check on the trains that would take me north. After eleven years, I'd decided, there was no reason to fly. I would sleep in a berth for a night or two. I would watch the country fall away, state by state, landscape by landscape, and only then would I begin my search for Bashir Ahmed in earnest.

I pulled down our old atlas from its place on our bookshelf and spread it open on my bed. The tops of the pages were black. Stella's dusting rag had evidently never ventured this far. And there it was: Kashmir, the ponderous head that had always seemed too much for its awkward, tapering body. For a while after Bashir Ahmed left us for the last time, I kept an ear open for a mention of Kashmir in the news. But it was always the same vague thing—two or four or five militants killed, an Indian soldier injured, a gun battle, rumbling threats from across the LoC. I'd listened to the names of unfamiliar towns—Poonch, Baramulla, Sopore—and wondered if they were anywhere near Bashir Ahmed's home. But it had been too abstract for me to grasp as a child, and besides I'd had my reasons back then for wanting to forget Bashir Ahmed and everything connected with him. Eventually, shamefully, I'd stopped paying attention.

Now I realized how little I knew about the place where Bashir Ahmed came from. I did not even know the name of his village. If he ever told us, I'd forgotten it. He had always spoken of mountains, but as I looked at the thousands and thousands of folded, crumpled kilometers, I understood just how useless that information was. The exhilaration I'd felt sitting across from my father slowly slipped away, replaced by doubt. I found myself scrolling blankly through train charts, days going by. The only practical preparation I made was to drive to the bank and empty out my checking account—I had a sum total of twelve thousand rupees.

I kept expecting my father to ask when I was leaving, but he didn't. The only mention he made of my supposed trip was to suggest that I might look up an old friend of his while I was there, a Sameer Reddy, who was supposedly a high-ranking officer, a brigadier, in the army. I'd nodded and entered the brigadier's number into my cell phone, with no intention whatsoever of calling him.

Several nights in a row, I woke from fretful dreams, sweating, gripped by the fear that I had been on the verge of remembering something important and had just missed it.

But the answer, when it came, was astonishing in its simplicity. I was lying in bed, drifting into and out of sleep, when I sat bolt upright, my heart racing. In less than a minute, I was at my computer, my fingers trembling as I typed in the words: *Shah Baghdadi. Son. Hindu friend revived. Kashmir. Story.* The third page of search results gave me the name I was looking for.

Kishtwar.

It was a town that lay on the Jammu side, six thousand feet above sea level. A town whose population was almost evenly split between Hindus and Muslims. A town most famous for its shrines, especially those of two legendary Sufi saints. Shah Fariduddin Baghdadi, and his son, Shah Asraruddin Baghdadi, who had once brought a dead boy back to life. I closed my eyes and thought of Bashir Ahmed, his hand resting on our gate, saying, *My wife's whole family is from there.*

It was the slimmest of clues, but it was enough.

II

5

A MAN IN A blue tracksuit was sleeping in my berth. One arm thrown over his eyes, gold ring on the thumb. I stood clutching my ticket and rucksack, while people surged up the aisle behind me, fragments of their luggage—tiffin carriers, jute bags, a table fan—jabbing me in the back.

"Excuse me," I said.

A frail old couple sat side by side on the opposite berth. He wore a sleeveless gray sweater over a neat white shirt and she a starched magenta sari. They could have been siblings as easily as husband and wife. Their single cloth bag huddled between their socked feet, their sandals carefully hidden away. I smiled at them to say, *Can you believe this?* but they simply stared ahead.

"Excuse me," I said, a bit louder, and tapped the man on the ankle. "This is my seat."

He raised his elbow and squinted up at me. "Lots of space there," he muttered, gesturing toward the empty spot on the berth next to the old couple.

All morning I'd braced myself for disaster. My father would confront me about the real reason for my trip; I would not find the right platform; the train would be canceled. Now all of it came flooding back as unreasonable anger. I lifted my rucksack and dropped it on the man's legs.

He scrambled up, yelping. "Are you mad?"

"Oh, I'm *so* sorry," I said. "It must have slipped."

Cursing under his breath, he slid over to the window, and with a sense of raw, breathless triumph I sat where his legs had been, the blue Rexine still warm from his body. All around us, the station frothed and bubbled. I looked at the crowds through the cloudy yellow window, seeing instead my father at his desk above the factory floor; Stella in our kitchen, palming a small red knife; Hari cross-legged, flicking ashes onto a dirty plate, and I very nearly stood up and pushed my way back onto the platform, but right then the train began to move, and I fell back in my seat.

Now there were acres of ugly buildings. Mud and metal shantytowns. Flat, scrubby countryside. For hours, nobody in my compartment spoke. The old man and woman took turns sipping water from a giant Bisleri bottle. The man in the tracksuit chewed his fingernails and spit the slivers discreetly on the floor. And, suddenly, I imagined that this was my family, that the old man and woman were my parents, and the man in the tracksuit my husband. It came out of nowhere, and I glanced around guiltily, as if they might have heard my thoughts. We were a family, on our way to Delhi for a holiday. I saw us posing stiffly for photographs in front of monuments. Saw us eating dinner at our hotel then climbing to our rooms. Saw the old couple wishing us goodnight. Saw my husband and me slipping into our own bed, his gold ring a point of ice against my skin.

I felt no attraction to the man, but the fantasy gave me a strange comfort, cast our single fraught exchange in a benign light, which perfectly matched the light outside, a sad and bottomless blue. I glanced at him from the corner of my eye. He looked tired, and I wished then I had just let him sleep. When a boy in a khaki uniform brought our bedding, blankets wrapped in brown paper, pillows like firm cakes of soap, I turned to the man, intending to offer him the bottom bunk if he wanted it. But before I could speak, he addressed the boy loudly: "Better give that girl hers first. Otherwise god knows who she'll hurt. People like that, they think the world was made for them."

My heart clenched, but I said nothing. The old couple might as well have been deaf, for all that they reacted. I waited until the boy had gone, and then I stood and made my way to the bogie door, which was open. The wind whipped my hair against my neck, stung my eyes to tears. I stared out at the darkening landscape, trying to fight off a sense of doom. I could make out fields in tight squares. Clusters of houses, light blooming in windows. Low hills wavering. Vehicles waiting at a railway crossing, the drivers' faces upturned. Trash lining the tracks, a rat's thick body streaking down a hole. And then, my mother. Standing with me at the train door, long fingers gripping the handle. Her thin body leaning far out, her mouth stretched wide in a soundless laugh. She would have laughed that man right off the train. He was nothing to us.

I stood there, calm now, until the wind turned cold. And then I returned to my berth, to the people who were not my family.

Delhi in the morning already showed signs of brutal heat. I sat in the station on a peeling red bench that was stained with various things I tried not to think about. The Jammu Tawi was scheduled to leave at 9:00 p.m. It was barely noon.

My cell phone vibrated in the pocket of my jeans.

"All okay?" my father asked. His machines thundered and roared in the background.

"Yes," I said. "I'm in Delhi."

"Hello? Are you there? You have to speak up."

"I'm in Delhi," I shouted.

"Good," he shouted back. "So everything's okay?"

"Yes."

The night before I left, he had given me money. "Here," he'd said, holding out a thick white envelope with a clear window through which I could see the first of a stack of thousand-rupee notes. I hesitated. It seemed a betrayal to use his money for what I had in mind to do, a betrayal worse than leaving, worse than lying to him. But he looked so imploring that I knew refusal was out of the question, so I took the envelope, silently promising myself that I would not open it unless I absolutely had to—a last, wretched bargain with decency.

"Well," my father said now, "have a good trip. Call me if you need anything. And you can always get in touch with Reddy, too, remember."

"Who?"

"The brigadier."

"Oh," I said. "Right."

There was another pause. Then my father said, "All right then. Bye. Take lots of pictures."

"Bye, Appa," I said.

He hung up. I sat still for a moment; then I started to laugh. In all the time I had been packing, it hadn't occurred to me to bring a camera.

The Jammu Tawi left on time to the minute. There was a family in the compartment with me this time. A young mother with her two children, who played Antakshari after dinner. One of them, a boy of seven or eight, sang in a pure, crystal soprano whenever it was his turn, and knew more old Hindi songs than it should have been possible for a child of his age to know.

Just before dawn, I woke. We had stopped at a station. A single lamp burned like a beacon over the long, deserted platform. I looked at it and thought of Hari, who woke early and would likely be standing on his terrace, smoking his first joint of the day, unaware I was no longer in Bangalore. I felt a pang of guilt. Perhaps I should call, at least tell him I would be away for a while, that we could talk about everything after I returned. I dialed his number, but the call died before it connected. I tried again then saw the phone had no signal. I moved it closer to the window.

"It won't work," someone said quietly.

It was the mother of the two children, lying on her side in the opposite berth. I hadn't noticed she was awake. Her son lay curled in the crook formed by her body, his mouth open, a damp and defenseless thing. "Your phone is prepaid?" she whispered.

"Yes," I whispered back.

"Outside prepaid doesn't work in J&K. It is the government rule." Her son's head rolled to the side, and she brought it back with a gentle palm. She reached around him into her purse and drew out a small Nokia in a pink rubber case. "Do you need to call someone?"

I stared at her phone, weighing the implications of what she'd just told me. I imagined my father frowning, rubbing his stubble as he listened to the impersonal recorded voice telling him over and over again that my number was no longer reachable. His confusion, his slow-building panic.

"No," I whispered. "Thank you very much."

"Please, it's not a problem," she said, holding it out farther. "Use it if you need to."

"I don't need to call anyone," I said. "But thank you."

After that we were both silent and the train began to move again. I closed my eyes and was aware of a sense of liberation, not exactly peaceful, and not detached from sorrow. Now, I thought, I was truly adrift. From now on, whatever happened would be my responsibility alone.

Jammu came in pieces, boxy houses, roads growing larger, busier. At the station, I waited until the compartment had emptied; then I reached for my rucksack and walked up the aisle. My fellow travelers were gone, leaving behind crumpled paper, candy wrappers, orange rinds, the smell of sweat. A woman in a blue sari was desultorily cleaning the first compartment. When she arrived at mine, if she was careful, she would find my phone tucked into the back of the seat.

The tout for the share taxi assured me that my bag would not fall off the roof, while at the same time hustling me almost bodily into the vehicle, which was a white Tata Sumo. He wore a red shirt, the sleeves rolled up almost to his shoulders. Sixteen or seventeen, his hair molded into an impossibly high, cresting wave, he stalked back and forth in front of the taxi, shouting, "Doda! Kishtwar! Doda! Kishtwar!" in a bored, imperious voice. From time to time, he stopped and scowled at the cloudless, innocent-looking sky. "Going to rain," he muttered darkly to nobody in particular.

After I'd relinquished my rucksack, I climbed in and found a seat at the very back of the taxi, next to the window. My fellow passengers were a bearded, scholarly-looking old man, and a teenage boy with his father, both of whom ate banana after banana from the largest bunch I'd ever seen, which they had placed like a third passenger on the seat between them.

Outside on the street, Hindu and Muslim women walked by, heads loosely covered. The young Muslim men had thin, angular faces, and I fancied I could see traces of Bashir Ahmed in one or two of them, which I took, in my tiredness, to be a good omen. I leaned my head against the window. Fatigue was setting in, two continuous days of travel stiffening my muscles, pulling at the backs of my eyes.

A thickset woman in a purple headscarf climbed into the taxi with her husband; the tout leapt in after them. There was now a plump man in the driver's seat, dusting the windshield with a cloth. Extremely businesslike, the tout collected fares from the others then turned last of all to me.

"How much?" I asked in Hindi, aware that every pair of eyes was on me. With my jeans and T-shirt and ponytail, I thought I knew what I looked like. A clueless tourist, a woman traveling alone. It did not occur to me that what they saw, first and foremost, was an outsider.

The tout made a great show of impatience. "To Kishtwar? Two fifty."

Flustered, I handed him two hundred-rupee notes, and he glanced down at them. "Two *fifty*," he muttered. "Another fifty."

"Oh." My face burned. "Sorry." I gave him another hundred, and he handed back fifty with a professional flick, then leapt out of the back door of the taxi, taking his seat next to the driver.

And just as quickly as it had arrived, Jammu dissolved, and we were on a highway that, but for the numerous security check posts, could have been anywhere in the country, surrounded by lorries piled high with timber, bricks, iron rods. I fell asleep for a while, and when I woke up, I looked out and saw fields of smooth white rocks, and I realized, with a shock, how far below they were.

We had entered the mountains.

On the other side of the taxi, the teenager sent another banana peel sailing out of the window. I saw the earth torn open, great wounds for new roads. I saw intermittent signs, some on neat diamond-shaped boards, some splashed messily on rocks.

Kashmir Is the Jewel in the Crown of India.
Watch for Falling Rocks..
Peep Peep Don't Sleep.
Be Gentle on My Curves.
From Kashmir to Kanyakumari India Is One.

After an hour, the driver stopped at a roadside shack with long wooden tables, and everyone trooped out. I watched them drift into groups, the brief, unconscious alliances of travelers. The teenager and his father with the driver and the tout. The scholarly old man with the headscarfed woman and her husband. I willed myself to leave the taxi, to ask if I could join one or the other of them, but all I saw was myself thrusting money into the tout's hand, his scornful young face as he said, "Another fifty," while the rest looked on, and, childish as it was, shame kept me pinned to my seat.

After a while, I heard someone tapping at my window. It was the plump driver, holding up a tiny plastic cup of tea. I shook my head without thinking.

"If you don't drink it, I'll throw it away. Very sad," he said in plain Urdu, not sounding sad at all. I opened the window, took the cup, and put it to my lips. The first sip brought a welcome heat to my cheeks, and I felt twice as stupid for refusing the first time.

"Thank you," I said as sincerely as I could.

"You are travelling alone." It was not a question.

"Yes."

He did not inquire further, some unwritten code of courtesy holding him back, perhaps, but I was so grateful for being spoken to at all that I thanked him again. He smiled slightly, told me we would be in Kishtwar in an hour, then climbed back into his seat, leaving the door open, one leg dangling out. It was clearly a tacit signal, because shortly afterward, the other passengers trooped back to the taxi, wiping their mouths with their sleeves.

The tout had been right, as it turned out. It began to rain as soon as we got back on the highway. Now the driver hunched forward in concentration, the wipers hissing. All the windows were closed, and our clothes steamed, their stink mingling with the ripeness of banana. Occasionally I caught sight of the valley as we turned a hairpin bend, all that hazy, endless space, and I had to close my eyes to ignore the drop in my stomach.

Out of nowhere, a convoy of gray-green army trucks and jeeps passed us, going in the opposite direction. Metal letters on their front grilles read *Vehicle Factory Jabalpur*. It took a minute for them to pass us completely; there must have been at least fifty trucks, each driven by a soldier, his face partially obscured by the visor of his cap. I guessed they were returning to the army headquarters in Udhampur. We had passed through the town of Udhampur a little while ago, and I'd remembered my father's friend, the brigadier, thankful I would never be obliged to meet him. I knew exactly what it would be, sipping weak tea in a stuffy, overdecorated living room, while the brigadier and his wife—both stout and hearty in my imagination—bombarded me with volleys of well-intentioned but tactless questions about my dead mother and why I wasn't married yet. All I saw of Udhampur itself was a few broad streets bristling with zigzag roadblocks that forced our taxi to slow almost to a crawl, soldiers who eyed our vehicle as it went past, and a tank hunkered in the middle of a grassy circle, its dark barrel painted in incongruous candy stripes. I was glad when we left it behind.

We arrived in Kishtwar at dusk. The tout hoisted himself up to the roof rack and flung our luggage down piece by piece. Blue-gray mountains curved steeply up on all sides, but the town itself appeared relatively flat. It was a little like standing inside a bowl. We seemed to be in a marketplace, surrounded by taxis, tea stalls and shops, most of which were already locked and shuttered. In one stall, men tore off chunks of bread and dunked them into tiny cups of steaming tea. A stray cow shambled toward a quiet corner.

It was all quite ordinary, but I could not shake my sense of bewilderment, perhaps because it *was* so ordinary. I didn't know what I had been expecting, but I was aware of a slight sense of disappointment as I looked around. Then my eyes fell on a strange sight, the burned husk of a large, partly demolished building with a charred tower rising on one end. As

I stood there, a voice rose from somewhere near or within the building, a man's low, keening voice, which held a knife-edge of sorrow and desperation. Not a soul in the marketplace reacted, and I stood frozen, afraid to move, afraid I'd lost my mind. Then I understood: the burned building was, or had once been, a mosque. When the voice fell silent, I walked over to the driver, who was inspecting a nick in the windshield.

"Excuse me," I said, "is there a hotel around here?"

He looked at me, his face neither friendly nor hostile. It was as though he'd forgotten he'd bought me a cup of tea, that we had ever exchanged words.

"Hotel?" he echoed. "You mean you don't have anyone to stay with?" When I shook my head, he appeared to consider. Then he said, "See the mosque? The burned one? Take a left there. After a shoe shop, you'll see some green steps. Go up."

"And that is a hotel?"

"People stay there, yes. Tell them my name, and they will give you a room."

"And your name?"

"Majid."

"Thank you, Mr. Majid."

He bent his head slightly in a decorous, old-worldly gesture.

"What happened to the mosque, Mr. Majid?"

"Better ask the people at the place you're going. This isn't my town."

I thanked him for the final time. Then I turned my back on him and the taxi and began walking toward the blackened, gutted mosque, which, I could see from patches of unburned wall, had once been pink. Once I was past it, I looked back, wanting to catch a final glimpse of the vehicle that had brought me here, of Mr. Majid, the first person who had been kind to me. But ours was one of several white vehicles in the bustling marketplace, and I could no longer see him.

* * *

There was a staircase leading up, as he'd said, and painted green. The door at the top was closed, but light leaked from a crack at the bottom. The middle-aged man who answered my knock had clearly just finished his dinner. I could see it still laid out on the ground behind him. His hair was graying and curly, and he wore glasses with thin, round, gold-wire frames.

"Yes?" he said in Urdu.

"I'm looking for a room, Uncle," I said. "Mr. Majid told me this was a hotel."

The man frowned. "*Who* said this was a hotel?"

"Mr. Majid," I said. "He drives a taxi. I asked him about a hotel and he sent me here."

"This tall?" He raised a palm to the level of his shoulder. "Slightly fat? Light eyes?"

"Yes," I said, though in all honesty I couldn't recall. The hundred meters or so I'd walked from the taxi had seemed to take years. The smell of gravy drifted from the room and hit me like a hard blow. I realized I hadn't eaten a proper meal in two days.

The curly-haired man looked down at my rucksack. "You've come on holiday?" he asked. He seemed not to know what to make of me.

Maybe it was because I was exhausted from traveling, or because of the food, but I told him the truth. I said, "I've come to find someone."

All at once, the man's face changed. It turned grim, but with a new softness, a sympathy. He moved aside from the doorway. "Come in," he said. "You will eat dinner?"

"So you do have a room?" I asked, confused.

"We will find one, don't worry," he said. "First eat. Then we can discuss it."

Too tired to wonder what this meant, I stepped into the hall. The floor was covered in a patterned cloth; colorful bolsters lined the walls. The man pointed to a small, salmon-colored sink in the corner. While I washed my hands, he carried my rucksack behind a curtain that obviously led to the rest of the house. Moments later, a woman emerged from behind the same curtain with a plate. She was stocky and broad-featured and unsmiling, and when she said, "Sit here," her voice was like iron. It brooked no indecision, and I was glad to obey. She heaped rice onto a plate and laid a large piece of chicken on top. "Eat," she said, and disappeared behind the curtain again.

Left by myself, I took a mouthful of chicken and nearly wept. The rice was fragrant, the chicken tender and flavored subtly with cardamom. I ate without grace or restraint, hunching low over my plate, shoving fistfuls of rice into my mouth. Only when the man came back out did I struggle to sit up straight. He sat cross-legged beside me, and once again I glimpsed his expression: sadness but no surprise. It was almost as if, I thought with a shiver, they had been *waiting* for me.

"So," the man said. "Where have you come from?"

"Bangalore."

"Bangalore," he said gravely. "I should have guessed from the way you speak. And you are looking for somebody."

I nodded.

"Have you tried elsewhere?"

"No," I said.

"Srinagar?"

"No."

"You haven't tried anywhere else?" he said, his voice intent.

I stared down at my food, which I badly wanted to finish. Why was he asking me these questions? He must have seen the confusion in my face, because he softened.

"I'm sorry," he said. "You are tired. We will talk about this tomorrow. Take your time to finish eating. Your room is ready for you."

He left me alone to finish my meal, and when I was done, the woman came back from behind the curtain. I thought I saw a glimmer of approval in her eyes at the sight of the empty plate, but when I praised the food, she did not react. I washed my hands again; then the man returned and led me past the curtain, down a small corridor with two doors on each side. The first door on the right led to a neat kitchen, where I saw the man's wife standing at the sink. She didn't turn.

The first door on the left was ajar, and I caught a brief glimpse of bright yellow walls, a terrific mess of clothes on the floor, the overpowering stench of sweat. Two skinny, bearded men lay on the floor, listening to a small radio, and a third stood at the window, smoking a beedi. All three followed me with their eyes as I passed, but none of them spoke.

The two far doors were closed. "Toilet," my new host said, pointing to the one on the right. "And you will be in here." He knocked smartly. A young man, about the same age as me, I guessed, came out quickly, shoving some clothes into a little backpack and apologizing. The curly-haired man waited for him to pass then led me into my new room.

It was so tiny I could have stood in the middle and touched any wall just by stretching. It had also obviously been cleared in a hurry. The pink sheet on the bed had been tucked in askew, the door to a low wooden cabinet hung open. There was a book of some kind under the bed; I could see its black corner jutting out. The walls were painted pistachio-green, and a purple banner with silver Arabic script hung from a hook. My rucksack had been brought ahead of me; it stood in the corner beside the cabinet. There was something soothing about it.

I looked around the room, then at the man. "I'm sorry," I said.

"Why?"

"This was his room. That man who just left. You gave it to me."

The curly-haired man smiled. "No, no, you mustn't think of it like that. He is leaving us soon, anyway. Now if you need anything else, please ask me or my wife." He touched his fingers to his chest. "My name is Abdul Latief."

"Thank you, Latief Uncle," I said. "How much—?"

But he held up a hand, cutting me off. "There will be time for all that tomorrow."

He shut the door, and I turned to face the room. It was the first time in three days that I'd been completely alone. For a second, I couldn't remember where I was.

Then I heard a soft, urgent knocking. I opened the door to find the young man I'd just seen leaving with his backpack. He smiled awkwardly, his eyes darting past me into the room.

"Your book," I said, following his gaze. "It's under the bed."

I picked it up and handed it to him, seeing as I did that it was a daily planner, turned threadbare and soft with use, the year 2002 emblazoned in gold on the bottom right corner of the cover. He opened it with a shy smile, inviting me to look. I hesitated, then stepped forward as he flipped through it. The pages were covered with a dense Urdu I couldn't read, interspersed with what appeared to be telephone numbers. Then he gently extracted a photograph from between two pages and showed it to me. It was deeply creased and showed another man with a similar face, though a few years older, a cheap studio portrait in which he stood against the painted backdrop of a lighthouse perched above a gloomy, whitecapped sea.

The young man tapped the photograph with a finger. In Urdu, he said, "My brother."

"Very nice," I said uncertainly. He seemed so much like a child, standing there with the photograph held out for my approval, but there was also a charged inquiry in his eyes, as if he was sure I knew his brother and was waiting for me to admit it. "It's a very nice photo."

He smiled, then quickly looked somber. "Tomorrow I will go to Bhaderwah," he announced. "Have you been to Bhaderwah already?"

"No," I said.

"Tomorrow I will go there," he said. He slid the photo back into the planner and closed it. Out in the corridor, he turned back and said, in shy and diffident English, "I wish best of luck."

Startled, I wanted to ask him what he meant, but I stopped myself. If it was luck, I'd take it.

"Thank you," I said. I held out my hand. "Best of luck to you too."

He grinned. We shook hands, and he walked back slowly to the room where I'd seen the three men, holding his precious book tight under his arm.

Once he was inside, I locked my door and sat on the edge of the bed. I took off my jeans and my T-shirt. I looked at my skin then at the green walls of this new room, and I tried to make sense of the two things together. My skin and this room. My skin in this room. There was a pause, a second of blankness, and then I began to cry, pressing my palms to my mouth to keep from making a noise. After the tears, I felt better.

I crawled under the pink sheet and gathered it tight in both my fists. I could still feel the lurching of the taxi, the valley below, the strange and terrifying pull of all that space. I tried to conjure up my mother to help me sleep, but what came instead, to my surprise, was the image of Abdul Latief's silent wife, piling rice onto my plate, the mound growing steadily higher and higher, and I fell asleep, comforted by the thought that she was close.

6

I WOKE IN THE green room with the sun streaming onto the silver Arabic letters. A gray towel had been placed on the cabinet, a fresh bar of soap nestled in its folds. It pleased me, the thought of Abdul Latief's wife walking around my room, noiseless and efficient, her capable eye deciding just what I needed. I gathered the towel and a fresh set of clothes and stood in their chilly bathroom, watching the bucket fill with steaming water. Later, I wrapped the gray towel around myself and rubbed a circle in the foggy mirror, staring at my face while I brushed my teeth.

In the hall, Abdul Latief was watching TV, elbow propped on a black-and-white bolster. In front of him was breakfast: a large blue thermos, a pair of white teacups and saucers, and a small wicker basket filled with gleaming triangular parathas.

"Good morning," he said, smiling and clicking off the TV as I entered.

He poured me a cup of tea, which was, strangely enough, pink-tinged, and then one for himself. I took a careful sip and was surprised to find it salty. Abdul Latief laughed.

"Noon chai," he said. "Here we drink our chai with salt. You don't like it?"

I took another sip. It tasted like a warm, slightly bitter broth. "I do like it."

"What do you drink in your home?" he pressed. "Lipton chai? The sweet kind? Shall I ask my wife to make that for you?"

"Oh no, please. I usually drink coffee at home anyway. But this is fine. Really. I like it a lot."

I took a few more sips to reassure him, and he settled against his bolster, cradling his cup in his hand. "So," he said, "you're looking for someone. That is what you told me yesterday, correct?"

"Yes," I said. In the mirror earlier, I had rehearsed what I would say. "I am looking for a man. He must be about fifty years old now. His name is Bashir Ahmed."

"Bashir Ahmed." He repeated the name slowly. "He is Kashmiri, this Bashir Ahmed?"

"Yes."

"And how do you know him?"

"He is my friend," I said. Then I corrected myself, "A friend of my mother's."

"I see. And your mother, she is Kashmiri?"

"No."

"Then where did you meet this Bashir Ahmed?"

"He used to work in Bangalore," I said. "Selling clothes. He used to come to our house, when I was a child."

"To sell clothes."

I hesitated. "Yes."

"And what happened to him?" Abdul Latief asked.

"I don't know."

He nodded, as if he'd been expecting it. "No one really does," he said. "When did you see him the last time?"

"Eleven years ago. When I was thirteen."

He glanced sharply at my face. "You are twenty-four years old now?" he asked.

I nodded. It seemed that he was about to ask something else, but, in the end, he just exhaled. "Eleven years. That is a long time," he said. "But you will find this Bashir Ahmed, inshallah." He set the cup down. "Now listen. There is a bus, which stops near the camp outside Kishtwar. If you can be ready in half an hour, I will take you myself."

I had no idea what he was talking about, but before I could ask, his wife entered. Her face was as unsmiling as on the previous night. "Good morning," I said, glad to see her.

She returned the greeting, albeit a bit stiffly.

"Our guest does not like our chai," Abdul Latief told her.

I tried to deny it, but he laughed without malice. "It's true. You have not touched it. Do we have any coffee?" he asked his wife. "She says she drinks coffee at home. Otherwise, Lipton."

His wife took one look at my cup and went back to the kitchen. Feeling slightly rebuked, I turned once again to Abdul Latief.

"So," he said, "you can be ready in half an hour?"

"I'm sorry," I said, "but I don't understand. Ready for what?"

"For the bus."

I shook my head. Abdul Latief looked at me sharply, as if he thought I might be joking, then took his elbow off the bolster and sat up. "Tell me again properly who this person is and why you are looking for him." His voice had a new, hard edge.

I stared at him. "I told you," I said. "He was my mother's friend."

"And he used to come to your house to sell clothes."

"Yes."

"Eleven years ago."

"Yes."

"And then he stopped coming."

"Yes."

"And that's *all*?" he asked incredulously.

I stared down at my untouched cup of tea. All the armor I'd gained from my night in the tiny green room, the bar of soap, the clean clothes, all of it fell away, and I felt gritty and vulnerable again. *That's not all!* I wanted to shout. But then Abdul Latief's wife came back in, holding a second white cup. He spoke to her in Kashmiri, and she listened without comment. When he was done, he turned back to me. "Tell me, why do you not just ask your mother where this Bashir Ahmed is?"

"Because," I said flatly, "she's dead."

After a moment's silence, Abdul Latief asked tentatively, "Your mother?"

I nodded, not trusting myself to speak.

His tone was much softer now, the hard edge gone: "And that is why you have come to Kishtwar? To find this Bashir Ahmed and tell him about your mother?"

I don't know if I nodded again, but this time Abdul Latief gave a long sigh. There was genuine sympathy in it, which seemed to go beyond ordinary condolence.

"I am so sorry," he said. "I did not understand. I wish you had told me this yesterday. Then I would have told you right away that we could not help you and we would not have wasted your time."

"Ah," I said.

"What we do," Abdul Latief said, and here he and his wife glanced at each other, a private, coded look I could not decipher. "What we do is—a bit different. You are not—I mean—" He broke off and shrugged.

"No problem," I said, starting to get up, but his wife stopped me. She took a step forward and placed the second white cup in her hand beside the one already in front of me.

"Drink that," she said firmly. "We have no coffee, but I made you another cup of tea. Sweet, this time. The way you drink it at home."

As soon as breakfast was over, I struggled into my shoes, muttering something about a walk, and left their house, pushing my way blindly down the green steps. A tiny boy in a skullcap was darting into the shoeshop with two cardboard boxes under each arm. I found that I was furious, not at Abdul Latief and his wife, but at myself, at my stupidity, my *complacency*, embarking on this journey with no concrete plan, with only a ridiculous story as my guide. What on earth had I imagined would happen? That I would arrive in Kishtwar and run into Bashir Ahmed on the street? Now I was here, in a foreign town, in a foreign house, without any idea of how to proceed.

The market was more crowded than it had been the evening before. Men stood in groups outside tiny shops crammed with radios and cheap watches; women walked in the shade of the mosque's smoke-blackened wall. I looked around for my driver, though I did not really expect to see him. But there were other drivers, other taxis and I knew it would be the easiest thing to climb into one going back to Jammu. Find a phone booth and call my father. Claim my phone had been lost, stolen. Ask him to book me on the next flight back home. Give up this search. Return to my father and to Bangalore and the life that was mine.

I turned away from the taxis and walked down one of the tiny streets that radiated from the marketplace, and soon I could no longer hear its bustle. I passed a boys' school, where a woman in a gold headscarf and matching stilettos was entering through the metal gates, which were partially blocked by security barricades. I passed an orphanage, a tailor, a few hardware stores. Then I saw what looked like a park, surrounded by a low compound wall. I could not bear the thought of more aimless walking, nor of returning to Abdul Latief's house, so I crossed the street, found the park gate, and went in.

It was enormous. At first glance, it seemed to hold the entire population of Kishtwar—families picnicking; boys playing cricket, half a dozen games in progress simultaneously; men walking in pairs for exercise. Briefly I envisioned a catastrophe, a great explosion or a massacre in the past, which might have caused such a large area to be leveled. But there was no indication of anything of the sort. The grass under my shoes was ordinary, yellowing, and speckled with trash. At the far end of the field, blocked off by a wire fence, sat a squat army helicopter, flanked by the silhouettes of two soldiers.

I lost track of how long I sat in the sun, arms wrapped around my knees, watching red cricket balls judder over the ground, fielders dashing after them. A young Hindu couple picnicked close by, eating chips and taking photographs of their daughter, who twirled in a spangled lavender frock. Eventually they left, as did most of the cricketers, except for a few who remained lying on their stomachs, talking. But then they, too, were gone, and I reluctantly returned to the street.

It took me the better part of twenty minutes to find the house again. My body sore, I mounted the steps slowly, but pulled my shoulders back before entering. I would not let them see my fear, my helplessness. I would pack my bag, pay them for the night, and I would leave. I did not know where I would go, but it did not matter, as long as I was away from their pity. But when I opened the door, I was greeted by a small crowd in the living room. Abdul Latief was there, as were the three bearded men I'd seen last night. His wife sat in another corner, a pair of knitting needles and some dark blue wool on her lap. As soon as he saw me, Abdul Latief got to his feet, relief spreading across his face.

"There you are," he exclaimed. "We were getting worried about you."

"I just wanted to look around. I'm sorry."

"No, it is fine. You saw a little bit of our Kishtwar?" His anxiety had abated by now, and he seemed to be asking it kindly, so I said, "Yes. I found a big field, and I sat there for a while."

Now he smiled. "Ah, yes, Chowgan," he said. "It is very famous, our Chowgan. There is a very interesting story about it, you know. Many years ago, a Muslim pir, Shah Asraruddin Baghdadi, performed a miracle close to there. He—"

"Yes, I know," I said flatly. "His friend died, and he brought him back to life."

Abdul Latief's eyes widened. "You know? How did you hear about this?"

"My mother's friend told me."

"The one you're looking for?"

I nodded.

"I see," Abdul Latief said. He glanced at his wife, who set her knitting in her lap. When he looked back at me, I knew something had been decided in my absence.

"Please sit down," he told me formally.

They were all watching me—the three men with their thin faces and dark beards, Abdul Latief, and his wife—so I had no choice. I moved forward and sat down before them.

"This man," Abdul Latief said, "Bashir Ahmed. How do you know he is from Kishtwar?"

"He is not from Kishtwar," I said. "But his wife's family lives here."

"You are sure about this? You visited them today?"

"No, I don't know who they are. I just know they live here."

He leaned back, lost in thought. *Now,* I told myself. *Stand up now and tell them that you're leaving. Ask politely how much they want, then pay double. That way, you will owe them nothing.*

I put my hands under me and began to lift myself up.

"We will help you," Abdul Latief announced.

I stopped.

"We will help you find this Bashir Ahmed," he said again. "Kishtwar is a small place, and we know many people. It should not be so difficult."

I allowed my weight to sink inch by inch until I was on the ground again. I laid my hands carefully in my lap. The three men were looking on with approval, as if they had something to do with it, and Abdul Latief himself was grinning, but I knew, immediately and without a doubt, that the person responsible for this was his wife.

"Thank you," I whispered in her direction. "Thank you," I said, louder, to Abdul Latief.

"It is our pleasure," Abdul Latief replied. Then his smile changed, turning bitter and slightly self-mocking. "At least," he said, "you have a better chance of finding your friend."

My *mother's* friend, I wanted to say. Instead I asked, "Better than what?"

But he was looking at his wife again. The same look as before, so private and profound it felt like an indecency even to witness it. Finally, he dragged his eyes away from her and looked at me.

"Better than the rest of us," he said.

We agreed on four hundred rupees a night, including breakfast and dinner. Lunch I would have to arrange for myself, since they both worked. Abdul Latief, it turned out, was a teacher at the same school I'd passed on my way to the Chowgan. I didn't know what his wife did, and her stony face made it impossible to ask. Four hundred rupees was not unreasonable; in my old life, I might have spent as much on a single meal. Now, however, it was more than I wanted to pay, but I did not haggle. My mother would have refused. She would have been immovable. *Two hundred or I'm leaving*. She once reduced a vegetable vendor to raging incoherence. He snatched up a tomato and flung it on the ground. "Just go! Take it and go!" My mother looked down at the ruined tomato, dribbling its juice all over the road. "It's a bit damaged," she said. "Do you have a different one?" He howled and flung another.

Abdul Latief said he and his wife were going to talk to some people, spread the word about Bashir Ahmed, and informed me, quite bluntly, that there was nothing I could do to help. And so, just like that, my days were barren again. I went to my room each evening, and brought out four hundred rupees, which Abdul Latief tucked into his pocket before going for prayers at the charred mosque. It had burned down a few years before, he told me, and the police claimed the fire was caused by an electrical short circuit. He snorted as he said this, though he didn't explain why. I had never seen his wife pray. She rarely addressed me, and it was not because she was a reticent woman. I once walked into the hall and caught her in mid-laugh, face contorted, chin tucked to her chest. When she saw me, the laugh evaporated. She made two thermoses of tea now, salty for them, sweet for me. For a couple of days, I rose and ate with them, but after it became clear that they had truly shouldered the burden of my search, I gradually began to sleep later, sometimes waking only to the afternoon azan. The hall would be empty, but my breakfast would be laid out on a tray, parathas and boiled eggs, or four slices of bread and some jam.

Looking back, it was astonishing how quickly I became accustomed to their house. Within a week, it all felt familiar: the salmon-colored sink, the tiny TV in the corner, the few leather-bound Urdu or Arabic books with gold-edged pages, the dense bolster at my back. I felt at ease there amongst the objects of their life, and sometimes, in the silence, I pretended they were mine.

In the afternoons I walked, the town slowly resolving itself into a pattern I could hold steady in my mind: the scuffs on a door, a shopkeeper's face, a street corner. The shops were sharply divided, as far as I could see, between Hindu and Muslim owners; their customers too sorted themselves accordingly. I could not escape noticing, either, the number of Indian soldiers and policemen in the town. They were everywhere, dressed in khaki or olive, congregating in tight groups on street corners or in tea stalls. Whenever I walked, a convoy of army jeeps would usually roll by, soldiers sitting in the back like bored tourists being ferried around yet another foreign city, but they mostly ignored the local people, who ignored them in turn. I never stayed away from the house long, however. The greatest pleasure was opening the door to find it as I had left it, all mine for the hours Abdul Latief and his wife were away.

I studied them as carefully as I studied their house. I knew that after dinner he always reached for a toothpick from the little box on the windowsill. I knew that when she washed her hair, she sat in the hall with it fanned out over her back, a towel thrown over her head. Neither of them hummed or sang, even unconsciously; there was a fundamental stillness to them both, despite Abdul Latief's jokes and joviality. Each night, they slept on the floor in the hall, unrolling a mattress and covering it with a sheet. Once, unable to sleep and going to the kitchen for a glass of water, I caught sight of them. His wife lay closest to the door, a solid barrier against anything that might burst in. Somehow, it was easier to fall asleep after that.

What else? I knew, from scraps I picked up, that his sister lived in Srinagar, and that there was a relative in Dubai. That the relative had two sons, and when they called, the air in the house was transformed. Abdul Latief spoke to them first, letting them tease him, pretending to be outraged, then pacified, then outraged again. His wife spoke to them next, and she was the one who teased her nephews, reducing them to helpless giggles I could hear across the room. That was really all I knew about their lives. Except, of course, the people who came to stay.

For the first few days I lived with Abdul Latief and his wife, the three bearded men joined us for dinner, eating little and speaking even less, but otherwise they remained in their room, smoking and listening to the radio. They went out for long periods each day. The young man with his black book had left the morning after my arrival, and the one time I asked Abdul Latief about him, he sighed. "Poor boy," he said. "He ran out of money and had to go back home. He'll try again next year." I'd nodded as though I understood. And after a few days, the three men disappeared, too, all of them in a single night, taking with them their gaunt faces and the smell of beedi smoke.

People were always coming and going in their house. Most arrived unannounced, the way I had, and were taken in. A few were prepared for and welcomed. There was a constant parade of faces, of shoes by the door, of bags and suitcases. None of these people were ever introduced to me, so I never quite understood who they were. Besides, they stayed only a day or so. A young girl with her grandmother. A pair of soft-voiced men. There was an old woman who shared my room for two nights, because the other one was occupied. The old woman was tiny, with gray hair that curled away on either side of her forehead like a ram's horns. She spoke only Kashmiri in a thick, phlegmy voice, as if she'd been sick for years, though she looked strong enough to have lifted me over her head. Abdul Latief dragged in a mattress, apologizing, and left it on the floor. That night, I tried to make her understand she should take the bed, but she gave me a look that shut me up in a second. The next evening, though, I saw her in the kitchen with Abdul Latief's wife, who had an arm around her. She was sobbing, dreadful sobs, as a stream of Kashmiri, which I could not understand, poured from her, and I stood there in shock, unable to believe this was the same woman. But when she came in an hour later, there was no hint of tears. Her face was like rock. She took the floor. I took the bed. The next day, she was gone, and Abdul Latief came in to drag the mattress from my room.

7

MY TENTH MORNING IN the tiny green room in Kishtwar, and I was awake before dawn. I could see a chunk of sky, feather-gray, like the pigeons that always surged and bubbled before the blackened mosque. I swung my legs out of bed and padded up the corridor toward the hall.

Abdul Latief and his wife were already awake. They were sitting next to each other in the dark, and they didn't seem surprised to see me. Abdul Latief nodded, beckoning me in. I went in and sat beside them without speaking. And suddenly it seemed like the most natural thing I had ever done in my life, sitting in comfortable silence with this somber couple in the predawn. When the azan began, it only seemed to reflect and deepen the tranquillity in the room. Abdul Latief rose to his feet, smiled at us, and left the house. I imagined him walking slowly toward the mosque, head bent, obeying the call of that voice.

His wife went to the bathroom and returned with a small prayer rug, which she unfolded in the middle of the hall. Then she began to pray, hands by her sides, eyes closed, mouth forming silent words. She knelt and pressed her forehead to the rug, then sat up and turned her chin first to one shoulder, then the other. I watched from my corner, oddly stirred by the intimacy of her gestures and unable to suppress a pang of longing for my mother and her idols.

She stood, folding up the prayer rug. Before I could lose my nerve, I asked her name.

"Zoya," she said, after a pause.

"Zoya," I repeated. "That is a beautiful name."

She smiled. It was not the smile she gave her nephews in Dubai, nor the smile with which she welcomed the people who came to stay, but I held tightly on to it. She went to the kitchen and returned with a thermos of sweet tea and a bowl of dried apricots. She sat beside me, and we ate and drank in silence. I did not want anything to disturb this comfort, but then she cleared her throat and said, in Urdu, "There will be people here today. We have a function."

"Oh?" I said, too brightly. "Someone's birthday?"

Her chin shot up. "No," she said, and to my surprise, there was anger in her voice, so flashing and unexpected that I flinched. She fought it back and said, in a dull, indifferent tone, "It is a function, that's all. You can join us, if you want. Maybe you can talk to the people there, ask them if they know your mother's friend."

I thanked her, but the intimacy that had lingered in the air a moment ago dissolved, as though it had never been. I felt my chest growing tight, and after I helped her clear away the thermos and bowl, I told her I was going for a walk. She nodded curtly but didn't look at me.

The marketplace was just coming alive, touts and drivers and early passengers milling around, tea stall owners sitting like rocks in the rivers of steam that rose from their huge metal vats of chai. The motion and energy was grating, so I plunged instead into the network of tiny alleyways and shops, all of which were still shuttered at this hour. Here the light was thin and feeble, smearing the ground, and sleep was thick in the air. It suited my sense of being an outsider, and I walked in the very middle of the road, taking a perverse satisfaction in making my steps as loud as I could—the misfit, the invader, stomping this tiny town to rubble in the early morning.

I stopped and raised my face to the mountains. They were pink, shadows running like deep cracks down their slopes. I lifted my hand and traced their wavering peaks with a forefinger. Somewhere in those mountains, I sternly reminded myself, was Bashir Ahmed. *That* was why I had come. To find him. Not to ingratiate myself with a woman who never smiled.

When I looked down, I saw I was not alone.

Standing at a Y-shaped intersection, before the rippling red-and-white cross on the shutter of a closed pharmacy, was an Indian soldier. I hadn't noticed him earlier, but it was clear that he had been standing in the same place for hours. He was tall and lanky, his rifle a thick black line that cut his body in half. His eyes, under his helmet, followed me as I walked.

As I've said, I'd seen plenty of soldiers in Kishtwar, but only ever in groups, huddled shoulder to shoulder, like teenagers. This was the first one I'd seen standing alone. My first instinct was to turn and walk away, but at the same time I was drawn forward by his solitude, which seemed somehow a reflection of my own. I approached slowly, pretending to be absorbed in reading the signs above the closed shutters. *Nashrah Fashions. Manzoor Photo Studio. Lal Ji Sweets.* A few downy chicken feathers blew across the street.

Then I heard him call out, in English, unexpectedly, "The shops won't open for some time."

His voice was boyishly high, and once he addressed me, I was able to look directly at him. At first, all I'd noticed was the uniform, the tall black boots, the dappled gray-green camouflage, but now I saw that he was young, not even twenty, with a wispy, carefully maintained mustache on an otherwise hairless face. He shifted from one boot to the other.

"Thank you," I called back cautiously. "Do you know what time it is?"

"Six fifteen," he said. "Which shop are you looking for? I can tell you when it will open."

His ears stuck out comically from under his bowl-shaped helmet. Now I was close enough to read the name tag sewn to his shirt: *P. L. Stalin. Malayali,* I thought, with a jolt of irrational relief. A fellow South Indian in the Himalayas. I felt myself starting to relax. It was also comforting to speak English again, after days of speaking with my hosts in an admixture of Hindi and Urdu, a hybrid language in which our communication was imperfect at best.

"It's nothing urgent," I said.

We stood there in silence.

Then he asked, shyly, "Where are you from?" When I told him, he beamed. "Bangalore!" he exclaimed. "I went there for three months, during my training. It is such a nice city."

"And where are you from?" I asked.

"Me?" He seemed gratified by my interest. "I am from Trivandrum. Have you ever been there? It is also nice," he said, when I shook my head, "but not like Bangalore. You know, for a while I wanted a posting in Bangalore itself, but then I thought it would be better to come here."

"Why?"

"More money," he said cheerfully. "And you? Why have you come to Kishtwar?"

"Oh," I said vaguely, "a holiday."

"A holiday? Here?" I noted the distaste in his voice.

"Why not? Don't you like it here?" I asked.

"The place itself is not so bad, but the people . . ." He shrugged.

"Why?" I thought of Zoya and Abdul Latief. "What's wrong with them?"

"I don't know," he said. His voice tumbled over itself in its eagerness. I had the feeling it had been a while since he'd talked to anybody. "They are not friendly, any of them. Actually, the Hindus are okay. It's mostly the Muslims." He removed one hand from under the rifle and gestured toward the deserted intersection. "They supported the militants, you know. Ten, fifteen years ago, militants used to ride motorcycles openly in the road and boys would run after them. That doesn't happen anymore, but the Muslims here still act like nothing has changed. Sometimes I try talking to them, but they always look the other way." He abruptly leaned in toward me. "You will see," he breathed in a low, confidential voice, his eyes fixed on my face. "These people, they are not like us."

It was the *us* that did it, the assumption of a shared intimacy, like a curtain pulled around our bodies. It gave me pause, and I wondered suddenly if he was right. Not about the Muslims of Kishtwar, but about the way they saw *us*. Was that the reason for Zoya's coldness? Because she thought soldiers like Stalin, named for a revolutionary turned dictator, and I were the same breed of creature, to be held at arm's length? Was that why she stopped laughing whenever I entered a room? No, it couldn't be. I had no weapon. He and I were not the same.

"Perhaps they're frightened of you," I said, looking at his gun more pointedly than I'd intended.

He gave me a look of genuine incomprehension. "Of me? Why should they be frightened of me? What have I done to them?"

I said nothing.

Stalin was now looking around, as if my suggestion had troubled him. Then he said, "Do you know what happened here?"

I shook my head.

"Well," he said, "it wasn't here exactly, but in a village about an hour away." He pointed toward the same range of mountains I'd been looking at earlier, which had turned now from dawn pink to charcoal gray. "A Hindu village, close to a forest. Five years ago, during the winter, a group of militants came out of the forest with guns early in the morning, and they went into every house in that village. They pulled out all the men from this village and forced them to sit on the ground. Then they shot all of them. Sixteen men."

After a moment of silence, I managed to say, "How awful."

He nodded sagely, as if I'd screamed. "Yes. And I heard that, on the same day, the Muslims held big parties in Kishtwar. Everybody could hear them."

At the word *party*, I remembered Zoya, her glittering, inexplicable anger. I swiftly crushed the memory and said, "That is a terrible story."

"And then the mosque burned down," Stalin concluded with satisfaction.

I recalled Abdul Latief's snort when he told me about the supposed electrical short circuit that had been the cause of the fire. For a few seconds, I felt light-headed.

"You were here?" I pressed him. "You saw all this yourself?"

"No," Stalin said, "I was only posted here this year, but I heard the whole story. You don't believe me? Ask anybody."

I could sense that he was becoming annoyed, so I quickly said, "No, no. I believe you."

Stalin nodded, grudgingly placated. As if to add a flourish to the end of his story, he drew a dented box of cigarettes from his pocket and lit one. The smoke reached me, blunt and warm and bitter, and I felt the twist of a craving in my stomach. I hesitated, then thought, *Why not?*

"May I have one?" I asked.

"What?"

"A cigarette."

He stared at me. "You want a cigarette?"

"Yes," I said. "Please."

For a moment, it seemed he might refuse, but then he shook out a limp cigarette from the pack. He handed it to me with his matchbox and waited while I lit it. "Thank you," I said.

He was watching me with a new expression. "I don't know any other ladies who smoke," he said, sounding suddenly like a child. Then he blurted out, "How long will you be in Kishtwar?"

"I don't know."

He took a deep breath. "Will you meet me again tomorrow?"

I started. "What?"

"Not here. There is a place," he said quickly, "very close to my camp. It is very beautiful, with a waterfall. I am on patrol there tomorrow. Take my number and SMS me, and we can meet there." He broke off and waited shyly.

The streets around us were turning brighter now, starting to fill. A Muslim boy on a bicycle, carrying a brown package, trailing the smell of fresh, warm bread. A pair of elderly men in skullcaps, neither of whom so much as looked sideways at us. A car with tinted windows rolled slowly by, and, in the backseat, a woman's head swiveled, her dark eyes fixed on me. And, as if those eyes were a mirror, I saw myself. Standing on the street at six-thirty in the morning, a cigarette in my hand, talking to a soldier.

"No," I said without thinking.

Stalin frowned. "You don't want my number?"

"No, that's not—" My skin itched to be away from him. I longed for the safety of my green room. "I just can't. I'm sorry."

I let the burning cigarette fall from my fingers and began to walk away as fast as I could.

"Wait!" I heard Stalin call from behind me, but I walked even faster, not turning my head, waiting for the pounding of boots behind me on the pavement. It didn't come.

Just before I turned the corner, however, I couldn't help glancing back. Stalin was standing in the same spot, arms cradling his rifle. His eyes were shaded, made invisible by the rim of his helmet, but I knew that he was watching me.

I turned the corner and broke into a jog, not stopping until I'd climbed the green stairs and let myself in. I tiptoed past the kitchen, where Zoya was cooking something. Then with relief I locked myself into my room.

Hours later, a burst of loud voices just outside my door startled me awake. I had fallen asleep at some point, and now I sat up in bed, heart hammering. The voices passed into the hall and dropped to a murmur. What was going on? Then I remembered: the function.

I went across the room and put my ear to the door. Abdul Latief's voice came to me, muffled, followed by the laughter of multiple people. I returned to my bed and sat there for a few minutes, trying to decide what to do. I was still smarting from my last interaction with Zoya, and I did not want to face her, but I dreaded what she would think of me otherwise. I imagined one of their guests glancing toward my door, mouthing: *Where is she?* And Zoya: *Who knows? I invited her, but she's obviously too good for us.* Besides, I desperately needed to use the bathroom.

Before I could reconsider, I stood up, crossed the green room, wrenched the door open, and stepped out into the corridor. At the same moment, the curtain separating the hall from the rest of the house was flung aside, and two little boys, perhaps six years old, burst into the corridor, evidently in the midst of some game, both dressed in shiny black kurtas over jeans. They stopped short when they saw me, mouths open.

"I was just—the bathroom—" I muttered like an idiot.

"It is behind you, aunty," the bolder one said politely, while the other stared at his feet.

"Yes, I know," I cried, my voice far too loud and hearty for the narrow space, and the boys prudently backed away through the curtain.

In the bathroom, water had spread all over the floor, and there was the smell of unfamiliar urine. A long brown hair, neither mine nor Zoya's, lay draped over the rim of the sink, and I stared balefully at it as I washed my hands. Then I took a deep breath, unlocked the door, passed quickly up the corridor, and pushed aside the curtain.

The hall was full of strangers, but the first one to see me was a balding man standing by the door. His remaining hair, which circled his large head like a corona, was hennaed bright orange; in one arm, he held a baby, smooth and pale as a large piece of soap, and in the other, a sheet of paper. The people in the room were angled toward him, sitting cross-legged, or leaning back on their elbows, and he was reading to them. When I entered, he made the briefest of pauses, then smoothly went on, but it was enough to make everyone turn and stare. I stood there, helplessly self-conscious, until Abdul Latief, who had been sitting on a stool in the back, slid off and carried it over to me, smiling. As I perched awkwardly on it, I felt myself sized up by a dozen pairs of eyes.

The balding man was still reading. His cadences were slow and musical, and even the baby in his arms seemed mesmerized. He read in Urdu, but a formal, elevated Urdu I had no hope of understanding. After a minute, I let my gaze wander around the room. I could not see Zoya anywhere, but Abdul Latief was now sitting next to a short, almond-eyed man, whose kurta was unbuttoned to reveal a shock of dark chest hair. Their shoulders touched in an easy, unconscious, way, and then I noticed that everybody in the room shared that same sense of ease, which could not be anything but the long association of blood. This, then, must be their family. I stared around, slightly taken aback by the depth and bitterness of my own resentment. I thought of how I'd sat with Zoya and Abdul Latief in this same room only hours earlier, the stupid joy that I'd felt at imagining us a kind of family, but which, I saw now, was only a pale shadow of what existed here, amongst these people, the ones to whom Abdul Latief and Zoya rightfully belonged.

The man with the orange hair finished reading, and applause broke up the concentrated air of the room. He handed the baby to a young, fair-skinned woman in a frilly hijab. People stood, stretched, and began to talk. I glanced around for Abdul Latief, but, to my alarm, he was gone.

Before I could move, two women approached me, one of them the baby's mother. She stayed slightly behind an older woman with a powdered, jowly face, whose maroon hijab was tucked behind her white, incongruously delicate ears. The older woman addressed me first, in brisk, slightly officious Urdu. "We thought you wouldn't come out at all," she said. She had large, yellow teeth and smelled strongly of floral perfume. "We thought you might be sick."

"I didn't realize it had already started," I lied weakly.

"It started an hour ago. Didn't Zoya tell you?"

"She did, but—" Both women were watching me closely. "She said it might start late."

To my relief, they seemed to accept this. The older woman nodded grimly. "It almost did. Nothing was ready, as usual. Good thing we came early. We almost didn't come at all, you know. My grandson was sick, and we were taking care of him all morning."

I made a sympathetic noise, and we all looked for a moment at the soap-like baby, who gurgled, not looking the least bit sick.

"What's his name?" I asked.

"Musa," answered the pale young mother, smiling at me.

"Alhamdulillah, he became better, or we could not have come," the older woman put in. "And then who knows what we would be eating now. The chicken was not even cooked." She sighed. "How many times I've told Zoya, this is too much for you, let me do it in my house. But she won't listen. As if she isn't under enough stress already, thinking about Ishfaaq, she wants to cook on top of that? But what to do? She is my husband's sister, and he is the same way."

I searched my memory but was quite sure I'd never heard Zoya or Abdul Latief mention the name Ishfaaq before. But I was more arrested by what she'd said about Zoya having a brother. I tried to conjure an image of Zoya as a little girl, running after a taller, laughing boy.

"Your husband . . . ?"

"Yes, the one who was reading. He and Zoya, they do what they want, and nobody can make them do anything else." The older woman held her arms out for the baby, Musa, and her daughter handed him over. She bounced him twice on her hip then said, "I'll go check on the chicken." She carried him off to the kitchen, and I was left alone with the young mother.

"I liked what your father read," I told her.

"Oh?" she said, smiling. "You can understand Urdu?"

I blushed. "Not really. I only speak Hindi. But I liked the *sound* of it."

She laughed. "Then you must tell him that. It will make him very happy. He wrote it himself, you know. He writes everything—stories, plays, poems, songs. And he writes in three languages, Kashmiri, Urdu, and English."

"I will tell him," I said, genuinely impressed.

"How do you like Kishtwar?" she asked me.

"I like it a lot," I said.

"My aunt told me you are from Bangalore. I've heard it is a big city."

"Yes," I said. "Very big."

"Then Kishtwar must seem so quiet to you. Nothing happens here."

I recalled the story Stalin had told me and shifted a bit uncomfortably on my stool.

"What about during the militancy?" I asked. "It wasn't quiet then, was it?"

"No," she said gravely. "It wasn't. That was a bad time for everybody, though, of course, it was worse for some people. Like my aunt and uncle." She sighed. "Excuse me," she said, before I could ask more, "I should go and make sure Musa gets his food."

When she'd gone, I looked about. People were sitting or standing in groups, chatting. The two little boys I'd seen earlier were doing somersaults in one corner. Nobody seemed to be paying attention to me, so I took the chance to slip behind the curtain and head back toward my room. I shut the door, and it was only when I turned that I saw I was not alone.

Zoya was sitting on my bed. She had half risen, but when she saw who it was, she sank back down. She'd taken off her headscarf, or it had slipped off, and she was gripping it tightly in her fists. It was a shock to see her head suddenly uncovered; it made her look younger, closer to the little girl I had tried and failed to imagine.

"I'm sorry," I said, automatically, turning to go.

"No, please—I just came to rest," Zoya said. She spoke jerkily, without her usual calm force. "The room was empty, so I thought you were—I'll go now."

She made a halfhearted move to stand.

"No, it's fine," I said quickly. "Please stay."

She hesitated, then sat down again. I could hear a swell of voices from the hall.

"Every year," said Zoya, "there are more and more people."

She was speaking in a lifeless tone, more to herself than me. Her face wore a look I'd never seen before, dull and disoriented.

"I was the one who started it," she went on. "In the beginning, it seemed like a good idea. But now I can't remember why. They come, they eat, they go. And what for?"

The last thing I wanted was to interrupt her trance by speaking, so I stayed mute, watching her face, willing her to go on.

"Is it helping anybody?" Zoya exclaimed suddenly. "Family is important, Latief says, and yes, I agree with him, but what does it have to do with Ishfaaq? I don't know how much longer I can keep doing this, how many more years. I'm getting tired. I think—"

She stopped and looked up, as if she'd only just realized whom she was addressing. I wanted to cry out, *No! Don't stop!* but she stood and wrapped the scarf firmly around her head.

"I'm sorry I bothered you," she said, and her voice had become itself again, remote and unyielding. "The food is ready, or it will be soon. Please come and eat."

And in three swift steps, she was past me and out of the room.

I sat down on the bed where she had been, feeling a loss I could not name. A few moments later, there was a knock and Abdul Latief poked his curly head around the door.

"Why did you run off?" he demanded gaily. "Come, come, meet some people."

I stood and followed him, shaking hands with various relatives whose faces I barely registered, politely answering their questions about Bangalore, but thinking the whole time of Zoya's bloodless face, her voice going on and on in that dead whisper.

"Now," Abdul Latief told me, "I want you to meet someone special."

He led me to the yellow room, which this afternoon resembled a sort of female durbar. In the middle, in a red plastic chair, sat a very old lady in a thick, shapeless garment. Around her were more than a dozen women, sitting on the floor with their knees drawn up. The air was stuffy with a mixture of perfumes. I quickly scanned the room; Zoya sat closest to the old woman, her head resting on the arm of the plastic chair. As soon as she saw me, she pulled herself straight.

"Ammi-jaan," Abdul Latief called loudly. "See who's come to meet you? Our new guest, all the way from Bangalore." To me he whispered, "Zoya's mother. She's ninety years old."

The old woman raised her head. Her thick eyebrows were spangled with silver and her eyelids drooped, but her voice was strong when she said, in Urdu, "Come sit down, child."

I picked my way across the room, the women pulling back the skirts of their kurtas to make room for me. As I approached her, I hesitated. There was nowhere to sit. But Zoya solved the problem for me by standing and abruptly leaving the room, not meeting my eyes.

I sat, very self-consciously, in her place at the old lady's knee. She held out her hand, and I placed mine in it. Her skin was disturbingly soft, almost without texture.

"How are you, child?" she asked.

"I'm fine, aunty."

"You are comfortable here, in my daughter's house?"

"Yes, aunty."

"And where have you come from?" She was running her thumb over and over my knuckle, the way one might absently pet a cat, but I liked it, the sensation of being so gently handled.

"From Bangalore," I said.

"Bangalore," she repeated softly. "That is far away. Your mother must be missing you."

She was an old lady, and it was only a platitude, but I found myself shaken. "She's dead, aunty," I said loudly. "My mother is dead."

"You poor thing," she murmured.

I was struck by a sudden, savage resentment at her tone, which was pitying, yet I took a strange pleasure in it too. I sat with my head held high, tasting bitter pride in my own weakness, and hating myself for it at the same time, because, cynical and hardened as I believed myself to be at twenty-four, I had never stopped to consider that pity might, in fact, be just another facet of love.

Suddenly, the pressure on my knuckle lifted away. I looked up to see the old woman sitting straight in her red chair. Her face wore a queer, intent look.

"My grandson," she said, "is also dead."

A peculiar reaction followed her announcement. The collective breath went out of the room. A stunning teenage girl with kohl-rimmed eyes shrank back against the woman sitting beside her. The old lady glanced around, a contemptuous amusement in her face. "What?" she asked. "Our guest has come from so far away, and we can't even tell her the truth about our Ishfaaq?"

That name again. Only then, slowly, did it began to dawn on me who this Ishfaaq might be. Who he must be. I'd seen no sign of him in the house where I'd lived for nearly a fortnight, had never heard his name mentioned, but the more I thought about it, the more sense it made. The sadness that seemed to blow over Abdul Latief and Zoya from time to time, for no apparent reason.

Still, I had to be sure. "Aunty," I said, "who is that?"

"Ishfaaq?" She barely glanced down at me. "Ishfaaq is my grandson. Zoya's son."

I closed my eyes, feeling a pressure in my chest, as if a hand were pushing down on it. How had I not known? How had I not sensed it, sleeping night after night after night in that tiny green room? A room perfect for a child, a son. But the old lady was not yet finished.

"For eight years," she went on, her hard gaze making the women around me cower, "all of you have been acting like he's just gone away for a holiday. Like he will come back. None of you will say the truth openly, not even my daughter, but I will say it." She tossed her head. "I will say—"

She broke off, her eyes fixed on the doorway. I looked up and froze. Zoya stood there, her left arm raised and her mouth half open. It terrified me to look at her. The other women dropped their eyes. Even the old lady seemed uneasy.

"Zoya," she said.

Zoya ignored her. "The food is ready," she said. "Come and eat, all of you."

Most of the women stood up. I did the same and began to file out with them, not daring to meet Zoya's eyes as I passed her. The old woman did not acknowledge our departure. She remained bowed over in her chair, looking exhausted.

Zoya followed us out to the hall, where platters and bowls of food had been laid out on a plastic folding table, paper plates in a stack at one end. Several people were already eating, lined up cross-legged against the wall. I saw Musa's mother, feeding him from a bottle of milk.

"Please help yourself," Zoya said to me stiffly.

I stepped forward to the table, where I recognized the first dish, a bowl of vermicelli cooked in milk, with raisins and cashews floating in it. "Payasam," I said involuntarily.

"Phirni," Zoya said from behind me.

"We call it payasam at home." Then I added, "My mother used to make it all the time."

For a while, she said nothing, but I could hear her breathing just behind my shoulder. Then she said, in a voice that was barely audible, "This is Ishfaaq's favorite dish. He used to wait all year for Ramadan, just so he could eat this after fasting."

She'd spoken thickly, but without anger. I hadn't missed her use of the present tense, either, and I said, taking a chance, "Then Ishfaaq and I are the same."

I turned just in time to catch her startled, vivid smile, full of pain. After another pause, she said, "I should have told you earlier."

"No," I said firmly. "There was no need to tell me anything. I'm nobody."

She shook her head. She still seemed a little dazed. "You are not nobody," she said. "You are—it is nice to have you here. For us—for me. A young person in the house after many years." She straightened up. "Please," she said again. "Start eating. I have to take some food to my mother."

I watched her walk away holding a plate with a few spoonfuls of rice and a tiny dollop of phirni; then I looked around the room, at their family, all of them bent over their plates, eating and talking, and I felt the absurdity of my earlier resentment. There was no reason to feel jealous of these people, who all clearly felt the same affection for Zoya and Abdul Latief as I did, who were here for the sake of Zoya's son, who may or may not have been dead. No sooner had I had the thought, however, than it was disturbed by another: Stalin, with his stories of militants riding through the streets and local boys running after them, and a doubt twitched at the back of my mind. But I pushed it away and concentrated instead on the echo of Zoya's voice. *It is nice to have you here. For me.*

I picked up a plate, helped myself to the phirni, and looked for a spoon. I saw one at the other end of the table, but as I picked it up, I heard a man's voice, "That one has been used."

It was the balding man, the one who had been reading earlier. He took the spoon from me and ran it under the tap of the small sink. The back of his neck was deeply veined, networks of blue that disappeared into the spray of dyed-orange hair. He shook the spoon and handed it back.

"Thank you," I said. "You are Zoya's brother, aren't you?"

"Yes." His speaking voice, too, was musical. "My name is Saleem."

"I heard you reading. It was beautiful. Your daughter said you wrote it?"

He nodded. "I do not get enough time for writing. But I try to do it whenever I can."

"And it is true you write in Urdu, Kashmiri, and English?"

"My daughter talks too much," he said, evidently pleased. "But she is correct. I find that different languages are useful for different things. For instance, it is best to write poetry in Urdu. Urdu words are made for poetry and songs. For stories, Kashmiri is the best."

"And English?"

"English?" He smiled. "English is excellent for signboards and maps."

I laughed. He was teasing me, but I didn't care. My conversation with Zoya had lifted my spirits, given me patience enough for anything.

"And you?" he asked. "What is your language?"

"Tamil is my mother tongue," I said. "I learned English and Hindi in school, so I can understand a little Urdu, but I can't read it."

"You should learn to read Urdu," he said seriously. "It is a beautiful language."

"I'd love to learn someday."

"I'd be happy to teach you if you want," he said.

It was just a politeness, I knew, but as soon as he said it, I wanted it to be possible. I wanted to stay in Kishtwar, become his student. I would wake each morning and walk the narrow streets to his house. Under a vast, luxuriant tree, he would teach me the elegant flowing Urdu alphabet. There would be a breeze, the jumbled shadow of leaves on the page. I would walk home in the afternoon, and wait for Abdul Latief and Zoya to return from work. We would linger over chai, and then I would recite for them what I had learned. They would listen, Abdul Latief leaning back against his bolster, Zoya knitting her blue garment, and they would praise me. Then the three of us would sit down to dinner. Why couldn't such a thing be a life I wondered suddenly. Why couldn't it be mine?

Saleem had been silent for a while, looking around the room. His right eye tended to drift slightly inward, barely noticeable except when he was looking to that side.

"Zoya told me about your mother," he said. "I was sorry to hear about that. It is a difficult thing to lose one's parent." He looked across the room. I followed his gaze, saw Zoya talking to the man with the chest hair. "As difficult as losing a child," he said.

I looked at him. "What happened to Ishfaaq?"

He sighed. "We've heard so many different stories that we don't even really know anymore. All we know is that he was walking home from school when he ran into them."

I digested this in silence for a moment. "And what happened?" I asked, thinking of the militants Stalin had told me about that morning. "Did he join them?"

He gave me a strange look. "Join them?"

I nodded. "The militants who took him."

"Who told you the militants took him?" he asked sharply.

"You just said—"

"It was the army," he said, cutting me off. "He was coming home from school, and an army vehicle stopped and made him get in. That was eight years ago. On this same day," he added. "And it was the last time any of us ever saw him. He was sixteen years old then." He paused to note my expression. I was thinking of Abdul Latief and the way he looked at me when I told him my age. Twenty-four. The age his son should have been. "Have you been to Zoya's office?" Saleem asked then, seemingly apropos of nothing.

I shook my head.

"You should go," he said. He was about to say more, but then he glanced over my shoulder and quickly arranged his face into a relaxed smile. I turned to see Zoya approaching us, clutching a bouquet of spoons in her hand.

"I forgot to put spoons out," she said.

"We know." Saleem smiled at his sister. "How did you expect your guest of honor to eat your famous phirni, hm? Good thing I managed to find one and save your honor."

"Oh, enough of your drama," she said to him, then turning to me, added, "Sorry."

Despite the shock of what I'd just learned, I still felt pleasure at the way she addressed me, not with her usual remote distrust, but with wry casualness, as if she had known me for years.

"I was just saying she should come with you to the office one of these days," Saleem said.

I saw the muscles of her face tighten. "With me?"

"Yes, why not?" Saleem said. "Maybe she could help you with some of the work."

Zoya looked at the floor. "She doesn't want to do that. It would be boring."

"Not at all. I'd love to help," I said quickly.

"See?" Saleem said. "She'd love to help." He turned to me. "Zoya and Latief told me about this person you are looking for. Bashir Ahmed, is that correct? I know a few people in the clothes-selling business. I will ask them, and together we will find him, inshallah." He smiled at us and walked away, his sparse flame-colored hair bobbing over the crowd.

Zoya stood there, gazing after him. "Saleem will be able to help you," she said quietly. She seemed abstracted again, though no longer aloof in quite the same way.

"He said I should help you," I reminded her.

She didn't reply.

"I won't come if it's any trouble," I added.

"No," she said thoughtfully, "it's no trouble. In fact, it will be nice to have company. I should have taken you with me before."

Right then someone called her name. She set the spoons on the table and looked at me again. And then she did something wholly surprising. She touched me lightly on the shoulder.

"Tomorrow," she said and headed across the room.

8

After my bout with chicken pox, I returned to school at my father's insistence, and my mother made no objection, or at least made none openly. But thus began one of their many wars of silences and recriminations. She spoke to him in an exaggerated mumble, an idiot's thick accent, which drove him crazy, and eventually caused him to ignore her for an entire week. To me, too, she was frosty, and whenever she called me down to dinner, she would add, "But you should probably check with your father first, in case he knows more than I do about the latest, scientific methods of feeding children." At the swimming pool, she sat with her arms folded, and when her new friends crowded around her, gossiping, laughing, trying to draw her out, their witty and scandalous leader, their outrageous queen, she stood up and said, loudly enough for everybody to hear, "If I spend another second listening to all of you whine about your good-for-nothing husbands and your lazy maidservants, I promise you that I'll slit my own throat and bleed to death right here in front of your precious children. So instead I'm going to go sit over there by myself, and I would like it if all of you left me alone." And she walked over to an unoccupied table, sat down, and folded her arms again, while I tried to avoid the furious eyes of the other women.

If he'd had the language, my father might have reacted to my mother's moods differently, but he had a young man's temper then, as well as a young man's pride, and she had an exquisite instinct for zooming in on his frailties. One evening, he came home late, grinning, and announced that my swimming coach had called his office to tell him about an upcoming competition, for which he thought I was ready. My father had stopped by the venue to register me on the way home, and now he sat back, enormously pleased with himself. I must have seemed reluctant, because he put his hands on my shoulders and fixed me with a solemn look. "Shalini," my entrepreneur father said, "tell me this. What do you think separates the successful people of this world from the ordinary ones?"

He did not wait for my answer.

"Hunger," he declared. "Pure and simple hunger. Nothing else. Talent, hard work, all of those things have their roles, yes, but they won't make any difference if you aren't hungry for success. How old do you think I was when I started my first factory? *Twenty-four*. I didn't know the first thing about running a company. All I knew was that I was going to do it, no matter what, and I did. Mind you, people also said I was crazy. Believe me, there were *plenty* of people who said that." He winked at me and put a finger to his lips. "They were right, but, shh, that's a secret between us."

He laughed lightly at his own joke. And it was that laugh, so calm and self-satisfied, that goaded my mother into speaking. "Yes, Shalini," she said mimicking his lecturing tone. "It was hunger, pure and simple. The twenty lakhs your grandfather put in, his important business contacts, all that was a complete coincidence, understand?"

My father slowly drew himself up.

"Why," he asked, "must you always do that?"

"Do what?" she said innocently.

For a long moment, he simply stared at her; then he stalked out of the house, grabbing the car keys on the way. I heard the engine roar and, a moment later, heard it fade. My mother shrugged. "Probably got hungry again," she said and went upstairs.

In the end, I took part in the swimming competition, and to my own surprise, I placed second in the freestyle. My father openly wiped tears from his eyes when they placed the medal around my neck, and I could tell that my mother, though she stood stiffly next to him, lips pressed together, was also pleased. In the car on the way home, she remained quiet, almost too quiet, until we were in the middle of bustling M. G. Road, vehicles blaring their horns around us, and then, as if she couldn't stand it any longer, she rolled down her window, climbed onto the seat, and stuck her entire torso out of the car. "My daughter is a champion!" she screamed to the vehicles whooshing by. An auto swerved away in alarm, and several motorists craned their necks back to goggle at her. "My daughter is a champion!" my mother screamed again. "A champion, a champion, a champion!"

My father, who was driving, seemed torn between joining her and maintaining the chilly status quo that had reigned in our household since their last argument. But she looked so happy, so wild, so glowing, her arms stretched high, that he couldn't help himself. He leaned hard on the horn, while she shrieked to the passing vehicles, "Hear ye! Hear ye! All of you will know my champion daughter someday!" I sat in the back, mortified, but with a wide, foolish grin plastered to my face, as my parents honked and hollered my success all the way back home, their rancor and bitterness forgotten in a miraculous instant. Those moments, when the two of them were in accord, came so rarely and with such blistering force that even now I can summon up the feeling they gave me, that we had all three lifted into the air and were flying.

But they never lasted. Soon he would become distracted, and she would become sarcastic; then he would be pompous and she would smirk; he would rage, and she would stand there coolly until he was gone, slamming the door. And there was one terrible time, when she asked him to turn up the volume of the evening news, and he said, half joking, "Since when have *you* been so interested in what goes on in the world?" The air around her went deadly cold, and, too late, he saw his mistake. "You're right," she said. "Your father sent you to IIT and Columbia. My father didn't think girls needed to go to college. So why should *I* be interested in the world?" He tried to apologize, but she cut him off. "Please. There's no need," she said. "I know what I am."

This, then, was the world into which Bashir Ahmed had now entered. The third time he came, he did not wait for my mother to invite him inside, but walked in as if it were his due. He laughed at everything she said, no matter how ordinary, and while she was in the kitchen, making tea, he drew from his pocket a tiny plastic box of saffron strands and presented it gravely to me. When she came back, he told us a story, this time a funny one about a man he'd known, who traveled from village to village, eating huge amounts at weddings to which he hadn't been invited. It got to be so bad that the headmen from several villages got together to concoct a plan to teach him a lesson. They gave it out that a huge wedding would occur in a remote hamlet, certain that the wedding crasher would hear of it, as he inevitably did. Anticipating a lavish meal, he made the arduous uphill trek, but when he arrived at the hamlet, he found only a bewildered cowherd in a stone hut, his cows peacefully grazing some distance away. "Where is the wedding?" demanded the crasher. "Is there no cause for celebration here today?" "Well, yes, sir, there is," the old cowherd replied. "Today my cows will be united with my bull in the hope of a good round of calves next year. It is for us a day of celebration indeed." The crasher, blushing with shame, went home and never tried to attend a wedding uninvited again.

It was a good story, and Bashir Ahmed told it well. My mother was slapping her thigh and wheezing with laughter by the time he was done. It delighted him, her unrestrained mirth, and he told her, "It was a good thing that you weren't the one who went up to the cowherd's hut."

"Why?" she asked, smiling.

"Because that poor old cowherd would have been finished. You would have sat down in the middle of his house and refused to leave. In fact, you would have probably forced him to get one of his daughters married just so you could get your wedding meal."

"Naturally," she said, pleased.

He left soon after, promising to return in a few weeks. And he did, with another gift and another story. He always addressed these stories to me, though I knew somewhere in the back of my mind that they were really meant for my mother. I had no proof of this, but when he was in the midst of telling one, I had the feeling that if I simply stood up and left the room, neither of them would notice. She would be lying back against the sofa, her eyes partially closed, and her face, if not precisely happy, was at least free of that vague, taut energy she so often carried around with her. When his voice fell silent, she would open her eyes to find his green ones waiting, and she would nod discreetly. Only then would he turn, smiling, to me, and say, "Did you like the story, beti?"

His stories. They all bordered on the fantastic, with gaping holes he glossed over with a cursory wave of his hand, as if details were beneath him. He told us about a boy in a village close to where he lived, who had found two leopard cubs in a cave. Thinking they were kittens, he brought them home. His parents, of course, had known better, and his father ran to return them, but the boy had by then fallen in love with the tiny creatures, so small they hadn't opened their eyes. He went back the next day and took them again, thinking he'd hide them under a basket and care secretly for them, but the next morning, the basket was overturned, one cub was missing, and the other lay ten feet away, its downy belly ripped open by birds. After that, Bashir Ahmed told us, the female leopard had started stalking the village. Before, she had been peaceable, almost courteous, taking only what she needed, a dog here, an old sheep there. But now she was anguished and indiscriminate. She was also strong; villagers would wake up to find the doors to their barns broken open, their livestock slaughtered. Not eaten, simply slaughtered. They began to speak of her as something more than an animal; the maulvi of the village was consulted. Men with guns sat up at night waiting for her, but she was too quick, too stealthy. The entire village suffered, and it wasn't until the boy confessed and the maulvi put him through a rigorous cycle of penitence that she left them alone.

Then there was the story of the chudail, a female demon who would take the form of a pretty young woman and accost lone male travellers, asking if they would escort her home. She would call out to them first from forty feet away; the next moment, she would be right beside them, and they would realize what she was and flee. When they turned back, she had vanished.

My mother never seemed bothered by the illogical elements of his stories, but I couldn't let them go. I tried to contain my questions in deference to the silence that prevailed whenever he came to the end of one, but sometimes I couldn't help myself. How could a leopard break locks? I demanded to know. How did she know that the boy that stole her cubs came from that exact village? Had any of the chudail's victims ever gone with her? What would have happened if they had? Bashir Ahmed answered my questions first with amused tolerance, but when they became too many, he would throw up his arms and plead for mercy. "Enough, beti, enough! You're too smart for me." And my mother, from her spot on the sofa, smiling that dreamy, content smile: "She's too smart for all of us, believe me." And he, turning immediately to her: "Just like someone else I know." And a startled softness coming into her face, changing it in a way I would have never believed possible if I hadn't been there to see it myself.

How many times did he visit? Not so many, I realize now, though it seemed to me then that he was always there. Twelve, perhaps fifteen times over the span of three years? I grew to expect, then to await him, once every couple of months, his arrival always coinciding with the thickest of the afternoon's shadows. He still brought his bundle, though he never again made the pretense of opening it. He would set it down by the door, where it would remain, forgotten, until he was ready to leave again. Sinking down into his place on the sofa, he would look around with a slight expression of anxiety, which cleared once he had made sure that everything was still the same. As a child, I never thought to ask myself what pleasure he gained from the quiet and comfort of our house, but it seems clear enough to me now when I consider the work he did—the long days; the callused feet; the aching neck; the endless, empty patter so inescapable for a salesman—that the pleasure must have been in part the sheer relief of being able to rest. As for what else might have kept him coming back to our house, I must have recognized it even then, in some wordless portion of my brain, and, surprisingly, it did not cause me jealousy, as perhaps it might have done for another child. I saw that he spoke to my mother in a way that nobody else did, and that because he spoke to her in this way, she responded to him in a way she did with nobody else. I saw that there was a brightness and merriment that strengthened in her while he was in the room and dimmed when he departed. And that was, for me, enough to begin to love him.

And he loved us, too, I am certain of it. I saw him once reach out to adjust a curtain that had blown over the arm of our sofa. He pinched it between thumb and index finger and, instead of letting it drop, he gently lowered it back into place. There was such tenderness in that act:

tenderness for this house, for my mother, for me, for the long afternoons when nothing beyond our living room carried any weight or reality. And when my mother was rude, when she interrupted him or laughed in a way that was mocking, he had a way of looking at me—eyebrows pulled down, stern yet humorous, warning me not to be angry with her—that produced in me a real flush of affection.

My mother, with her typical, bizarre confidence, never once asked me to keep Bashir Ahmed's visits a secret, but I did. It seems astounding to me now that I never let it slip out, even by accident; but children are, in their way, the most secretive of creatures, and it was, at the time, the ruling principle of my life: the two of them, Bashir Ahmed and my father, represented different worlds, and to cause those worlds to overlap, even slightly, would have brought nothing short of disaster. To my child's mind, Bashir Ahmed belonged exclusively to the world of afternoons, with their high, walled shadows and elongated silences, to strange stories and unusual gifts. My father, on the other hand, belonged to the steady world of evenings, to comfortably rumpled office clothes and the house lit up, to homework and dinner, to the fading of energy and the coming of sleep. And it began to seem to me that as long as I kept the two separate in my mind, I could have my reward, which was to continue in this way forever.

Then came the afternoon when my mother fell asleep on the sofa. Bashir Ahmed was with us; he had just come to the end of a long story. He seemed quiet, more so than usual, and I knew better than to ask any questions. We both looked at my mother. Her kurta had bunched up on her lap, and, as we watched, her knee slipped sideways. Then I noticed that her salwar was torn, a little to the left of her crotch, exposing a strip of her pink underwear and a section of thigh. I was mortified, yet afraid to stand up and cover her, irrationally believing that if I made no move, he would somehow miss it altogether. But after a while, he stood up himself and walked over to her. He lifted the edge of her kurta, the way he had done with the curtain, and resettled it so that the material covered the tear. All this he did with the utmost gentleness, and she did not wake up.

I walked out with him to the gate, where he turned. And instead of saying, as usual, *Tell her I will come again soon,* he said, "Tell her I might be away for longer than usual, beti."

I was immediately afraid. "Why?"

Because your mother has exposed herself in this indecent way. Because she does not behave like a woman is supposed to. Because I'm sorry to say I do not like her—or you—any longer. Goodbye.

He sighed. "There are some bad things happening in Kashmir. I have to go back to my family."

"What kind of bad things?"

"I'll tell you all about it when I come back, okay?"

"But when will that be?"

He closed his eyes. "Beti, please. No more questions right now."

"I'm sorry."

He put his hand on the gate and smiled. "It's all right. Just tell her. Promise?"

I nodded. And as he was walking away, it struck me for the first time that there might be far more to his life than the little bits he gave us, bound up in his gifts and his stories. That, perhaps, we were not quite as important to him as he was to us. It was a strange and painful revelation, and, in the way of children, I was utterly convinced it had come to me alone. My mother did not know, and it was my duty to shield her forever from this knowledge. I watched Bashir Ahmed turn the corner with his bundle, and then I went back inside to where she was sleeping on the sofa, her head lolling to one side, her nakedness so carefully concealed.

9

I ENTERED THE HALL the morning after the function to find Zoya ready. She stood by the door, her dark green handbag at her feet, reading an Urdu newspaper, as if she were waiting for a bus. My breakfast was on its tray as usual, two boiled eggs in a dish, along with a few slices of bread and a thermos. When I poured, however, the smell was different, and I glanced up in surprise. Zoya was smiling.

"Coffee," she said. "That first day, you said that's what you drank at home. I went out and bought some this morning."

I'd completely forgotten having mentioned it and was, for that reason, doubly moved. I thanked her, took a sip, and nearly spit it out. It was instant coffee, and she had made it blindingly strong. She was watching me with a worried frown.

"What's wrong?" she asked. "Don't you like it?"

"Mm hm," I lied. "It's very good."

"Good. I put in extra powder," she said proudly. "Three full spoons extra."

I couldn't help myself; I began to laugh. At first, she stiffened; then she came forward and took a cautious sip from my cup. Her eyes went wide and she wrinkled her nose like an offended cat, which only made me laugh harder. For a moment, she pressed her lips together in disapproval; then she, too, gave up and began to laugh. The sound of our laughter rang through the hall, which, without all those bodies, felt vast and peaceful.

"I'm sorry," Zoya said, wiping her eyes. "It tastes so bad."

"No," I said. "It's the best coffee I've ever tasted." To prove my point, I drank the entire contents of the thermos. Then I washed the dishes in the kitchen, laced up my shoes, and, for the first time, Zoya and I walked together down the narrow green steps and into the day.

In the street, the morning haze moved like a living thing and landed cool on my skin. I had to walk slowly to keep pace with Zoya. She was quite a small woman, I realized. All these days, she had seemed so powerful, looming over me to fill my plate. I wondered briefly, with a thrill, if anyone who didn't know us might think I was her daughter.

We made our way up the streets of Kishtwar, now so familiar to me. Zoya's green bag thudded occasionally against my hip. "Sorry, sorry," she murmured in a distracted tone. Then she stopped altogether at a corner, seemed to think, then said, "Come this way, I want to show you something." She went right then cut sharply right again, through a small, dark alleyway between a tailor and a tiny dry goods shop that smelled of cloves and cinnamon. The alleyway led out onto a wide, tree-lined street with large old houses on either side. Zoya came to a stop before a house with a tall black wrought-iron gate and waited for me to catch up to her.

"Here," she said.

"This is where you work?"

"No." She pointed to a patch of pavement. "This is the place from where the soldiers took Ishfaaq. We found his schoolbag here." Behind the wrought-iron gate was a cracked pathway, overgrown with weeds, which led to a large, crumbling house. I found that I couldn't speak.

"Right after they took him, I used to come here," she said. Her eyes were still lowered, fixed on the pavement. "I thought I would find something. I didn't know what. I found a pencil once, but it could have belonged to anyone, any schoolchild. After a while I stopped coming this way. This is the first time I've stood in this spot in almost five years."

I wanted to touch her arm, but I felt very clearly the distance of those years between us. Yet I was unutterably grateful that she had trusted me enough to bring me here, to show me this thing. I closed my eyes and imagined hands pulling at a boy's school uniform, a door slamming, tires screeching, an eerie, ringing silence afterward.

"Bastards," I said in English.

Zoya raised her head.

"Bastards," she repeated, and the careful way she said it made the oath sound even more obscene. She took a deep breath and drew herself up. "Let's go," she said.

We walked away from the quiet, leafy street and the elegant old houses, and entered another neighborhood, smaller and more cramped, where Zoya stopped again.

"This," she said, "is my office."

She pushed open a low gate and led me through a tiny unkempt garden. At the end was a tiny, dilapidated bungalow, its hay-yellow paint all but peeled away. A single chipped step led up to a little verandah, covered in shoes. We slipped ours off before entering.

Inside was a large main room, with two folding tables in the center and multiple chairs arranged around them, in the style of a conference room. Half a dozen people sat at the tables, poring over thick cardboard files. I caught the comforting smell of aged paper, the scrape of chair legs, the murmur of voices. At the end of one of the tables was a desktop computer, its screen blind with dust. I watched as a plump man with inky fingers flipped through a register like the one I'd pretended to keep at the agency. A young woman wearing a sky-blue hijab carefully copied something from a yellow form into a large legal pad. The whole place felt like an antiquated library minus its books, or some sleepy backwater government office.

People looked up and smiled as Zoya and I crossed the room, wishing her a low, "Salaam alaikum," and leveling curious glances at me before returning to their work.

We stopped before a door that led off the main room. It stood slightly ajar, and I heard the rapid clicks of typing from within. Zoya entered, and I followed her into the room, which was lined with tall metal racks filled with dozens and dozens of cardboard files.

A woman sat at a tiny desk in the middle, her hijab slipping back over her thick, cropped gray hair, a pair of thin spectacles balanced on the tip of her nose. She was somewhere in her mid-fifties, I guessed, and was peering closely at a computer screen. She waved us in without glancing up.

Zoya stood patiently until she had finished. Then she said, "Salaam alaikum, Zarina," adding in respectful Urdu, "This is my guest, the one I told you about."

"Yes, you did," the woman, Zarina, responded. Her voice was low-pitched and somehow ragged, as if it had caught on a nail and torn. She had gray eyes and a cool, direct gaze that now fixed on me. Switching smoothly to English, she said, "Which part of India are you from?"

"Bangalore," I said.

Zarina raised an eyebrow. "A long way from home," she said. She spoke casually enough, but something about her tone made me think that she had sized me up and was not particularly impressed with what she saw. "We don't get many tourists from Bangalore coming to Kishtwar."

"I'm not a tourist," I said. "I came here to find someone."

She was unfazed. "Oh, yes," she said. "Yes, I think I remember Zoya mentioning something about that. Well, you're in good hands with her and Latief." She nodded at Zoya. "Between the two of them, they know everybody in town. Good luck to you."

She was about to turn back to her computer when Zoya asked her hesitantly, in Urdu, "Is there any work she can do, Zarina? She wants to help us."

"Help us?" Zarina sounded surprised. "Here? In the office? We have all the help we need."

"Yes, I know," Zoya said eagerly, "still I thought maybe she could—" But she broke off, seeing the expression on Zarina's face. It shocked me to witness this flinching, deferential woman who had so suddenly taken the place of my formidable host. I could not suppress a surge of protective anger on her behalf, but I forced myself to keep my mouth shut.

Zarina seemed to be thinking. Then she said something clipped in Kashmiri to Zoya, who nodded and looked relieved, touched me lightly on the arm, the way she'd done the night before, and quickly walked out of the room. Left alone with me, Zarina leaned back in her chair and regarded me for a long moment. I tried to make my spine straighter.

"So," she said, this time in English again, "has Zoya explained to you the work we do here?"

"A little," I lied.

"I see. Has she told you about Ishfaaq?"

I nodded.

"All right, you know about him. Then you probably also know Ishfaaq isn't the only one. A friend of mine—we were in law school together—runs an organization in Srinagar for the families of those who have been arrested by the army. I do something similar here—on a smaller scale."

"You find them?"

She winced. "We try. We help people file habeas corpus, police reports, petitions. Mostly we collect cases, record testimony that kind of thing." She waved toward the stacks of files on the metal racks.

"*All* of these?" I asked, unable to hide the wonder in my voice.

"Yes," she said. "And we get new ones all the time." She tapped the top file in the stack on her desk. "For example, this young man came to see me last week. His older brother had vanished about four years ago, right from their family fields. All this man knew was that, a week before it happened, his brother had some kind of disagreement with an army captain. Over a cigarette, if you can believe it. So he went to the captain, begged for the release of his brother. The captain pretended to know nothing, obviously; then he very offhandedly mentioned an amount of money. The poor boy ran around the village for weeks, trying to raise it. Then he invited the captain home for lunch, had his mother cook a huge meal, and presented the cash. A month of silence went by, then two, and the boy went to see the captain again. Do you know what the captain said?"

I shook my head.

Zarina leaned forward. "He said, 'You shouldn't have fed me rice. Rice in the afternoon makes me sleepy.'"

She watched me, cool and evaluative, from behind her desk, the tall gray metal towers full of files rising like rows and rows of teeth around her.

"What happened in the end?" I asked. "Did you find him? The brother?"

She shrugged. "Like I said, this man only came to see me last week. I don't know what we can do, frankly. Last I heard, he was on his way to the army camp in Bhaderwah."

I gave a start, thinking of the earnest young man with the black book, wishing me luck.

"This man," I said, "did he happen to show you a photograph of his brother?"

Instead of answering, Zarina simply opened the top file and turned it to face me. And there was the same man, standing before the same painted backdrop of lighthouse and ocean, his hands stiff by his sides, staring up at me.

"I met that man," I said softly. "He was staying with Zoya when I first arrived."

Then, all of a sudden, it hit me. I raised my head to stare at Zarina. "All of those people," I said, "the people who stay with Zoya, are they—I mean, do they all—"

She nodded. "Yes. They're all looking for someone. They go out to the camp, trying to find whatever information they can. Sometimes one of the soldiers might feel sorry for some of them and tell them he saw the person they're looking for, three months ago or three years ago, but most of the time, they just make them wait all day, then chase them off without telling them anything. But what can these people do? They have to try."

I gazed around at the files, some of them dusty, clearly untouched for years.

Zarina looked toward the door. Her face had changed, grown softer, more contemplative.

"You know," she said, "when I began this organization, Zoya was the first person who started working with me. I met her the week Ishfaaq was taken. She was completely devastated, and she couldn't think of anything but finding him. She came to ask me for help filing his FIR and then simply never left. Now I don't think I would be able to run this place without her."

Zarina took her glasses off and wiped them on the edge of her hijab. "Sometimes I worry that she takes on too much. Especially letting people stay in her home." She gave me a quick glance that was nonetheless full of meaning. "Zoya's problem is that she gets too close, if you know what I mean. She wants to help everybody, no matter who it is. I understand why she does it, but all the same it takes a toll on her. And each time someone leaves, as everyone does in the end, it breaks her heart all over again. Even though she'd never show it." She paused "I've told her so many times not to do it, not to let people stay with her, but—"

"But she's stubborn," I finished for her.

"Yes," Zarina said, "she is."

We were silent, watching each other with, I thought, a degree of wariness. I was trying to work out what her speech was meant to convey, whether she was merely warning me of Zoya's fragility, or whether it was something else, a way of expressing suspicion of me. The thought made me bristle, and I responded more harshly than I might have otherwise; and only now, from the remove of so many years, does it also occur to me to wonder exactly what sort of danger she thought I represented. Was it the same danger Hari had seen the night he said I frightened him?

"Look, I just want to help Zoya," I said firmly. "If there's something you can think of for me to do, I'd be happy to do it. Otherwise I'll leave and won't trouble you anymore."

Zarina opened her mouth to reply, but she never got the chance, because at that moment, Zoya herself came back in waving a sheaf of old papers bound with twine. There was a smudge of dust on her nose, and it struck me as a very tender thing. I suddenly wanted to hug her.

"I found them!" she announced happily in Urdu. "They were right at the bottom of all these boxes, so it took me a while."

"Thank you," Zarina said, gravely accepting the sheaf. Then she said, "Zoya, do you remember those old bills we have? From '98–'99? They're in a file somewhere, I'm almost sure." She glanced toward me. "Maybe your friend can enter them in the computer. What do you think?"

"Could you do that?" Zoya asked, turning toward me eagerly.

"Yes," I replied, and she beamed like a little girl.

"Then it's settled," Zarina said. She was already turning back to her laptop screen. "I hope the rest of your stay in Kishtwar is pleasant."

* * *

Zoya led me back to the main room, over to the old desktop computer. I touched the mouse, and the screen flickered to life after a long moment. While she went off in search of the files, I sat before the blinking cursor, trying to make sense of everything I'd just learned. The people who passed through Zoya's house, Ishfaaq, the stacks and stacks and stacks of files. The boy and his brother and the army captain, the disagreement over cigarettes. *Cigarettes.* I felt my stomach drop, thinking of the cigarette I'd shared with Stalin. While I sat there, trying to wrestle down the fear that Zoya would find out about him, she returned holding aloft a dusty file bulging with multicolored scraps of paper.

"Here," she said, setting it down beside me. "These are our bills from the first two years. We didn't have a computer then. Can you make a spreadsheet of this?"

"Yes," I said.

"Good. I'll be here if you have any questions," she said, touching me once on the shoulder. Then she left me to my work.

I opened the file and began to sort through the papers. They consisted of taxi booking forms, invoices for stationery, bills, receipts, all of them thrown together haphazardly. I began sorting through them, separating them into neat, chronological piles, looking up from time to time at the others bent over their own files. It reminded me of Ritu Shah, of the agency, and I was seized all at once by vertigo, by a sense of how far I'd come from everything I'd known. I had no business being in this room with these grave people absorbed in their work, and yet, at that moment, I had no wish to be anywhere else in the world. I saw Zoya going into and out of Zarina's office, saw her talking for a while to the young woman in the sky-blue hijab. Then I didn't look up until I felt Zoya touch my shoulder again.

"I think that's enough for today," she said gently.

We said goodbye to the people in the room, and then we went out into the afternoon sun. As Zoya closed the low gate, she looked at me and said, "Thank you."

"I'm happy that I could help," I answered automatically.

"No," she said. "Thank you for listening about Ishfaaq. For giving me company today."

My heart swelled. I recalled Zarina's gray eyes, her dry voice saying, *She gets too close,* and I felt a swoop of dark foreboding. But I could not hold on to it. The sun was so bright, the mountains seemed unreal, like they were cut from gauze, I was going to walk back home with this fierce, extraordinary woman who was finally speaking to me, and—this was the truth—I was content.

It took me three days to organize the papers in the file, after which I began to enter the information into an Excel spreadsheet. It was rote, mindless work, but that did not matter—what gave me pleasure were the murmurs of the other people in the room, the scent of those tiny white flowers in the garden, the ruffling of papers, and the clearing of throats. Zarina occasionally came out of her room, and her manner to me was unfailingly polite, though reserved. My favorite part of the day, however, was the walk home with Zoya. After the first day or two, we took to stopping at a little hotel for lunch, sitting at the same kind of long wooden table I'd once observed with envy from the back of a taxi. The skinny boy who worked at the hotel grew to expect us at the same hour. We would eat, elbow to elbow in the sun, and Zoya would talk. Most often, what she talked about was Ishfaaq. How he disliked cricket but pretended to like it because all his friends did, how he had grown three inches in a single month, how he loved food, especially phirni. Sometimes she spoke of her own childhood, the girls she'd once played with, now married and with children of their own. Back at the house, Zoya would hand me a bowl of rice from which to pick out the small, black stones. While I did so, she would cook, now and then breaking the silence to ask me to fetch an egg from the fridge, or the bottle of turmeric from her fragrant cupboard of spices.

Each evening, I still went into my room and peeled from my diminishing stack another five hundred rupees, which I had come to think of as payment for the continuation of this peace. They would be in the hall, Abdul Latief flipping through channels on TV and Zoya knitting her mysterious blue garment. Tea would be laid out already, a third white cup set aside for me, and so would pass the evening. When the azan sounded, and Abdul Latief left us to go to the mosque, Zoya and I would heat up the food and set it out on the living room floor, and when he returned, the three of us would eat, sitting in a close semicircle. Afterward, Abdul Latief would reach for a toothpick; Zoya would close her eyes; and I would lean back against a bolster, happy just to be in the room with them, snug in the certainty that tomorrow would bring more of the same.

Then one afternoon, perhaps five days after I'd begun going with Zoya to the office, as we were walking home in the afternoon, I saw Stalin. We turned a corner and there he was, standing at the end of the road. There was no mistaking those long legs, that lanky torso. I almost tripped; my blood ran cold. Since the day of the function, I'd faithfully avoided the intersection with the pharmacy, determined never to encounter him again. What was he doing here?

Zoya hadn't noticed my agitation; she was busy talking, telling me about a friend she once had on this road, who now lived in Jammu. Stalin's head was turned the other way, but at any moment, he would look in our direction. I could think of no way to divert her, to suggest another route home. There was nothing between him and us except twenty meters of bare pavement.

I tried to think rationally, bravely. So what if he did see me? What did I have to fear? He might have forgotten me entirely. But even as the thoughts raced through my mind, I knew I didn't believe them. And before I could make up my mind to do anything at all, Stalin turned. His eyes caught mine. I saw a flicker of surprise, followed by confusion, saw it darken to recognition.

I dropped my gaze and stared at the pavement. Zoya was still talking, oblivious of my silence. I watched the ground slide back under our feet, bracing myself for that high-pitched voice, that reedy whine, but second after excruciating second went by, and I heard nothing.

We were almost upon him. I caught a flash of gray-green from the corner of my eye, heard the dry scrape of a boot on the pavement.

And then we were past. I started to let out the breath I'd been holding.

But then he giggled. A weird, high-pitched giggle, more chilling for being devoid of humor.

"You two," I heard him say in Hindi, though without the respectful address that a woman of Zoya's age should have merited. "Come here."

I waited as long as I could before obeying. Zoya had already turned. She showed no fear, no surprise, but waited calmly for him to repeat himself: a short, fearless woman built like a mountain, a bottle-green bag stuffed under her arm.

"Yes. You two. I'm talking to you." Stalin nodded. "Come here."

We walked back toward him. I moved slowly, my legs uncooperative. Zoya, on the other hand, walked briskly up to him, as though she might embrace him. But I knew her well enough by now to recognize the strained muscles in her neck, her barreling gait. She was furious.

Stalin surveyed us for a moment, like a man considering a purchase. His helmet had fallen forward over his eyes, and, rather than adjust it, he raised his chin to look at us. This might have been amusing in other circumstances, but his eyes were half-closed, a faint sneer hovered on his lips, and I found that I was not inclined to laugh.

Fear roared in my ears, an oceanic sound. I tried to keep my head up, my face expressionless, fully expecting him to address me. But, to my astonishment, it was to Zoya he spoke.

"Show me," he said.

I looked at her, baffled. Show him what? She was opening her bag, fumbling around inside. She brought out a laminated card, which she pinched at one corner and held out to Stalin, who gave it the most cursory of glances, and said, "What nonsense is this?"

For the first time, Zoya's iron composure wavered. "Sir?"

"I'm asking," he said, insultingly slow, "what rubbish this is that you're trying to show me."

"My ID card, sir," she said.

"Is that so?" he jeered. "'My ID card.' You think I'm stupid?"

She didn't answer. It hadn't been a question.

"Show me another one," he snapped.

Zoya opened her mouth. Then, slowly, she closed it.

"Quickly!" Stalin squeaked. He was toying with her, taunting her with this parody of a schoolteacher's severity. "Don't waste my time."

She let her hand hover over her bag then let it fall.

"I don't have another one," she said, and then her face was no longer made of iron, it was flesh again: gray and blue capillaries, puffed fat beneath waxy skin. She was probably twice his age.

"I don't have another one, *sir*," he corrected her.

"I don't have another one, sir."

"Then what are you doing outside?" he demanded. "Want me to arrest you, huh?"

Only then did he look at me, and there was nearly enough malicious delight in that look to make me speak, to defend her. My mother would have spoken. She would have eyed him, and, with a few precise words, reduced him to nothing. She would have, but I did not.

The seconds passed, and then he smiled at me. It was not a nice smile.

"I'll let you go this time," he said to Zoya, sounding bored now, assured of his victory. "But this is your last chance, hear me? Next time I catch you without a proper ID, you won't escape so easily." He waved a contemptuous hand at her. "Now get lost, go home. I don't want to see your face here again. I'll be looking out for you."

Zoya spun on her heel and walked away, so quickly I had to jog to catch up with her. We trudged home, speaking not a word to each other until we reached the house. Finally, unable to stand it any longer, I burst out, "How can he *do* that?"

Zoya didn't respond. She began to climb the green stairs.

"Zoya!" I called up after her again. "How can he do that?"

She turned. "What do you want me to say, Shalini?" she asked with weary patience.

"I don't know," I cried. "Say something!"

"I think we should leave it," she said.

I heard the warning in her voice, but, childishly, I pressed on. "I can't leave it! How could you stand there, listening to that—to that—"

Then she lost patience. "What should I have done instead?" she asked. "Should I have hit him, hm? Should I have shouted at him?" She paused. "Asked him for a cigarette?"

I stared openmouthed at her.

"So just leave it," she said. She turned and went inside the house, but I remained rooted to the same spot. What had she meant? Had she seen me with Stalin? Had someone told her?

I longed to flee, but I forced myself to walk upstairs. She had already begun cooking, and I silently began to help her. After dinner, as the three of us sat in the hall, Zoya as always reaching for her knitting, I leaned toward her and whispered, "Sorry."

She did not stop knitting, but her hands seemed to soften. She angled her face toward me and smiled, shaking her head slightly to show she was not angry. I felt a wave of relief wash over me. Abdul Latief soon found a channel playing Bollywood songs from the seventies, and we listened in silence for a while to the scratchy old music. I thought of my father's collection of records, his hands moving over the spines, a silent incantation, and, briefly, I missed him.

"What are you making?" I asked Zoya.

"A hat," she said. "For Farzana's baby."

"Farzana?"

"Saleem's daughter," interjected Abdul Latief. "You met her and the baby the other day."

"Musa?"

"Good memory," he said and smiled at me.

Then Zoya, not taking her eyes off her knitting, said, "The first thing I ever knitted was a hat for Ishfaaq. Just after he was born."

Abdul Latief shifted onto his side. "Oh no," he laughed. "*This* story again."

"I was just learning," Zoya said. "I didn't want to rush."

"She took five months to make it," Abdul Latief put in. "Five months for one hat."

"I was following a pattern," Zoya said. "The pattern was very important to me."

"*Very* important," Abdul Latief agreed solemnly, clearly enjoying his role.

They both giggled, sounding for a moment like impish children. And then I felt a desperate need to laugh, and at the same time, a ferocious desire to hug them, to fight for them, to keep them safe from everything in the world that might ever want to harm them.

"So what happened?" I asked.

"It came out as big as a bag," Zoya said. "We used to put Ishfaaq inside it in the winter."

She and Abdul Latief gazed at each other, their expressions sad and tender, and, for a moment, the full force of their loss blew through the room like a cold wind.

There seemed to be no more to say after that. Zoya's needles ticked, keeping erratic time. The black-and-white lights from the TV streaked Abdul Latief's glasses, and his eyelids began to droop. I kept watch over them both, wishing for nothing to disturb this extraordinary peace, wishing for no intrusion, no stranger at the top of the stairs tonight, seeking a loved one vanished, his whole body burning with his great and terrible hope.

But what disturbed us in the end was the phone on the windowsill. It shrieked its loud, burring sound and Abdul Latief blinked and leaned over to answer. "Hello," he said. "Walaikum salaam. Yes, she's here. Tell me."

He listened, then sat up, switching over abruptly to Kashmiri. I became aware that Zoya had stopped knitting and was listening intently. My first thought was that it was news about Ishfaaq, and my heart quickened. Then Abdul Latief hung up the phone. He was smiling.

"I knew it!" he burst out. "That was Saleem." To my astonishment, he pointed the TV remote straight at my heart. "He was calling about you."

"Me?"

"He has found the family of Bashir Ahmed's wife, the people you were looking for."

Next to me, Zoya set her knitting down, as if she had just discovered a mistake in the pattern. I knew that I should express joy, gratitude, but I felt nothing.

"That's very good news," I said finally. "Thank you."

He grinned. "Saleem has told them that you wish to see Bashir Ahmed."

"And what did they say?"

"Saleem didn't say on the phone, but he did mention that this Bashir Ahmed's village is quite close to Kishtwar. I'm sure as soon as he finds out you are here, he will come." He laughed. "See, I *told* you we'd be able to help you find him! Didn't I tell you?"

This whole time, Zoya had not spoken. Now she picked up her knitting and began again, her eyes firmly lowered. I could not bear to look at her either. I opened my mouth, though I had no idea what I would say, but her gray needles clicked and clicked without pause, a barrier against any kind of speech, any expression of regret or sadness. Like that, we sat in silence for the rest of the evening, Zoya knitting, the TV blathering on, until Abdul Latief fell asleep with the remote still in his hand.

10

Every March, when I was a child, my father took precisely five days off from the factory, and the three of us went on a holiday to a resort. It didn't much matter where; the point, I see now, was the ritual. Like so many Indians scaling the middle-class ladder in the early nineties, my father believed it was an annual comfort owed to us, like regular electricity or tax breaks. There was always a clubhouse of sorts on the premises, a swimming pool, a table tennis room, a library filled with dog-eared *Reader's Digest*s, and a wood-paneled card room, where men gathered in the evenings to play gin rummy. My mother never failed to mock these places and their occupants, especially the spoiled, noisy children, whom she called "resort rats," and whom I thereafter avoided. As if to counter her cynicism, my father became doubly enthusiastic about everything. He was up at dawn for long walks around the golf course; he was ready to drive an hour to see a waterfall, even in the dry season; he was a regular at the gin rummy evenings. And I understand it, or at least I think I do. A man with his education and his experience of the world, with the income he was making, with a three-bedroom house and no great tragedy in his past—what else could he have done but celebrate his success with others like us? I think now that for him there might even have been something of the sacred in the whole thing. He rejected my mother's idols and prayers, but he constructed his own system of worship that was no less rigorous. All year he toiled for the sake of those five days in March, and it was both reward and punishment, for it took him away from the work he loved so much and landed him in a world with my mother, who could be joyous one minute and vicious the next, so that when he returned to the factory, it was with an air of distinct relief and the washed soul of a penitent.

Bashir Ahmed had been gone perhaps a month when the three of us went to Kerala, to a resort beside Lake Vembanad. Thousands of water hyacinths floated on the choppy brown surface, a living green carpet. My mother, who was in one of her irascible moods, dragged a chair onto the little pier and sat there watching them. I hung about her, dangling my legs off the warm wood, letting my toes skim the water, until she looked down and said, her tone distant, "You know what I hate, Shalini? It's when you just *sit* there at my feet, like a sad little mouse, waiting for me to do something to entertain you. For god's sake, can't you leave me alone for once in your life?"

Deeply wounded, I went and found my father, who seemed surprised and flattered at my sudden appearance. He and I spent the next few hours exploring the resort, finding in the process a stinking wire cage that housed a single obese rabbit, whom we named Garfunkel, and a badminton court with a sagging net, where we played until it was time to wash up for dinner. I ostentatiously ignored my mother throughout the meal, not even smiling when, in a poor attempt to win me back, she spoke to our waiter in an exaggerated Dracula accent, which caused the poor young man so much consternation I thought I saw tears in his eyes, and after dinner, I curled up beside my father to watch TV in our room. My mother noticed this but said nothing, instead disappearing for over an hour. She often went off like this, usually to find the nearest temple, so neither my father nor I worried too much about her. When she came back, she was smiling to herself.

That night, I was shaken awake in darkness. My mother stood over me, fully dressed.

"Get up," she said.

I asked no questions. The old excitement had ignited my belly as soon as I heard her voice, and I did not think of refusing. Anger forgotten, I scrambled out of bed. What were rabbits and silly games compared with this covert nighttime operation? I found my shoes and followed her out to the gate of the resort. The security guard was asleep in his little cabin, left hand tenderly cupping his crotch. From the dregs of pink in the sky, I guessed it was nearly morning. We walked along a wet, narrow street, canals cut deep into both sides, wide enough for little wooden boats. Little wooden bridges led to brightly painted houses. At one of the bridges, a small boy in shorts was waiting. He led us across to a mud courtyard at the back of the house, and I gasped. Tied to a stake in the corner, half-asleep on its feet, was a baby elephant. The boy pointed to a bucket with a mug bobbing in it. "I think," my mother murmured, "you're supposed to give it a bath."

I clutched her hand, grateful enough to be mute, and stumbled forward. The little creature was trusting; as soon as I got close, it bumped its forehead against the front of my shirt and nuzzled. With trembling hands, I poured a mug of warm water over its back, and it squeaked with pleasure. For the next thirty minutes, I forgot everything else. When all the water was gone, I went to my mother and wrapped my wet arms about her, a wordless apology. She bore my hug with a pained smile, and then she brought her lips down to my ear.

"We have fun together, don't we, little beast?"

"Yes," I whispered. I was starting to shiver, my lips painfully cold.

"Tell me, do you have fun like this with anyone else?"

I looked up at her face. "No," I said. "Nobody else."

"Good," she said, straightening up, and paid the little boy with a fistful of coins.

My father was still asleep when we got back to the resort. I changed into my pajamas, hung my wet clothes out to dry, and climbed, trembling and exultant, into bed. Needless to say, I never mentioned the incident to my father.

She wanted to prove to me, I think, that I was bound to her, as if I'd ever doubted it. Though now I think it must also have been her way of testing me, preparing me. A handful of minor secrets to pave the way for the final one.

It is surprising, looking back, that it took as long as it did for my father and Bashir Ahmed to meet. The day came, shortly after our trip to Lake Vembanad, when the bell rang, my father opened the door, and there was Bashir Ahmed, already slipping off his sandals, ready to enter. My father had stayed home from the factory that day, nursing a bad cold. He was grumpy; he and my mother had tussled that morning over the question of medicine, about which they held entirely contrary positions. My father, who sermonized science and logic, hated taking pills of any sort, whereas my mother, her faith notwithstanding, was pragmatic about the treatment of illness. It had ended with her saying, "Well, if you won't take a single tablet of Crocin, maybe you should go into the garden and dig up a few leeches instead," and shutting herself in their bathroom.

I did not see Bashir Ahmed at first, but I heard my father sniffle then say, in peremptory Hindi, "Thanks, but we don't want anything."

And I remember this particularly: instead of protesting that he knew my mother and me, Bashir Ahmed stood meekly in the face of the closing door. If I hadn't been passing, he would have walked off into the afternoon, and we would never have known.

"Appa, wait!" I shouted.

My father turned, hand still on the doorknob.

"I know him," I said quickly. "I mean, Amma and I do. He's from Kashmir."

Then Bashir Ahmed called from the other side of the door, "Janaab, I have not come to sell anything. Madam is my good customer, and I have brought her and beti a small gift."

My father opened the door and scanned him again, the enormous yellow bundle, the large hands, the weathered skin, the thick hair under the knit skullcap. "Please wait here for a minute," he said. Then he closed the door and, after a moment's consideration, locked it.

"I'll go tell Amma," I said, already starting up the stairs.

"Stop," he said, and I froze. "I'll come with you."

We went upstairs, leaving Bashir Ahmed locked out on our doorstep. It took all my self-control not to sprint ahead, to warn her. My father rapped on the bathroom door.

"There's a man here," my father said. "From Kashmir. Says he knows you."

From the other side of the door came the sound of water splashing on tile. For a while, she did not reply; then I heard her say, "Where is he?"

"Waiting outside," my father said.

I could smell her Pond's soap in the steam seeping from under the door. "All right," she said.

"What do you want me to do?" he asked. "Shall I send him away?"

"No. I'll come down in a minute."

My father glanced at his feet. "Are you sure that's a good idea?"

The water stopped falling. In the new silence, her voice rang out appallingly loud. "What," she asked evenly, "do you mean?"

"I'm just saying, if you've been watching the news at all these days, there are some pretty gory things going on up there. It doesn't hurt to be careful."

There was a long silence. Then she said, "All right."

"All right what?"

"Let's be careful."

"What does that mean?"

"I have no idea," she said coolly. "You tell me."

My father exhaled slowly through his mouth then sniffed once. Then, without another word, he went back downstairs, and I followed him. I half expected Bashir Ahmed to have left, but he was still there, back bowed under the yellow bundle. He had slipped his feet back into his sandals.

"Come inside," my father ordered him.

For the first time in my memory, Bashir Ahmed slunk into our house without anything resembling pleasure. He stood next to the sofa, bundle huddled at his feet.

My father did not invite him to sit. "What is your name?" he asked.

"Bashir Ahmed."

A long silence followed this.

"Where is Madam?" Bashir Ahmed asked.

"She's coming," my father said.

"Ah," Bashir Ahmed said. He turned to me. "How are you, beti?" he asked, trying and failing to sound cheerful. "How is everything? Are you studying hard?"

I gaped at him. He sounded like a nervous, fussy uncle, with no children of his own, who arrives with pockets full of sweets to cover up his awkwardness.

"Yes," I said.

"Good, good," he said miserably.

My father stood with his arms crossed, making no effort to speak. Then, thankfully, my mother came down the stairs, her hair wrapped in a towel. Bashir Ahmed turned to her with relief.

"Aadaab," he said, a greeting he'd never used with her before. It sounded sad and solemn.

"You said you'd brought something," my father reminded him.

"Yes," Bashir Ahmed said quickly. From his pocket, he drew out a peach, round and green, but with the lightest flush of pink. He handed it to my mother, who hardly looked at it.

"Thank you," she said.

An oppressive silence descended over our living room. Bashir Ahmed cleared his throat in desperation. "I also brought this," he said, diving into another pocket. "For beti."

And he placed in my hands a small piece of wood, carved into the shape of an animal I couldn't identify. It might have been a lion, a cow, or a horse. I ran my thumb over the featureless face. There was a curving scar on its belly, where the knife had slipped.

"My son made it," he said, still with that strained cheer. "I told him there's a very sweet, intelligent girl in Bangalore, and he made it just for you. He made me promise to give it to you."

The lie was obvious. The wood was years old, rubbed to the shiny smoothness of a beloved object, but I closed my fingers over it and thanked him, deciding I would return it to him later.

My father, in the meanwhile, had softened the slightest bit.

"You're from Kashmir, you said?" he asked Bashir Ahmed.

"Yes, janaab. Not from the valley, though. From the mountains."

"You live there?"

"I work here, janaab, but I was just there, visiting my family."

"Things are getting worse and worse over there. I've been reading about it," my father said, nodding seriously. "These poor Pandits leaving their homes and running away in the middle of the night, because they might be killed for being Hindu! It's sheer madness, and these militants sound like animals. Frankly, I'm a little surprised you're even here at such a time, Mr. Ahmed. I would have thought you'd prefer to stay with your family."

"Ah," Bashir Ahmed said. He glanced at my mother, but she seemed to have gone blind and deaf. He looked back at my father with difficulty.

"It is very sad about the Pandits, janaab. But that is happening in the Valley. In my area, no Hindus are being killed."

"And all those Kashmiri men crossing the border into Pakistan," my father went on unheeding, "for training, or whatever nonsense they're being fed. Calling themselves freedom fighters, waving guns, and shouting slogans like they have any idea what they're talking about! I've been reading about them too. The army killed seven of them just yesterday, I think."

In an even softer voice, Bashir Ahmed said, "Yes, janaab."

"And so?" My father leaned forward with the keen air of a courtroom lawyer. "What do you think, Mr. Ahmed?"

"About what, janaab?"

My father waved his hand. "All of it."

I looked to my mother, but she was staring down at the peach in her hand.

Bashir Ahmed did not respond for a long moment. Then he said, "Janaab, I am just an uneducated man. I have not even studied up to class five. I can hardly even read. These are not matters for me, they are for important and educated men like you."

My eyes opened wide. Bashir Ahmed's tone was one I'd never heard from him before, not even during his stories. It was the whining, servile tone of an obsequious servant. I saw my mother's eyebrows shoot up, but she made no comment.

"Come, Mr. Ahmed, you must think *something*," my father pressed.

But Bashir Ahmed shook his head stubbornly, his eyes still lowered. "No, janaab," he said. "Please do not ask me about such things. I am just trying to live and work so I can feed my family, and I wish for all Kashmiris, including the Pandits, to be free to do the same. That is all I know."

Next to me, my mother shifted. My father had his head cocked; he seemed to be considering this speech. Then, to my surprise, he grinned and clapped Bashir Ahmed on the shoulder.

"I like you, Mr. Ahmed," he announced. He drew out a handkerchief and loudly blew his nose. "If you ask me, we need more men like you around, especially nowadays."

Now Bashir Ahmed looked up, as if he suspected he was being mocked. "Janaab?"

"I mean it," my father insisted. "There are far too many people in this world who stick their noses in things that they don't understand and wind up making a mess of them. I'm glad there are still some of us around who know that the most important thing a man can do is to take care of his family and leave the rest to those who know what they're doing."

"I agree, janaab," Bashir Ahmed said, not sounding as though he agreed at all.

But my father nonetheless nodded, satisfied. "You're a good man, Mr. Ahmed," he said, sniffing. "I'm glad I met you."

Clearly relieved at having ended the discussion, but at the same time flattered, it seemed, by my father's praise, Bashir Ahmed turned again to my mother.

"Madam," he said with exaggerated formality. "Would you like to see anything today? Kurtas? Shawls, maybe?"

She shook her head.

"Then I should go," he declared. "My other customers will be waiting."

"I'll come out with you," my father offered.

He accompanied Bashir Ahmed to the gate, speaking to him the whole time. When he came back in, he looked satisfied with himself.

"Nice chat?" my mother asked, and I marveled at her. Her expression was ironic, amused, utterly uninterested. It was as if she'd never laid eyes on Bashir Ahmed before.

"You know, I'll admit than when he first came in, I thought he was a bit unsavory," my father said, sniffing noisily. "But then he doesn't seem like the rest of them, the Kashmiris you read about in the newspaper these days, anyway. That's obviously why he's here, working, instead of creating mayhem over there. He seems quite sensible, actually."

"Oh, I'm *so* glad," my mother murmured.

My father was grinning. He had, it appeared, forgotten all about that morning's quarrel, the scene at the bathroom door. "I told him if he ever needed any help, he could come to us. I'm sure he doesn't make any money doing what he does. Especially with a wife and son to support." He snorted. "Selling clothes. What kind of life is *that*?"

That was the first I heard of the events that were taking place in Kashmir in the nineties, and for a long time, it was all I heard. Bashir Ahmed came back three days later, and neither he nor my mother mentioned my father, or the peach my mother had cut up for our breakfast the next morning. I remember being nervous about seeing him again, because in the few days that had passed, I had lost the wooden animal. It had somehow disappeared from my bedside table. My mother had been typically unconcerned. "Must have fallen behind the bed," she said. "I probably swept it up and threw it out." I crawled around my room on my hands and knees, but the animal was truly gone. I finally screwed up my courage and confessed it to Bashir Ahmed, who assured me that it was all right, though I could not help noting he looked a bit disheartened.

He sat for a while on our sofa, hands on his knees, then launched into a story about a poor, beautiful woman with an extraordinary voice. I never heard the end of the story, however, because my mother, who had been getting more and more restless while he spoke, suddenly jumped up.

"Let's go," she ordered, clapping her hands.

He looked up in bemusement. "Where?"

She gave him an incredulous look. "To buy a carpet, of course. Where else?" When he still seemed baffled, she sighed and explained that she'd always wanted to buy a Kashmiri carpet for our living room, and since Bashir Ahmed was here, he would be able to help her choose one. There was a shop she'd heard about, and she wanted to go.

Bashir Ahmed shook his head. "But I don't know anything about carpets," he said. "I'm not from Srinagar. I already told you, I am from—"

"Yes, yes, the mountains. I know. Come on, just go with me."

"But—"

Like a child, she clapped her hands over her ears. "I'm not listening," she sang loudly. "I'm not going to listen to anything you say until you get up and come with me."

Unsurprisingly, she got her way. She chivvied us up the road and into an auto, with me sitting between them as usual. It was a tight fit with the three of us plus Bashir Ahmed's fat yellow bundle, but my mother seemed oblivious. Despite her injunction to hurry, she gave the auto driver interminable instructions about which route to take, then leaned back and started to hum.

The driver took us to Commercial Street, a wide shop-filled central street with countless forking alleyways, each of which contained hundreds of shops. She marched us like a general halfway up the street then down a flight of steps to a low, wide basement shop filled with carpets, mirrored tapestries, and carved wooden boxes. A short, obsequious man wearing a huge ruby ring greeted us. He called out and a boy sprang from nowhere, and together they began a dance of lifting and unrolling, spreading carpet after carpet before my mother. The owner spoke in a crooning voice, explaining the firing of the carpet, the warp and weft, inviting my mother to take off her shoes and walk on the silk, which she did with unfeigned pleasure.

This whole time, Bashir Ahmed had not said a word, sitting hunched next to me on the wooden bench. After about fifteen minutes, my mother politely turned to him and indicated a carpet the owner had just shown us. It was small and dusky red, the color of an apple on the verge of rot. "What do you think?" she said.

"It's nice," Bashir Ahmed said uncertainly.

"Yes," she said. A smile appeared on her face. "I think you are absolutely right."

Then she began to haggle.

She was implacable. The owner tried to pretend injury when she named a price far lower than his, but she ignored him and kept repeating the same number over again over again, like it was the only one she'd ever learned. The owner's expression changed from unctuous welcome to irritation, then to outrage, and finally to dour exhaustion. Bashir Ahmed sat to her side, wearing a look that seemed to ask the same question I was asking myself, which was why she had brought us here at all. For this escapade with the carpet, diverting as it was, could not be the end of what she had in mind. She was after something more, and we both waited to see what it was.

Finally, the owner excused himself and went into a back room, where he stayed for a while. When he returned, he gave the boy terse instructions to pack up the carpet. He did not see us out.

Back on the street, my mother turned to Bashir Ahmed, the carpet rolled and tucked under her arm. Her face was flushed. "Did you get a look at his face?" she whispered hoarsely. "He wanted to *kill* me, didn't he?" She laughed. "And he would have, too, if it weren't bad for business." She laughed again then became serious all at once. "Let's find an auto," she said.

Bashir Ahmed hailed one. My mother got in with the carpet, and I followed. Bashir Ahmed, however, remained standing on the pavement. My mother stuck her head out.

"What's wrong? Why aren't you getting in?"

"I can walk from here," he said. "This is close to my home."

"It is?" she asked innocently, and every one of my senses pricked up. "I've forgotten—where did you say you lived?"

"Near Russell Market," he said.

"Oh, that's just ten minutes away!" she exclaimed. "Get in. We'll drop you at home."

"No," he said, a little too quickly. "No, thank you. I'll walk."

She frowned. "Don't be ridiculous."

He shook his head again. My heart beat faster. It was as clear to me now as if she had whispered it in my ear. *This* was what she had been after all along. She wanted to see his home.

"Bashir," my mother said with deceptive sweetness, "get in and don't be a fool."

He cast around a final look of desperation, then flung himself into the auto. Once again, we juddered through the streets. Bashir Ahmed sat very still on one side of me, and on the other side, my mother bounced her knees, her eyes restlessly scanning everything we passed.

Then Bashir Ahmed said, "Stop."

The auto stopped.

"Which one is it?" my mother asked, peering out.

He pointed to an ugly building on the corner. The ground floor operated as a halal butcher, rosy skeins of goat hanging from ceiling hooks, and I saw my mother's nose wrinkle. Rickety balconies jutted from the upper floors, and weeping pipes had streaked the walls black.

Bashir Ahmed climbed out but didn't walk away yet. He glanced at the building then back to my mother. "Please come upstairs and have a cup of tea before you go," he blurted.

"Upstairs?" She even contrived to look surprised, my charlatan mother, who knew very well that, having come this close, he would be forced to invite us up. "Why not? Thank you."

She paid the driver and we followed him up the dingy stairs, the walls stained with dark, ominous liquids. The bottom two balconies were covered in shoes, but the top one was dusty and imprinted with a single set of footprints. Bashir Ahmed took his sandals off. We did the same.

Before he opened the door, he half turned and said in a rush, "It's very small. I'm sorry."

The dim room beyond was filled entirely with beds. Lumpy mattresses lay edge to edge, with only a narrow gap in between. Stepping carefully, I caught the smell that rose from each mattress, a smell that was neither sweat nor oil nor piss nor musk, but something so private and deeply human that it made me want to weep. There was a barred and netted window, which let in almost no light. Only one mattress had a sheet; it lay wrung and twisted, like a man fallen from an immense height.

The sight of the mattresses seemed to momentarily subdue my mother. She gazed around for a long moment, then said, "I didn't know there were others."

"Yes," he said, "there are usually eight of us."

"And all of you are Kashmiris?"

He nodded.

"Where are they?"

He shrugged, staring at his feet. "They've all gone back home," he said.

She gave him a look. "Because of what's happening?"

"Yes," he said.

She gazed around again, still hugging the rolled carpet to her chest. There were no chairs; he could not invite us to sit. He kept his eyes down and, after a moment, said, "I'll make tea."

He went into what was presumably the kitchen, and I heard the clinking of steel vessels. My mother, once he was gone, began to pace up and down in the narrow gap between two mattresses. "It can't be," I heard her whisper to herself. "It can't be."

"Amma," I said, putting my hand on her arm. "Please, let's go home."

She shook me off and kept pacing. Then she stopped, her eyes darting around, and without any warning at all, her face cleared. It was as remarkable and frightening a transformation as watching a roiling sea go flat. She dropped the carpet with a thud that seemed to make the cheaply tiled floor quiver. After a second, Bashir Ahmed came hurrying out of the kitchen.

"Is everything okay?" he asked in panic. "What was that sound?"

"What sound?" she asked, looking around. "Never mind. Listen, I have a question for you."

He went rigid. "Yes?"

My mother took a step toward him. "How bad is it in Kashmir?"

"What?"

"Don't pretend you didn't hear." She took a step toward him. "All your friends have gone back to Kashmir, so how bad is it?"

"I—" For the first time since I'd met him, he seemed to have no ready reply, no witticism to make her laugh. But then it was the first time they had talked about Kashmir. "It is bad," he said quietly.

"I see," my mother said. "In that case, I have another question."

He looked up.

"Why are you still here?"

"Here?" he asked hesitantly.

"Yes," she said. "Here. In Bangalore. Why are you here?"

"To earn money," he said finally.

"To earn money," she repeated mockingly. "Really, Bashir? You expect me to believe that?"

He did not reply.

"What about your friends? What are *they* doing to earn money?"

"I don't know."

"Are they training to be militants? Have they crossed the border? Are they fighting?"

"I don't know," he said.

"Are they at least with their families?"

"Yes. I don't know. Probably."

"So they're doing *something*." Her voice dropped several notches until it was a cold whisper. She took another step toward him, so that her face was barely a foot away from his. I could see his fingers curl, his muscles twitching with the desire to flee. And I did not blame him. Her lips were dry, she was rocking back and forth on the balls of her feet, and her voice trembled with a barely controlled violence that made her frightening to me. I watched as this stranger, this madwoman, fixed her eyes on the cowering Bashir Ahmed. "And *you*? Shall I tell you what you're doing? Hm? Shall I tell you why you're here and not there? Shall I?"

He glanced at me. I saw that he was terrified of what she might say, embarrassed by my presence there, and I would have turned away to spare him, except at that moment my mother exploded into motion. She spun and kicked the rolled-up carpet with all the strength she had. It made a dull, muffled thud that seemed to please her, because she kicked it again. Finally she turned back and pointed at his chest with a thin finger.

"Because you're a coward," she said coldly. "A coward. Your home is full of fighting, and you're here, carrying around your *stupid* clothes, telling your *stupid* stories, whining, 'Yes, janaab, no janaab,' as if nothing is happening. Are you a child? My god, what's *wrong* with you?"

She glanced around, and her eyes fell once again on the much-abused carpet. "You want money?" she asked with unconcealed contempt. "Is that all you want? Here. Take that. It's yours. I'm giving it to you. You know how much I paid for it and you're ten times better as a salesman than the idiot in the shop. You'll get ten times as much."

She fell into an abrupt silence. Nobody moved for a long time. I wondered if the people in the apartment below were listening.

Then Bashir Ahmed said quietly, "You're right."

What?" She seemed confused all of a sudden. "What? What did you say?"

"You're right," he said again. He was still speaking quietly, but there was more force in his voice than there had been all afternoon. "What *am* I doing here? What did I think I was going to achieve by coming back, leaving my family? There *must* have been something wrong with me."

Then he raised his finger and pointed to the front door.

"Get out," he said.

My mother stared at him. "Excuse me?"

He didn't flinch this time. "Get out," he repeated.

It seemed for a moment that she might pounce on him, attack him physically; but she only spun around and strode to the door.

Opening it, she half turned and said over her shoulder, archly, "Go home, Bashir. There's nothing for you here."

He did not respond. She picked her sandals up in one hand and began walking, chin lifted, down the filthy staircase. Not daring to meet Bashir Ahmed's eyes, I followed, stopping only at the very bottom of the stairs to wriggle into my shoes.

My mother, meanwhile, was standing barefoot in the street. I rushed up to her.

"Amma," I cried. "What's going to happen? Is he going to leave?"

She looked down at me. There were tears in the corners of her eyes, and this terrified me even more than the ugly scene upstairs. But at the same time, I saw that the madwoman was gone, that, tears or not, she was my mother again.

"Shalini," she said hoarsely, "I've made a mistake."

I waited, certain that she was going to say she had been too harsh, that she had not meant to lose her temper, had not meant to wound him. I waited eagerly for the words, ready to race upstairs and apologize to Bashir Ahmed on her behalf, ready to beg him to forgive her.

"I shouldn't have let that auto go off," she said impatiently. "Now it'll take *forever* to find another one."

That evening, when my father came home from the factory, he almost tripped over a thick cylindrical bundle left on our doorstep, which, upon unrolling, was found to contain a small, exquisite Kashmiri carpet, the color of a late-season apple. He looked inquiringly at my mother.

"Delivery people," she sighed. "You know how careless they can be."

III

11

I DID NOT GO back to the office with Zoya. Instead I stayed at home, as I had done in the beginning, waiting for Bashir Ahmed. Zoya began leaving my breakfast on a tray again, and however early I rose, she was gone by the time I came out of my room, as if avoiding me. She said nothing to make me believe this was so, but I knew she felt betrayed. The tenuous affection that had begun to grow between us was arrested, and, though she must have known, as I had, that this day would come, her hurt was palpable, and I was helpless to change it.

Once again, I passed my days in Kishtwar doing nothing. I did not sleep or watch TV or go for a walk, afraid I would miss Bashir Ahmed, afraid that he might knock once, twice, then give up and go away. It was not pure anticipation I felt, waiting for him, but a murky mixture of fear and impatience, eagerness and reluctance. What was he like now? Would he recognize me? What if he never came at all? I asked this of Saleem, who occasionally visited in the evening for tea and a game of cards with Abdul Latief. He laughed, "He will come, child. These mountain people, they follow their own time, unlike those of you from the city. You must be patient."

Then, on a Tuesday afternoon, shortly before lunch, there was a knock at the door. I opened it, and for a second I could not speak. The bearded man who stood outside wore a brown kurta, muddy and stained at the hem. He had obviously spent most of his life outdoors; the skin around his nose was like treebark. His mouth was small and sensuous, with a faint overbite. His hair was thick and dark, except for a smudge of gray at his right temple, and it fell over his forehead in a way that was so familiar it was like a slap. I had to remind myself to say, "Yes?"

"My name is Riyaz," he said in Urdu. And when I did not respond, he added, "Bashir Ahmed is my father."

It took another moment for me to say, "Salaam alaikum."

It was the first time I'd greeted anyone that way, and I was relieved when he responded, though without enthusiasm, "Walaikum salaam." I glanced behind him, but there was nobody else on the stairs. As if he'd read my thoughts, he said, "I came alone."

"Oh," I said. Then I realized I was blocking the doorway. "Please come in," I said.

He seemed to hesitate, then stepped past me. While he was looking around the hall, I seized the chance to observe him again. There were hints of Bashir Ahmed in his neck and jaw, but whereas Bashir Ahmed had been tall and hefty, a pillar of a man, his son was smaller and neater, more compact. There was a lethargy to his body, which suggested, not laziness, but its opposite, a barely coiled energy. He swept the house with a single glance then turned back to me. "You are the one who was asking about my father?" he asked. All this time he hadn't smiled.

"Yes," I said. "My name is Shalini. I knew him years ago, when I was a child. In Bangalore."

He nodded, but it was evident he was not listening. He glanced once more around the room then drew himself up, as if he'd come to a decision. He fixed me with a gaze that was stern and oddly aloof, and, just before he spoke, I had a flash of something. Call it an omen, foreshadowing, what you will—but if I could have leapt forward and clamped my hand down on his mouth, if I could have thrown myself on him to prevent him from speaking, I would have.

He said, "My father is dead."

I don't know how long we stood there. Riyaz's face had closed like a door after his announcement. And I? Absurdly, my first thought was that at least I would now be able to stay here with Zoya, return to my work at the office, but it did not take me long to realize that this would be an impossibility. The green room, which had once been Ishfaaq's, and for a short while had been mine, would be required by others, who were far more desperate than I was. Once I'd understood this, it was all I could do not to turn away from him and weep.

Bashir Ahmed was dead. Dead, like my mother, both of them gone forever from my grasp. I knew I should express my condolences to the man standing before me, but I could not bring myself to speak. Riyaz, in the meantime, was starting to look uncomfortable. His fingers twitched, as if in search of some familiar object, and he glanced over my shoulder at the doorway.

"Where are the people whose house this is?" he asked abruptly.

"They're at work. They'll be back in the evening."

"Then I will come back in the evening," he declared, and before I could reply, he stepped past me and ran lightly down the stairs. Left alone, I closed the door and looked around the empty hall, which suddenly seemed strange and unfamiliar to me.

Abdul Latief came back first, and I told him what had happened. He looked sad and patted me on the shoulder. "I am sorry," he said. I could not bear telling Zoya, so I excused myself and went into my room. I heard her come in, heard their voices as a low murmur, and I waited, half hoping she would knock on my door, half hoping she wouldn't.

She did not knock.

And then, in the evening, as he said he would, Riyaz returned. Saleem was there, too, shuffling the deck of cards. I was sitting with them in the hall, not drinking my tea, letting a rippled brown skin congeal on the surface. Zoya opened the door, and there he was again, looking startled and not entirely pleased to find so many people on the other side of it.

"Salaam alaikum," he said gruffly to Zoya.

"Walaikum salaam," she replied. "Please come in."

While he greeted Saleem and Abdul Latief, Zoya brought a cup and poured him some tea, which he drank in one long, uninterrupted swig, setting the cup down and staring at it angrily. He was, I thought, either extremely surly or extremely shy.

"So," Abdul Latief said in Urdu, trying to put him at ease, "how was your journey?"

He did not look up. "Fine."

"You did not have any trouble finding our house, I hope?"

"No."

"I'm glad to hear it," Abdul Latief said, throwing a glance at his brother-in-law.

Saleem interjected, in his low, musical voice, "I was sorry to hear about your father."

Riyaz ducked his head in acknowledgment but did not reply.

"I am also sorry because this young lady"—Saleem nodded at me—"has been wanting very much to see him. She came all the way from Bangalore. Did she tell you that?"

I waited for Riyaz to look at me, but he didn't.

"I don't know if you know this, but Bangalore is at the other end of India," Saleem said casually. "It is a long way for anybody to travel."

Abdul Latief, apparently grasping something I did not, echoed, "Yes. A very long way."

Zoya finally looked up from her knitting. Only I was still puzzled.

"Since she has come such a long way," Saleem went on, "I was thinking it might be nice for her to at least visit your village for a few days. What do you think?"

Now Riyaz looked at me, sharply and with accusation. I wanted to shake my head to show I was as surprised as he was, but he looked away almost immediately. Then Saleem switched to Kashmiri and spoke for a long while. His tone never meandered away from utmost politeness, but it was evident, even though I could not understand what was being said, where the authority lay. Saleem was polished, educated, and at least thirty years older than Riyaz, who, as I could see, was only a few years older than me. As Saleem spoke, a sullen, resigned look came over Riyaz's handsome face. I glanced at Abdul Latief, who was suppressing a smile, then at Zoya, who had returned to her knitting. When Saleem finished speaking, Riyaz sat motionless, staring at the patterned yellow cloth that covered the floor, then stood up all at once and walked out.

I thought he meant to leave, but he went only as far as the landing, where he pulled out a small cell phone and made a brief, muttered call. When he hung up, he pocketed the cell phone and came back in. Ignoring Saleem and looking only at me, he said, "Do you want to see our village?"

What was I to say? The truth was that at the moment I could not think of anything I wanted *less* than to see his village. All I wanted was to go back to my green room, crawl under the sheets, and fall asleep. And, when I woke, I wanted to eat breakfast with Zoya and walk with her through the streets of Kishtwar to the office. I wanted to sit by her side on our wooden bench in the sun and listen to her talk. I wanted to pass the evening in this very same hall, while Zoya knitted and Abdul Latief watched TV, until it was time to sleep again. So, no, I did *not* want to see Riyaz's village, but even less did I want to admit my hesitation and risk being sent away altogether, back to Bangalore, to my grieving father, to the job I no longer had, to the parties on the weekends, to all those deadly barren hours in between. So I said, "Yes. If it isn't too much trouble. Thank you."

Riyaz nodded. "I'll go find a taxi," he said. "Be ready in ten minutes."

"Wait." My stomach dropped. "*Now*? You want to leave now?"

He scowled. "Is there something wrong with now?"

To that, I could find no satisfactory reply. Riyaz nodded at Saleem and Abdul Latief, who seemed as taken aback as I was at this sudden acceleration of events, and strode out. After a moment of stunned silence, Abdul Latief laughed shakily.

"Well," he said, "at least you know he won't make you tired with talking."

I stood and went to my room. I dragged my rucksack, which was dusty, from under the little bed and placed it on the pink sheets. My clothes—jeans and T-shirts, underwear and bras, a sweatshirt—lay in two piles in the low cabinet. I carried them over and placed them in the rucksack. Then my comb, my sandals, a scarf hanging on the hook with the Arabic inscription, my toiletries. In less than five minutes, I had packed everything I'd brought here, and the green room looked undisturbed, its surfaces closing, like water, as soon as I was gone.

Walking amid the fleet of white taxis was exactly as I remembered it, all of them covered in the dust of a hundred roads, giving off heat like circus behemoths. I followed Riyaz, hunching under my rucksack, bumping it into shoulders and cars. After a terse exchange in Kashmiri with a yawning, uninterested teenager, Riyaz indicated a particularly run-down vehicle, whose seats spit jaundiced foam from long rips. Again, my rucksack was strapped to the roof. Again, I climbed in and found a seat in the back corner, next to the window.

Riyaz had come back to the house in ten minutes as he promised he would. He wouldn't come inside but stayed downstairs, waiting. I walked to the door with Abdul Latief and Zoya. Saleem had just wished me goodbye and left.

Abdul Latief smiled and shook my hand.

"All the best," he said. "I am only sorry that you will not get to meet your mother's friend."

"Thank you for everything," I said.

"No thanks are needed. Come back and see us whenever you want."

Zoya stood next to him, her face expressionless. This evening she wore a light green headscarf, patterned with leaves veined in thin gold thread.

"Do you have our phone numbers?" Abdul Latief asked suddenly. I shook my head. "Wait here for a minute," he said and went inside.

I looked at Zoya.

"Will you tell Zarina?" I asked. "That I've left?"

She inclined her head slightly, and I was conscious of my disappointment. But what right, I scolded myself, did I have to be disappointed? How many times had she stood right here, at this same door, with someone about to depart, someone she had fed and sheltered and protected, as she had fed and sheltered and protected me? Fifty times? A hundred? Wasn't that what Zarina had been trying to tell me from the beginning? And so wasn't it an absurdity, arrogance, to imagine it would somehow be different with me, simply because I had stayed a little longer, because I had walked with her for a few days in the sun?

The azan began, sung by an old man. We listened in silence as he made his precarious way through the long minor notes. Then I heard her say, "When Ishfaaq comes back, I will tell you."

I looked up. She still wasn't smiling, but there was a liquid quality to her face, as though something had softened for a moment and flowed toward me. I had the urge to sit down right there, on their doorstep, and burst into tears.

"Yes," I whispered. "Please. Tell me. I would like that very much."

Abdul Latief came back, brandishing a pen and a sheet of paper. In a large, elegant hand, he had written their two cell phone numbers.

"In case you need anything," he said.

"Take mine, too," I said on impulse, before I remembered I no longer had one to give them. "I mean, my number in Bangalore. If you ever come, you must stay with us."

He laughed. "I think your family would not want two old people to trouble them." Nevertheless, he handed me the pen. I tore off a corner of the sheet and wrote our landline number on it, making sure every digit was legible.

"It's just my father," I said, handing the paper to him, "and he will enjoy meeting you."

"Maybe one day," Abdul Latief said.

"Inshallah," I added, and he laughed again.

Halfway down the green stairs, I stopped. I was trembling. I rested my hand on the wall, then, aware that Zoya was still watching me from the doorway above, made myself continue. When I reached the bottom, I resisted the temptation to turn, instead pushing out into the dusk, to where Riyaz was waiting.

A door slammed, startling me. The driver was in his place. Riyaz had taken the seat in front of me, and I kept my eyes on the point where his hairline ended, the vertical furrow that hid the top of his spine. Beside me was a Hindu woman in a bloodred kurta with girlishly puffed sleeves, typing something rapidly on her cell phone. Her lipstick and bindi were the same shade of lurid red, and her black hair had been ironed straight and hung over her shoulders like straw. Her two sons, twins, sat on the other side of her, already asleep, wearing identical striped T-shirts tucked into jeans. Her husband, a burly man with close-cropped hair, sat in front beside the driver. Now and again, he turned and called out something to her, and without looking up from the little screen, she responded in a voice that could have sawed bone.

A tout came around collecting fares, and I paid without hesitation, a fact that caused me quiet pride. Then the taxi pulled out of the marketplace, leaving behind the tea stalls and the vendors and the grand, charred mosque. Shops were beginning to close for the evening, people were going home. I had a last glimpse of the Chowgan, immense with shadows, and then it was the highway and the mountains again. Lights on the valley floor, lights on the distant slopes, lights from the vehicles we passed, a glow that fell around my shoulders and died away. Lights from an army checkpoint, where a bored soldier waved us through. Lights from the dozens of highway food stalls, exposed bulbs dangling and waving in a warm breeze. And all of a sudden I was exhausted, by the thought of having to do it all again, the arrival, the introductions, the discomfort, the explanations. I longed for my warm, familiar home in Kishtwar, where Abdul Latief would be right now stretching out against his favorite bolster and Zoya would be in the kitchen, boiling water, though tonight there would be only one kind of tea, only one blue thermos.

I had no idea how long we'd been traveling when the taxi stopped. I sat up. The darkness around us was nearly complete; all I could tell was that there was a river close by. I could hear the pounding, the full weight of water on earth.

In the seat before me, Riyaz rose and beckoned to me with a finger. The driver had already hoisted himself onto the roof of the taxi. I pointed out my bag, and he freed it from the others, flinging it down to Riyaz, who grunted at the impact. The driver leapt down, bare feet landing without sound. He climbed back into his high seat, gave us a last nod, and drove off.

I looked around. We seemed to be still on the highway, but there were small closed shops on either side, topped by little rooms, all of which had the hastily improvised yet durable look of a shantytown. There was no one in sight, and all the windows were dark.

"This is your village?" I asked Riyaz, whispering though I didn't know why.

"No. We will go there tomorrow."

"Why not now?"

He picked up my rucksack and swung it onto his own shoulders. "You want to break your legs in the dark? Go ahead."

He walked away from me, going about ten feet along the narrow pavement. Then, without warning, he was swallowed up by the earth. I shivered and yet I wasn't entirely surprised. Any kind of magic seemed possible in this place. I hurried to the place where he'd disappeared, only to find a steep flight of stairs that cut between two buildings, going down the mountain.

I descended cautiously and was amazed to find more buildings behind the single dark row along the highway. An entire town had been built into the side of the mountain, houses hanging one above the other, sewn together with tiny streets. I saw homes, shops, restaurants, barbers, even a little school. Most lights were off, except for the occasional glowing bulb in an upstairs window.

Riyaz led me swiftly through, until we came to a house with a raised concrete verandah, its lights still on. The door was opened by a young woman with a long, sad face, who showed us past a small hall crammed with dark furniture, and into another room filled with gunnysacks and a cot.

"You can sleep here tonight," Riyaz said.

"What about you?" I asked.

He scowled. "Don't worry about me. Be ready early tomorrow morning."

The sad-faced girl shut the door, and then I was alone in the room. It smelled like the cool loam of a graveyard. Illogically fearful, I pulled open one of the gunnysacks and pushed my hand inside to find something smooth and knobby.

Potatoes.

I started to laugh, weakly. What was I doing here? Starting out on this journey, I'd been so *certain* of finding Bashir Ahmed, certain that something vital would be settled if only I could see his face again, but had that been only the warped logic of grief? For Bashir Ahmed was dead, and where was I? In a room filled with potatoes, in a town hanging over a river, in the company of a surly stranger, and with my own life, as I had known it, vanished utterly.

I heard a noise and peered out of the window. Riyaz was leaving. The front door closed behind him, and he walked to the raised edge of the concrete verandah. He stood there silently for a while, looking out at the tiny street, and then I saw his shoulders shift. He bent his knees, and in a graceful, unexpected motion, launched himself off the edge. Arms thrown out, toes pointed like a dancer's, he hung suspended for a fraction of a second, every line of his body etched in sharpest relief against the dark. Then he landed, and, without breaking stride, walked away around the corner.

The next morning, I woke to the sound of bells. A pair of mules stood outside my window. Swollen white sacks hung down on either side of their backs, and they swiveled their necks like slow, ancient machines. One of them stretched its neck up and brayed, dark lips pulled back over enormous teeth.

The door to my room opened, and the girl stuck her head inside. In the light, I saw she had pocked skin and sweet brown eyes. "You are awake?" she asked. "Riyaz bhaiyya has already come three times. I told him you were still sleeping."

She gave me a simple, plentiful breakfast of milk, roti, and butter, and showed me to a chilly bathroom where I dabbed water on my face and under my arms. Then, carrying my bag herself, she led me into the little town above the river. The shops were open now, some owned by Muslims, others by Hindus who had lit sticks of incense in front of tinseled portraits of Lakshmi. The ground was littered with fruit rinds, plastic cups, pellets of goat shit, and runnels of brown water.

Riyaz was waiting in front of the tinted glass of a barbershop, visibly impatient.

"Don't you know what 'early' means?" he snapped in Urdu at the girl, who flushed.

"It's not her fault," I said loudly. "It was mine. I was tired."

He shot me an irritated glance. "Well, I hope you're ready to get even more tired," he muttered. "It's a long way up."

He pried my bag from the girl's hand and walked off. "Thank you," I said to her.

"Don't let Riyaz bhaiyya scare you," she whispered, reaching for my hand and clasping it in her damp one, smiling her sad smile. "He likes to get angry, but actually he is very nice."

I looked at his receding back. "I'll try to remember that," I said.

Then I left her and followed Riyaz down toward the river.

We made our way down a mud track littered with animal shit and plastic bags, broken shoes and chocolate wrappers, to two thick concrete pillars supporting a bridge. We passed between them, and here I stopped, because below us was the river. I'd learned its name as a child in school, and that it was one of the five mighty rivers of the north, but I had not been prepared for such a vital, living thing. The water was gray in places, slate blue in others, and, farther off, a tawny green. The roar was so loud it seemed to dampen the sun's glare, so that it felt momentarily as if we were standing in shadow. The bridge itself was of old wood, its green paint flaking, the beams cradled within twisted metal cables as thick as my calves. It looked solid, immovable, but as soon as I was a little way out onto it, I realized that the bridge creaked and swung wide above the roiling river, and my stomach began to churn. I took each step slowly, keeping my eyes fixed on my feet, but when I reached the middle, I could not resist looking up. I could see miles and miles up and down the river, mountains looming dark on both sides, all that tall blue sky held between. It was terrifying and exhilarating, and a sound—a laugh of delight or moan of fear, I couldn't tell—escaped me, torn away in an instant by the gale that funneled through the valley.

On the other side of the river, a Hindu temple stood on a flat, grassy patch, which gave way to a rough upward track, strewn with sharp, glittering stones. Riyaz was waiting here for me to catch up. I remembered what the sad-faced girl had said, and I said with as much friendliness as I could muster, "Thank you for taking me to your village, Riyaz. It's very kind of you. Your father used to talk about it all the time. I'm so happy that I'm going to be able to finally see it."

He gazed down at me, and I thought for a moment he might not respond at all. Then he said, "If you want my advice, try to contain your happiness, at least while we're walking uphill. Otherwise you'll be crying for rest every two minutes, and it will take us even longer to get there than it already has."

With that, he hefted my rucksack onto his back and began walking. Part of me wanted to turn on my heel and go the opposite way, but now I had no choice. I followed in silence, partly because I did not know what else to say to him, but soon because—he was right, as it turned out—I had no breath to say anything at all. The incline, which hadn't been noticeable at first, quickly became punishing. My panting sounded obscene in the hot, still air. Stones dug into the soles of my running shoes. Pain shot through my hamstring, an old swimming injury. Occasionally, people passed us, carrying their belongings on their heads or slung over their backs: cloth bundles or tin boxes, and once even a gray sheep straddling a man's shoulders, gazing gloomily back at me.

Riyaz, meanwhile, kept climbing. I suspected he was testing me, trying to wear me out, so the few times he turned, I forced myself to walk erect, a careless half smile pasted to my face. As soon as his back was turned, though, I slumped over like an abandoned puppet. The slope of the mountain dropped away to our right, and I saw where it had been leveled into terraces, each holding a field of corn. Along the path were trees with twisted trunks, which threw a shade as thick as syrup. I longed to curl up beneath them, close my burning eyes, but after what Riyaz had said, I did not want to ask him for a break. And the sun—the sun was everywhere, between two branches, leaping from leaves, shimmering in the sand. My clothes were drenched with sweat. My vision blurred; at one point I thought I saw a tall, thin figure standing just behind my shoulder. I nearly screamed, but realized in time that it was just the shadow of a tree whose limbs stretched out over the track.

Later I would find out that we climbed four thousand feet that day. I saw one mud-walled house, then another, built into the mountainside. I saw cornstalks with their tapering, swordlike leaves. I saw a pumpkin vine snaking across the path, leaves splayed broad and shining dark as an oil spill. Riyaz abruptly cut off from the main track and began to lead us downhill on a trickle of a path, stepping over a leaking water pipe, to a small mud house, its walls painted sky blue, with a flat roof of pressed dirt. A pressed mud porch extended in front; in the far corner was a magnificent buckled tree with delicate pink blooms. A honey-colored spaniel raced up, barking, and flung itself against Riyaz's shins then sniffed my ankles vigorously.

Through the haze of my exhaustion, I saw an older woman on the porch. Her face gathered in wrinkles, her eyes set deep in her skull, the same eyes as those of the man in front of me. Her legs bowed in a faded green salwar. Her head covered in a faded scarf too warm for the weather. Her feet bare. Her mouth set in a line that did not betray the slightest welcome.

"My mother," Riyaz said. "She has been waiting to meet you."

12

I SAT ALONE IN a room with mud walls, the bottom half of which was painted the same sky blue as the outside of the house. The top half was bare, the line between blue and brown running along the periphery of the room like an inverted horizon, broken only by a wooden cupboard sunk into the wall and painted white. Bolsters were scattered about, exactly as in Zoya and Abdul Latief's home, but here they were old and faded and misshapen from years of use. A threadbare mattress lay under a single large window, which framed an astonishing view. I could see peaks upon peaks, the farthest of them pale and watery, as if some trick of light threw an endless reflection.

I heard a noise at the door and looked up. It was the woman, Riyaz's mother. She did not enter, but stood at the doorway, watching me. I opened my mouth to speak, but something stopped me, and instead I sat there while she took me in. She seemed to be in no hurry, her face dispassionate as a surgeon's before an anesthetized body. I could not read her expression, could not ascribe to it welcome or curiosity or pleasure. I know it sounds strange, but the closest I could come was to say that she was *memorizing* me, learning my features for some purpose of her own. I shivered under the gaze, but also, strangely enough, was comforted by it.

The old woman looked at me a moment longer, then turned and left. Five minutes later, she came back with tea and some flaky buns on a plate. Riyaz accompanied her. He'd splashed water on his face and on his hair, which glistened where the drops still clung to the tips.

"My mother asked me to tell you there is more tea in the kitchen if you want it," he said.

"She doesn't speak Hindi?" I asked. "Or Urdu?"

"No, just Kashmiri."

I looked again at her. Bashir Ahmed's wife. This was the woman whose absence had been present all those afternoons when Bashir Ahmed told his stories, when my mother had laughed and smiled, when I had not dared to take my eyes off either of them, as though they might be snatched away if my attention slipped even for a second. This woman had been there with us the whole time, the invisible one that nobody dared to mention. I felt suddenly shy before her, embarrassed.

"What is her name?" I asked Riyaz.

"Khadijah."

"Could you tell her that I'm happy to meet her?"

Riyaz translated into Kashmiri. She listened then said something brief back to him. He nodded. "She says you should drink your tea before it gets cold."

They left the room together, and then I was alone again. I picked up the chipped cup and took a bun from the plate. It was warm and light and delicious, and the tea was the salty kind. I ate and drank everything the old woman had placed in front of me, then waited for them to return. But they did not, and as hard as I fought to stay awake, it was as if my body had absorbed every one of those four thousand uphill feet, and they now became four thousand weights inexorably pulling my aching muscles down to the cloth-covered floor. I crawled over to the mattress under the window and fell asleep. At some point, I clawed my way briefly to the surface to find that my cup and plate had been cleared away, but before I could wonder which of them had been in the room, I was asleep again.

* * *

The next time I woke, my head was relatively clear. I had no idea of the time, but the dense haze of sleep that had enveloped me had gone. I was still alone in the same room. It was broad daylight, and the mountains were sharp as paper cutouts in the window. I gingerly got to my feet. My muscles ached, but I appeared to be not too much the worse for wear. I made my way out into the narrow corridor and toward the front door. To the right was a small smoke-stained kitchen I had no recollection of passing on my way in. It was empty of human occupants; only a round, soot-blackened iron pot sat on a mud stove that had been built into the wall at floor level. Where on earth were Riyaz and his mother?

The mud porch was as empty as the house. Half a dozen or so chickens plucked desultorily in a bed of large orange blooms, and when I emerged from the house, they abandoned their scavenging and came to crowd hopefully around me.

Right then, a young woman came around the corner of the house, stopping short at the sight of me. Then her face broke into a huge smile.

"You're finally awake!" she exclaimed in Urdu, as though we'd already met.

"Yes," I said, blinking.

"Did you sleep well?" she asked. "How are you feeling? Are you still tired?"

"A little, but I'm fine, thank you." She had clear brown eyes, and a crooked, humorous mouth. Her long headscarf hung down the back of her kurta, dyed in vivid streaks of purple and red. "I'm sorry," I blurted finally, "but who are—"

She laughed. "I'm Amina," she said, "I am Riyaz's wife. He did not tell you?" She used his name without shyness.

I shook my head. "Do you know what time it is?" I asked.

She seemed to find the question hilarious, because she laughed again. "Time? It is the next morning! You slept for, oh, I think fifteen hours. I have never seen anybody sleep that long."

I blushed. "I'm sorry."

She waved her hand. "No, no, you were tired. Now come and have breakfast."

In the kitchen, which was immaculate, lined with mud shelves on which were stacked a few dented tins, a handful of steel plates and tumblers, and three or four fire-blackened pots, she began to select sticks from a pile in the corner and place them deftly in the mud stove.

"Sit," she said, indicating a woven straw mat on the floor. I lowered myself onto it and watched her light the sticks, leaning forward and blowing to encourage the newborn flame.

"You said your name is Amina?" I asked. She nodded without taking her eyes off the slowly growing fire. "My name is Shalini," I said.

"I know who you are," she said smiling. "I was the one who told Riyaz to bring you up."

I could not hide my surprise. "You?"

"Yes," she said, then her face softened. "He told me that you were looking for Abbaji."

"Yes."

"You used to know him?"

"A long time ago," I said. "When I was a child. I thought he would be . . . I mean, I didn't know until Riyaz told me that he—"

I broke off. The young woman looked sympathetic, then she clapped her hands together in a brisk way and said, "Well, you are here. Once you eat something, I will show you around the village."

"Thank you," I said, adding, "I won't trouble you for long. I'll leave in a day or two."

The merriness had now returned to her face. Raising her eyebrows, she said, "You've just arrived, and you are already talking about leaving? You hate this place so much?"

"That's not what I meant at all," I said, quickly. "I just meant—"

Again, she burst into laughter. "I'm teasing," she said, "but, really, there is no need for you to run away so fast. You're like one of my murgis outside. Come here a second. I'll show you."

She picked up one of the battered cans from the mud shelf above the stove, and went to the kitchen window, which overlooked the front porch. She dug in the tin, pulled out a fistful of rice, and flung it in a shower on the ground outside. The half-dozen chickens rushed up with amazing speed from all corners of the porch. They scrabbled at the earth with their strong claws, their beaks jabbing furiously as they fought for space, a riot of feathers and dust.

"See how fast they are?" Amina said. "I'll call you Murgi from now."

She was grinning at me with such infectious humor that I couldn't help smiling back. She possessed none of the sullen heaviness that had marked Riyaz, nor his mother's aloof scrutiny. She went back to the stove and began making parathas, which she cooked in twos, pulling them apart into impossibly thin, translucent halves when they were done. These I ate with a generous dollop of butter and several cups of tea, and then she stood up, wiping her hands on the front of her kurta.

"Are you feeling all right? Do you want to go on a walk?" she asked.

I nodded. I felt surprisingly good, given yesterday's grueling climb.

"Then let's go," she said.

First, she showed me around their house. It was very small, consisting of a single short central corridor, which branched off into the kitchen, the little room in which I'd slept, and another room, of which I got only a quick glimpse before Amina closed the door. I saw a mattress laid out on the floor and surrounded by untidy stacks of clothes, a large colorful sheet tacked to the wall like a tapestry. It was,

I assumed, the room in which she and Riyaz slept. After this, Amina took me outside onto the mud porch and showed me the outhouse, which was a basic, though spotlessly clean, concrete room with a raised toilet and a drain. We descended a mud track that led down to a rough stone structure with an opening instead of a door. It had, I realized, been built into the slope directly below the porch itself, which formed its roof. A red-and-white cow and a tiny black calf were tied to a log outside, their tails swishing.

"He was born last month," Amina said, nodding at the calf. "We also have two mules."

"Where are they?"

"Riyaz has taken them. He uses them for his work."

"His work?"

"Yes. He does transport. Building materials, rice, wheat, oil—people tell him what they want, and he brings it up from the town below, where you spent the night."

"He walks that distance every day?"

She laughed at my surprise. "Sometimes twice a day."

We climbed back up to the porch, and she pointed out the boundary of their land, a massive pine tree that marked the place where their fields ended and the neighbors' began. The pine seemed to be somehow writhing, and I thought my eyes were playing tricks on me, until Amina said, in a grim voice, "Crows. There are too many of them to get rid of. They eat everything. Corn usually, or one of our chicks. They even carry off puppies sometimes."

She then gave me a tour of the village itself. In my urban imagination, I had always pictured villages as tight-knit clusters of homes, limited by size and proximity, but here the houses were flung wide upon the mountainside, like a handful of brightly colored toys tossed by a careless hand, separated by narrow rocky ridges and terraced cornfields. The paths skirted close to the edge of the mountains; stones occasionally slipped from under my feet and bounced down the slope, farther down than I cared to look. The third time I stumbled, Amina turned and looked at me clinically. "Bend forward a little," she instructed me. "That way you won't fall." I did as she said and felt immediately more secure. "And when you walk downhill," she added, "bend back."

She took me to what seemed to be the closest thing they had to a village square, a flat patch of land that housed a tiny shop, made entirely of dark wood and stone, and a small whitewashed mosque, whose corrugated iron roof culminated in a glinting tower. A man in a kurta was painting the tower, his body lashed to the metal with a single rope, bright green streaming from his brush. A narrow wooden bench ran along the outer wall of the shop, and a row of very old men with wrinkled, mottled skin, dressed in dark, bulky jackets, were arranged on it like dolls in the sun, all of them watching the painter, but when Amina and I came up, they transferred their collective gaze to me. Amina greeted them and introduced me. They nodded once in unison, then resumed watching the painter. Amina winked at me and ducked inside the shop. It smelled richly of paraffin and grain; the walls were lined with close-built shelves that seemed to hold everything from towels and belts to hand mirrors and biscuits. Without bothering to get up, a tall shopkeeper in a cream kurta reached for the small bar of soap Amina requested, giving me a curious look as he did so.

We walked back to their house in the bright sunlight, and all the while I tried to adjust to the strangeness of this place, its vastness. I had not, I realized, been prepared for it at all. Bashir Ahmed had spoken to us so many times of mountains, and yet the images evoked in my mind had been imprecise and clichéd, all of them stolen, no doubt, from some book or film: gentle, sloping meadows dotted with tiny yellow flowers and vast herds of cows, peacefully grazing. This place with its steep, rugged drops; its narrow, glittering pathways; its tiny mud houses that clung like limpets to the face of the mountain—I had imagined none of it. From our vantage point, I could see, on far slopes, other glinting roofs which were, I presumed, more houses, more settlements.

We arrived back at the house at the same time as Riyaz's mother, who was coming from the opposite direction, a curved sickle hanging low in one hand and her face obscured by a massive sheaf of grass, which she had perched on her head. Amina and I stood on the porch, watching as she tossed the grass to the cow, who dropped her neck and fell to munching. I realized Amina was looking at me.

"Your home," she asked, "is it very different from this?"

"Very different," I said, unable to begin to describe it.

"Good," she said simply. "Then you can enjoy it even more."

"Thank you," I said. "But, as I said, I won't trouble you for long."

She grinned. "Still trying to run away? Murgi is the perfect name for you."

Riyaz's mother tossed the last of the grass to the cow and came up to the porch. She started taking down clothes that had been pinned to a clothesline stretched between two wooden poles. She did not speak to us, and I felt the same shyness in her presence as I had before.

Amina said, "Let's go in, Murgi. I have to get lunch ready."

We went back to the cool, dark kitchen, where Amina began to cut up spinach-like leaves into a bowl. As I watched her, a boy, about five years old, came into the kitchen, trailing a backpack. He wore a school uniform, a checked blue-and-white shirt tucked into dark blue pants, and, as soon as I saw him, I felt the blow of recognition. His face was Bashir Ahmed's. He had the same green eyes set in the same dark skin, which made them seem even more luminous. The only difference was that whereas Bashir Ahmed's features had been craggy and carved, this boy was daintily beautiful, with thick, curling eyelashes and a sweet, lopsided mouth like Amina's.

"Aaqib, come here," Amina ordered him. To me, she said, "This is my son, Aaqib."

I held out my hand, and he shook it solemnly, a smile lurking in the depths of his lovely face.

"Quick, go change out of your uniform," Amina said, and he scuttled off, still with that secret smile, dragging his backpack behind him.

I couldn't help myself. "He looks just like Bashir Ahmed," I said.

Amina smiled but made no comment. She tossed the spinach into a pan of frying onions, and the hiss and smell engulfed me. I suddenly realized I was ravenous.

A while later, Riyaz's mother came in, as did Aaqib, now dressed in jeans and a dirty white T-shirt that read *Superstar Happy* in pink curlicued letters, and the four of us ate together, the silence broken only by Amina urging me to take second and third helpings of everything. The food was spicy and extraordinarily good. Aaqib ate like a cat, crouched close to his grandmother's body, cleaning his plate fastidiously with small, deft fingers. Riyaz's mother ate very little, betraying no sign of contentment or pleasure, and as soon as she was finished, she stood up and left the kitchen. A moment later, I saw her from the kitchen window, vigorously sweeping the mud porch with a dried-grass broom. Amina smiled. "Ma does not like to sit still," she said.

Amina would not hear of me helping her to clear up, but insisted that I rest for a while. So I returned to the room where I'd spent the night and sat on the mattress looking out of the window at the hazy mountains. I was here. What would my mother have thought of this place? I tried to picture her sitting on the mattress across from me, chin propped on one knee, gazing out at the view. But the image would not hold, and eventually I gave up and fell into a pleasant doze, only dimly aware when the light began to leach from the sky.

What roused me was the evening azan, floating up the slope, sung by an adolescent boy in a croaking but determined voice. I went out onto the porch to find Amina picking up an iron pot from beside the front door. "Are you rested?" she asked.

"I am, thank you."

She lifted the pot. "I'm going to milk the cow. Do you want to come with me?"

I accompanied her down to the barn. The sun had just set, and above us, the sky tore itself apart in bloody strips of orange and burgundy. The cow and calf were no longer outside the barn, but I heard their shifting and shuffling from within. Amina ducked inside, and I followed.

The interior of the barn was dark and damp and smelled of hay, hide, and old, sweet shit. The cow stood tied up along the far wall, rump facing us, and as we entered, she turned her head and rolled her suspicious eye at us. The calf was a small shape beside her, tied up just out of reach. Amina set down the pot and untied the calf, who rushed to its mother and began suckling. She allowed the calf to drink for a while, then pulled it back to its post and tied it up firmly again.

Now Amina picked up the pot and squatted beside the cow, whose red hide seemed nearly black in the dimness. Her fingers quickly found the mottled pink teats, tugged a few times, then curled in an elegant wave, thumb to pinkie. A jet of milk shot into the vessel with a soft, metallic ring. Like this, she quickly established a rhythm, and standing over her, I could see the milk starting to froth inside the pot, ivory yellow and glistening. I found the whole thing hypnotic, and I watched mesmerized until Amina turned and peered up at me.

"Want to try?" she asked.

"Me?"

She laughed. "Why not, Murgi?"

Why not, indeed? I squatted and she showed me how to hold the pot between my knees, how to grip the teats whose texture was rubbery and velvet at the same time. I fumbled with one of them and squeezed. Nothing. The cow rolled her dark eye back at me, unimpressed.

"Try again," Amina said.

After what felt like hours, I managed to elicit a weak, pathetic trickle. Muscles aching and inordinately pleased with myself, I stood and handed the pot back to Amina.

"You did very well for the first time, Murgi," she teased. "From tomorrow, I'll sleep and you work."

We emerged from the humid barn, the cool evening air instantly drying the sweat on my skin. Despite my tiredness and disorientation, I felt a spark of genuine pleasure.

"Thank you," I said to Amina.

"What for?"

"For letting me come here."

She opened her mouth to respond, but before she could, I heard the clink of approaching bells, and her head cocked. "That is Riyaz," she said.

Two brown mules, like the ones I'd seen in the town by the river, but sleeker and fatter, came thumping down along the side of the barn. They came to a halt before Amina and me, the one behind bumping its soft black nose against the other's rump. Empty sacks were tied to their flanks.

A few second later, Riyaz appeared, a long switch in his hand.

"Salaam alaikum," he said gruffly.

"Walaikum," Amina answered. "How was it today?"

"Same as always," he said. "I had to wait two hours for the same driver, as usual."

"But he came? You got paid?" she asked with a touch of worry.

He nodded without looking at her and flung the switch away into a patch of tall grass.

I cleared my throat. "Good evening," I said.

He started, then nodded in my direction. To Amina, he said, "I'm late for namaz."

He herded the two mules inside the barn, the bells around their neck softly clanging. Amina began walking up to the house, gripping the iron pot carefully with both hands. I followed her.

Dinner was as silent an affair as lunch had been. After Riyaz came back from the mosque, we ate in a semicircle around the fireplace, Amina on one end, ladling out rice and dal and the same spinach we'd had for lunch, and Riyaz on the other, eating stonily, his face drawn back into shadow. Again, I noticed, I was served more than anybody else, and again, Amina would not allow me to clear my own plate, but stood and beckoned me to go with her. She opened a tall cupboard built into the wall at the far end of the corridor and pulled out a thick, synthetic, candy-pink blanket. She placed it on the mattress in my room and said, "Do you need anything else, Murgi?"

I looked around. "Where will Khadijah Aunty sleep, Amina?"

"She sleeps in the kitchen, with Aaqib."

Another stab of guilt. "I haven't taken her room, have I?"

"You worry too much." Amina smiled at me. "She prefers to sleep there, by the stove. Her legs hurt in the night sometimes, and she needs to keep them warm. And Aaqib won't sleep anywhere else but with her. Now, tell me, is there anything else I can bring you?"

"No, thank you. You've already done too much."

"Now go to sleep," she ordered. "Don't forget, you've got to wake up early tomorrow." Seeing my perplexity, she burst into laughter. "The cow, Murgi! Remember? Who else is going to milk her if you don't, hm?"

I couldn't help laughing. She was so charming. "All right, all right. I'll go to sleep."

But once she left me, I could not fall asleep right away. I sat at the window, resting my arms on the rough wood of the windowsill. The mountains were now the darkest blue I'd ever seen; the sky above them was a powdery lavender. I thought of Zoya and Abdul Latief in Kishtwar, but they seemed small, impossibly far away. A light breeze came through the window.

I saw a figure walk out of the house, and I stiffened. It was Riyaz. He walked to the edge of the porch, then, as if someone had whispered in his ear, he turned his head sharply in my direction. Without thinking, I ducked below the windowsill, then instantly felt stupid. What was wrong with me? Why was I hiding like a child? If he'd had a poor opinion of me before, then this had surely sealed it. I took a deep breath and prepared to explain myself—I'd dropped something on the floor, I'd been searching for it—but when I sat up again, my eyes sweeping the dark porch, it was empty.

13

For weeks after the terrible scene in Bashir Ahmed's apartment, I found it difficult to look at my mother. I kept recalling his stunned face, the way he had raised his finger and said, "Get out," and shame would fill me like a boiling liquid. What made it worse was that my mother seemed entirely unaware of what she had done. When we got back home, she fell right away to cooking, banging about in the kitchen, telling me about a cauliflower dish she remembered her mother making once when she was a girl, and which she was sure she could reproduce only if she spoke the whole recipe out loud. By the time my father came home, she'd calmed somewhat, though the meal we finally sat down to that evening was inedible. The whole thing could have been comedic, my father's valiant chewing, my mother's hard gaze challenging him to speak even a word of criticism, but I felt no desire to laugh. Before going to bed that night, I swore to myself that when Bashir Ahmed came back, the first thing I would do was apologize to him.

But he did not come back. For weeks afterward, coming home from school, climbing off the rusty, groaning school bus at the end of our road, I would manage to convince myself that he was there, and I would start to run, my backpack jouncing against my spine, my feet pounding the pavement, my heart tapping out a painful staccato in my chest, and I would shove the gate open and race up to the door, hoping to find his familiar sandals splayed on the mat, his bundle in the corner, and Bashir Ahmed himself rising from his end of the sofa, gravely saying, "Beti," while my mother smiled from her place on the other end. But it never happened. I would burst in to find the living room desolate, often cluttered with the remains of some project my mother had begun and abandoned halfway through, a set of curtains or a crocheted tablecloth, mounds of loose cloth and thread everywhere. And, as the weeks turned into months, I began to hope less and less, until, at some point, I stopped expecting him at all.

I was now swimming every day and slowly starting to take part in competitions around the city, where I usually managed to snag a medal or two in the freestyle or breaststroke events. My coach, pleased with my progress, told me he would start training me for national-level competitions. I began going to practice earlier and staying later, so my mother, no longer able to spare the time to accompany me, remained at home, and I went instead with a friend, whose family employed a driver. I grew to love the constant and unvarying demands of swimming, the shock as my body broke the surface of the water, the silky parting of it, the reliability of my legs propelling me forward, the rhythm of stroke, breath, kick. I loved the atmosphere of competition: swimmers shaking out their long arms, sizing each other up; the chlorine-scented air; the breeze fluttering the pool's surface; the crack of the gunshot and the controlled insanity of the race; the muted, faraway cheers of the spectators; the pounding of blood in my ears; and the beautiful, floating exhaustion later on.

And my mother? Was she happy that I had ceased to trail after her, that I no longer watched her every move with the fiery, unblinking concentration of an acolyte? Or did she mourn what must have felt like an abrupt desertion by her most faithful follower, her audience of one? It was impossible to tell. Sometimes it seemed as if she noticed nothing at all, borne along instead by her usual erratic bursts of energy, followed by long periods when she did nothing but sleep on the sofa. At other times, however, I could sense her watching me, a perplexed look on her face, and I was torn between a perverse satisfaction at thwarting her attempts to win me back and a strong desire to give in. The time I remember most particularly was when she found a squirrel's nest in her window, lodged between the glass and the mesh screen. While I was in the bathroom, she brought it into my room and carefully placed it, with four blind, squalling pups inside, on my homework. I froze in horror when I walked in, then cautiously approached, both repulsed and drawn by the tiny cries. As I was peeping in at their naked, red bodies, my mother appeared at the door, arms crossed over her chest, the expression on her face both expectant and exasperated, as if to say, *Satisfied? Is this what you wanted from me?* The look galled me, so instead of exclaiming over the pups, as I might have done, instead of helping her turn the house upside down for an old plastic syringe we could use to feed them, I stepped back and said, "It's dirtying my homework." I went downstairs to fetch a broom, but by the time I came upstairs again, the nest was gone, save for a few bits of straw, and my mother was calmly reading a book on her bed. Guilt bubbled in my gut, but I did not dare ask what she had done with the pups.

My father accompanied me to my first few junior national-level swimming meets. I remember those trips only as sensations now: the squeaky berths of the train; the yellow glow from his side of the room as he riffled through papers before bed; the haze of new faces that slowly crystallized into names, personalities, or an occasional flirtation; the dizzying range of languages spoken by my peers; the constant sense of disorientation and excitement. Then, once I turned thirteen and my father's workload increased at the factory, I was put in the care of other swimmers' parents, unpacking my bag in strange hotel rooms, warming up in the chlorinated air, checking the schedule board, calling my parents every evening. My father spoke to me first, asking me detailed questions about the conditions and the competitors before handing the phone to my mother, who always said, in a tone that suggested she'd been interrupted in the middle of a very important task, "Yes, tell me." And all the little stories I'd stored up to tell her, mildly nasty tidbits I knew she'd enjoy—a referee's comical accent, a misprinted and unintentionally funny signboard—would evaporate on the spot, and I'd say, "Nothing to tell, Amma," and hang up as soon as I could.

It was during the championships in Vizag that the incident with Zain Shafi occurred, bringing about the ignominious end of my brief career as a swimmer. It was the final day of competition, and Zain and I had been running into each other, not wholly by accident, since the beginning of it. The sense of departure hung heavy in the air, the knowledge that we would all be parting ways soon, returning to our respective cities, and it lent to every interaction a frisson of urgency. I was sitting in the stands, watching some boys warm up for their two-hundred-meter butterfly finals, when Zain came up behind me. He was a few years older, a handsome, broad-shouldered swimmer from Delhi. He tapped me on the shoulder. "Come on," he whispered.

I got up and followed him. I knew what was coming and felt no fear. We left the pool area and I followed him through a warren of corridors that smelled of mothballs and mouse droppings, the forbidden domain of the referees and competition judges. It was empty now; everybody was at the pool, watching the finals. Zain glanced over his shoulder, then opened the door to what seemed to be a small storeroom, crammed with boxes of T-shirts and dusty, unused medals. He closed the door, then looked gravely into my face without speaking. When he moved toward me, I had the urge to giggle, but I choked it down. His mouth tasted of spearmint and something oniony, and while I was still getting used to that odd combination of tastes, his hand came out of nowhere and slipped down the elastic waistband of my track pants. My breath caught in my throat. With his other hand, he guided mine into his. I focused all my attention on the warm, smooth hardness my fingers were suddenly wrapped around, trying to ignore the noises Zain had now started to make. I moved my hand resolutely, and after a minute, I forgot about his noises, because my fingers were covered with a warm sticky liquid. I drew my hand out and stared at it.

The handle to the storeroom door suddenly rattled. Zain jumped back and pulled his T-shirt down over his track pants. I held my hand out stiffly, as if for a handshake, not wanting it to touch any other part of myself. Before he and I could so much as make eye contact, the door was shouldered open, and three referees were looking down at us, first with surprise, then with horror.

The news spread with bewildering speed. I faced the adults' reproving stares and the swimmers' giggles with the same flinty expression. The parents of the swimmer I'd been sent with, my chaperones, did not speak a word to me on the train ride back to Bangalore. I sat hunched by the window, alone, dreading the thought of facing whichever of my parents had come to pick me up. But when the train pulled into Cantonment, I saw the last thing I expected so see. My mother and father stood next to each other on the platform. They had come together. Held for an instant in the frame of a train window, it was a view of them I'd almost never had. Exactly the same height, they stood shoulder to shoulder, like warriors of some ancient tribe, holding themselves perfectly erect and looking straight ahead, while people scurried around them. I grabbed my bag and jumped off the train before it had fully stopped.

They saw me right away. I hesitated, suddenly timid. What would their first reaction be? Anger? Disgust? Disappointment? But they settled the question for me by starting to move forward in unison, their shoulders still touching, the crowd on the platform parting to make way for this tall, serious couple. They cut a path right up to me, then, in a single, clean motion, as if they had melded into one body, one parent with a shared mind, they pulled me into a hug, my father's right arm crossing over my mother's left, pulling me close, shielding me from view. In the car, my mother did not sit in front with my father as she usually did, but climbed into the backseat with me. While my father drove us home in the gentlest way imaginable, maneuvering around every single pothole, my mother, her lips pressed together and her eyes shining, put her arms tightly around me and drew me down, inch by inch, into her lap. I tried to resist, but her tenderness was as devastating as her viciousness could be, and I finally gave in and sank down, abandoning the pretense of toughness and self-control I'd been maintaining so rigidly for the past twenty-four hours. Wrapped in my mother's arms, I broke down and sobbed.

14

AMINA WAS AS GOOD as her word. She knocked softly at my door the next morning, and after I'd used the chilly outhouse and splashed water on my face from the outdoor tap, I followed her down to the barn to milk the cow. The sky was overcast, the color of concrete, and I could feel the morning chill even through the sweatshirt I'd pulled over my jeans and T-shirt. Within the barn, however, it was as warm as a sauna. This time, Amina let me milk the red-and-white cow for longer than before, issuing brief instructions from time to time: "Don't be scared, you have to be stronger than that. Yes. Now try the other side. More smoothly. Good, that's good." When I returned the iron pot to her, she nodded approvingly. "If you keep going like this, you can start a milking business in Bangalore," she said and went into gales of laughter.

Afterward we went back up to the house, where Riyaz's mother was making tea and parathas for breakfast. The parathas were hot and dripping with butter, and I asked Amina to tell Riyaz's mother that they were delicious, but I got only a curt nod from the old woman in response. Like her son, she seemed to feel no pressure to communicate with me. Soon Aaqib came in, dressed in his uniform and chewing on a stick to clean his teeth. He ate and drank beside his grandmother, whom he obviously adored, his long lashes blinking at me from over the rim of his cup. Then he ran to join another little boy in a similar uniform, waiting outside. I heard their laughter and chatter in Kashmiri fade as they ran off across the mountain.

"How far away is Aaqib's school?" I asked.

"Oh, about half an hour's walk."

"He goes by himself? Aren't you worried?"

"Worried?" She laughed. "Why should I be worried? Everyone in the village knows him. If he tries any mischief, somebody or other will drag him back home. Besides," she added, "I have enough to do here without wasting time worrying about him."

She was not exaggerating. It did not take me long to see that these were people unfamiliar with idleness. As soon as the kitchen was cleared, Riyaz's mother picked up her sickle from a long nail beside the door and went off to cut grass for the cow. Amina washed clothes at the outdoor tap, hanging them end to end—her kurta, Riyaz's, Khadijah Aunty's long scarf, Aaqib's T-shirts—then swept the porch and fed the chickens. And I, who had never in my life been required to consider the contours of poverty, understood quickly that theirs was not industriousness for its own sake. Their need was obvious—it was in the bare upper half of their walls, the hissing pipe that needed fixing, the meals at which everybody ate less than was strictly adequate. They could not afford idleness. I thought guiltily of the white envelope in my rucksack, bulging with notes I had not earned.

In the late morning, Amina came to me, wiping her hands on the front of her kurta.

"Let's go, Murgi," she said in the brisk tone I had quickly come to expect from her.

"Where?"

She smiled. "I'm taking you to meet somebody."

We walked uphill to where the track split in half. There Amina turned right, and we followed a narrow path cut into the side of the mountain, the spaniel racing ahead of us, a honey-colored blur. Dotted on the steep slopes to our right was a herd of goats, who looked up curiously as we passed. A very old man in a gray kurta was watching over them, leaning so far forward on a long staff I was afraid he would tumble right off the mountain, but when I said something about it, Amina laughed. "Him?" she asked. "He's like one of his goats." I walked in the way Amina had instructed me to, bent at the waist. When she linked her hands behind her back, I did the same.

We passed other houses, some low and simple, like Amina and Riyaz's, others with additional rooms built on top to form a second story. Then the houses gradually ended and we were surrounded by nothing but steep slopes, scrub, rock, and above us, swathes of dark pine trees. Amina hopped down onto a tiny track that split off from the main path, which meandered for a while before it curved sharply, revealing a large, beautiful house built alone on a ridge. I could not help exclaiming out loud. The walls were whitewashed and lustrous in the late morning sunlight. The roof was two sheets of shimmering tin that gently sloped over wooden window shutters, which were painted a dark green. In front of the house were neat wire fences enclosing a vegetable garden, a tidy cement path stretching beside it, leading up to the broad, shaded front porch. "Isn't it lovely?" Amina asked with pride, as though she had built it herself.

"Very lovely," I agreed. "Who lives here?"

"The village sarpanch," she told me. "Mohammad Din. He's the one I want you to meet. He gives Riyaz most of his work."

We walked up the path to the front door, which stood open, and took off our shoes. Amina poked her head in and called out. A few seconds later, a tall, slender man with white hair came to the door, his arms spread open in welcome. He wore a stone-gray kurta with a black wool waistcoat, from whose breast pocket peeped the head of a sleek black fountain pen.

"Look who's here!" he exclaimed in Urdu to Amina. His voice was soft and musical, reminding me briefly of Saleem in Kishtwar. "I thought you had forgotten all about this old man."

"Me?" she replied, laughing. "How could I forget? Salaam alaikum."

"Walaikum," he replied. His eyes, which seemed tired though bright, landed on me. "And this must be the guest who everybody has been talking about."

"This is Shalini," Amina said. "She's from Bangalore."

The man took my hand in both of his. "Come in, both of you."

We followed him just off the entrance into a large sunny room, whose tall windows overlooked nothing but forest and dappled valley. He gestured for us to sit on the floor, which, I noticed, was covered in a real wool carpet, instead of plain cloth. Stacks of official-looking papers were strewn all about the floor, a pair of thick-rimmed spectacles resting on top of one pile. There was a low bookshelf in one corner, filled with volumes of Arabic or Urdu. A wooden stand on the bookshelf held an open leather-bound Quran.

"Forgive this mess," Mohammad Din said. "My wife is not here, you see, and my daughter is at school, so I take my chance and throw my things around everywhere. Now what will you drink?"

We demurred, but he went off anyway, coming back with two glasses of juice, which he placed on the ground in front of us before sitting down.

"Tell me, first of all," he said to Amina, "how is everybody at home?"

"Fine, alhamdulillah" she responded. "Except Ma's legs are paining her a lot these days."

Mohammad Din nodded gravely. "She works too hard, your mother-in-law."

"I keep telling her that," Amina said, "but she just won't listen."

He thought for a moment. "I'll tell you what," he said. "When the doctor comes up on Friday, bring her early. I will make sure he sees her first. Also, before I forget, tell Riyaz I will probably need him and his mules tomorrow. I have some things being delivered early in the morning, and I want them as soon as possible."

Amina nodded quickly, and the white-haired man turned to me. "And now," he said, smiling, "I'm afraid it's your turn to answer this old man's questions. Are you enjoying yourself in our village?"

"Yes, thank you."

"You are from Bangalore, yes?"

I nodded.

"Bangalore," he mused. "I have been to Delhi many times, and to Amritsar, and once even to Hyderabad, but I have never been to Bangalore." I stayed quiet, afraid he would ask me what had brought me here—I did not want to talk about Bashir Ahmed or my mother—but he only said, "And what do you think of our village so far?"

"Oh," I said. "I think it's beautiful."

"But not as developed as Bangalore." He used the English word *developed.*

"Well—"

"We are trying to become developed, you know," he said, cutting me off. "The problem is the government doesn't care about us mountain people, so we have to do everything ourselves. All the money that Jammu and Kashmir gets, half goes to Srinagar, Gulmarg, places like that, and the other half goes to the yatras. So, tell me, what is left for us?"

Next to me, Amina was listening as intently as if to a sermon.

"We don't even have a proper hospital here," he went on, "just a young doctor who comes up once a month. He tries his best, poor chap, but he doesn't have the right equipment, the right medicines. If you are sick, like Khadijah Begum, or like my wife, then it is difficult, because often you have to go to Jammu for treatment. That is where my wife is now, in fact. Her heart is weak, and the air up here isn't good for her. Next year, once Sania, my daughter, finishes school, I will send her off to Jammu as well. She can go to college and be with her mother at the same time."

"And what will she study?" I asked politely.

"She says she wants to study politics," he answered, chuckling, "but I think it's only because she hears me talking about politics all the time. But I am not worried about her. She's a good girl, and will do well whatever she chooses. The only worry I have is that her English is not so good, and for these colleges in Jammu, especially, you must speak good English to be accepted."

I liked the way he spoke, slow and intense, as if he were considering the merit and validity of each word before he allowed it to pass his lips.

"Amina told me that you are the sarpanch for the village," I said.

"I am," he replied. "For this village and also for the Hindu village that is close by. We share a panchayat—three members come from our village and two from theirs."

"There's a Hindu village close by?"

"Of course." He must have seen my expression, because he added, smiling, "You are surprised to hear that Muslims in Kashmir are able to live peacefully with Hindus. In India, that is not what they say about us, yes?"

I was about to deny it, but Mohammad Din seemed more amused than offended, so I took a chance and said, "Well, it's just that I heard this story." Stalin's thin, querulous face flashed briefly before my eyes. "I heard that a few years ago a group of Hindus were killed up here by militants, so I was just surprised, I guess."

Mohammad Din and Amina glanced at each other. I could not read the quality of the glance. Was it shock? Anger? Had I upset them?

"Where did you hear this story?" Mohammad Din asked, his tone carefully neutral.

"Oh, just from someone I met in Kishtwar," I said vaguely, adding, "I'm sure it never even happened. It was probably all nonsense."

He cleared his throat.

"Actually," he said, "it did happen. The village is about two hours away from here."

I glanced for corroboration at Amina, but she was staring down at her lap.

"*Sixteen* men?" I asked.

"Twenty were shot," Mohammad Din said grimly. "Sixteen died." He leaned forward. With an odd vehemence, he said, "They were foreigners, those militants. Not Kashmiris. A Kashmiri would never do something like that to his own people, and when it happened, we were all shocked. We sent food to that village for an entire month. It was a very sad thing."

I nodded a bit numbly. So Stalin had been telling the truth.

"And *that* is why I keep saying we need development," Mohammad Din declared, after a few moments of silence. "Because when you have schools and hospitals and roads, then people like that have no power. Alhamdulillah, it never ever happened again, and those militants are gone now, chased out by the army. It has been quiet in our area for the past year. Next month we are going to have local elections, and if I am elected sarpanch again, I will make sure that things remain this way."

The three of us were silent for a while. Amina, I noticed, seemed subdued.

"Tell me, how long are you planning to stay with us?" Mohammad Din asked. "I would love for you to meet my daughter, Sania, before you go. Perhaps tomorrow, if you are free, you could come and have lunch with us?"

"That sounds lovely," I said, glancing at Amina. "But I don't want to trouble—"

"Oh, don't start talking about troubling us again!" she exclaimed. "Stop trying to run away, Murgi." She explained the joke to Mohammad Din, who laughed.

"Tomorrow, then," he said. "I will come to fetch you after prayers. And you," he said, looking sternly at Amina, "promise you won't forget me again. Come visit more often."

We rose to go, Mohammad Din again shaking my hand in both of his. As we were leaving, an extremely old man was slipping his sandals off on the porch. His hands were covered in faint blue liver spots, and he seemed wobbly on his feet. Mohammad Din took him gently by the elbow. "Salaam alaikum, uncle. Come in and sit down. Let's see what we can do for you today."

As we were walking away from the house, I caught Amina looking at me strangely.

"Yes?" I asked.

"Nothing," she said quickly. Then she added, "So? What did you think of him? Isn't he wonderful? He helps everybody."

"He seems very nice," I said truthfully.

"*Nice?*" She shook her head. "You'll see, Murgi. He's the nicest person in the world."

When we returned to the house, I sat with Riyaz's mother in the kitchen as she cooked lunch. Aaqib came home, immediately changing out of his school uniform—I suspected he owned only the one set—and giving me a shy, mischief-filled glance before running off to climb the tree in the yard. I followed to find him hanging upside down by his knees from one of the low branches.

"Oh, hello," I said, pretending surprise. "I'm sorry, I was looking for Aaqib. I didn't mean to disturb you, Mr. Monkey."

He giggled, blood blooming in his cheeks, T-shirt slipping over his belly.

"I think your tree is beautiful, Mr. Monkey," I said. "Could I live in it with you?"

"No!" he shouted, still giggling.

"No?" I pouted. "You won't let me live in this tree with you? Why? Is it because I'm not a monkey? Are only monkeys allowed to live in this tree?"

He nodded, then abruptly swung himself up, dropped down to the ground, and scampered off into the house, leaving behind the echo of his laughter. I shook my head, smiling.

After we'd eaten lunch, Amina took me down to their field, and showed me how to look for the thin vines that snaked around the cornstalks, how to search with my fingers and eyes to find the ripest kidney bean pods and drop them into a little bag.

Riyaz returned with dusk and the evening azan, sung tonight by a man with a breathy, feminine voice, and after he'd finished praying at the mosque, we sat down to dinner in the darkening kitchen. The fire leapt and threw its erratic light, Amina served us one by one, and I realized that I had gone nearly all day without thinking of my mother or of Bashir Ahmed. The thought both buoyed me and caused me a strange pain. Perhaps, I thought, this was all I had needed, in the end, to see the place from which Bashir Ahmed had come, which my mother and I had been hearing about for so long, and which she would never see. I walked out onto the porch after dinner, watching as lights from other villages flickered on across the mountains.

The spaniel, who'd followed me out, leaned against my shins, worrying her fur with her sharp front teeth, and I was conscious of an unexpected contentment. But then she shook herself and trotted away to someone behind me, and I turned to see Riyaz coming out of the house. My heart quickened. I did not want another unpleasant interaction. He was walking in my direction, but I was standing beyond the light cast from the kitchen window, and I knew he could not yet see me.

I cleared my throat. "Hello, Riyaz."

He stopped, peering into the shadows. Then he said, his tone unreadable, "Hello."

I saw him turn his head, as if debating whether to go back inside, but in the end, he came to stand with me at the edge of the porch, pointedly leaving between us a gap of several feet. We watched the dark rise of the mountains, freckled with their hundreds of glittering homes.

"It's so beautiful," I said finally, just to break the silence.

He snorted. "If that's what you want to call it."

"You don't think so?"

"Maybe I do or maybe I don't." He was still looking ahead. "It's not really important, is it?"

"What do you mean?" I asked.

He didn't answer, instead squatting down to scratch the ears of the spaniel, who promptly rolled onto her back, offering him her soft belly. He said, "Have you always lived in Bangalore?"

"Yes," I said. "All my life."

"And do you think it's beautiful?"

"Bangalore?" I paused. "I've never really thought about it. It's just where I was born."

"This place is like that for me. My whole life, I have been looking at these mountains. There is nothing in this place, not one person or one tree, that I haven't seen ten thousand times."

I was silent, surprised to hear him address me at such length. He seemed to have had the same thought, because he abruptly stopped talking.

"I think I know what you mean," I said slowly. "But I don't think it's quite the same thing. Bangalore is a city, just like any other city in the world. But this place . . . I've never seen anything like this in my life. It's like heaven," I added lamely.

To my surprise, Riyaz rose quickly to his feet, and the spaniel did the same. He looked at me for the first time since we'd begun talking, and what I saw in his eyes was anger. "Maybe it is," he said coldly, "but one thing I can tell you for certain. If I had been born in a place like Bangalore, or any other city in the world, believe me, I'd have done the smart thing and stayed there."

I blinked. "What are you saying?"

He stared directly into my eyes, and I felt a prickling on the back of my neck. "You should not have come here," he said. "Heaven is not at all what you think."

With that, he strode down along the side of the barn, vanishing a minute later into the cornfield, the spaniel trotting in energetic pursuit. I stood in silence, not knowing what to make of his display of anger, or of the strange sensation I'd had when he looked at me.

I did not have time to consider it further, for a second later, the spaniel began barking furiously, and there was a deafening explosion of wings. I jumped. An enormous cloud of crows rose from the pine tree at the far end of the field, the one that Amina had told me marked the end of their property, and spread out in the air, cawing and screeching. I waited, expecting them to scatter off into the night, but they did not. They simply circled the pine for several minutes, before returning one by one and settling down in the branches, still and watchful.

15

IT SOUNDS STRANGE TO say, but the time after the incident with Zain Shafi, the time of my disgrace, became the calmest time we had known as a family. I fully expected a stern lecture from my father, or an inscrutable remark from my mother, but neither of them breathed so much as a word about what had happened. On the contrary, I began to sense that it had rattled them, brought about a new tentative affection that centered on me, although the way they behaved with each other was altered too. My father seemed to be making an effort to come home earlier from the factory, and I watched in disbelief as my mother sauntered out from the kitchen one evening, kissed his cheek, and asked lightly, "Had a good day?" Night after night, she cooked all of my favorite dishes, while my father sat with me at the dining table, teaching me to play chess, and later, she would come to stand over my shoulder and suggest outrageously illegal moves with a perfectly straight face, while he groaned. "Yes, yes, do what your mother says. And while you're doing it, why don't you just hit me over the head with the board and rearrange all the pieces while I'm unconscious? At least *that* would be less painful." And they would look at each other in their new shy way, which both disturbed and thrilled me. It was as if they were trying to lure me toward them, and I alternated between a willing complicity and a dark reluctance I could not fully explain.

Then my father came home one evening, bursting with some great secret and making hints all through dinner. When my mother curtly ordered him to spill it, he laughed and announced that, instead of our annual five-day resort trip, we would be going to Italy for an entire month; he had just bought the tickets. I was thrilled beyond measure, and even my mother could not keep her pleasure from showing in her face. We applied for visas and landed in Florence a few weeks later, tired from the flight and made quiet by the grandeur of the streets, the weight of so much ancient stone.

We were dutiful tourists. We walked in the Florentine sun until our feet cramped; we waited for hours in line at the Uffizi, we leafed through our guidebook until the pages smudged with the sweat from our fingers. I was put in charge of the camera and took pictures of everything. From the outside, we must have seemed like any other tourist family, but I never lost sight of the fact that we were nothing short of a miracle. Here, amongst these giant buildings with their carved dates of long ago, surrounded by hordes of alien pink faces, wrapped in the buzz of so many languages we could not speak, my parents were renewed. My mother mercilessly teased my dark-skinned father when he was mistaken for a local and harangued in Italian by a woman cradling a tiny pig in her arms. And when, in a crowded piazza, my mother was accosted by an elderly man, quite obviously drunk, who insisted upon dancing with her, my father laughed so hard people backed away from him. My mother allowed herself to be led in a weaving circle, then gravely patted the old drunk on the cheek. He beamed, bowed gallantly to her, and lost himself in the crowd.

After Florence, we went to Rome, where we pressed with the gawping crowds through the Colosseum. Then to the Vatican, into the room where everyone stood with an upturned face and a middle-aged American woman clutching a rosary began to sob at the sight of the ceiling. From there, we went to Venice, and when the first murmur of an evening breeze touched the canals, we took a gondola ride. My father got shakily to his feet and announced he would serenade us, but he couldn't finish because my mother was giggling too hard. That set him off, too, and then they couldn't stop, both of them with their hands pressed over their mouths, tears running down their faces, while the grumpy gondolier muttered to himself and savaged the water with his single oar. And because I didn't like his muttering, I laughed along with my parents, the three of us cackling like the insane as we slid through the green water under an arched bridge.

Looking back now, it was as though we were under some kind of spell. I remember nothing of what we saw, the old churches, the dark paintings of tortured saints, the famous squares roiling with pigeons. I remember the ease with which my mother touched my father's arm as she pointed out the bell on a tower. I remember my panic when I lost sight of them in a crowd, my relief when I spotted them again, dark heads bent over a map, almost touching. I remember my mother at a pizzeria, nodding when my father asked, a little shyly, if she would like to try the house wine. My mother—*my mother!*—drank a glass of wine. A small glass, barely enough to make an infant unsteady, but she drank it. Afterward, she claimed that the moon seemed tilted to her, and laughed.

I see us now during that trip as three people who had drawn a shining circle in the ground around themselves and were trying as hard as they could not to leave it. It was as though we had all made the same tacit decision, to pretend to be the kind of family we had never been, and, as the days went by, I started to fear that it would end. Cracks began to appear. My father's tiredness revealed itself in his face, his impatience to return to his work and factory. My mother became more prone to spells of abstraction, standing lost before a painting or some unremarkable shop, until we were far ahead and would have to trudge back to find her. The churches started to blend together, the food to seem repetitive and heavy, the crowds to press in. Still the circle held and we kept our new lightness, until the last couple of days, when we went to the Alps and met the Soods.

The Soods were the first Indians we'd spoken to in Italy. Like us, they were tourists, going up to the same Alpine town as we were. Our glass-sided cabin swayed back and forth on its metal cable, suspended far above the pines and mirrored mountain lakes, and Mrs. Sood was complaining loudly about nausea to anyone who'd listen. Glad, perhaps, of fresh company, my father moved over to their corner and struck up a conversation. It turned out they were from Bombay, where Mr. Sood was involved in real estate. They were a middle-aged couple, both built like gone-to-seed wrestlers, his pressed polo shirt the same shade of peacock blue as the glossy Dior handbag she carried.

With the rushed, slightly false bonhomie of fellow nationals in a foreign land, my father and Mr. Sood fell into an amiable discussion. Mr. Sood told my father about the real estate market in Bombay. My father laughed the way he did with strangers he wished to impress, a lighter, more urbane laugh than usual. Mrs. Sood, meanwhile, tried to flag my mother's attention with a breathless, banal comment about the view, but without success; my mother seemed to have become suddenly mesmerized by a loose thread on the sleeve of her kurta.

"We like Italy," Mr. Sood was saying to my father. "A charming country. Full of variety."

"Oh, absolutely," my father said.

"Not that the same can't be said of India, too," Mr. Sood added.

"Of course, of course," my father agreed pleasantly. "You can't beat India for variety."

"Indeed. I mean, where else in the world can one find all that in a single country?" Mr. Sood said, with the air of a tycoon listing his various holdings. "Cities, palaces, temples, lakes, deserts, jungles, mountains, you name it. I know it isn't fashionable to say these sorts of things, especially abroad, but let me tell you, I'm damned proud to be Indian."

"Oh, yes, me too," my father cried.

After that, they fell silent, each content with the other's accord. The cabin rose. The lakes shimmered and winked below. Then Mr. Sood said, with a chuckle, "Lovely, but doesn't really compare to the Himalayas, does it?"

"Not in the least," chuckled back my father, who had never set foot in the Himalayas.

"And, of course, there's Kashmir," Mr. Sood added.

"Kashmir!" cried his wife. She had given up trying to get my mother's attention. "I *adore* Kashmir! I always tell Prakash that I'd like us to live there forever."

My mother raised her eyes, and I felt the beginning of an old, familiar dread.

"We used to go almost every year for a while," Mr. Sood said. "Shame it's been ruined now. It's not even Kashmiris doing the fighting anymore, you know. It's these foreigners—what do you call them?—jihadis. Fellows from Afghanistan, Pakistan, and god knows where."

"It won't last," my father said confidently. "The army's out in full force. They'll get those chaps sooner or later."

"I hope so," Mr. Sood said darkly. "All I can say is, I hope so."

I'd been listening to their talk, but now I turned away from them to look at my mother. She had ceased to play with her sleeve and was sitting bolt upright. Her hands were clenched in her lap and her eyes were open and fixed, but the rest of her face was a mask. My first thought was that she looked like someone staring at an oncoming vehicle, with enough time to register the impact that was milliseconds away, but too late to do anything to avoid it. Unfortunately, Mrs. Sood happened to glance over at my mother at the same moment and promptly flew to her side.

"What's wrong, darling?" she cried. "Do you have nausea too? Such a *curse*, isn't it?"

Wordlessly, my mother nodded.

"Don't worry," commanded Mrs. Sood, rising to the occasion. She probed around in her bag and drew out a round yellow tablet and a small plastic bottle of water. "Here, take this."

My mother obediently put the tablet into her mouth and swallowed it. Mrs. Sood placed a plump, motherly arm around her shoulders. "Take my advice and don't leave the resort for a couple of hours, darling," she warned. "Thin air."

There was just enough magic left to carry us through those final days on the pine-carpeted mountain, but on the flight back to Bangalore, with the cabin food that was too hot to taste, and the wintry blast that came through the vents, I could feel the last of it draining out of us. The morning after we landed, my father slipped off early to work, and my mother didn't get out of bed until noon.

I hung around the house uneasily until she woke. She took one look at the open suitcases we'd lugged all around Italy, clothes and shoes and souvenirs flowing haphazardly from them, and went to bathe. Then she went downstairs to light the lamp in her kitchen shrine. She remained standing before the metal faces of her idols for a long time, her own face just as blank.

When the doorbell rang, she did not move immediately. I could feel her weariness, black and dense, like we were connected to the same ball and chain and it was dragging us down, down to lingering sleep. Then she left her gods and went to open the door.

Bashir Ahmed stood on the mat outside. He had lost a frightening amount of weight. His beard was overgrown, and his eyes were red. He had no yellow bundle with him, but a small brown suitcase hung from his hand. We had not seen him in four years.

"Aadaab," he said.

She said nothing, but stepped aside and let him in.

16

My mother led Bashir to the living room. He stood gazing around, as though surprised to find it the same—the dark maroon curtains, the clock on top of the television. His green kurta was dirty, and sagged a little at the shoulders. His hair was greasy and unattractively long. He sank down onto the sofa without being asked. My mother did not sit, but remained on her feet.

"I've been coming every day," he burst out. "You weren't here."

"I'm sorry," she said.

And then I knew without a doubt that the last of the shining circle that had protected us in Italy was gone, that we were as vulnerable as we had been before. Bashir Ahmed had done what he had always done, arrived without warning and plucked her away. Rage suddenly surged up in me. I forgot the affection I had once felt for him, for his stories, for the easy and thrilling way he had with my mother. I forgot my guilt over the terrible things she had said to him in that musty apartment, forgot all those weeks that I had waited so desperately for him to return. I thought only of my mother in Italy, laughing, the stem of a wineglass between her fingers; of my parents' dark heads bent together over a creased map; of my father singing loudly and off-key as a gondola glided smoothly up a canal, and I felt a pure, vast, consuming hatred. I *hated* Bashir Ahmed. I hated his unwashed clothes, his hollow face, and most of all, I hated the way he sat there and talked to her as though he had every right to arrive on our doorstep after four years and find her waiting.

"We went on a family trip," I said loudly. Bashir Ahmed started and blinked, as if he had not noticed I was there until that moment.

"Beti," he said, but he could not replicate his old gravity, his old decorum.

"We went on a family trip," I repeated. "We went to Italy. In case you don't know where that is," I added cruelly, "it's in Europe."

"Very nice," he said, without conviction.

"I'll make tea," my mother offered, too hastily. Bashir Ahmed looked away from me and nodded. She nodded, too, clearly relieved to have something to do, and went off to the kitchen. I wanted badly to follow her, but I stayed where I was.

"Where are the clothes?" I asked.

He glanced up slowly. "What was that, beti?"

"The clothes. Where are they?"

"Here, beti." He gestured to the brown suitcase at his feet.

"Not *your* clothes," I said, my heart pounding. "The clothes to *sell*. Where are they?"

Understanding dawned on his face. He let his hand fall. "I didn't bring them."

"Then why did you come back?" I cried. "If you didn't have any clothes to sell, why did you come back here?"

I left him sitting there and ran into the kitchen, where my mother was standing before the stove. I opened my mouth to speak, but something about her posture, the rigid set of her shoulders stopped me. I stood behind her, unable to make a sound. And when she didn't move, even after minutes had elapsed and the water started to hiss in the pot, I tiptoed away.

By the time she returned to the living room, Bashir Ahmed had washed his face and regained a bit of his old composure. My mother handed him his tea and, after a pause, sat down in her usual spot. The space between them—mine—was empty, and I knew they were waiting. *No!* I wanted to scream. *I won't do it!* But some inexplicable force compelled me to sit, and as soon as I did, time dissolved and it was the three of us again: my mother, Bashir Ahmed, and me.

Despite everything, I could feel the excitement building in my stomach, the same excitement that always preceded his stories. Bashir Ahmed raised his eyes to the ceiling, then brought them down to my mother, seeking permission. She leaned back and nodded once. Then he began.

"I did what you said," Bashir Ahmed told my mother. "I went back. Not right away. After the last time"—here his forehead creased—"after that last time I saw you, I stayed in Bangalore for another week. One day I went to the house of one of my customers, an old Hindu lady who had bought from me for years." He smiled slightly. "She would always give me biscuits, this old lady. Her son lived in London, and he sent her a box every month. She would tell me, 'He sends so many, eat, eat, you are like my son too.'" The smile faded. "But this time, her daughter opened the door. I never even knew she had a daughter. She looked at my cap and my beard, and she wouldn't let me inside. I could even see the old lady, sitting on a chair. But the daughter said, 'There's no need for you to come back. My mother won't buy from you anymore.'"

He paused, collecting himself, then went on.

"That was the night I decided to go home. It took me three days to get there. There was an army curfew in my village—nobody was allowed outside after four o' clock. Soldiers were everywhere. I've never seen so many soldiers in my life. They said they were searching for militants, but to us it seemed like they were only searching for trouble."

It was a story like no other he'd told us, and he did not tell it with the elegant narrative tricks that had been his trademark. He spoke in bursts, urgent strings of words followed by long pauses. But it did not matter. Already I could see the changes being wrought in my mother. Her shoulders had relaxed, and her face had lost its frown lines, making her seem years younger.

"I found a job as a laborer," Bashir Ahmed went on. "I hated it, but there was nothing else available. Half the time the people who were hiring me did not pay. Even if they did, the money was barely enough for rice, assuming there was rice to be bought at all. Plus it was getting close to winter, and my wife fell sick. I did not know what to do. So I—" He stopped.

We waited, but he did not start again. He simply sat there. Then my mother, who had been leaning back all this while, said in a quiet voice, "Bashir."

He looked at her without recognition.

"Go on," she said.

Something flared in him, some last fragment of defiance, and I thought he might refuse her. But it went out of him, and he seemed to slump over.

He began to tell us about the militants.

"I did not want to get involved," he said quietly. "In the beginning. Most of us didn't, at least the older ones. The younger boys, they got excited much more quickly, especially the ones who were picked up and beaten by the army. Some of them joined militant groups, many of them were arrested or killed. My own son, alhamdulillah, was too young for all of that. But it was hard to ignore, if you know what I mean. Every night, you could hear gunfire from the forest, and you would lie awake, hoping that it did not come closer."

He took a breath. He seemed calmer now, as if in submitting to my mother's command he had found rhythm, a measure of peace. "After prayers one evening, a friend of mine pulled me aside. He knew that my wife wasn't well, and he asked if I wanted to earn some extra money. All I would have to do would be to help a few militants. They would pay me," he said. "Not a lot, but . . ."

He fell silent, looking straight into my mother eyes. "It's not what you might have done," he said quietly and with dignity, "but I *did* something."

They gazed at each other for a long time. Then she nodded once and lowered her chin. It was as close as she would ever come to an apology.

"It wasn't much, in the end," Bashir Ahmed continued, "what they wanted from me. There were men hiding in the mountains, men who were from other countries, and they needed a place to stay for a short time. I said okay. And soon they started coming—"

"Who were they?" I burst out, suddenly remembering what Mr. Sood told my father. I regretted my enthusiasm instantly, but Bashir Ahmed was too absorbed in his story to notice.

"They never told me their names," he said. "All I knew was that they were foreigners. My wife knew they were there, but she pretended not to see anything. After a day, they went away. I didn't know what they did once they left, or what they had done before they got there. I didn't ask. All I knew is they were fighting for us, for Kashmiris, and that was enough for me. Maybe if I had known earlier . . ."

He fell silent again, and this time my mother said nothing to make him continue.

"Anyway, I had already agreed to help them by then, so there was nothing I could do now," Bashir Ahmed went on. "Every few weeks, a man would come to our house in the middle of the night and the next morning he would be gone. Most of them were all right, I mean they were polite, they didn't give me any trouble, but I was afraid all the time—that the army would find out and arrest me, that my family would suffer because of what I had agreed to do, even if I had agreed to do it to help my family in the first place. Still it went on for a long time and nothing bad happened. Then a few months ago, there was a knock, and I knew it was another one of them. I'd never seen a man so tall. His eyes, I swear, they were red. I don't know why, maybe from smoke. I gave him dinner, and he didn't speak a word the whole time, didn't say thank you or anything. There was something about him that was not . . ." Bashir Ahmed shuddered. "Anyway, that night I heard a sound and woke up. And there he was, standing next to our bed, watching me and my wife. I couldn't even tell if he was awake or asleep, and I didn't want to scare him, but I thought we were as good as dead. But then he turned and went back to his room."

There was perfect silence in our living room.

"That was all I could stand," Bashir Ahmed said quietly. "I went to my friend and told him to find someone else to help." He looked down at his hands, which had been lying very still in his lap. "But the next month, another militant came. I tried to send him away, but he got angry and took out his gun. If my wife had not come in at that moment, I don't know what he would have done to me. She asked him to come in, she gave him dinner, and he went off the next day. As soon as I could, I found my friend and asked him why the militants were still coming. "He said, 'I've tried talking to them, but they won't listen. There is nothing else I can do.' We had a big fight, and in the end he told me, 'If you did not want to get involved, then you should not have taken the money.'"

Bashir Ahmed nodded bitterly. "My friend said the same thing to me that you did. He said, 'Bashir, you are a coward. It's not as if you're fighting. You're just giving these men a place to sleep. You're giving them a meal, as you would to any Muslim. They are the ones doing the fighting, and they're doing it for you, for your son, for Kashmir.' Yes, and that is what I told myself, too. But it was not as simple as that. These men, these militants"—and here Bashir Ahmed's tone grew hard—"they were supposed to be fighting for us, for Kashmiris, but they were becoming bad, arrogant. Some of them started working for politicians, demanding money in exchange for protection, troubling women . . . Not all of them were like this, of course, but enough. The army was getting worse, too, coming around almost every week, beating people up. I thought I would go mad if I didn't do something."

His voice dropped. "I knew that as long as I remained in the village," he said, "nothing would change. So I left. When the militants see that I am no longer there, they will find another place."

He looked at my mother, who did not speak. Who merely looked back at him.

"They will be fine," he cried, and for a second I thought he still meant the militants. "My wife understands, and she will take care of my son. They will be fine. The militants will stop coming soon, the army will leave us alone, and then I can go back home."

My mother did not respond to this outburst. "When did you get here?" she asked.

"Five days ago. I didn't know where else to go." Then, as if he could stand no more, he closed his eyes.

And my mother? She did not call him a coward. She did not make a wry remark or stand up and walk away. Instead, she did something she had never done before. She reached out and took his hand. His eyes flew open in panic and immediately flickered to me, but she didn't seem to notice, and he gave up, letting his hand rest in hers, letting his chin fall toward his chest. Her face was flushed but serene, and his was uneasy. We sat like that for several minutes before she spoke.

"Your flat," she remarked. "The one you had last time—you're not staying there again?"

He shook his head, and I remembered the dim, greasy light, the battered mattresses.

She nodded, letting his hand fall. "So then it's all right," she said.

He looked up. "What is all right?"

Picking up his teacup from the table, where it had left a thin brown crescent, she stood.

As if it were the most obvious thing in the world, she said, "For you to stay here."

17

The next afternoon, as he said he would do, Mohammad Din came to fetch me for a visit. Amina, saying she had work to finish, didn't come along. As we approached his house, a girl of about seventeen emerged from the front door. Her pale, round face was moonlike, her eyes were a light hazel. She wore a pink kurta with a matching headscarf thrown loosely over her brown hair.

"This is Sania, my daughter," Mohammad Din said in Urdu.

In soft, labored English, Sania said, "It is nice meeting you first time, ma'am."

"She has been practicing," Mohammad Din told me proudly. "Ever since she heard you were coming to visit, it's all she has done."

I smiled, touched. "It's nice to meet you, too, Sania."

We went into the same sunny room, which today had been cleared of Mohammad Din's papers and was immaculate. Mohammad Din and I settled down on the carpet beside the window, while Sania went to the kitchen and came back with a feast: a mountain of deep-fried chicken legs, rice, egg curry, curd, and a stack of parathas. She unrolled a long plastic mat in front of me and her father, and insisted on washing my hands with a mug of warm water poured into a bowl.

"Please, you must eat all of it, ma'am," she said. She had lapsed into Urdu. "Don't be shy."

"There's so much food!" I exclaimed. "If I eat all this, I won't be able to walk back."

"Good," Mohammad Din said, leaning forward and beginning to eat. "That means you can stay here and have dinner with us, too."

Sania laughed. She had a loud, frank laugh, and I liked her immediately. She watched me with fascinated eyes as I bit into a chicken leg, as though she expected me to conduct the business of eating differently from other human beings.

"Your father told me you want to study politics," I said to her.

She nodded eagerly. "Yes, ma'am."

"What do you want to do afterward?"

"I want to run for elections, ma'am, like my father."

"And you?" Mohammad Din asked me. "What work do you do in Bangalore?"

I explained to them about the agency, choosing to omit the fact that I no longer had a job there. Sania listened, rapt, and even Mohammad Din seemed interested, asking several questions. Their attention was gratifying and had the effect of making me talk longer than I would have done otherwise, and I found myself talking about Ritu's various pet projects with an enthusiasm that I'd never felt, even while I'd been working on them. When I finished, Mohammad Din nodded gravely. "It sounds very worthy, what you are doing." He wagged a finger at Sania, a gleam of humor in his eyes. "See? If you want to be like her, you have to study much harder than you do now. And stop watching all those Bollywood movies you like so much. They're not helping you in any way."

Sania dropped her eyes in embarrassment, and I cleared my throat, feeling like a fraud. Mohammad Din shook his head indulgently at her then turned back to me. "Please," he said indicating the food, "eat some more."

While I ate and drank, Mohammad Din told me more about the village, returning to what was clearly his favorite theme: development.

With Sania hanging on his every word, he told me of the vision he had for a road connecting the village to the highway, for a modern hospital and a college, for a reliable electricity grid that would cover the entire mountain region. I found his earnestness poignant, and I remembered again what Amina had said. *He helps everybody.*

When I could not eat a bite more, even for politeness' sake, Sania washed my hands and passed me a towel to wipe them with. She began to clear the dishes and carried them away. While she was in the kitchen, Mohammad Din said in a low voice, "Thank you for talking to Sania. I can see how happy she is to have met you."

"It was my pleasure," I said. "I'm glad I was able to meet her before I left."

"Have you decided when that will be?"

"I'm not sure," I said. "Amina and her family have been very kind, but I don't wish to trouble them. I think whenever Riyaz goes down the mountain next, I'll go with him."

"He's going tomorrow," said Mohammad Din. "I'm expecting some goods, and I've asked him to bring them up for me."

"Then I'll be leaving tomorrow." I tried to speak lightly, but as I said it, I realized with a pang that this meant the end of my journey. I had tried my best to stave it off by coming here, but it had nonetheless arrived. Soon I would have to face the people from whom I'd fled so ungracefully, Hari and Stella and, above all, my bewildered and hurt father, who would be waiting for me to explain myself. My throat all of a sudden was dry and painful.

"In that case," Mohammad Din said, "we shall hope to see you back here again soon."

"Uncle," I said in a rush, "could I ask you a question?"

He nodded, pressing his fingertips together in his lap in a posture of attention.

I took a deep breath. "Did you know Bashir Ahmed?"

That seemed to surprise him. After a pause, he said, "Yes. I knew him."

"He was a friend of yours?"

"You could say that, yes."

"Could you tell me what happened? How he died, I mean?"

His eyebrows rose. "Amina hasn't said anything to you?"

I shook my head.

Mohammad Din looked out of the window at the expanse of the valley. Then he turned back to me. "I'm sorry," he said at last. "It is not something I like to talk about."

"Oh. But I just—"

"I'm sorry," he said again, sounding firm, though regretful. "It is a very sad memory for me, for all of us in the village. Besides, I believe the dead should be undisturbed once they are with Allah, no matter who they are. There is no point discussing things endlessly."

Right then, Sania came back into the room and Mohammad Din's expression cleared. He got to his feet; I did the same, trying to fight back my disappointment. Shaking my hand, he said, in his grave, pleasant way, "It is a shame that you are not staying longer. If you were, I would have asked you to help Sania with her English."

"It's very good already," I said, glancing at Sania, who reddened charmingly.

They walked me out onto the porch. "I'm afraid I have some panchayat work to finish. May I send Sania to walk back with you to the house?" Mohammad Din asked.

But I declined, and so they stood together on the porch, waving as I walked away. The afternoon was warm, the corn whispering in the fields, and a desultory breeze hurried a few dried leaves across the path. I stopped on a ridge to watch it all, trying at the same time to make sense of what Mohammad Din had said just before I left, his reluctance to talk about Bashir Ahmed. Had they been such close friends that the mention of Bashir Ahmed's death had caused him pain?

I found my way back, stepping over the broken pipe, but when I arrived at the house, it was empty. I called all their names, but there was no answer, so I went back to my room and sat on the mattress, looking out of the window at the sunset. Gradually a strange lassitude settled in my mind, a combination of sadness, relief, and regret. Soon Amina would return to the house with Khadija Aunty, Aaqib would run to hide in his tree. Soon Riyaz would return from work or the mosque or wherever he was. In a few hours, we would eat dinner around the leaping fire, and tomorrow I would be gone.

Without knowing it, I briefly dropped off to sleep.

A hot breeze blew again, and I woke. Then I heard, quite distinctly, a cough. Rasping and filled with phlegm, it seemed to me to be coming from very close, from inside the house. I listened carefully, and when it did not stop, I got to my feet, my heart quickening. Perhaps one of them had come back and I hadn't realized. Perhaps Riyaz's mother was in the other room and was having a coughing fit. I stuck my head into the corridor, but at the same instant, the coughing stopped. I waited for several minutes but there was only silence, and I began to think I'd imagined it. I was about to return to my mattress when it began again, even more violently.

I quickly checked the kitchen, but it was empty, the fire cold and dead. That left only Amina and Riyaz's room. I walked up the corridor to their closed door and knocked softly. "Hello?" I called. "Khadijah Aunty? Do you need some water?"

There was no answer. I put my ear to the door then took hold of the handle and pushed. The door swung open noiselessly. The lights were off and my eyes adjusted slowly to the dimness. I could make out the shape of a mattress, thick and rectangular, in the middle of the room, and I could tell at once it was unoccupied. The dark, indistinct shapes of crumpled clothes lay all around. An emergency lantern sat silhouetted on the windowsill, its plastic dome reflecting a dull crescent of light. A dark shape on the wall marked the colorful sheet I remembered seeing when Amina showed me around on my first day, the only attempt at decoration anywhere in the house. I stood in their room with the sense of guilt that always came with entering the private spaces of others, and I nearly forgot about the cough until it sounded again, this time coming from an altogether different direction. Could it be some trick of the wind, a scrap of sound torn from its origin and conveyed uphill? I turned my head, trying to gauge whether the sound faded or grew. Then I noticed a thin, cylindrical shape propped in the corner beside the tapestry, and my stomach cramped with fear. It was a gun. A rifle. I didn't realize they owned one. I moved forward warily, keeping my eyes trained on it, as though it might spring up at any moment and attack me.

In my distraction, my foot caught on something soft, a bit of clothing, and I tripped, stumbling forward and at the same time stretching my arms out to save myself. My palms hit the sheet, but instead of the impact of brick I was bracing for, I felt nothing but air. I regained my footing and cautiously pressed against the sheet again with both hands. Once again, there was no resistance. Forgetting about the gun for the moment, I knelt down. Grasping at a corner of the sheet, I pulled it back as though it were a curtain.

And, with a dreamlike amazement, I saw that it *was* a curtain. The sheet was no mere decoration, as I thought, but hid a narrow opening, barely two feet wide, leading off into a dark passageway, whose end I could see only as a lighted rectangle. Stunned, I tried to map the house in my mind, and slowly I understood that the passageway was built *behind* the tall wooden cupboard that stood at the far end of the house, the same cupboard from which Amina had taken the pink blanket she'd given me. Or, more accurately, the cupboard had been made much shallower than I'd imagined, leaving a gap behind it, large enough for a person to squeeze through.

Without thinking, I stepped into the passageway, which smelled strongly of sawdust. My shoulders brushed the walls; splinters caught in my sleeve. Now I could almost see the other side, could feel warm, stale air eddy about my ankles. I ducked my head and stepped out, blinking.

I stood in a room more cheerful than any other in the house. Paper streamers hung from the ceiling—blue, yellow, and pink, twirling slowly, as if in preparation for a child's party. A red kerosene lantern sat in a corner, casting an arc of oily light. A low table held a white skullcap, a clock, and a steel plate with a handful of chewed-up fruit pits. The only other furniture was a bed, covered in a fleecy pink blanket, the twin of the one Amina had given me.

And sitting up in the bed, hands folded in his lap, was an old man wearing a brown, oversized jacket, whose buttons were done up all the way to the throat. An old man with a gaunt face, greasy white hair, and green eyes that, at this moment, were staring at me with an expression that was neither fear nor shock, but something so feral and primitive that, for a second, I did not recognize him. We stared at each other for what felt like entire lifetimes, and I'll never know how, despite the chill that had seized the base of my skull like a vise, I managed to take a step forward and speak the only phrase that came to my mind.

"Aadaab."

Bashir Ahmed opened his mouth. For a long second, no sound emerged.

Then I heard him say, "Get out."

His voice cut deep into me, straight to the place of memory. It was the same voice. The voice from my childhood. The voice of his stories. The voice that said, *Tell her I will come again soon.*

"Get out. Get out. Get out."

On and on his voice went, rising in pitch and excitement until he was screaming at me, that single phrase twisting and swelling to become a vast and violent tide.

I stumbled backward into the dark passageway and fled.

IV

18

"MURGI?" AMINA STOOD AT the doorway, wiping her face with the corner of her long scarf. "You're back already? I thought you'd still be at—" She stopped in mid-sentence, peering at me. "What happened?" she asked sharply. "What's wrong? Why are you sitting in the dark?"

When I did not reply, she took a step inside the room. "Murgi?" she asked.

"I saw him."

She went rigid. "Who?" she asked carefully.

Suddenly the numbness that had filled my head for the last thirty minutes exploded into rage. "What kind of joke is this?" I shouted. "What are you people trying to do to me?"

"Murgi—" she began.

But I didn't let her finish. "Why did you lie to me?" I shouted. "He's not dead! He's not dead! Why did you lie to me?"

"Come to the kitchen," she said, and there was such authority in her voice that I found myself obediently standing, shuffling behind her to the kitchen, where a fire was now crackling. "Sit," she ordered, pointing to the straw mat, and I sank down, hugging my knees to my chest.

She squatted on a piece of sackcloth across from me and adjusted a stick in the fire. A round orange ember leapt out from the flames. I watched it sail in a perfect orange arc, leaving the afterimage of a tiny comet's trail, landing at her feet on the coarse material. I stiffened, seized by a vision of the house engulfed, but Amina calmly reached out and laid her palm over the ember, killing it. I felt foolish, then all of a sudden exhausted. What was I doing in this place, with these strange people and their still stranger secrets? I did not belong here. Riyaz had been right; I should never have come. I needed to go home.

Amina was still gazing into the fire. Finally, she looked at me.

"Murgi," she said, in that same firm tone, "I am sorry that we did not tell you before about Abbaji, but you must believe me when I say there was a good reason."

I could not reply.

"I will try to explain everything to you now," she continued, "but I need you to do something for me." She reached out and placed her hand on my knee, in the same calm way she had placed it over the ember. "Please don't tell anybody you have seen him."

"Not even Mohammad Din?"

"Not even him, and I'll tell you why," she said. She drew in a deep breath. Then she said, "That story you were asking about yesterday? The sixteen Hindus who were shot by the militants? You said someone in Kishtwar told you about it, remember?"

What did this have to do with anything? I nodded.

There was movement at the doorway to the kitchen. Riyaz's mother had entered with an armful of washed and dripping vessels. She set them down in the corner and began to dry them with a rag, cloth squeaking against metal.

I turned back to Amina, whose eyes had not left me.

"It happened five years ago," she said. "Like Mohammad Din Uncle told you yesterday, the militants who did it were not Kashmiris. And they were never caught."

I nodded again, unable to fathom why she was repeating this grisly story. Hadn't she and Mohammad Din assured me those militants were now gone from these mountains?

"The thing was—" Amina hesitated, then continued. "The thing was that some people started saying that the commander of those militants *was* a Kashmiri."

I looked sharply at her.

"It was just a stupid story, Murgi," she said. "Nobody who knew Abbaji, nobody who had any *brains,* actually believed in it."

"Wait." I stopped, staring at her in horror. "Do you mean they were saying that *he* was—that Bashir Ahmed was the one who killed those—"

"No, no," Amina said hastily, making Riyaz's mother glance up from her work. We were speaking, as we always did, in Urdu, which I knew Riyaz's mother could not understand. She looked from her daughter-in-law's face to mine, then went back to wiping.

"Nobody was saying that," Amina went on, in a quieter voice. "But"—and she dropped her gaze to the sackcloth—"some people, even in this village, said that maybe he gave the order."

I felt a churning begin low in my stomach.

"It wasn't true, Murgi," Amina said. There was a pleading note to her voice. "You *know* Abbaji. You know he would never do anything like that."

It was all too bizarre, too fantastical to be believed. *Hindus killed. Never caught. Gave the order.* I could not connect the gaunt old man I'd seen buried under his pink blanket, to the words emerging from Amina's mouth.

"I don't understand," I said finally. "If he didn't do anything, then why is he hiding?"

At that moment, Riyaz's mother got to her feet, and we fell quiet. She surveyed us for a long moment, then left the kitchen. Amina's eyes trailed after her, a bit sadly. "She knows we're talking about him," she murmured. Then she straightened. "Murgi, something happened. To Abbaji."

"What do you mean?"

She was silent for a beat. Then she sighed. "All of this was before I married Riyaz. I've heard this story from him, but neither Ma nor Abbaji has ever spoken about it to me. Not even once. After those Hindus were killed, Ma, Riyaz, and Abbaji were at home, when they heard a knock in the middle of the night. There was a lot of snow that year. Five or six feet maybe. Anyway, Abbaji went to open the door, and there were these soldiers standing outside. They asked him for his name, and when he told them, they caught hold of him and took him away."

Some sticks fell apart in the fire with a hiss, giving off a bright shower of sparks. I started.

"I don't know what happened next, Murgi," Amina said. "Ma and Riyaz don't know, either, because Abbaji has never told them. They stayed in the house waiting. Ma didn't want to leave the house in case he came back, and she didn't want to send Riyaz in case the soldiers were still around. After a long time, many hours, they heard a noise outside. Ma went and opened the door, and Abbaji was standing there holding the door. He seemed fine at first. But as soon as he walked inside, he fell down and couldn't get up. Then Ma saw that he was crying."

She looked up at me, with a pitying sort of resolve, as if she had wanted to spare me this.

"They had broken his legs, Murgi." She tapped each of her knees once. "They left him and went away, thinking he was already dead, maybe, or that he would die soon in the snow. To this day, I don't know how he managed to get back home."

What followed was not silence. I could hear sounds as though from a great distance—the hissing of the fire, the gloomy bark of a dog from somewhere down the mountain, followed a second later by a responding bark from Riyaz's honey-colored spaniel. But each sound, as soon as it formed, seemed to drop into a deep ravine of silence, never quite reaching me.

"It was Ma's idea, Murgi. She didn't want the soldiers to come back and try to kill him again, so she said he'd been arrested, and when he didn't come back, everyone just assumed he had died. It has been like that for five years, and even Aaqib has been taught not to talk about his grandfather. Have you noticed that nobody comes to visit us, Murgi? Except you, of course. The villagers stay away from this house, because of what they think Abbaji did. Mohammad Din is the only one who still talks to us, but even he doesn't know about Abbaji. That's why we couldn't say anything to you." Her voice had returned to its normal volume. "And now you know," she said, sounding slightly relieved.

"Yes," said a dry voice from the entryway. Amina and I turned to find Riyaz standing there, one shoulder leaning lightly against the wooden doorframe. He was dressed in a cream kurta, and his dark hair glinted in the light of the naked bulb that hung in the corridor.

"Now you know," he said, his voice heavy with rage and sarcasm. "Now you know all of our dirty secrets. Congratulations."

I sat on my mattress in the dark, eyes closed, while behind their closed bedroom door, Amina and Riyaz fought. Their voices reached me, the crackle of anger unmistakable.

Riyaz had not come in for dinner. I'd eaten in silence with Amina, Riyaz's mother, and Aaqib, who had taken one look at our faces when he walked in, and pressed closer than ever to his grandmother, his beautiful eyes cast down. Feeling a surge of sympathy for his obvious distress, I tried to distract him with jokes, but he gave me a look that was both reproachful and surprisingly adult, and went on eating. I fell silent, gripped by a sense of guilt. *I have done this to him,* I thought. I had thrown his family into disarray with my invasion and my probing questions, but this thought was quickly followed by resentment. I might have been the one to arrive here, but I was not the one who had lied, who had dissembled. It was not only my fault.

There was a sudden uptick in the volume of their voices, and I glanced up. I saw the shadow of a body momentarily block the light that leaked under my door, and then it was gone. Riyaz, I guessed. Sure enough, a moment later, I saw him walk out onto the porch. This time, I was prepared for him to turn, to look accusingly and angrily in my window, but he did not. He went swiftly down along the side of the barn and soon disappeared from sight.

There was a soft knock at my door. Amina peeked inside.

"Murgi?" she whispered. "Are you asleep?"

"No," I said.

She groped for the switch beside the door, and the room flooded with light. When my eyes adjusted, I saw that her face was suspiciously raw and scrubbed, as though she'd been crying.

"Are you all right, Amina?"

She nodded. "What about you?" she asked. "Are you still angry with me?"

I shook my head. "I'm not angry. I'm sorry for shouting at you before."

"You *do* have a loud voice for a murgi," she said with a weak, crooked grin.

I smiled then glanced down at the floor. "Amina, can I ask you something?"

She nodded.

"Did you tell Bashir Ahmed that I was here? Before today, I mean. When I arrived."

She seemed surprised by the question. "No, Murgi, we didn't tell him. Why do you ask?"

"No reason," I said.

For a second, she looked as though she might press me, but then she said, "Sleep, Murgi. We'll talk more about all of this tomorrow." She turned to go.

"Amina," I said.

"Yes?" she said.

"Can I see him again?"

I saw her shoulders fall.

"Maybe in a few days, Murgi," she said. Her voice was apologetic but firm. "He has not been well. He needs to rest." Without waiting for my response, she added, "Now go to sleep. I'll wake you in the morning. For the cow, remember?" she added with the faintest shadow of a smile.

She flicked off the light and closed the door. But I sat there, unmoving. Bashir Ahmed was on the other side of the wall, behind a mere foot of mud and paint, and the knowledge was like a drum, beating, beating, beating a relentless rhythm in my chest. I forgot that I'd intended to leave. I forgot my exhaustion and bewilderment with this place. I kept returning to the memory of his room, the blanket, the kerosene lamp, the paper streamers, and finally, to his stunned face, to his voice saying, "Get out, get out, get out."

The very same words he had once addressed to my mother, long ago in an apartment filled with mattresses. And then it occurred to me, the source of that howl of animal terror in his eyes when I stumbled, dazed and blinking, into his room.

I'd always known that I resembled my father. I had his shoulders, his carriage, his jawline, his hands, his laugh. But now, all of a sudden, I wondered whether I might not also carry something of mother within me, in my gestures and skin and posture.

Whether, for the space of a heartbeat, he thought I *was* her.

19

I DON'T KNOW EXACTLY how my mother explained Bashir Ahmed's sudden reappearance on our doorstep to my father, but, in retrospect, it was possible that no real explanation was necessary. I recall Bashir Ahmed emerging from the guest bedroom, where my mother had installed him and his brown suitcase, recall my father squeezing his shoulder and saying, "Don't worry, Mr. Ahmed," the self-conscious paternalism in his tone, as if Bashir Ahmed were a teenager in trouble, instead of a man only a few years younger than himself. Because it must have been his own offer he remembered, of course, walking out to the gate with Bashir Ahmed, telling him to come back if he needed any help. Maybe that was all the explanation my mother had needed to give.

The first evening, we all sat down to dinner, my father in his usual place next to me, my mother across from us, and Bashir Ahmed, after a moment's hesitation, took the remaining chair next to her. He had bathed, and was now dressed in a black kurta with a high Nehru collar. I could see just how thin he had become, and moreover, I could see a new look in his eye, which did not allow him to meet anyone's gaze for long. He cleared his throat.

"Janaab," he said in formal Urdu, "I wish to thank you for allowing me to stay."

My father smiled his most magnanimous smile. "Mr. Ahmed," he said, "you must stop this 'janaab' business. We're happy to be able to help."

"It will only be for a short while."

"Stay as long as you need," my father said. "I only hope that your family is safe."

"Yes, janaab. They are fine for now."

"You have a son, don't you?"

"Yes, janaab."

"How nice," my father said. "Has he ever been to Bangalore?"

"No, janaab."

"You must bring him someday. And your wife, of course."

Across from me, my mother served herself some carrots. I stared deep into her face, willing something from her, though I didn't know what. A clue, perhaps, an indication that my fears were unfounded, that his coming had altered nothing, that she was still the woman she had been in Italy.

"So things in your area are not good?" my father asked, taking a sip of rum.

"No, janaab," Bashir Ahmed mumbled, "not so good."

"Hm," my father murmured. "That's sad to hear. But what about the army? Aren't they keeping things under control?"

After a pause, Bashir Ahmed said, "The army is there, janaab."

"Well, that's good, at least." My father nodded. "You haven't been back to Bangalore in a while, have you?"

"Not for four years, janaab."

"A long time," my father said. "We were worried about you." My mother's eyes flashed fire at this outrageous lie, but my father didn't notice. Bashir Ahmed mumbled something then fell to eating with cheerless determination. Staring at his haggard face from across the table, the blunt fingers that stabbed so inelegantly at the rice on his plate, his mechanically moving jaw, I was seized by a revulsion so strong my stomach cramped.

Nobody was paying attention to me. My mother was eating as though this were an evening like any other. My father was still talking—government, army, firm response—his lips wet with rum. Bashir Ahmed simply appeared to be in a daze. And just when I couldn't bear it anymore, when I thought I would stand up and scream, I heard my father pronounce the words, ". . . a party."

Bashir Ahmed looked up, his hand suspended in midair. "Janaab?"

"A party," my father said again, looking pleased with himself. "Nothing big, just a few friends of ours. They'd love to have a talk with a real Kashmiri, especially one as fair-minded and reasonable as yourself. It's a rare opportunity for them. For all of us, to tell the truth. Maybe a couple of weeks from now? You'll stay that long, won't you?"

Bashir Ahmed glanced at my mother.

"What do you say?" My father also turned to my mother, who blinked. We all waited for her to speak. I found myself holding my breath, not knowing quite why. It was a bizarre notion, entirely unfounded, but it seemed as though by speaking, by uttering judgment on this absurd party, she would set our course of action, decide our collective fate. She swallowed another bite of food before answering.

"Why not?" my mother murmured. "Who doesn't love a party?"

For the first few days he stayed with us, Bashir Ahmed spoke very little and did not stray more than a few feet from my mother's side. He said no more about the militants. He told no stories at all. In fact, he behaved more like a solicitous servant than anything else. He stood in a corner of the kitchen while she cooked our meals, leaping forward to wash every dish she dropped into the sink. He collected and neatly folded the clothes that hung on the line. He kept a watchful eye on the stove while my mother's back was turned, switching off the heat the instant before the milk erupted. The rest of the time he spent shut away in his bedroom. The few times I surreptitiously listened at the door, I heard nothing from within, only a prisoner's silence.

He was quiet and clean and unfailingly polite, but I watched him like a hawk, as if at any moment, he might steal something and escape. I knew he sensed my hostility, and though he never gave any indication of it, I knew that it hurt him, but I refused to let myself care. My father, immersed as always in his work, might have been fooled into accepting Bashir Ahmed's return as something innocuous, but I swore I would not make the same mistake.

I watched my mother just as closely, though this gave me far greater pain. In Italy, she had come as close as I'd ever seen her to ordinary human contentment, but no trace of it remained now. She became industrious, frantically so. One morning, she decided that every curtain in the house needed washing, which resulted in Bashir Ahmed spending an entire day on a rickety stepladder, sliding the plastic rings on and off curtain rods. When a puff of dust blew into his face, he sneezed eight times in rapid succession, and my mother giggled in a way that reminded me of something. I puzzled and puzzled over it until I remembered: she'd sounded exactly like one of the mothers who sat and gossiped beside the pool, the ones she'd called stupid cows.

And yet I said nothing. What could I have said, and to whom? At thirteen, I was without the language to articulate the fears that were beginning to consume me with greater ferocity each day. My father's behavior seemed to suggest that Bashir Ahmed's presence was nothing other than welcome, and my mother's mind could not be accessed, and Bashir Ahmed himself seemed torn between gratitude and misery, which was of no help to me whatsoever. So I did the only thing I could do. I waited, trying to stay alert, trying to keep them all in view, these shifting, traitorous pieces—mother, visitor, father—trying to keep track of their masked sentences, their mutable moods, waiting for a clear sign of what my next move should be.

And, all the while, a sense of urgency was building. The summer was almost over. And with the end of summer would come my inevitable return to school.

Then only the two of them would remain. The two of them in the dense hush of noon, the curtains drawn, sitting at either end of the sofa, not speaking, but looking only at each other.

It was as far as I dared to think, let alone speak of to anybody.

I can speak of it now, of course.

And I also know now that it didn't happen.

She never touched him.

20

THE TAIL OF THE red-and-white cow swished slowly as I approached, and her black eye rolled back, but this time with no suspicion, only a gleam of familiarity.

"See, Murgi?" Amina said. "She already knows you."

Her face was tired this morning, as though she had slept very little. I had not slept much either. I'd woken several times, gripped by fear, thinking I heard sounds from Bashir Ahmed's side of the wall. It was as if, now that I had found him, I expected him to suddenly be spirited away.

I squatted and began to work, gripping the pot between my knees. The cow seemed to wait for a moment, then dropped her head and began to nose about in the warm, flattened straw on which she'd spent the night. My mind, which all night had been restless, calmed a little, and soon I was thinking only of the rhythm, the warm pliable teats in my fingers, the stirring ring of the milk in the pot. When I handed the pot back to Amina, I lifted my chin, challenging her to find fault with my work, but she only nodded and smiled.

I pulled off my sweatshirt as we walked up to the house, shivering with pleasure as the morning air touched the crooks of my elbows. The far mountains were sharply outlined against the sky, the closer ones soft and shadowed. Strangely enough, I felt good. Even a few days of walking on these slopes had strengthened my legs, awoken muscles I hadn't used since my swimming days.

"Murgi," Amina said. She spoke with a jaunty haste, keeping her eyes fixed on the pot, in which the bright milk sloshed. "I was thinking, maybe you would like to go back to Mohammad Din Uncle's house again today?"

"Oh," I said. "I'm not sure I —"

"They said you could come back whenever you wanted," she urged. "And didn't you say something about teaching Sania?"

It was clear enough she was trying to distract me. For some reason, she was reluctant to let me see Bashir Ahmed again. I could not say I disagreed with her. All night I had dreamed of his face as I had glimpsed it yesterday, the immensity of the loneliness that had emanated from the gaunt figure in the bed. Perhaps, I thought suddenly, it would not be such a bad idea to visit Mohammad Din and Sania again in their sunny house perched on its ridge.

"All right," I said. "I'll go."

Amina looked pleased that I'd agreed without a protest. We delivered the pot of milk to Riyaz's mother in the kitchen, and then we sat down to breakfast.

Aaqib came in in his uniform, blinking the sleep from his green eyes. He sat next to his grandmother, drawing his limbs tight to his little body, like a soft animal ready for an attack. I felt sorry for him, and I wanted to make a gesture of friendliness.

"Aaqib," I said, "Which class are you in?"

He glanced at his mother, who nodded encouragingly at him. Looking back at me, he held up one soot-smudged finger.

"And do you like your school, Aaqib?"

He shrugged.

"I have an idea," I said. "What would you say if I walked with you to your school today?"

"That's a very good idea!" Amina exclaimed quickly. "You must take her, Aaqib. Show her the school."

He gazed at the ground, and I saw his natural reticence wrestling with his desire to be obedient. Then his face broke into a sweet, shy smile. "Okay," he said finally.

He fetched his backpack and we walked out of the house. Unexpectedly, when we reached the top of the track, he tucked a small, warm hand into mine. Other children raced by in identical blue uniforms, staring and giggling and whispering to each other in Kashmiri, but Aaqib paid them no mind, walking at my side, holding on tight to my hand, and pointing out various items of interest—a tree he liked, the house where a friend of his lived. I felt unaccountably flattered.

"You saw my dadaji yesterday," Aaqib said suddenly.

I looked down at him, not sure how to respond. "Yes," I said finally.

"People want to hurt him," Aaqib informed me seriously. "Government people." He paused as something occurred to him. "Are you from the government?"

"No," I said firmly. "I'm not."

He considered my answer. "Okay," he said, then pointed. "That's my school."

The government school was a small, whitewashed building set in a shallow valley, which echoed at the moment with the screams of children. Aaqib slipped his hand from mine and set off down the hill, his backpack jouncing on his shoulders. I stood and watched as he reached a small knot of children, who surrounded him, glancing curiously up at me. They ran into the school building, and after a moment, I turned and walked back to the house.

* * *

I stepped over the broken pipe, a gesture that had become habit in the space of a few days, but before I turned the corner of the house, I could tell that something was amiss. I heard Amina's voice, but it was stilted, formal, absent its usual warm and teasing mirth. Then I turned onto the porch and found myself facing a sea of uniforms. At least, it seemed like a sea at first, but I quickly realized I was looking at about eight or nine Indian soldiers, all of whom had turned to stare at me. Some of them wore caps, others backpacks. A few had their sleeves rolled up. All of them carried rifles. In their midst stood Amina, her arms crossed in front of her chest, speaking to a handsome, dark-skinned soldier with a luxuriant mustache.

I paused, then, aware that they were all watching me, walked forward until I was beside Amina. I could see the mustached soldier's eyes making rapid calculations, trying and failing to fit me, with my jeans and ponytail, into this setting. I glanced quickly at his name tag: *A. S. Bakshi.*

"This is the visitor you were speaking of?" the soldier asked her in crisp, nasal Hindi.

"Yes," Amina said.

"What is her name?"

"Shalini," I told him.

His gaze seemed casual but I could tell it missed nothing, from my untidy ponytail to the mud stains on my jeans. "You are not Kashmiri," he said.

"No."

"Subedar, sir," one of the other soldiers called. He had a face full of pimples and a red bandanna tied guerrilla-style around his head; in his hand was a small cell phone. "I'm not getting any signal here."

"What do you want me to do about it?" the subedar answered, not taking his eyes off me. "Carry a cell tower for you everywhere we go?" The soldier in the red bandanna flushed and stepped back.

The subedar looked at Amina. "Where is your husband?"

"Working."

"What work does he do?"

"Transport. He has two mules."

"Hm." The subedar glanced at his men, who were milling around. "Sit down, all of you," he called out, and they scattered, spreading themselves across the porch, like boys at a picnic. A few slumped at the base of the pear tree, another dangled his legs over the edge of the porch. The rest sat in a small circle in the dirt and picked their teeth with their fingernails or fiddled with their cell phones.

Riyaz's mother came out of the house bearing a plastic tray with eight cups of tea. She held the tray out to the subedar, who took a cup delicately between his thumb and forefinger. He watched her as she carried the tray around the porch, the young soldiers reaching for their cups with muttered thanks. When the tray was empty, she handed it to Amina and went back in the house, not so much as glancing at the subedar, who, I noticed, seemed mildly intimidated by this rock-jawed old woman. I felt a flare of admiration for her.

"Your mother?" he asked Amina, when Khadijah Aunty had gone inside.

"My mother-in-law."

"And who else lives in the house?"

"My son. He is five years old."

"That's all?"

"That's all."

The subedar turned to me. "And what about you?"

Panic dripped like acid through my chest, burning at the lining of my stomach. I was surprised at the control in my own voice when I said, "I'm from Bangalore."

"And what are you doing here?"

"Staying with my friends."

"Your friends? You mean these villagers?" he asked, as if Amina were not there.

"Yes."

"I see. And how many of your friends live in the house?"

"Five."

"Five?" he echoed.

"Yes."

He leaned forward slightly. "She said she lives with her husband, her mother-in-law, and her son." He counted them off on his fingers. "That is four people. Why did you say five?"

"I'm the fifth," I said.

His expression didn't change. I desperately wanted to look at Amina but forced myself to keep my eyes on him. He seemed to be pondering, sipping his tea. Then he said, "All right."

He signaled, and his soldiers began to unfold themselves. They came up to Amina one by one and clinked their empty cups down on the tray. She stood straight, her eyes staring unseeingly over their heads. When they were done, the subedar stepped forward and set his down.

"One last question," he said to Amina. "Have you seen anyone around here that you don't recognize? Strangers? Outsiders? Other than her, of course." He nodded at me.

Amina shook her head.

"You're sure about that?"

"Yes," she said.

"All right," he said, and crooked his finger at his men. "Thank you for the tea." The eight of them fell into a ragged line and began walking. Amina disappeared indoors as soon as their backs were turned, but I stood and watched them head up the track until they turned left and were lost to sight.

Amina was by the outdoor tap, on her haunches, scrubbing hard at each cup. Silently, I joined her, and together we washed them all, setting them back on the tray to dry. Finally, she looked up. "Thank you, Murgi," she said softly, touching her dripping fingers to my wrist.

"How often do they come?" I asked.

"Once every few months. Different soldiers every time, but asking the same questions. I was mostly surprised because there was a group here a week ago, just a few days before you arrived. Usually they don't come back so soon." She looked worried.

"What would they do to Bashir Ahmed?" I asked after a pause. "If they found him?"

She shrugged. "I don't know. Maybe they wouldn't do anything. Or maybe they would. We have no way of knowing." Her face cleared. "But, they're gone, so forget them. Tell me, Murgi," she said, a little too brightly, "have you thought about what you're going to teach Sania?" The way she spoke made it clear she wanted the subject closed.

"No," I admitted. "I haven't thought about it at all."

"She's a bright girl," Amina declared. "She'll learn anything you teach her."

Sunlight filled the room with the tall windows as I walked in. Sania had her schoolbooks ready and waiting for me, and while she went into the kitchen to make tea, I paged through them. They were all standard government-issue textbooks—poorly printed and abounding in errors. I was not quite sure what I was meant to do here, what Sania or anybody could be expected to learn from me. I wanted to say as much to her, tell her there had been a mistake, I was no teacher, but when she came back in and sat across from me, she looked so sweetly expectant I could not bring myself to say more than, "Shall we try some reading first?"

I picked the first textbook that came to hand—history—and opened it at random. Sania tucked her chin so it was almost touching her chest, and with grim determination began mangling the long, abstract English words: doctrine, annexation, treaty. I let her get through three sentences before stopping her. She looked up, blinking.

"Good," I said uncertainly, "that's good. So you understood all of that?"

She blushed and shook her head.

"You didn't understand any of it?"

She shook her head. "Our school was closed for a long time, ma'am, and the teachers we have now aren't good," she said shyly. "They just give us the answers during exams, so we can pass and get good marks."

"Oh." I took a deep breath. "Well, let's forget about reading for today, okay? Let's just talk, you and me. But in English. Why don't you tell me, I don't know, some things you like?"

"Ma'am?"

"Like this." In slow English, I said, "I. Like. Bollywood. Movies."

"I like Bollywood movies," she repeated.

"Good. What else?"

"I like family."

"I like *my* family," I corrected. "That's very good. What else?"

"I like *my* village." Her nostrils flared with the effort of concentration. "I like *my* friends. I like *my* house."

"Very good," I said. "Now tell me what you *don't* like."

She dutifully listed the things she didn't like: winter, milk, hospitals, and eggs. I made her construct dozens of simple first-person sentences then made her write them down, looking over her shoulder to correct her spelling. She was smart, as Amina had said, soon anticipating what I was going to ask, catching her own mistakes after a while. I felt myself slipping into the kind of rhythmic absorption that came over me when I was milking the red-and-white cow. When I finally glanced out the window again, I was shocked to see that the sky had gone the softest gray.

Sania was beaming. "Thank you, ma'am. You are a very good teacher."

"I hope it was helpful, Sania."

"It was, ma'am. You will come again tomorrow?" she asked eagerly.

I was about to answer, when Mohammad Din walked in with another man. He was compact and stocky, like men in these parts, but his fingers were unusually thin and long. Sania muttered a quick, "Salaam alaikum," then disappeared to fetch tea. Mohammad Din smiled at me. "I see you've decided to stay longer," he murmured. "I'm happy for that."

"A little longer," I said. For a moment I wanted to blurt out to him everything I'd discovered since last night: Bashir Ahmed, the hidden room, the soldiers. But I remembered my promise to Amina and said nothing.

Mohammad Din invited the other man to sit. They began speaking in Kashmiri, the other man doing most of the talking, with Mohammad Din putting in an occasional, "Hm" and asking now and then what sounded like a question.

Sania brought their tea, then sat beside me, listening intently. Finally, the man fell silent and Mohammad Din spoke a few sentences, of which the only word I understood was *tomorrow*. The man seemed satisfied and stood up to go.

"Khuda hafiz," he said, nodding to us.

"Khuda hafiz," Sania murmured. But once he was gone, she turned to Mohammad Din, her eyes shining. "Is he telling the truth, Papa?" she asked excitedly. "Who can those people be? They don't sound like militants."

"Calm down," he told her. Seeing my confusion, he said, "That was one of our villagers. He came to tell me he saw two men, strangers, hiding near his house last night. He thinks they were robbers, because they were wearing black. But they didn't steal anything, so I'm not sure what he wants us to do about it." Seeing my expression, he added firmly, "It's nothing to be worried about. This same man once went around telling everyone in the village that he'd seen an elephant near his house. It's best not to listen to everything he says."

I smiled then thought of the questions the soldier had asked Amina, and I told Mohammad Din about their visit. His brow creased. "That could be a coincidence," he said. "It's the army's job to ask those kinds of questions. I'm sure it will turn out to be nothing."

"But what if it *isn't* nothing?" Sania demanded excitedly. "What will you *do* about it?"

"How should I know, child?" Mohammad Din's voice was still pleasant, but I heard the edge of annoyance. "First, we will discuss it at the panchayat meeting tomorrow."

Sania looked crestfallen. Mohammad Din shook his head indulgently at her then turned to me. "Thank you for helping my daughter," he said, "even though she asks too many questions."

"It was my pleasure," I said. "And," I added, "if she wants, I'll come again tomorrow." At that, Sania's face lit up with a smile so wide I thought it would split right open.

That evening after dinner, I went out to stand at the edge of the porch, as I always did, to look out at the valley. Dinner had been, on the whole, less unpleasant than yesterday's. Amina and Riyaz were stiff with each other, but civil, and Aaqib surprised everyone by leaving his grandmother's side and flopping down next to me, his knee touching mine throughout the meal.

The valley was shifting to night, lights dotting the slopes. This time, when I heard footsteps come out of the house, I knew who it was. I was prepared for him to avoid me, as usual, but then I heard his footsteps stop, heard his breathing, the whisper of cloth.

"Ten years ago," Riyaz said, "all of this used to be dark."

He stepped up beside me, looking not at me, but straight out over the valley.

"There was no electricity in those years," he continued. "And in the winter, no electric heater, obviously. The temperature would go down to minus ten, minus fifteen sometimes."

"What did you do?" I asked.

"We used to light a fire in the kitchen, lock the door, and stay there until summer."

I glanced sidelong at his profile. I could not tell whether he meant the last bit to be funny.

"Sounds cold," I said finally.

He laughed. The sound sent a queer jolt through me, and I immediately wanted to make him laugh again. "It was," he agreed. After a while, he added, rather gruffly, "I heard about what happened today with the soldiers. Thank you for doing what you did."

"I didn't do anything," I said.

He made a mock bow. "In that case," he said, "thank you for doing nothing."

"You're welcome," I said. "Nothing is what I do best."

He laughed again.

What surprised me was how natural it felt to stand there with him, the silence between us as easy as breathing, as though we had known each other for years. I was keenly aware of the regular rise and fall of his chest just a few feet away from me, the shifting of the muscles in his legs, and I felt a strange excitement mounting in my chest.

Then Riyaz said, "You know, my father used to tell me about you."

I glanced at him, but he was still gazing out at the valley.

"He used to say that there was a girl in Bangalore, about my age, living in a big house with a garden. He used to tell me that one day he would take me with him to meet you." Riyaz shrugged. "Well, he never did, as you know."

I was silent for a while, watching the pine tree that marked their property's end. Fewer crows than usual were roosting in it tonight.

"Your father used to tell me about you, too," I said. "He once gave me something you'd made. An animal. You'd made it from wood. All this while I thought it was lost, but I recently found it again." I was about to say more, but I noticed that his face had gone rigid. "What's wrong?" I asked.

Without a word, he dug into the pocket of his kurta and held something out on his upturned palm. At first I could not make out what it was, but just then a cloud shifted, and I saw it was a piece of wood. Barely three inches long and shapeless, the bark had been stripped away in places by a knife, leaving patches as pale as skin. I reached out and took it from his hand.

"You still do this," I said. For some reason, my throat was painfully tight. I was aware of his face near mine, his steady breathing, and I felt the heat of his breath flush my skin.

"You come to stand out here every evening, don't you?" he asked softly.

"Yes."

"Will you be out here again tomorrow?"

"Yes."

"Good," he said. And that ended the conversation, but we stayed there without moving. Behind us the house glowed and faded, but the line of firelight stopped a few feet short of where we stood. If Amina had looked out of the kitchen window right then, she'd have seen two shadows, nearly indistinguishable from the darkness, a foot of empty space between them.

21

BASHIR AHMED LIVED IN our house for nineteen days in the summer of 1995 and with the passing of each of those days, he became increasingly withdrawn. By the end of the first week, he'd stopped slinking after my mother like a whipped creature. He still obeyed when she called him to help with some task around the house, though it was no longer with the broken submissiveness he had displayed in the beginning. Once the task was complete, however, he shut himself into his room again, emerging only when it was time for dinner. Slowly, he came to seem to me less like a prisoner and more like a king, albeit a king in exile, old and ravaged and tragic, sinking slowly into his madness and his remote world of memories. My mother's first response to this was an attempt to wrest him back toward her and the world of the living. She did this by increasing the number and urgency of her demands. It was as if she believed she could bind him to her by sheer force of will and a never-ending list of household tasks. In a single week, the floors of our house were washed and rewashed, wooden railings were shined, brass pots polished, carpets smacked with broom handles, cupboards emptied and relined with newspapers, mothballs placed in drawers, but none of it helped. Bashir Ahmed drifted further and further from her, and my mother became desperate.

There was, of course, the obvious irony. My mother, who had always herself been a drifter, tugged along by the mysterious and unknowable currents of her mind, and whom I'd spent so much of my life chasing, was now unashamedly pursuing Bashir Ahmed, battling for his attention, and it felt like nothing less than an outrage to me. And yet it was not so simple as outrage, either, for in those weeks that he lived with us, weeks in which she always seemed to be calling his name, I began to feel for my mother something else I'd never previously imagined possible. Pity.

I pitied her for the way she listened, head cocked, for the sound of his bedroom door opening and closing. I pitied her for the way she found reasons to tiptoe past his room a dozen times a day. I pitied her for the excuses she made for him, for the way he often kept us waiting at the dinner table. *I think he must be asleep. He looked tired. Or maybe he's praying.* And because I hated the idea that my flashing, unconquerable mother could ever be the recipient of anyone's pity, let alone mine, I reacted in a way that any child would. I transformed my pity into anger, my helplessness into spite, and laid all of it squarely upon the shoulders of poor Bashir Ahmed.

One evening after dinner, I followed him back to his room. I did it very quietly, so that it wasn't until he placed his hand on the doorknob and pushed it open that he realized I was right behind him. Hurriedly, he yanked it shut, but not before I caught sight of his bed, rumpled and piled with clothes, and smelled the lonely, cold stench of cigarettes. I had never seen him smoke.

"Beti," he said, attempting a watery smile that quickly dissolved. "Do you need something?"

"I'm *not* your beti," I hissed.

He reared back, as if he'd been slapped. I felt a raw, sick pleasure at having hurt him, followed instantly by the desire to hurt him more. Was this the kind of joy my mother felt, I wondered, when she was cruel to my father, to me, to people like the plump floor manager at my father's factory? Was this what made her tilt her chin back and gaze down at you with contempt and say those unfeeling things? This terrible, ungovernable anger, which threatened to sizzle a hole through her veins unless she turned around and poured it into somebody else?

"Why can't you just go home and leave us *alone*?" I hissed.

I waited, a little afraid of what I'd said, bracing for his anger. But Bashir Ahmed transferred his gaze over my shoulder. He said nothing for a long time; then he sighed and looked back at me.

"Beti," he said quietly, "I am going."

Now it was my turn to feel as though I'd been slapped. "What? When?"

"Sunday. The day after the party."

"What party?" I'd completely forgotten my father's impulsive, enthusiastic plan.

"The party," he said. "The one with your parents' friends."

I was silent for a while. How could my mother have not said anything to me about Bashir Ahmed's departure? How could she have kept such a thing from me?

"What did my mother say when you told her?" I asked finally.

But Bashir Ahmed wouldn't answer. There was a strange look on his face, and he seemed reluctant to meet my eye. A little louder, I repeated, "What did she say?"

Suddenly something snapped in him. "Why don't you ask her yourself?" he cried.

I took an involuntary step backward.

Swallowing hard, he said, "I'm sorry, beti, I'm sorry. I didn't mean to shout at you. I'm just tired, that's all. I'm going to sleep now, okay? Goodnight. I'm sorry."

He opened the door a crack, just enough to let his body slip through, not enough to afford me a view of his room. Then, very softly, he closed the door in my face.

* * *

The next morning, the morning before the party, I watched my mother in front of her gods. With a pair of kitchen scissors, she snipped a long garland of marigolds and tucked the shorter, snipped strands around the necks of her idols. She placed individual flowers at their molded brass feet and then stood with her eyes closed. She knew I was there, of course, but she did not look at me. When she finally opened her eyes, five minutes later, the first thing she said, in a wry, impatient tone, was, "Trying to read my mind, little beast?"

This was so close to the truth that I shivered. But I recovered myself enough to say, "I need to tell you something, Amma." I dropped my voice to what I imagined to be a level suitable for urgency. "Bashir Ahmed is leaving. After the party."

She nodded.

"You knew? How did you know?"

She brushed a stray yellow petal from the sleeve of her kurta onto the floor. "Because it was my idea, little beast."

I was flabbergasted. "Your idea? You told him to leave?"

"Yes. I did."

I looked up into her face. I'd always been so certain I knew what she was thinking. Like my father's work and my mother's shrine, it was a central tenet of my faith, that she and I were linked, in body as in brain. That I could feel what she felt, and yes, even read her mind. But now I looked at her and could read nothing. All this while, she had tried so hard to hold Bashir Ahmed here, inventing tasks to keep him busy, and now she'd suddenly changed her mind and told him to leave? It made no sense. There was something else, something she wasn't telling me.

"Will he come back?" I asked.

She thought about it. "No," she said at last. "I don't think there'd be any reason for him to."

What did *that* mean? "You should have told me, Amma," I said, a bit uncertainly.

"Why?"

"Why what?"

She fixed me with a calm look. "Why should I have told you?"

"Because—" I fell silent. What was I supposed to say? *Because I have always been loyal? Because I have sat in the same room, day after day, with you and Bashir Ahmed, and I have said nothing to anyone? Because if I'm not your secret-keeper, your little beast, then what am I?*

She sighed. "You can't know everything, Shalini," she said, and this time it was as if she were the one who'd read my mind.

"But I—"

My mother drew herself up to her full height. "Must I confess every thought that goes through my head to you? Are those the rules? According to whom, hm? You? And who are you supposed to be, may I ask—my best friend? In that case, I have something to tell you, since you're so interested in what I'm thinking. You are *not* my best friend. You are a *child*. A very clever, compassionate child, to be sure, but a child nonetheless."

I gaped at her. I wasn't unfamiliar with this tone of hers, icy, high-handed, but full of fury. She'd used it many times with my father during their arguments. She'd used it with Bashir Ahmed four years before when she told him to leave. She had never used it with me.

"I have a life," my mother informed me. "And that life, whatever you or anyone else might think of it, is something I intend to protect. Against everybody. Even you." Perhaps it was something in my face or perhaps she suddenly became aware of her tone, but she relaxed. "You're going to be fine, Shalini. You're smarter than most adults I've ever met. You're certainly smarter than me. You'll be fine, no matter what happens."

I shook my head.

"You *will*," she insisted, making it sound like a command, an injunction. "Remember that time I took you to a shop and you wouldn't stop crying? Maybe you don't, you were just a baby."

"No," I lied, "I remember it perfectly."

"We were waiting for Appa to come, right? Well, I got so frustrated with your crying that I left the shop and stood outside. I could still hear you sniffling; then suddenly I couldn't hear you anymore. I came back and peeked inside the shop, and there you were, happy as anything, playing with a packet of biscuits and laughing. And the people in the shop, all these strangers, were watching you and smiling. And that's when I thought, *She'll be fine*."

She touched her hand to my cheek, then turned and left the kitchen, leaving me standing there with the bedecked gods in their alcove.

I stared at their smug brass faces. Then, on some chaotic impulse, I reached out and, one by one, I ripped the fat marigolds from their brass chests, shredding each flower, smashing them in my fists before letting them fall to the ground.

When I was finished, the floor was covered in tiny yellow petals and green stalks, the air was filled with the vegetal smell of night and soil, and my hands were sticky and hot. My mind felt hollow, empty but for a single thought. It was a thudding, shrieking certainty, and it echoed so loudly within the confines of my head, I could not believe that I was the only one hearing it.

She meant to leave with him.

22

THE DAY AFTER THE soldiers passed through, the house seemed especially quiet, as in the aftermath of a storm. As Amina and I walked down to the barn, a thin fog clung to our hands and faces, and I was grateful when it was dispelled by the warmth that steamed from the hay and from the broad, damp flanks of the cow. While I was crouched next to her, Riyaz ducked under the opening of the barn. He was evidently late, for he began untying the mules in a hurry, glancing neither at me nor at Amina, who had started to chew on her lip. Just as he was about to leave, she began, "Try to be careful. With those soldiers around the place—"

"I know," he said irritably, cutting her off. "Don't you think I already know?"

"Okay, okay," Amina said, her tone soothing. Perhaps to change the subject, she drew his attention to me. "See how much she's learned in a few days?" she said, and pride was evident in her voice. "She'll be an expert in a few more days."

I could feel his eyes on the back of my neck, which grew immediately hot. I waited for him to speak, but all he said was, "Hm," and despite myself, I was disappointed. I heard him leave, the mules clanging mournfully after him. When he was gone, Amina sighed and squatted next to me.

"Murgi," she said with a wry shake of her head, "don't get married."

I smiled slightly, not taking my eyes off my hands.

"Sometimes I think," she said, "that the only way to make him even see that I'm there is to put my nose in the air and bray like one of his mules. Otherwise? Forget it." Then she sighed again and tapped me on the shoulder. "All right, that's enough for today. I'll finish up here."

I handed the pot to her and stood, stretching my legs, while she worked deftly. I felt an elusive uneasiness that lasted all through breakfast. Afterward, instead of going to fetch a broom, as she usually did, or starting to wash a load of clothes, Amina spoke a few words in Kashmiri to Riyaz's mother, who was sweeping the morning's ashes into the smoldering fireplace, and turned to me. "Put on your shoes," she said.

"Why?"

"Uff, not your questions again," she said. "Just do it, Murgi."

By now, I knew better than to argue with her. I laced up my sneakers and soon we were walking away from the house. At first I thought we were going back to Mohammad Din's, but halfway there, Amina chose a different path, a switchbacking trail that swung uphill and seemed to lose itself high in the pines. I tried again to ask where we were going, but Amina turned around and put a stern finger to her lips, so I shut up and gave myself over to the pleasure of the walk.

The path veered back and forth, glittering with dust and stones, and at some point, I realized I could no longer hear the crunch of our footsteps; the stones had given way to pine needles, the air was tinged with the medicinal sharpness of pine sap, and we were passing under the long, thick shadows of the trees themselves. They grew at impossible angles from the slope, their trunks bursting horizontally from the ground before changing direction and curving straight up, rising a hundred feet or more above us. Whatever sunlight reached us was soft, velvet; and in some places, partially covered by beds of dry, brown needles, were enormous, moss-spattered rocks. I could hear nothing apart from the wind and the soft rustle of our progress.

Then, without warning, the trees ended, like curtains being drawn away, and we scrambled up a steep stretch of path that dipped and terminated in a wide, rocky bowl, around which the boulders formed a sort of natural amphitheater. In the very middle of it, a thin white waterfall speared down. Amina and I slithered down to the base, and I could not contain a cry of surprise.

Under a jutting lip of rock was a pool. The water fell into it from an opening in the rock above, churned to a filigreed white froth that spread and calmed over the moss-green rocks, a perfect and private cascade in the sun. Amina was grinning at my obvious delight.

"Isn't it beautiful?" she asked. "It comes from high, high up the mountain."

I shook my head in disbelief.

"Go," she said.

"Where?"

She motioned toward the falling water.

"You're joking! I'm wearing jeans!"

"Go, Murgi! The sun will dry you off in ten minutes." She pushed me, laughing, and I felt the spray from the waterfall graze my face, cold enough to make me gasp.

"Wait, wait, let me at least take my shoes off!" I peeled off my socks and tucked them into the toes of my sneakers. I looked at her. "What about you? I'm not doing it if you don't."

"After you finish," she said, giving me another playful push.

"Fine." I stared at the waterfall then took two steps forward. It was like being picked up and flung into a wall. The water drove into me with incredible force. I gasped at the cold, at the same instant feeling my blood, startled awake, surging hot through my body. When I stepped out, I was laughing uncontrollably. "Now you!" I cried.

Calmly, Amina removed her headscarf and placed it next to my shoes, then walked forward. For an instant, I couldn't see her as she went behind the veil of water; then she was there, smiling as it poured down her face. When she stepped out, the kohl had run from her eyes, and she was laughing too.

She led me to a wide, flat rock in the sun, and we sat there squeezing the water from our soaked clothes. Amina lay back and closed her eyes, and I followed suit, feeling a lovely, tingling warmth spread slowly across my skin.

Amina let out a long sigh. "I haven't come here since Aaqib was born. I'd forgotten how nice this feels. Lying in one place, doing nothing." She raised her arms over her head and stretched like a cat, toes and fingers curling slowly.

The sun burned hot and orange against my closed eyelids, its warmth broken only when a cloud passed above us. I could hear the whirring and clicking of insects.

"Can I tell you something, Murgi?" Amina said. Her voice seemed to come from far away. I opened my eyes to find her on her side, head propped on her elbow, watching me. "I'm very happy that you came here to the village."

I opened my mouth to reply, but she put up a hand.

"I wasn't sure in the beginning how it would be," she went on, "but it has been so nice, having you stay with us. For me, especially, to have someone to talk to. So thank you."

An echo rang in the back of my head. Zoya saying, *For me, it is nice.* Zoya, to whom I had given no more than a passing thought since my arrival here. Guilt made my tone more curt than I intended when I said, "There's no reason to thank me, Amina. I've done nothing."

"But you have," she insisted. "You don't understand what I'm saying. Listen, Murgi, I have no reason to complain. Allah has given me a lot in my life, but sometimes it is so quiet in the house I think I might go mad. Aaqib is just a small boy, and you know Ma doesn't like to talk more than she has to. And Riyaz." She shrugged. "Well, you've seen what he can be like, no?"

She was smiling, but I could sense the loneliness that lay behind her smile, and I could hear, too, the entreaty in her voice, for a woman's understanding, a woman's sympathy. And to my lasting shame, I denied her both. I recalled, with an admixture of guilt and pleasure, how I'd stood with Riyaz at the edge of the porch just the previous night, gazing out at the darkening valley, the thrilling, wordless accord that had existed between us, which contained both comfort and its opposite, and which I'd felt with nobody else in my life, and I could not bring myself to agree.

I didn't know whether or not my silence disappointed Amina, but she said nothing further. Instead, we continued to lie on the rock, our clothes drying slowly.

Finally, Amina rolled onto her other side and sat up, reaching at the same time for her headscarf. "We should go back, Murgi," she said. "Ma will be waiting."

I nodded and pulled myself upright, feeling the blood rushing from my head. A thin bank of clouds had come from nowhere and covered the sun, and I shivered.

"Amina?" I said. She was shaking out her headscarf, pine needles falling to the rock below our feet, and she looked up. "Why don't you want me to see Bashir Ahmed?" I asked.

She stood gazing down at the colorful ends of her scarf drooping from her hands. "It's not that I don't want you to see him, Murgi," she said finally. "It's just that after what happened, Abbaji hasn't been the same. Small things upset him. Like if I bring his dinner five minutes late, or if he cannot find his jai namaz. He falls sick, and it takes a long time for him to recover. So if you tried to talk to him, I don't know what might happen."

Perhaps she sensed I was about to object, because she added, in a firmer voice, "I'm sorry, Murgi. I have to think of Abbaji's health first. In a few days, if he's feeling better, I'll ask him. But not before then." She glanced at me. "And, anyway, what's the hurry? Stay a few more days. We can go for walks, or come back here to the waterfall, whatever you like."

She trailed off, chewing a corner of her lip. It was a habit with her, I'd noticed, whenever she was expecting resistance or argument. But I did not argue. She sounded so pleading, and what harm would a few more days do?

"Then at least let me pay you," I said. "For letting me stay with you, I mean. You've been so kind and I don't want to—"

But this time, she wouldn't even let me finish. "Murgi," she said in a colder, loftier tone than she'd used with me so far. "Didn't I just tell you how I was happy that you are here? Didn't I just say that I liked talking to you? You're my friend, and I don't take money from friends, understand?" Her tone was light, but there was a trembling edge to it that warned me to drop the subject, and I did.

"I understand," I mumbled. "Thank you, Amina. I'm sorry."

"It's okay," she said, still in that lofty tone. "Now we should get ready to go back home."

Amina wrapped her scarf over her head, tossing each corner over the opposite shoulder. I pulled my socks on and quickly laced up my shoes. When I stood, I noticed that she was looking at me.

"Murgi," she said, "can I ask you something?"

I nodded.

"What happened to your mother? How did she die?"

A moment passed in which I wanted to reveal everything to her, this woman whom I had known barely four days, but who had showed me such impossible kindness, and I still don't understand why I was unable to speak the truth. Perhaps there is no explanation other than that I had been weaned too long on secrecy, taught by my mother from earliest childhood the strange and unquantifiable power of keeping one's counsel. But that is probably too generous an assessment. I suspect the truth was that, like so many who cloak themselves in mistrust and call it independence, I was merely a coward.

"It was an accident," I said softly, hoping it would be enough.

It was; all at once her brow relaxed. Putting her arm around my shoulders, she squeezed. "Come on, Murgi," she said gently. "Let's go back home."

That evening, I sat in my room beside the window, with the lights off. Earlier in the evening I'd had a lesson with Sania, during which I was thrilled to see that she'd retained everything I'd taught her the day before. Mohammad Din had come in toward the end for a cup of tea, giving us an amusing account of the panchayat meeting. The stocky man with the complaint about the robbers had apparently gotten his story so garbled that by the end he was claiming a horde of fifty men had been hiding behind a single tree. It felt good to laugh with the two of them, and as I walked back, looking down the cornfields, golden in the evening sun, my mood was hopeful. It stayed with me through dinner, during which Aaqib insisted on serving me, which Amina, with an amused smile, allowed him to do. With his lips pursed in concentration, he carried my plate to me, collapsing in high-pitched laughter when I accepted with a stately bow.

I did not go out to stand on the porch after dinner, instead returning straight to my room. Now I sat by the window in the semidarkness. Soon enough, as I knew he would, Riyaz appeared on the porch. He walked to the edge, just beyond the line of light, to where we'd stood the night before. I saw his head swivel, looking left and right for me. Then, slowly, with every appearance of casualness, he turned so that he was facing my window.

Part of me longed to stand up and join him, to resurrect the thrilling ease of yesterday, but I thought again of Amina, her sweet declaration of friendship, and I did not move. I knew that he could see my shape in the window, even if he could not see my features. I felt his eyes, expectant, waiting, boring into mine.

A second went by, then ten. Then a long, excruciating minute.

Riyaz shifted. His right hand dropped into the pocket of his kurta, and he turned back to stare out at the dark valley. I saw anger and humiliation in the stiff set of his shoulders, and my heart sank. He walked down along the side of the barn and was quickly lost to my sight.

23

THE PEOPLE MY PARENTS invited to dinner were not their friends. The men were not men my father met for golf or beer or a game of cards, nor were the women those whom my mother would dream of inviting over for a cup of tea. At best, my parents saw them twice or thrice a year, whenever they took it into their heads to host one of these dinners, and their relationship with them rarely, if ever, cracked the shell of lighthearted banter. I never considered it, but looking back now, I realize that my parents, despite their drastically different personalities, were both essentially guarded and solitary people, who found it difficult to form true friendships, which would have required risk and revelation beyond what they were prepared to provide.

When I woke up on the morning of the party, my mother was already on the move. I found her on her hands and knees, swabbing under the sofa. After that she proceeded to carry in from the garden heavy stone planters, each containing a tall, luxuriant ficus, and arrange them around the house. All the while, the smell of frying onions and spices haunted the kitchen. On any other day, she might have enlisted my help, handing me a lapful of peas to shell or a dusting rag but today she worked alone, and it made me afraid. My father had gone to the factory for half a day's work, and, more unusually, Bashir Ahmed, too, had gone out. My mother and I were alone for the first time in what felt like months, and as our house was transformed, under her hands, from an ordinary, worn place to a dazzling, glowing stage, I found myself more and more agitated. But I said nothing. I did not accuse her, or burst into tears, or threaten to tell my father. I did none of these things. It was as if I believed that speaking would hasten the disaster, make it real. So, paralyzed, I did what I had always done: I kept her close in my sights, watched her as though my life depended on it.

By 3:00 p.m. Bashir Ahmed had still not returned, and my mother, glancing at the clock and taking a last look around at her work, went upstairs to nap. Shut out of her bedroom, I moped around, half hoping Bashir Ahmed would not come back at all, but I heard him shortly afterward, the front door softly opening and closing, followed by the still-softer click of the guest bedroom door. My father returned at 6:00 p.m., carrying a black plastic bag full of brown Kingfisher beer bottles, which he arranged in the fridge. Coming up to me, he put an arm around my shoulder. "Look," he said softly, with a gesture intended to take in our whole house, which glowed under the various lamps my mother had switched on before she went upstairs, the ficuses fluttering in an invisible draft, the table covered in a snowy white cloth, the Kashmiri carpet a pool of dark velvet in the low-lit entryway. There was pride and more than a little pain in his voice.

He went over to the bar, where he dumped ice into two glasses, pouring me a Coke and himself a rum. "Cheers," he said solemnly, and we clinked glasses. Then we went into the living room, where I sat on the sofa, while he ran his finger along his LPs, settling on Joni Mitchell's *Blue*. When her plaintive, nasal voice began, soaring above the vulnerable, open chords of her guitar, I held on to my glass even tighter. Something would happen tonight. I was sure of it.

A door opened, and my father and I turned. Bashir Ahmed had emerged from his bedroom. Tonight, he wore his black kurta, his hair combed back, the lower lids of his eyes darkened by kohl. With his gaunt face shaded in his trimmed beard, he looked especially handsome. He came to stand before my father, and, for some odd reason, they shook hands.

"Mr. Ahmed," my father said with formality.

"Janaab," replied Bashir Ahmed.

Another movement at the top of stairs caught our attention. We raised our eyes to see my mother walking down. My mouth fell open. She wore a red-and-gold sari I'd never seen before, its folds shimmering and shifting color with each step she took. Her hair, which she normally tied in a careless bun, was tonight loose around her shoulders. Her diamond earrings were twin points of light, and she wore a single gold bangle on each wrist. Her eyes, like Bashir Ahmed's, were lined with kohl, and her lips, slightly parted, were dark with a touch of lipstick.

She looked like a bride.

At the bottom of the stairs, she paused. "Hello," she said.

My father and Bashir Ahmed were both staring at her, their expressions nearly identical. The silence started to become strained, but thankfully just then the doorbell rang. My father cleared his throat. "You look nice," he muttered then went to open the door. My mother glanced once at Bashir Ahmed, then joined him at the door to receive our first guests, Bharti and Joshua D'Silva.

Bharti, a trim, no-nonsense woman in gray slacks, had for a few years been my father's boss at a German engineering firm before he quit to start his own company. Joshua, her husband, was a huge, unkempt man, nearly seven feet tall, whom I'd always liked for his shambling, bearlike aspect, his deep voice that contrasted with his gentle manner of speaking.

The two of them hugged my parents, and then my father introduced Bashir Ahmed, who bowed his head and murmured, "Aadaab."

Joshua peered down at him as if he were an interesting new species of animal, but Bharti just blinked her cool gray eyes and said in English, "Nice to meet you, Mr. Ahmed."

Almost immediately, the bell rang again, and the door was opened to admit Govind Narayan and his plump wife. Govind, a thin fellow with a high, whinnying laugh, had gone to college with my father. His wife, Sudha, was the headmistress of a girls' school. They both hugged me and shook hands with Bashir Ahmed, who shrank visibly from the onslaught of so many strangers. Now that he was standing beside me, I could see that he looked especially haggard tonight, the skin under his eyes puffy and raw. Had he been crying?

There was no time to wonder further because my father swept him away toward the bar. The others were laughing and seating themselves around the living room. My head spun with the sudden movement and commotion. Bashir Ahmed returned to the living room with a glass of Coke, and, after a moment of hesitation, took a seat next to the massive Joshua.

When everyone had been seated, the buzz of conversation died. My father stood, surveying all of us gathered about him. Then he raised his rum glass with a dramatic flourish.

"There comes a time in a man's life," he announced in English, "when what he begins to value is not the future and its possibilities, but the past and its comforts. I have known most of you for many years, and I am grateful for each one of those years."

He paused, eyes shining. He swung his glass around to Bashir Ahmed, who looked alarmed, as if a gun were pointed at him. Switching to Hindi, my father said, "But never let it be said that life holds no surprises. New friends can always be made, and this evening is for our newest friend, all the way from Kashmir. Mr. Bashir Ahmed."

Lifting their glasses, the others drank to him, including my mother, who pressed her red lips to her glass of water, her eyes fixed on Bashir

Ahmed, who was staring in obvious embarrassment at the floor. Beaming, my father flopped down in his chair and stretched out his long legs, every inch the genial host. I wanted to leap across the room and shake him.

"Thank you, janaab," Bashir Ahmed began, his ordinarily firm voice the weakest flutter. "What you have done—I mean, what your family has done—what I'm trying to say is that I am—"

He stopped, and again I thought, *He has been crying.*

My father reached over and squeezed him sympathetically on the shoulder.

"Mr. Ahmed has told us a little bit about the problems Kashmir is facing," my father announced in English, his hand still firmly on Bashir Ahmed's shoulder. "I wanted to host this dinner, partly to have the pleasure of your company again, of course"— he smiled around at the gathered guests—"but also because I was hoping that he might do the same for all of you. Living as we do in the south, it's rare to hear a firsthand account of the situation up there. I have no doubt that you will find the things he has to say about Kashmir very interesting."

Before anyone could say anything more, my mother leaned forward.

"What are you doing?" she hissed at him. "You can't just invite people over and ask him to perform. He's not some circus monkey."

"I'm not asking him to perform," my father hissed back. "I'm asking him to *talk*. Like a human being. Do you have any objection to that?"

The others kept their eyes tactfully lowered during this exchange, except for Bashir Ahmed, whose gaze darted between their faces, trying to understand the barrage of English words. My mother stared at my father, then leaned back and made a gesture with her fingers, which was all the more chilling for being so careless. *Carry on,* the gesture said. *This is nothing to do with me.*

"Go on, Mr. Ahmed," my father said in Hindi, turning back to him. "Tell us all what you told me."

"About what, janaab?"

"What do you mean? About Kashmir, of course," my father said impatiently. "The militants, the army. You know. All of that."

The guests were turned to him with varying degrees of interest and expectation. My mother's kohl-lined eyes were unreadable.

Bashir Ahmed cleared his throat. "I have nothing to say, janaab."

"Oh, come now," my father said. "There's no reason to be shy. We're all friends here. You told us that the army was there, in your village, keeping things under control. Remember?"

Bashir Ahmed shook his head. "I never said that, janaab."

"Of course you did," my father snapped.

Bashir Ahmed shook his head. There was an uncomfortable silence, and then Joshua D'Silva cleared his throat and shifted, making the whole sofa creak.

"It's been thirty years," he said in soft, rumbling Hindi, "but we fell in love with Kashmir when we visited. It was for our honeymoon. We stayed on a houseboat, and every morning this old man would float up in a tiny boat full of these beautiful flowers. He would give us this huge handful, and he would never take any money for them either. Remember the old man, Bharti?"

His wife nodded.

"Those houseboats are beautiful, Mr. Ahmed," Joshua said.

"I don't know about houseboats," Bashir Ahmed said stubbornly. "I am from the mountains, and there is no use for a boat on a mountain."

At that, my mother let out a bark of a laugh, which made the others whip their heads around to look at her. All except my father, who did not take his eyes off Bashir Ahmed.

"I don't understand you, Mr. Ahmed," he said slowly. "When you arrived, you had a very different attitude to all this. You told us that militants were causing trouble in your area, but that the army was keeping them in order."

"No, janaab." Bashir Ahmed raised his chin. "*You* said that."

My mother's shoulders were now shaking with silent laughter. My father whirled to face her. "Would you stop that?" he snapped in English. "What the hell is wrong with you?"

"Me?" She wiped tears of laughter from her eyes. "Nothing's wrong with me."

My father got heavily to his feet. His eyes went slowly from Bashir Ahmed to my chuckling mother. For a minute, it seemed he might speak, but then he simply turned on his heel and went to the bar. Without thinking, I followed him. I didn't know why. I wanted to say something to him, but his face was a warning to leave him alone. He was pouring rum into his glass, and I watched the level of amber rise well beyond where he usually stopped. He took a long draught, stared for a while at the shining wood of the sideboard, then went back to the others in the living room. Left by myself, I glanced over my shoulder, then tipped a generous splash of rum into my Coke and stirred it quickly with my finger. Imitating my father, I closed my eyes and drank, tasting the rottenness of the rum under the bubbling soda, feeling it coat the back of my throat.

I returned to the living room to find Sudha, Govind's wife, a plump woman in a magenta sari, telling a story. Trying, perhaps, to draw attention away from my scowling father and my still-smirking mother, she was going on and on about the girls' school where she was headmistress. My mother listened, head cocked, tapping her finger on her cheek. Then she stood with an abrupt motion, causing everyone to jump and cutting Sudha off in mid-sentence.

"Sorry," she said casually to their startled, upturned faces, "It's just not a very interesting story, is it? I'll go get the food heated up."

She sauntered off, and another shocked silence followed. Sudha glanced at her husband with raised eyebrows; then they both turned and gave my father an openly pitying look. Thankfully, he was slumped over his chair, turning his rum glass around in his hands, and he didn't notice.

After five minutes, during which nobody spoke except to make half-hearted comments about the weather and traffic, we heard my mother's voice calling us to dinner. I stopped short when I saw the table. She'd prepared a feast. Our best bone-white crockery was laid out: dishes filled with fluffy steaming rice, dark channa with a swirl of cream, mounds of potatoes and cauliflower garnished with coriander, rotis glistening with ghee, platters of fried okra and green beans. A jug of water sparkled in the middle, encasing a tall sprig of mint. My mother stood at the entrance to the kitchen, arms folded. "Go on," she called out. "What are you waiting for, a red carpet?"

One by one, we filed around the table. When my plate could hold no more, I returned to the living room and began to eat. For once, my mother had made no mistakes in her cooking; the food was perfect. I ate fast, suddenly ravenous, alternating with swigs from my tainted glass of Coke. The others sat around me: Joshua's huge hand dwarfing his plate, Bharti delicately using a fork to cut into a chunk of potato, Sudha and Govind eating with unabashed appetites, and my father not eating at all. His plate remained untouched on his knees, and as soon as I noticed, my own hunger vanished. My muscles tensed, ready for danger, though I didn't know from which direction it would come.

My mother came back into the living room with a plate of her own. She fell to eating with enthusiasm, seemingly oblivious to the furtive, wary glances of the others. Curd stained the corners of her mouth, and she chewed so loudly, it made me wince. From time to time, she smiled, apparently to herself, the gleefully unconscious smile of a little girl. My father, looking up, caught one of these smiles and stiffened. He set his plate down on the table beside him with a loud clink and went to the bar, coming back with still another sloshing, overfull drink.

Standing over her, he said in Hindi, "You know. I'm starting to wonder something."

Everybody looked up. My father, no longer the benevolent patriarch, no longer the jovial host, his face suddenly looking a decade older than his forty-two years, turned to Bashir Ahmed.

"I'm wondering, Mr. Ahmed," my father said "what it is you *do* think. It's funny, but I've been sitting here for the last ten minutes thinking about it, and you're right. You've been living in our house for almost three weeks, and you haven't told us"—here his eyes traveled briefly to my mother, who still wore a smile—"well, at least you haven't told *me* what you think about these things happening in Kashmir. And I really would like to know."

"I told you, janaab," Bashir Ahmed said, "I have nothing to say about that." He sat very straight in his black kurta, returning my father's unfocused gaze with a blank one of his own.

"Well, if *you* won't say anything," my father declared, and now I heard the slurring in his voice, the way it slithered over certain sounds, ground others down to nothing, "then *I'll* tell you what *I* think. *I* think that for more than forty years, India has taken care of Kashmir. We've given you jobs and roads and power and hospitals. Our taxes have provided education to thousands of Kashmiri children. So it doesn't seem like too much to expect some gratitude in return, instead those people you have up there blowing up buildings, shouting slogans for Pakistan, burning Indian flags and whatnot. Wouldn't you agree, Mr. Ahmed? Doesn't that make sense to you? If someone takes you into his home and gives you a bed and puts food in your mouth without asking any questions, don't you think you owe him something in return?"

Bashir Ahmed stood up. If the room had been quiet before, it became deathly silent now. I glanced at my mother. She had stopped eating.

"Janaab," Bashir Ahmed said quietly, "you are an intelligent man. Anyone can see that. You have a big business and a big house, and I respect you for that. And you are correct: you *don't* know what I think. I have been working and traveling in this country for many years now, and I have seen a lot. But I will tell you this: you are not the only one who believes as you do. There are many others who think the same way, who think that people should be happy with whatever they get, even if it isn't what they want. And I will also tell you this: as long as people like you believe the things you do, then those people in Kashmir, as you call them, will not go away. No, janaab. They will become more and more in number, and soon other people will join them. Ordinary people like me. And, for your sake, I hope that day doesn't come, because that is when you will *really* have something to worry about."

I'd never heard him speak at such length, except during a story, but the voice he addressed my father in was not the intimate voice of his stories, the one with the dramatic swoops, the repetitions, the one that accompanied the rise and fall of his hands, nor was it the weak and fragmented voice that had told us about the militants in his home. He spoke to us from a great remove, as if he had left the room and was looking down at us from some high place. And even then, young and frightened a child as I was, I felt sure that neither my father nor Bashir Ahmed was talking only about Kashmir. Now, of course, I know that for certain.

"As for me, janaab," Bashir Ahmed went on, "when I came here, I promised you I would not stay for long, and I am going to keep that promise. I am leaving tomorrow. I will never be able to thank you properly for your kindness in letting me stay, but please believe that I will never forget it."

With quiet formality, he bowed his head, first to my father, then to the group of stunned people in the room. He carried his plate to the kitchen, from where we heard the sound of water running. He came out, and without looking at us, went into his room and closed the door.

"Well!" Sudha, the plump headmistress, burst out in English. "*What* was all that? What on earth was he talking about? Did he mean terrorists? My God! I mean, I've never—" She looked desperately around the room for confirmation. "That was quite rude of him, wasn't it? To just walk off like that? *Wasn't* it?"

Nobody replied except for my mother, who said absently, "Oh, be quiet."

Sudha puffed up like a wounded hen, and her husband said, "Excuse me, I don't think there's any reason to talk to my wife that way."

The trim, bespectacled Bharti D'Silva cleared her throat. "Joshua," she said. "I didn't realize it was so late. We should probably get home. I've got that early meeting, remember?"

Her husband nodded, retrieving her plate from her outstretched hand and lumbering off to the kitchen. Sudha and Govind Narayan got to their feet at the same time. "We should get going, too," Govind said to my father, pointedly ignoring my mother, who seemed oblivious to him in any case. "Thank you so much for having us over."

My father nodded, his face expressionless.

And all of a sudden there were the flurries of departure around me. People standing, carrying their plates to the kitchen, looking around in search of their belongings, feeling in pockets for keys. I threw my head back and finished the last of my secretly spiked drink. My eyes stung, and all I could think was that once they left, it would all be over. She would leave. I would never see her again.

"Wait!" I burst out, and they all paused around me, blinking, as if they'd been shaken from a dream. I felt, rather than saw, my mother's head turn in my direction.

It was my father who responded. "Yes, Shalini?"

"I have something to say," I went on in a desperate rush. "About Kashmir."

The corners of his eyes tightened. "Not now, Shalini."

"No, please," I insisted. "I think—" I paused, desperately thinking of something to say. "I think Bashir Ahmed is right. I mean, I know the militants are doing some bad things, but all the people in Kashmir aren't militants, are they? So maybe we should be talking to the ordinary people instead, the ones Bashir Ahmed was telling us about. The ones who are good. The ones who . . ." I paused, then rushed on quickly. "And then we would at least be *doing* something, right? And isn't that the important thing, to *do* something? So, yes. I think we should find those people, we should talk to them, ask them . . ." I swallowed. My throat was so dry. I knew I was blabbering. "Anyway, that's what I think," I finished in a hoarse whisper.

It was the last thing I'd intended, but my words had the effect of releasing some of the tension that had built in the room. I saw their brows clear, saw them glance tolerantly and sadly at each other, as if to say, *Hear that?* Even my father allowed himself a smile.

"That's a noble point of view, sweetheart," he said, "and maybe you're right, maybe talking is the best solution, but I think we've talked enough about it for one day."

"But if you were a politician, I'd vote for you," Joshua rumbled.

Then they resumed looking for car keys, picking up handbags, making their little noises of farewell, the longing for home etched into every face.

Unnoticed, I slumped onto the sofa. I had failed. I had tried, and I had failed. Now there would be nothing to stop them from leaving, and once they left, she would leave too. Joshua and Bharti shook my father's hand and nodded once to my mother, who smiled as if the evening had gone splendidly. Govind and Sudha were already outside, pulling on their shoes, Sudha speaking furiously to her husband under her breath. I heard their car engines rev and fade. My father closed the door, and, with dreadful swiftness, the house was silent again.

For the first time all evening, amid the ruins of crumpled napkins and cloudy, half-full glasses and chairs left askew, my parents faced each other. Neither of them moved. Then my mother raised her chin, her earrings glinting.

"Not a bad party," she remarked. "Don't you think?"

My father's shoulders fell.

"I'm tired," he said. "It's been a long day. I'm going to sleep."

He took a last look around, then climbed the stairs slowly, each step seeming to cost him all the strength in his body. I heard their bedroom door softly close.

My mother looked down at me. "That was quite the speech you made, little beast," she said, in that same bright, brittle tone she'd used with him.

But I didn't respond, and then she seemed all at once to change. She dropped to her knees.

"Shalini," she said. "Look at me."

I did not want to, but I looked at her.

"You are not me," she told me. "What I am, what I say and do and think, none of it is your responsibility. You're allowed to do something else, be something else. You're allowed to hate me."

"I don't hate you," I mumbled.

"No," she said gravely. "Not yet. But you will." Then she gave me a long, tight hug. "Come on, little beast," she whispered. "Let's go to sleep."

She rose, gathering up the folds of her sari and gazing around the wrecked expanse of the room. Then she sighed, turned off the lights, and we went upstairs. She disappeared into her bedroom, and I entered mine. I looked around at all my things, my posters and books, my bed and cupboard, and I felt only a faint ache as though I had already left them far behind. Unzipping my school backpack, I emptied the contents onto my bed: brown-covered notebooks and pencil shavings, stray erasers and empty pen refills. Then I opened my cupboard and began pulling out clothes at random. I stuffed as many as I could into the bag, adding, as an afterthought, the white blouse, which was the first and only thing we had bought from Bashir Ahmed, and which I'd never worn. I added a comb and a pair of bathroom sandals, and I couldn't think of anything else to add, so hiking the backpack onto my shoulders, I crept out onto the landing and listened. There was still light leaking from beneath my parents' door, but as I stood there, it went off. I slunk downstairs, peering into the darkness and trying to avoid stray chairs. I found my shoes by the door and, crouching, I laced them extra tight. Then I sat down on the sofa to wait.

I don't know how long I'd been asleep, but I was woken by the soft click of a door. My eyes flew open and my heart began to pound. It was time. I didn't know how I would convince them to take me, but I would think of something. She would not leave me behind. Standing, I listened for voices, but there were none. Then I saw a figure moving outside the guest bedroom: Bashir Ahmed.

He was bent over, looking for his sandals in the pile of shoes beside the door. His suitcase stood on the ground beside him. He found the sandals and straightened up; then, catching sight of me standing in the darkness, he uttered a cry of fear and stumbled back.

"It's me," I whispered, taking a step forward.

"Beti," he whispered back. "What are you doing? Why aren't you sleeping?"

"I'm coming with you," I said. "With both of you," I added.

Even in the faint moonlight that came in, I could see his face blanch. "Beti," he said.

"Where is my mother?" I whispered.

"She—" he began. Then he pulled his shoulders back. "I'm going alone."

"She's not going with you?"

He shook his head.

"You're leaving her?"

He sank down on his haunches, gripping a sandal in each hand, and I realized, with an uncomfortable shock, that he was weeping. Not knowing what else to do, I sat down beside him. "Are you okay?" I whispered.

He coughed quickly into his hand. "I'm fine, beti. I'm fine. Don't pay attention to me."

I searched for something else to say, but the truth was I was no longer thinking of him. What was uppermost in my mind was my mother, asleep upstairs next to my father. My mother, who would wake up tomorrow to find Bashir Ahmed gone. What would she say?

Then he stood. "I have to go, beti," he said. The tears were gone, and there was a dull conviction in his voice. I knew he would not be dissuaded.

"What about the militants?" I asked. "What will you do about them?"

He raised his head, and I saw the glimmer of a smile. "You're a sweet girl, beti," he said. "You don't need to worry about me. I'll think of something."

For the very last time, I accompanied Bashir Ahmed out to our gate. He lifted it carefully before pushing—he knew its peculiarities as well as any of us—and its hinges made no sound. Once he was outside, he looked down at me again. His expression, I thought, was the same as it had been the first time, all those years ago, when he had appeared from nowhere on our doorstep with his yellow bundle, changing everything in a single afternoon. Wry and a little sad.

"Please tell her, beti," he said, "that I am sorry. For everything."

I did my best. I lifted my chin.

"I will tell her," I said.

Now that he was at the gate, he seemed not to want to leave. "Maybe I'll see you someday," he said. "Maybe you can come and see my home."

"I would like that," I said.

"So would I."

He turned and began walking. I waited until he reached the end of our street and turned left. Then I went back inside the house, pried off my shoes, and locked the front door. I crept upstairs to my room, hid my backpack in my cupboard, and slipped into bed.

I lay on my back, staring at the ceiling, at the slow-spinning fan.

Thinking only:

She is here. She is still here.

24

SANIA WAS READING. HER finger followed the length of the printed line, chin tucked almost to her chest. Her other hand was balled in a fist in her lap. I sat to her side and listened. When she reached the end of the chapter, she stopped. In the silence that followed, I put my hands together and started to clap. She looked up and blushed. With a quick, self-conscious laugh, she closed the book.

"That was very good, Sania," I said. And it was true. In the span of a week, she had shown real improvement. She could now recognize most simple English words and could sound out the more complex ones through a combination of context and instinct. And though I knew it mostly had to do with her innate grasp of language, its logic and exceptions, and nothing to do with my ability to teach, I could not help the pride that welled up in me when I looked at her, a frown of concentration creasing her forehead as she sat hunched over a book.

While she went off to make the cup of tea that had become our custom after these sessions, I leaned back against my bolster and looked out at the green valley winking in the late afternoon sun, thinking about this place and its people, all of whom until so recently had been unknown to me, strange as that was to think. Mohammad Din's conversation, Sania's finger traveling across the page, Aaqib's hand finding its way into mine, even Khadijah Aunty's stoic face—they all felt as if they had been part of my life for years, and it was hard to believe I'd ever lived without any of them. Then, of course, there was Amina's friendship, which I'd done nothing to deserve, and when I thought of it, I felt my first prickle of discomfort. I'd done my best to avoid Riyaz for the previous week, which had not proved especially difficult, since he seemed equally keen to avoid me. The few times our paths crossed in the narrow corridor, he pressed himself to the wall and allowed me to walk past him, his eyes fixed over my head, which was more hurtful than I'd expected. But the rest of the time, when I was crouched in the barn in the mornings, my cheek an inch from the warm, sweating flank of the red-and-white cow, or when I was working with Sania, the two of us bent over a page written in a language that was slowly unraveling for her like a scroll, I forgot about Riyaz completely, and all I thought about was the work itself, the unwavering sense of a goal, the bodily contentment and pleasant inertia that filled me whenever I was finished.

And yet, despite my growing affection for this place and its people, I could not forget the person I had come to find: Bashir Ahmed, still on the other side of my bedroom wall, still hidden, still unreachable. If I put my ear to the wall that separated us, I could sometimes hear him clear his throat or shift in bed, and I wondered what my mother would do in my place. No doubt she would find a way to get in, by lying and sneaking if necessary, but I could not bring myself to betray Amina's trust. She had promised me, on the day of the waterfall, that she would broach the subject with Bashir Ahmed again, but each evening, after she returned to the kitchen with his dinner plate, I would glance questioningly at her, and she would shake her head. *Not tonight.*

Sania came back into the room with three cups of tea and a plate of cream biscuits, and shortly afterward, Mohammad Din joined us. "How was the lesson?" he asked.

"Very good," I told him. Sania's moonlike face glowed. "She won't need me soon."

Her father smiled. "I'm glad to hear she's doing well," he said. "But you're wrong about her not needing you. It was one of the luckiest things in her life that she got to meet you. In fact"—and here he exchanged a glance with Sania, who grinned back mischievously—"we have been talking about something for the past few days. Sania wants to be the one to tell you about it."

I turned to Sania, who blushed, then suddenly reached out and took my hand in both of hers. Looking into my face, she blurted, "Ma'am, would you like to become a teacher in my school?"

"*What?*" I glanced from her to Mohammad Din, who nodded.

"Yes," he said. "That's where I just came from, actually, a meeting with the headmaster of the school. He said that we would have to seek official permission from the education board, but that it may be possible to hire a teacher without a B.Ed. I didn't want to ask you until I knew whether it could be done. We would pay you, obviously, and our students would benefit so much."

I stared at both of them. "I don't know what to say."

"Say yes, ma'am," Sania urged, shaking my arm.

"Don't pressure her," Mohammad Din told his daughter. To me, he said, "I know this is very sudden, and I would understand if you said no. I know you have a good job in Bangalore, and you will probably not want to leave it, but this would be a very big thing for us. And more important, it would be a big thing for our children; it would give them a chance to progress. So, speaking for the whole village, we would be very happy if you decided to stay. All I am asking—all *we* are asking—is that you think about it before you answer. Will you think about it?"

I nodded, as if in a dream.

Satisfied, Mohammad Din went on to talk about something else, the upcoming elections, most likely, but I heard none of it. Stay? Become a teacher? It would have seemed laughable even an hour before, but now that they'd said it, I saw myself strolling with Aaqib down the grassy slope toward that bustling, whitewashed building nestled in its shallow, sunny valley, walking into my classroom and setting down my books, saw myself cleaning the blackboard and straightening chairs, humming to myself as I waited for my students to come bursting through the door. Soon they would, in a flurry of energy and activity, calling, *Good morning, ma'am!* I saw myself bending over their shoulders, correcting mistakes, and gently disciplining a rude or careless child, who would love me all the more for my restraint; saw myself laughing and waving goodbye as they ran off across the mountains at the end of the day; saw myself exchanging familiar greetings with villagers as I walked back to the house and to Amina, who would rise from the outdoor tap, shading her eyes from the sun, calling, *How was your day, Murgi?* But here the fantasy faltered. How could I continue to stay with Amina, who had sworn not to take any money from me? Would she reconsider if I were working, making an income? Could I persuade her to let me pay rent? And what about Riyaz? How would he react when he heard? Riyaz, who so obviously wanted me gone?

I was still thinking about all of this as I pulled on my shoes outside, shook hands with Sania and Mohammad Din, and walked away from their pretty house, tinted pink in the evening light. Halfway down the path leading back to Amina and Riyaz's house, I hesitated, then doubled back fifty feet and instead took the trail that I knew would lead up to the waterfall.

The path folded and unfolded exactly as I remembered, twisting back and forth, rising sharply, then flattening out into a grassy lawn, then rising again. Once I was amongst the pines, I knew I had to be close. I put my head down and listened for water, certain that I would hear the telltale murmur any minute, but the only sounds that reached me were the wind snaking through the trees and the droning legions of invisible insects. Had I missed a turning somewhere? Had there been a path I hadn't seen, which Amina had taken me up the last time? Where was the amphitheater of rock, the pool of water? I climbed a little farther, hoping to emerge from the trees into a place I knew, but the path only narrowed and became less defined, finally losing itself altogether in a mess of rock. I then tried to retrace my steps, but before I'd gone even a hundred feet, I realized with a sinking heart that the way back did not look familiar either.

I slowly sank down onto the bed of pine needles, wrapping my arms about my knees, trying to think calmly. Surely somebody would come along soon enough, a village woman out to cut grass for her animals, a man shooing his goats toward home, a child sent to fetch firewood. All I would need to do was wait, and someone would point me in the right direction. But I sat there, the wind growing colder by the minute, sneaking glances at the sky, which was already starting to show stains of inky black, and it seemed less and less likely that anyone would appear.

Finally, I stood, pine needles falling in showers from my clothes, and began to walk downhill, though by this time I was so disoriented that the path seemed to swing the opposite way to the one I expected. My only hope was that the lower I got, the better chance I had of running into someone. I was losing daylight faster than I'd imagined. I emerged into a sort of clearing, empty of trees, though their stumps remained, broken off like teeth poorly extracted. My first thought was that this was a place frequented by woodcutters, and I experienced a brief surge of hope. Then I saw that the stumps were charred, that blackened woodchips lay everywhere, that the ground was stained dark and ashy. What could have done that? Lightning, I realized with a shudder. I was about to back away, when I caught sight of what was unmistakably a human figure. He or she was on the other side of the clearing, back turned to me. I thought of the black-clad robbers Mohammad Din had mentioned and felt a moment of panic, but my fear of being lost on the mountain quickly outweighed it. It was probably just a shepherd, I told myself.

"Excuse me?" I called out, starting to move forward. "Hello? Excuse me?"

The person did not turn right away. My eyes strained to make him out, for now I could tell that it was a man. Then he made a hitching motion with his pants, smoothly zipping them up with one hand as he turned around. I stopped in my tracks. It was a soldier.

"Who's that? Come forward so I can see you," the soldier called out in Hindi. It took me a second, but then I recognized his voice. It was the cool, mustached subedar, the one who had come to the house a few days ago, the one who had asked all those questions.

I remained frozen. He took a step forward. I saw, or perhaps imagined, his right hand twitch his rifle, and, shamefully, I felt a few drops of warm urine trickle out of me. "No, wait!" I called out, hearing the squeak of terror in my voice. "Please. My name is Shalini. You met me the other day."

Now I could see his face, his eyebrows drawn together in a mistrustful frown, which did not fully relax when he saw me emerge into the open. "You," he said slowly. "You're that girl."

"Yes," I said.

"The one staying with those villagers."

"Yes," I said.

"What are you doing here?"

"I was going for a walk and now I can't find the way back to the village. Could you tell me which way to go?"

But he didn't seem to hear me. He was staring at me, not in the dry, impersonal way he had looked at me the last time, but with a touch of knowing amusement, and it made me squirm.

"So you are lost," he said. His accent, I could hear, was different from that of Amina and Riyaz and the rest of the villagers, and different from my own. It was a flatter, more nasal accent, each word dropping without flourish or song, like a stone into a dry well.

"Yes."

"I see." Then, instead of answering, he fell silent again, and just as I was about to repeat my request for directions, he said, "Why did you lie to me the other day?"

My knees nearly buckled. "Excuse me?"

He gave me a reproving look. "Come, come. There's no need to pretend. That day at the house. You lied to me, didn't you?"

I stared at him. He knew about Bashir Ahmed. There was no other explanation. How had he found out? And what would he do to him now? I willed myself to think, to come up with a plausible excuse, but my mind wouldn't cooperate.

"Why so quiet?" he asked dryly. "You might as well tell me, since you have nowhere to go."

"I don't know what you're talking about," I said finally.

"Fine," he said, as if he'd abruptly lost patience with our little game. "Then I'll tell you. It was obvious from the beginning, so I don't know why you still feel the need to lie about it." He drew his head back and with a triumphant twist of his lips, he said, "You are a journalist."

He must have read my dumbfounded expression as one of dismay at being unmasked, because he smiled scornfully. "You really thought I believed you when you said you were *friends* with those villagers? Come on. How stupid do I seem? People like you don't have friends in Kashmiri villages. Only journalists and human rights people come to places like this. So tell me, what story are you searching for?" He pushed his lower lip out and dropped his voice to an effeminate whine, presumably meant to mimic me. "Are you going to write about how those poor, sweet Kashmiri villagers are suffering so badly under the army?"

I shook my head.

"Good," the subedar said curtly. He took another step toward me. "Because you won't find that story. Those people are not what you think they are. They've given help to militants in the past, and they will do it again in the future. Do you know about the Hindus who were killed in this area?"

I don't know how I found the wherewithal to nod, but I did.

"You know?" He seemed momentarily taken aback, but his eyes soon narrowed again. "Well, then maybe you should remember it before calling them your friends."

Even then, I had enough sense to see that the things he was saying were not, in substance, unlike the things Stalin had said to me in Kishtwar. But, unlike Stalin, who had, in the end, been a lonely boy far from home, this man, this *soldier*, seemed to have himself perfectly in hand. He was not trying to flirt or impress. In fact, he seemed to want nothing whatsoever from me, as Stalin had, and for that reason, what he was saying chilled me all the more.

Guessing, I think, that his words had had their intended effect, he said nothing further. Instead he glanced around at the piles of woodchips, at the charred and blasted stumps, then pointed over my shoulder. "Your friends' village is behind you," he said curtly. "Keep going that way, then, where the path splits, go left. It'll take you straight down to their mosque."

I managed to stammer out my thanks. I expected him to turn and walk away, but I was wrong. He said, "One more thing. It would be better if you didn't go wandering around by yourself. There have been stories of troublemakers in this area lately, creating mischief, scaring people. As if the army doesn't have enough to do already, we must now also be village watchmen. Good thing I saw who you were in time. Otherwise I might have thought you were one of them, and then . . ." He shrugged. "It would have been very sad if you had gone and gotten yourself hurt." This time it wasn't my imagination; his fingertips brushed his gun. "Now go home," he told me.

I started to walk but my legs felt like melting rubber. I could not help imagining him raising his rifle, pointing it between my shoulder blades. I tried as hard as I could to conjure up Amina's face, the way she had held herself so straight while the soldiers plunked their teacups one by one down on the tray. She would have kept her chin high; she would have walked away from him as if he was less than nothing, but I could not. As soon as I was sure he was out of sight, I began to run.

Panting, I skidded and slid inelegantly down the path, hoping against hope that I would not fall. Where the path split, as he said it would, I went left. I came out onto a ridge and looked down the mountain, and there, outlined against the sky, was the familiar green spire of the mosque, its windows lit up a welcoming yellow. Relief hit me so hard in the gut that I dropped to my knees, my chest heaving with dry sobs that could have just as easily been laughter.

Just then, floating on the air, I heard my name. Someone was calling me. My head shot up, and I strained to hear it again. Was it the soldier? Had he followed me? I held my breath and did not move for fear of giving myself away. For seconds, there was nothing but the evening breeze and insects. And then I heard again: "Shalini!" It was not the soldier. I scrambled to my feet and began to jog forward. Then, turning a corner, I saw the source of the voice.

Riyaz was standing a little way downhill, hands on his hips, looking around with a worried frown on his face. When he saw me, his eyes went wide, then almost immediately narrowed with resolution. "Stay there," he called out, starting up. "I'll come to you."

But I didn't listen. I was so glad to see him that I started to run down even faster, no longer caring enough to look where I was stepping. My left foot found a loose stone, and I crashed hard on my hands and knees, letting out a shriek of pain. In an instant, he was beside me. His arm was around my shoulders, and his face was close to mine, I watched a bead of sweat sink down his neck and soak into his collar.

"Are you okay?" he demanded.

"Yes," I panted. "How did you know where I was?"

"One of the villagers saw you go up this way a while ago. He came up to me after namaz and said you were by yourself. When I got home and you still weren't back, I came to find you."

My cheeks burned. "I'm so stupid. I don't know what I was thinking. I just—"

"Can you stand?" he interrupted.

I nodded and got gingerly to my feet. Then I realized his arm was still around me, his other hand gripping my elbow. My shoulder was pressed against his chest, and his mouth was inches from my hair. He must have realized the same thing, because he swiftly let go, stepping away and saying, in a gruffer voice, "Do you think you can walk? Should I go bring one of the mules?"

"No," I said. "That's all right. I can walk."

"Okay." Riyaz started to move away. Then he turned back to look at me, and in his face were desire and reluctance, loneliness and confusion, and something else, close to despair. I was sure that something almost identical showed in mine. But when he said, "Are you coming?" his voice was impersonal. I nodded and followed him back down the mountain.

As soon as I stepped onto the porch, Amina burst out of the house and hugged me. "What *happened*, Murgi?" she cried. "Where did you go? I was so scared!"

"I'm sorry," I mumbled. By now, the last of my adrenaline had drained away, and I was thoroughly tired and ashamed. "I wanted to go back to the waterfall, the one you showed me."

"Why didn't you just come and ask me?" she demanded. "I would have gone with you."

"I thought I could find it on my own but—" I was on the verge of telling her about the subedar, but it stuck in my throat. I thought of my abject terror, the way I'd fled like a child, and I compared it with the way she'd held the tray as the soldiers set their empty cups down, the unbending iron in her spine. I couldn't tell her.

"I lost my way," I said, as calmly as I could "but I found it again. I'm fine, Amina, really."

She still looked worried. "Are you sure?"

I glanced over her shoulder. Riyaz was standing in the doorway and our eyes met. A second later, he turned and disappeared indoors.

I took a deep breath and made myself focus on Amina's face.

"I'm sure," I said, forcing my lips into a smile. "Please don't look so worried, Amina. Tell me, what kind of murgi would I be if I didn't try to run off from time to time?"

25

THE NIGHT OF THE party, the same night Bashir Ahmed sneaked out of our house like a thief, I slept more deeply than I had in weeks, not waking until almost noon the next day. It was Sunday, and when I opened my eyes to the afternoon light pouring in my window, the house felt different, lighter, as though an extra force of gravity that had been operating upon it all these days had been removed without warning. I bounded out of bed, and ran downstairs to find my parents.

They were sitting on the front porch together, drinking coffee from their white cups, and even this seemed like a sign of recovery, of imminent health. There were still some traces of the previous night in their faces; my mother's eyes were smudged dark with the kohl she hadn't washed away, and the skin around my father's lips resembled wax paper, but he smiled when I appeared, and gave me a peck on the cheek. "Hello, sweetheart," he said. "Did you sleep well?"

I glanced at my mother's face, trying to read her expression. Did she know yet that Bashir Ahmed had left, or did she believe he was still in his room, asleep? I went back inside and peeked into the guest bedroom. It was spotless, the soiled and crushed sheets removed from the narrow bed, leaving the frayed edges of the bare mattress, the floors and table wiped clean. The smell of disinfectant hung in the air, reminding me of the rotten sweetness of the rum from last night. So she knew. I closed the door then jumped in fright. My mother was standing at my elbow, two empty cups in her hand.

"Amma, I was just—" I began, but stopped.

She said, "He's gone. He took his things."

"Oh," I said.

"All his things," she said. "You know what that means?"

I nodded, not daring to look into her eyes. And, in that moment, I knew that I would never be able to tell her what I had promised Bashir Ahmed I would. I would never be able to admit that I had been there, awake in the middle of the night, to see Bashir Ahmed leave. That I'd watched him walk up the road, suitcase in hand, and had not come to wake her.

"So," she said, after a moment of silence, "there you have it."

Then she turned on her heel and carried the cups to the kitchen, while I stood rooted to the spot, my heart hammering. Surely she guessed I knew. Surely she'd read it in my face. But I waited all day, and she did not ask me about Bashir Ahmed. My father read the newspaper on the porch, while she cleaned up the things from the party, the cloudy glasses like crystal balls, the plates streaked with gravy. In the evening, we sat in the living room while my father looked through his LPs, selecting one and placing it with especial care on the turntable. The voice that began was one I hadn't heard before, a deep voice that seemed to emerge from a well of sorrow, soaring on spikes of pain. My mother, who hadn't spoken since that morning, looked up.

"Who is that?" she asked.

"Nina Simone," my father answered. As far as I knew, these were the first words they'd addressed to each other since the previous night.

He came back and sat on the couch next to me, and, together, we listened to that voice that was more than a voice. Looking at the two of them, their faces pinched and tired, their bodies hunched and closed off from one another but at least occupying the same sofa, the same space, I thought, like the child I was then, that we would be okay.

And we were, for a while. Neither my mother nor my father so much as mentioned Bashir Ahmed's name again. It was as though they'd made a covert pact to pretend that he had never existed, a pact into which I threw myself with great willingness. It was unsettlingly easy, I discovered, this project of forgetting, and within a few weeks, I found it difficult to recall that he had ever lived with us, that he had sat across from me at the dinner table, that his clothes had ever swung next to ours on the line, that his sandals had lain upside down by the front door. School had started again, with all its chaos and crises, and though I never went back to swimming, I had more than enough to keep me occupied. And, at some point that year, I made a startling discovery: in attempting to forget Bashir Ahmed, I'd begun paying less attention to my mother. I was less attuned to her moods, less watchful of the expressions that flitted across her face. It was both a disturbing and a thrilling idea, that I could, in fact, lead a life separate from her without anything falling apart. She was still in my consciousness, of course, but whereas she had previously been its center, a colossus towering above all else, now she was at the periphery, a tiny figure lurking in the corner of my vision.

Perhaps it was because of my new sense of being free and unmoored, but it took me longer than usual to notice that she had, in fact, changed again after Bashir Ahmed's departure. She slept a great deal. I would return from school, and she would be asleep, stretched out on the sofa in the middle of the afternoon, like a lizard on a rock, one hand tucked under her cheek. No matter how much noise I made, how I clomped up and down the stairs, she would not wake. And when she finally did, well after sunset, she drifted around the house with a dreamy absence of purpose, setting a pot of water to boil then forgetting about it, leaving wet clothes in the washing machine for days until they acquired a green patina of mold and had to be thrown away. I would like to say that I tried to comfort her, that at the age of fourteen or fifteen, I was mature enough to see that she was genuinely struggling, but I cannot. "You're allowed to be something else," she'd said to me, and so I was.

Once I brought a classmate home after school, a boy. To study, we told each other, and would have told my mother if she'd asked. But she was asleep on the sofa, as usual, so we crept up to my room and closed the door. As his palms brushed my nipples, I listened for any sound from downstairs, but, of course, there was none. When I led him downstairs again, it was nearly dusk, and my mother was still asleep. Her mouth hung open, and spit emerged from the corner of her lips, like the head of a shy worm. The boy, my classmate, paused, a faintly sickened look on his face. And suddenly I wanted him gone. Gone, not merely from the house, but from the earth. Because he had witnessed her in this state, and because—this with a quake of guilt—I was *ashamed* of her. I'd adored and pitied her, but now I was ashamed of my mother. I walked him to the end of the road and watched him climb into an auto and putter away. It was the last time I brought anybody home.

My father, at the factory all day, did not know about the sleeping, as far as I was aware. But he must have noticed something, because one evening he made the suggestion of a maid, someone, as he said, to help her with the day-to-day. She shrugged. The first maid left in tears after my mother complained that her hair oil stank and was giving her a headache. The second maid was a strapping, gray-haired woman called Amba, who talked loudly and volubly, mostly about her own daughter, who had been born with cerebral palsy, and whom she had nursed and fed until the girl died at thirty-three. But my mother made so many acid comments that Amba soon walked out, saying that she was too old to be treated with disrespect by anyone. Then followed a series of other maids, who never lasted more than a few months, and whose faces and names I can no longer recall, until, finally, there was Stella. Impeccable sari, tiny gold cross. She seemed immune to my mother's barbs, her periodic outbursts of savagery, and, eventually, they reached a kind of stalemate. My mother, who would never admit it but was, I think, grateful to her, slowly abandoned the tasks of housekeeping, falling deeper into her world of sleep, while Stella, in her efficient way, cooked and cleaned and, by and by, came to take care of us all.

26

I slept badly the night after my run-in with the soldier. Tossing on my mattress, I finally gave up and resigned myself to sitting by the window, watching the lone pine tree at the edge of the property. The nights were mostly cloudless, and I could see the shapes of the crows like heavy, upright fruit in the branches. Now and again, one would dislodge itself, swooping silently away on goodness knows what mission. When the morning came, my eyes itched for sleep, but I still went down to the barn with Amina, who herself looked as if she'd spent a restless night. After breakfast, Aacib fetched his schoolbag, the straps dangling behind him, and we set off, hand in hand, toward the school. He had grown comfortable with me, and, as we walked, he kept up a steady stream of patter about his school and classmates, in his enthusiasm slipping for minutes together into Kashmiri, forgetting that I could not understand. When we reached the top of the slope, he let go of my hand, and ran down toward the school. I stood a while longer, listening to the screams of the children, trying to fit myself back into yesterday's fantasy of teaching, but it felt cold and unnatural in the wake of my encounter with the subedar. How could I have been so foolish, so misguided, as to imagine I might live here, when I couldn't get through a walk on my own without needing to be rescued?

Amina was sweeping the porch when I got back to the house.

"Anything I can do to help?" I asked, going up to her, but she shook her head and kept sweeping. "Are you sure I can't help, Amina?" I pressed.

With a burst of irritation she said, "Why do you keep asking the same question again and again, Murgi? Are you deaf? I told you there's nothing you can do!"

It was such an unexpected response that I could find nothing to say. I stood there in silence, and slowly Amina stopped sweeping altogether. She wiped her mouth with the edge of her headscarf, then took a long breath. "I'm sorry, Murgi, I didn't mean to shout at you."

"If you're angry about yesterday, Amina, you're right to be. I know I scared you."

"No," she said, "it's not you. It's—" She hesitated. "It's something else."

"What is it?"

Amina looked down. "You know the story you told me last week, about that man, the one who said he saw those people hiding outside his house? In the middle of the night?"

I nodded.

"Last night, a woman was going to the bathroom, and a person came up behind her in the dark and pushed her. She didn't get hurt, alhamdulillah, but she says she heard two men laughing."

"Who do you think it was?"

"I don't know," she said darkly. "But I'll tell you one thing. It's all because of these elections next month. Whenever there are elections here, funny things start to happen. I don't know, Murgi, it makes me worried."

"Because of Bashir Ahmed?"

"What?" She looked up as if startled. "Oh, no, not him." She paused. "Because of Riyaz."

I looked away. "Oh," I said.

"This morning, I asked him not to go down to work for a few days. The mountain will be full of soldiers, I told him, but he wouldn't listen to me." Her lips were pressed into a white, bloodless line. "See, he has problems with the soldiers, Murgi."

"What kind of problems?" I asked.

She looked down at the broom in her hand. "You've seen yourself how they like to ask questions. The best thing to do is answer them, and most of the time they let you get on with your business. Well, Riyaz doesn't answer. He just stands there, so they get angry and kick him. It's happened so many times over the years." She was toying with the broom now, picking out bits of straw and crushing them in her fingers, then letting them fall to the ground, where a few chickens came scurrying up to investigate. "The rest of us," she went on, and now there was a flare of anger in her voice, "we try and avoid the soldiers. Even babies try. But him? He always finds them. Every single time. Sometimes I think, Murgi, he *wants* them to beat him up."

For the first time since she'd started speaking, she looked at me, and, as if she'd suddenly had an idea, her brown eyes lit up. "Murgi," she said suddenly. "Could *you* talk to him?"

I could not hide my incredulity. "To Riyaz?"

She nodded. "Could you ask him not to go down to work for a few days?"

"But why me?"

She shrugged. "Why not you?"

"Because I'm not—" I swallowed. "Why would he listen to me?"

"He respects you," she said. "You don't know this, but he's always talking about how you're from outside, how you're from a city, how you've traveled and seen all kinds of things, and how we shouldn't embarrass ourselves in front of you." She gave me a small smile. "If you ask me, I think he's a little scared of you. If you told him not to go down, he would listen."

I squirmed, unable to fathom the notion of Riyaz being scared of me. But what really gave me pause was the memory of his face when he found me lost on the mountain, the way he'd gripped my arm before leaping back. My stomach twisted, and I tried pleading with Amina again. "I don't think I'm the right person to talk to him. Isn't there someone else? Mohammad Din?"

"Please, Murgi," she said, catching hold of my hand. "I wouldn't ask if it wasn't so important. Would you please try? For my sake?"

There was such appeal in her voice that I was trapped. I nodded.

"Thank you, Murgi," she breathed. She released me, and as soon as she did so, my hand felt heavy, as though it would snap off.

I waited until after dinner, once the plates had been cleared and Riyaz's mother began sweeping the ashes back into the fireplace with her stubby broom. Aaqib had once again insisted on sitting by me, and he was now leaning against my shoulder, his long lashes fluttering, battling sleep. Riyaz rose first, as always, and left the kitchen, and Amina's eyes met mine across the room. I gently lifted Aaqib's head. He grumbled something under his breath, but I laid him down on the mat, and he curled up like a puppy. I left the kitchen, feeling Amina's eyes trailing after me.

Riyaz was standing at the edge of the porch, his hand fumbling in the pocket of his kurta. I stopped a few feet behind him and cleared my throat. He froze, glancing quickly over his shoulder, then glancing back again.

"I'm sorry to disturb you, Riyaz," I said. Earlier in my room, I had rehearsed what I would say. "I just wanted to thank you again."

His head didn't turn. "What for?"

"For coming to find me. On the mountain."

"What else should I have done? Left you to spend the night with the bears?"

In spite of myself, I smiled. He could be very funny. "I would have deserved it."

He did not respond. I stepped up beside him at the edge of the porch, aware of our reversal of roles. That last time we had stood out here together, he had been the one to approach me.

"Did you hear," I said, "about the woman who was pushed down? It happened last night. She says she heard some men laughing."

He made a noncommittal grunt.

"Who do you think is doing it?" I asked.

"How should I know? Kids, mischief-makers. It's not my problem."

"Amina thinks it's because of the election."

He shrugged. "Could be. As I said, it's not my problem."

I took a breath. "But doesn't it frighten you?"

"Me?" He glanced up with suspicion. "Why would it frighten me?"

"Oh," I said, trying to sound casual, "I don't know. You go up and down the mountain every day, completely alone, except for your mules, of course. What if something happened to you?"

He had tilted his head forward to listen, but now he reared back and fixed me with a sharp look. "What are you doing?" he asked disgustedly.

"What do you mean?"

"All this nonsense about being scared. It doesn't sound like you at all."

"I just thought—"

"Never mind," he said. He threw a glance over his shoulder at the house. "I know exactly who's putting these ideas in your head. You can stop now."

"I don't know what you mean."

"Shalini, please," he said, sounding tired, "don't you start too."

As much as I wanted to do what I'd promised Amina, I felt relief at being able to drop this charade. He almost never said my name, and it gave me more pleasure than I cared to admit to hear it from his mouth. I fell quiet, and in the silence, I could feel the ease again, building between us, taking a shape that was exactly the shape of the air that separated us, an ease that nonetheless had at its core something primal and alive. I wanted to stand here, not talking, letting that something swim through my body. And, more, I was sure, as sure as I'd ever been of anything, that he felt it too.

Riyaz scratched at the beard on his cheek. "Anyway," he told me, as if we had just left off speaking a second ago, even though several minutes had passed. "I'm not going down tomorrow."

"You're not?"

"No. There is a panchayat meeting after namaz. All the men are supposed to attend, even those from the Hindu village. We're going to discuss the things that have been happening."

"You mean these robbers?"

"Robbers." Riyaz snorted. "They haven't robbed anyone, have they? Probably don't exist. The meeting will be a waste of time, like all those meetings, and it will take at least four or five hours, enough time for everyone to disagree with everyone else, but at least Amina will be happy."

After a while I said, "Amina told me the soldiers sometimes beat you up because you don't answer their questions."

Riyaz glanced sideways at me, then nodded. "It's happened once or twice, yes."

"I don't understand why you'd let them do that to you. Why don't you just answer?"

He fell silent again. I got the sense that he was not used to speaking so much. Then he said, "You already know what the people around here say about my father. What they think he did."

I nodded.

"Then it shouldn't be hard to understand," he said flatly. "My father has decided to hide. That's his choice. But I've done nothing wrong, so I won't hide from anybody. Not from the villagers, and not from the soldiers.

I'm not going to say, 'Yes, sir,' 'No, sir,' 'Sorry, sir' just because some idiot with a gun wants to feel like a king by treating me like a servant."

"You'd rather get beaten up?"

He shrugged.

"And what if they do something worse?" I pressed. "How would your family feel if something happened to you? How would Aaqib feel?"

Even in the shadows, I could see the flush rise in his neck. In a low, stiff voice, he said, "Why do you care? He's not your son."

He was right, of course, but it was like a slap in the face. I thought about Aaqib's damp hand clinging on to mine, his dark eyelashes throwing filigreed shadows on his cheeks, the warm pressure of his head against my arm as he fell asleep in front of the fire.

Minutes passed. "Riyaz," I said, "I'm sorry for what I said. About Aaqib, about the soldiers, your father. You're right, it's none of my business. I shouldn't have said anything. I'm sorry."

He didn't answer me right away. Instead, he drew the piece of wood from his pocket and turned it over a few times in his fingers. I could see that he'd made progress on it in the last few days. I saw a blunt snout, two pert, upright ears.

"I'm sorry for being rude," he said. "Actually, I don't mind talking about it with you." He licked his lips, then gave a short laugh. "To tell you the truth, I've never spoken about these things to anyone else. Not even my own family. But with you, it's different. Easier. I don't know why." He glanced at my face, then back down at the animal in his hand. Then he said, with every appearance of nonchalance, "What is Bangalore like?"

"Bangalore?" I asked, taken by surprise.

"Yes," he said, and I heard a suppressed excitement in his voice. "What is it like?"

I cast my mind back, but Bangalore was very far away, blurry, impossible to envision, let alone evoke. I saw only the shadow-filled living room of our house, my mother's sleeping form. "Well," I said lamely, "there are lots of cars, for one thing. A lot of noise."

Riyaz nodded intently. "Yes, my father told me," he said. "I remember."

And then I thought, with a sudden pang, how dissimilar our lives had been, and yet how similar too. We'd each grown up chasing after a parent, only to lose that parent, though in different ways. I felt a rush of sympathy for him. For a second, I longed to reach out and put my hand on his face, the coin-sized patch of gray hair at his temple. But I controlled myself, and instead I said, in as even a tone as I could manage, "And there are tall buildings everywhere. Fifty, a hundred feet tall."

I went on speaking like this, and slowly his expression relaxed, acquiring an abstract sort of peace. It was as if he'd left me and was walking down a busy Bangalore road, his eyes pulled in a thousand different directions by hawkers, scooters, pedestrians, shops, beggars, and temples competing for his attention. And, as I watched him, a memory lurched to life. My mother, her head lolling against our sofa, listening to Bashir Ahmed's stories. I faltered and fell silent.

Riyaz's head jerked, as if from sleep. "What? Why did you stop?"

"No reason," I said hastily. "I mean, there's too much to tell. It would take a long time."

He smiled. It was the first unguarded smile he'd ever offered me. In mute wonder, I watched as it altered his entire aspect. He looked happy and naughty and self-conscious, as if he were suddenly a kid spending a night away from his parents, instead of a husband and father.

"Well," Riyaz said teasingly, "if there's one good thing about this place, it's that we have nothing but time. I want to hear everything."

I went back up to the house. Riyaz stayed outside, saying he wanted to check on the animals in the barn. I passed the kitchen quickly, not wanting to be stopped and questioned by Amina about how my talk with Riyaz had gone. I caught a brief glimpse of her through the doorway. She was sitting on the straw mat where I had been, her back half turned to me, Aaqib's head resting on her lap. She was stroking his forehead very gently, her own dark head bent toward him. When I saw that, a sharp thread of pain stretched from my chest all the way under my left armpit, as if I'd run into a length of barbed wire, and I quickly moved out of sight.

I put a hand on the rough mud wall of the corridor, trying to ease the pain. Then I made a quick decision. It was risky—Amina was barely ten feet away and Riyaz might return to the house any minute—but I was determined. I tiptoed up the corridor to their bedroom, then, peering once over my shoulder, slipped inside.

Their bedroom was exactly as I remembered, the mattress, the piles of clothes, the rickety chair, the slender shadowy barrel of the gun propped up in the corner, but I gave it all no more than a glance. I made straight for the white curtain, pulled it aside, and entered the passageway. There was the smell of wood and varnish, and, as before, a warm draft gusted about my ankles. But no light leaked into the passageway; the room on the other side was in darkness.

I stepped into Bashir Ahmed's room. The jagged silhouette of the paper streamers shivered above me. I had to take only one look at the shape under the blanket to know that he was asleep. I hesitated then quietly approached the bed.

He was on his side, facing the entryway. The cheek that was not pressed to the pillow had sunk under the tug of gravity, making him seem especially skeletal. His beard was only a few days old; Riyaz probably helped him shave from time to time. His eyelids were waxy and creased, and they twitched slightly as I bent down, causing me a moment's alarm, but his eyes did not open. I bent even closer, absorbing the features of his face with hunger, but more than that, with a sadness that took me by surprise. As a child, I'd never thought to wonder about his age, whether he was an old or a young man, but now it occurred to me that he looked much older than his years should have allowed. For his hair had gone completely white, and there was an unhealthy pallor to his once dark forehead. His lips were slack and undefined, and his frame itself had shrunk to half its size. I felt an emotion I could not put a name to, though in it was a widening sense of loss, the loss of the tall, strong man who'd grinned and swung his yellow bundle onto his shoulders like it was nothing, who'd walked all day in the sun to reach the cool shadows of our house. In his sleep, Bashir Ahmed moaned and shifted onto his back, his lips falling back to expose teeth that were no longer white, no longer even. I straightened up, looking down at his gaunt, sleeping face.

"You're afraid of something," I whispered. "I don't know what, but I can promise you one thing. I'm not going anywhere until you talk to me."

Touching the blanket with my fingertips at the place over his chest, I backed away toward the entrance. Ducking into Amina's and Riyaz's room, I saw that I'd been lucky. It was empty. I quickly slipped out of their room and up the corridor, closing the door as soon as I was in mine.

27

THE MORNING I LEFT for college, my mother, for the first time in my life, asked me to prostrate myself in front of her gods. She stood beside me as I did this, and the whole time my forehead was resting on the cold kitchen tiles, I watched her feet, the silver rings on her second toes, her cracked heels and unpainted nails. Then, feeling a little light-headed, I stood and faced her. She was dressed in an old kurta, her hair dry and split at the ends, her lips as cracked as her heels. Pulling my head down to her mouth—by eighteen I was taller than she was, and she was not a short woman—she planted a dry kiss on my forehead. I'm not proud to admit it, but I was at that point in my teenage life when the prolonged touch of either of my parents was unwelcome, and as soon as I'd left the kitchen, I wiped away the imprint of her lips with the edge of my sleeve.

The university at which I'd been accepted was on the coast, a seven-hour drive from Bangalore. *Accepted* was a generous word; my final school grades had been mediocre at best. In fact, my father had been required to make a "donation" to the institution just to secure a seat for me in the Bachelor of Commerce stream. To everybody's surprise, he'd been adamant about my attending this college, which was an overnight bus journey away, instead of any one of a dozen colleges within the city, which would have been just as easy, and probably less expensive. Now I wonder if his insistence might not have had something to do with my mother, a lingering instinct, perhaps, that it might not hurt me to be parted from her a little. For, in the years since Bashir Ahmed and the dinner party, my father had changed too. It is only fair, I think, to mention this. In my lifelong preoccupation with my mother, I do not wish to forget him, the man whose life has always been present, unfolding beside mine and my mother's, even if I did not always see it back then. For so many years when I was younger, he had seemed so wrapped up in his factory and its mysterious workings, so sure of himself and of the world, so full of lectures and judgments and certainties, that he appeared to exist beyond my sight, and it wasn't until just before I left for college that I realized all the ways he'd softened, grown unsure and therefore understandable. He was more private, less inclined to speak, and though he still lectured me from time to time, his lectures took on a wry, self-mocking tone, as though he knew his tendency toward bombast and was asking me, with a sad, fatherly wink, to indulge him. He was more patient with my mother, her sleeping, her moods, her anger that leapt from nowhere and disappeared into the same unfathomable place. None of this happened overnight, of course. He lost his temper often, and every time he did so, he would grab the car keys and slam the front door, returning sometimes within ten minutes, sometimes not for an hour or more.

He was forty-seven when I left for college, as handsome as he had always been, the owner of a company that was fast becoming a significant local competitor to long-established foreign firms, and he was successful and accomplished by nearly all the world's metrics. Nobody who looked at him would have felt sorry for him, and yet, when he appeared at my bedroom door as I was packing the last of my things, I felt a sadness for him that had nothing to do with my departure.

"All set?" he asked.

I nodded. He looked around my room, the cupboard hanging open and mostly empty. He came in and sat down on my bed. "You know," he said, "I never went back to my own parents' house after college. This could be the last time you live in this room."

It wouldn't be, of course. I would sleep in this same bed the night after my mother's death, but neither of us could have known that then.

"I just want to say—" he began, but I would never know what it was he wanted to say. My mother came to stand in the doorway. Her cheekbones carved her face in half.

"Having a little heart-to-heart?" she drawled. "How adorable. Like a movie."

My father actually blushed. As always, she had the power to make him falter. "We should go," he said, standing up. "I just came to take Shalini's suitcase downstairs."

We piled into the car, my suitcase in the boot, and began the drive down to the coast. My mother slept in the car, and I sat in the back and watched her face in the round bowl of the side mirror. Villages, hamlets, towns slipped by; lorries wheezed under loads of iron rods and bricks and timber. The car pitched over a pothole, and my mother's head banged off the closed window. Her eyes flew open, and she stared ahead at the road, though without terror or recognition or any kind of emotion at all. A second later, she was asleep again.

Seven hours later, we arrived at the campus, a dozen dreary vanilla-and-charcoal buildings with slivers of grass wedged between them. My father, who wasn't allowed up into the girls' hostel, stayed with the car, and it was my mother who walked me up to my room, with its two narrow plywood beds, who greeted my shy roommate, Rupa. She looked around, and I imagine she was thinking of the college life I was to have, the one she never did. We went downstairs, and she waited to the side until my father had hugged me. I expected her to speak, to say something cryptic, faintly sarcastic, but she merely took hold of both my shoulders and stared into my face, a long stare that I desperately wanted to break, but forced myself to hold. I also had to will myself not to cover my nose; she had neglected to brush her teeth before we left the house, and her breath stank of coffee and sour, half-digested food. Then they got into the car and my father carefully reversed.

I was on the verge of turning away, to face the bland building that was now my home, when the passenger side window came down, and my mother's head appeared. It was followed by her shoulders, then her entire torso and hips. The car was now moving at full speed. Sitting in the open car window, her hair loosened from its messy bun and streaming in the wind, my mother raised both arms into the air. "My daughter is a champion!" she screamed. "Do you hear me, all of you? My daughter is a champion!" My father hit the horn hard. Curious faces appeared at the windows of the buildings around me, and I had to turn my head to hide the tears in my eyes.

28

RIYAZ, AS HE HAD promised, did not go down the mountain the next day. He hung around the house all morning, instead, ostensibly doing things that needed doing—using a rusted pair of pliers to fix a wire on the makeshift chicken coop at the side of the house, darning a tear in one of the sacks that he threw over the backs of the mules—but it seemed that each time I looked up from whatever task Amina had assigned me, he was no more than ten feet away, watching me. It discomfited me and at the same time sent a wave of warmth shooting over every inch of my skin. In the late morning, when I came out of the house to shake the dust from the straw mat in the kitchen, he came up to me and said quietly, "Do you know what I was thinking?"

I shook my head, hoping Amina would not come out and see us.

"I was thinking how much fun it would be to work in a shop. My father used tell me about all the different shops in Bangalore, you know, how they sold everything you could ever think of. Even shops full of new cars! What do you think? Could you see me doing that?"

I looked down at the dusty mat. "What kind of shop would you want to work in?"

"That's the only problem," he said with enthusiasm. "I can't make up my mind. Clothes would be nice, don't you think? Or shoes? I could see myself selling shoes. Couldn't you?"

I thought of the shoe shop that stood beside Zoya and Abdul Latief's house in Kishtwar, the boy in the white cap I'd always seen scurrying around with boxes under his arm. Then I thought of the Kashmiri shop on Commercial Street where I'd gone with my mother and Bashir Ahmed, the overly polite man with rings on his fingers. I thought of all the shopkeepers my mother had insulted and ignored over the years, the vegetable vendor who'd flung the tomato to the ground in rage. But Riyaz was watching me, expectation written all over his face, so I said, "Yes."

My answer obviously pleased him, because he winked—as if we now had some sort of secret between us—and wandered back into the house, whistling, on the way passing Amina, who was emerging from the house, wet clothes in her arms. She stared at him as though he were a stranger then looked quickly at me. There was nothing accusatory in her gaze, but still I couldn't hold it. I pretended that a bit of the soot from the mat had got into my eyes and squeezed them shut.

Riyaz remained in a good mood for the next few hours, and when Aaqib came home from school, he chased him all about the front porch, growling, "I am one of the robbers! Watch out! I am going to eat you!" Aaqib squealed and took refuge in the gnarled peach tree while Riyaz paced around below, snarling, pretending to be a robber or a lion or a leopard, I couldn't tell what. I watched them from my window, until I saw Amina step out from the house. She was watching them, too, and smiling. I turned away quickly, a strange hot feeling in my chest.

Riyaz strolled off to the mosque for the afternoon namaz, after which, I knew, would be the panchayat meeting. I went over to Sania's house but found her distracted, her attention wandering away from our work. All she wanted to do was talk about the meeting, what her father might say or do, what decisions would be made. Eventually, I ended the lesson early and trudged back home.

Riyaz's mother was in the kitchen, stoking the fire.

"Amina?" I said, making it a question; it was as far as our communication could go. She nodded toward the back of the house. I sat down to wait, and soon Amina came to the kitchen holding a glass and a plate. Seeing me, she stiffened, as if she had been caught doing something illegal. I knew right away that she had been with Bashir Ahmed. "Back so early, Murgi?" she asked, attempting casualness.

"How is he?" I asked.

"The same."

"Did you ask him about me yet?"

"No," she said quickly. Then she added, "But I will, Murgi. I promise."

There was a spot of color in each of her cheeks, and I knew, looking at her, that on this point she would not yield. Was it because she was afraid for Bashir Ahmed's health, as she'd claimed, afraid that he would fall sick from the shock of seeing me again? Or was there something else? Was she trying to keep me here longer, perhaps? As a companion, as a friend, or whatever she imagined me to be, someone to help her ward off the solitude of her days? She had already confessed as much, hadn't she, that afternoon at the waterfall? And, if so, what did that say about me? If, as I had come to believe, I considered her a friend, too, then how could I allow myself to stand with Riyaz in the intimacy of darkness? How could I allow his gaze to linger on me, indeed, half desiring it myself? What sort of friend did that make me? Strangely, the mustached face of the subedar came into my mind. *People like you don't have friends in Kashmiri villages.* I felt a rush of guilt, then of anger, though I did not know if it was directed at the subedar or against myself.

Now she walked over to the window and looked out. "It's getting late," she murmured. "I don't know what's taking so long. The meeting should have been over long ago."

"Riyaz said it would probably take a few hours," I said, regretting it instantly.

But she didn't reply, didn't even seem to register that I'd spoken. For a long time, she looked out at the yard and the mountains; then she turned to Riyaz's mother and said something brief in Kashmiri. Riyaz's mother nodded, and Amina turned to me.

"Want to go for a walk, Murgi?" she asked.

"A walk? Now?"

She shrugged. "I just thought we could go to the mosque and back. It won't take long."

I raised an eyebrow. "You mean, where they'll be having the panchayat meeting?"

"We would never *disturb* them, of course," she said with a show of wide-eyed innocence. "I mean, if we're *close* by, and we happen to hear *some* of what they're talking about, well, then where's the harm?" She smiled wryly. "Lucky for us, Murgi, men usually like to shout."

We heard raised voices long before we approached the mosque. Instead of arriving at it dead on, as she ordinarily would have done, Amina beckoned to me and skirted through the tall grass and weeds around to the back. "Up here," she said, and shimmied neatly up a walnut tree.

From up amongst the branches, she peered down at me. "Need my help?" she whispered.

I shook my head, eyeing the tree. It was a thick one, and there was only one reasonable hold in the bark, which Amina had found with ease. I put my palms against the trunk and took a breath, then hauled myself up. My heel slipped, but I managed with an ungraceful flailing of my right leg to keep my footing. Once I was perched beside her, Amina gave me a nod. "Not bad," she whispered.

We arranged ourselves where we could see the men, gathered before the mosque. Most were standing, but a few—the members of the panchayat, I guessed, for Mohammad Din was amongst them—were sitting on plastic chairs. There seemed to be very little order, for several people were talking at once. Then someone called impatiently for quiet, and in the silence, the stocky man with slim fingers, the same one who'd first complained to Mohammad Din of the robbers, stepped forward. "Enough of this. All day we've been here, arguing about who saw what, and whether they really saw it, and the whole time, our wives and children are alone at home, where anything might be happening to them. Why won't you just believe us? Are you calling us liars?"

Everyone, instinctively, it seemed, looked toward Mohammad Din. He pinched the bridge of his nose in a tired way before replying, "Nobody is calling anybody anything. We are trying to understand exactly what happened, so we can all be prepared."

The stocky man snorted. "Prepared? You want to be prepared, why don't you ask *them*? It's *their* political parties doing this." He nodded to a small group of men standing slightly apart from the rest. Each of them wore a red tilak on his forehead, and I remembered Riyaz telling me the Hindu men would be attending the meeting, too.

There was a threatening stir in the crowd at his words. Mohammad Din glanced warningly at the stocky man, who subsided, but the damage was done.

"What do you mean by that?" one of the Hindu men called out shrilly. "*Our* parties are doing this? As if these same things aren't happening in our own village. As if *we* aren't worried about our families. You say you've been here all day. Then haven't you heard us telling the same stories that you have been telling? Are *we* the liars, then?"

"Please, let us not argue," Mohammad Din said firmly. "All of you listen to me."

He didn't raise his voice, but there was a hush nonetheless at his words. He stood up from his plastic chair and looked around at them, with the same grave, intent expression he gave me during our conversations, when, over a cup of tea, he outlined his plans for the village, when he invited me to stay and be a teacher.

"This is our home," he said. "It has always been our home, and we are the only ones responsible for it. Nobody, here or anywhere else, is going to help us. We already know that. You people want to fight about politicians, about elections? Fine. But then leave me out of it. That's not why I joined this panchayat, to sit around and argue about which party is to blame for what. If there are men in black clothes going around and making trouble in the middle of the night, whoever they are, we'll have to catch them. That is all I know. Hindu or Mussulman, your politician or mine, it makes no difference to me." He raised his voice slightly. "Our Hindu brothers want proof of our loyalty? Then here is your proof: We will come and stand before your houses at night to protect your families." He hit his chest softly with his fist for emphasis. "I am an old man, but I will come myself and do it."

There was a hush. Both the stocky man and the man from the Hindu village who'd responded looked shamefaced. Mohammad Din gazed around gravely then said, "Now, we must end this silly fighting and discuss seriously what we can do. How can we help each other?"

"We could make a committee," someone suggested.

"Good," Mohammad Din said. "A committee. That's a good idea."

"We could do night duty," someone else piped up.

He nodded. "Yes. Yes. That is also a good idea."

"I do not doubt your loyalty." This was the same Hindu man who had spoken before. "I respect what you said, but what I want to know is this: What happens if things become worse?"

"Worse?" Mohammad Din frowned. "What do you mean?"

"I mean, worse." The man hesitated. He was middle-aged, with a prominent Adam's apple and deep-set, mournful eyes. "Today we may only be dealing with loafers and mischief makers, but what if the next time, it is something else? We all remember what happened five years ago. Those men who were killed were Hindus too, and their Muslim neighbors did nothing. What if the same thing happens again?"

Amina's arm flinched against mine. The crowd seemed to grow agitated, and at the same time I caught sight of Riyaz. He was leaning against a tree at the edge of the gathering. At least five people had been blocking our view of him all this while, and though I could have sworn that none of them had moved an inch, all of a sudden, he seemed to be standing alone in a pool of silence, the men on either side melting away like ice, their eyes on the ground.

Mohammad Din cleared his throat. "That will never happen again," he declared, but it seemed that he, too, was reluctant to look very long at Riyaz.

"But can you promise us such a thing?" the Hindu man asked. Emboldened, another Hindu man called, "Yes, can you promise? Mischief makers are all very well, but will you still be standing in front of our houses, protecting our families, when some militant is holding a gun to your face? Will you be standing there when you know that the person who ordered such a thing is one of your own?"

And as much as I willed him to, Mohammad Din did not reply. He stood there, leaning on his cane, speechless for the first time since I'd known him.

"That is what I thought," the first Hindu man said with bitter satisfaction. "All of this talking, this discussion, it sounds nice, but it comes to nothing when there are real lives at risk."

All this while, Riyaz hadn't stirred, but now he detached himself from the tree and began to walk, people stepping aside as he approached, faces turned away. Mohammad Din went quickly up to him, put a hand on his shoulder, and began talking softly and urgently to him. I couldn't hear what he was saying, but Riyaz shook his head and pulled away. He gave the gathering a last glance of profound contempt, then began walking away, in the direction of home, a solitary figure.

There was a flash of movement beside me. Amina was clambering out of the tree. I tried to follow her but soon fell behind, and for once she did not turn around to check that I was all right. She caught up to Riyaz just before the house.

He turned and stopped. She did the same. Neither of them knew that I was behind her.

Then she touched his face. She put her hand over the smudge of gray hair at his temple, the very place I had imagined touching, and left it there, looking into his face. Watching that was more painful than I could have anticipated, and I hated myself for it. Then, after what felt like hours, she let her hand drop and went inside, but he remained where he was. At last, he lifted his eyes and saw me standing there. He came toward me, and I didn't know what I wanted. To hug him tight or to run, though I didn't know from or toward what.

"You saw it, too," he said. It wasn't a question. "You were there."

"I'm sorry," I said. "It was horrible."

He shrugged. "I'm used to it by now."

"But it's so unfair," I said.

"That is why I hate this village, Shalini," he told me, "and all the people in it. After what happened, not one person, not even *one*, came up to my mother and offered support. We were completely alone. And when you're alone like that, you have only two choices." He looked over my shoulder. "You stay and put up with it. Or you leave."

A single crow swooped down from the pine tree. Its black shape made a slow circle. There was a heavy feeling of nausea in my stomach.

"Sometimes," Riyaz said. His voice was strange, and there was a weird, fixed smile on his face. "I have a feeling that this isn't my life. That I'm not even here. That I'm somewhere else . . ."

The crow swung up, hovered in midair, then dropped into the corn as neatly as a stone into a pool of water. I waited but it didn't come up again.

"Where?" I asked finally.

"Does it matter?" he asked with the same fixed smile.

"Of course it matters."

"To whom?"

"To everybody. To Amina, obviously. To your mother."

Then he asked, "Does it matter to you?"

The question caught me unawares, and it took a second before I said, softly, "Yes."

But he'd noted the pause and, to my dismay, he misread the reason for it. "Clearly you're not sure," he said. His smile became hard.

I wanted to shout, *No, no, you're wrong!* but my tongue had turned to stone.

"And what if I told you I saw myself in Bangalore?" he asked.

It shouldn't have surprised me, but it did. It was a measure of how naïve I was, that I had assumed that all these days when he looked at me, when we stood together on the porch and I heard his breath quicken, it was out of mere physical desire. I had yet to understand just how many shapes a person's desire could take, and how few of them, in the end, took the shape of the body.

"Would that matter to you?" he went on in that same softly insinuating voice. "Would it matter so much that you'd be willing to take me there?"

I didn't answer. His face was a mere inch from mine. Amina could have walked out and seen us. Anyone could have seen us, but I still didn't move.

"Would you take me, Shalini?" he repeated. "When you go?"

I thought of Amina squeezing water from her clothes, lying in the sun, eyes closed. Walking ahead of me, hands clasped behind her back, turning around to say, "All right back there, Murgi?" I thought of the job that had been offered to me, the life I could have here if only I chose to accept it.

Riyaz's mouth twitched, but he continued to hold my gaze, waiting for me to reply.

I see us as we were then, standing eye to eye, laboring hard under the illusion that we were cynical and cold, that our respective tragedies had inured us, put us permanently beyond the reach of further suffering, when the truth was that we were as terrified and lost as babies. Aaqib was probably wiser than the two of us put together.

"I don't know," I whispered.

A laugh escaped him, a huffing, wheezing laugh that came through clenched teeth. "You don't know," he said, nearly spitting the words. He stepped back and gave me a look that held just as much contempt as the one he'd given the men at the meeting. "That's what I thought. You're the same as all of them."

29

I HAD NOT EXPECTED to like college. I wasn't sure why. But from the minute my parents drove away, my mother's hair snapping in the wind, I was armored, prepared to dismiss each of my lecturers, my fellow students, to look down on all of it. I suppose it was, like so many other things, a trick I'd learned from my mother. To keep approval in reserve, to lead with mockery and distrust, for to reveal affection was to reveal weakness. In a few short weeks, however, I found myself genuinely interested by the things I was learning—accounting, economic theory, commerce. I liked sitting in the tiered hall listening to my balding professor drone on about partial returns, pleasantly conscious of the anonymity of it all, the long, curving desks scratched by a hundred bored students, the screech of chalk, the cleared throats, the scrape of pen on paper. I raised my hand to clarify doubts and made copious notes, taking pleasure in the neat rows of definitions, the columns of numbers, each question tagged gratifyingly with an answer, and bit by bit, I felt my resistance falling away.

Every Sunday, I talked to my parents. It was 2000, and most students still did not own a cell phone, unless their parents were diplomats or very wealthy. There was a mounted landline phone the color of curdled milk by the staircase at the end of my hostel corridor. I'd stand, absently wrapping the spiral cord around my finger, looking down from the window at the parking lot and, beyond that, at the basketball court. There was a group of girls who played sometimes, always at night, their legs long and liquid in the floodlights, their hair whipping, making dark shapes about their heads, the ball ringing loud on the concrete. I'd watch them as I listened to my parents' voices. "When are your first tests?" my father would want to know. "Have they started microeconomics yet? You'll enjoy that. What about Rupa, how is she? Tell her to come stay with us in Bangalore." Then, his voice changing, "Hold on a second, here's Amma." Sometimes she wouldn't come to the phone for nearly a minute. I'd wait, growing edgier by the second. Then I would hear her voice, far away, as if she hadn't bothered to lift the receiver to her face. "Tell me," she'd say, "how are things at the big, fancy college?" And that would set off in me a wave of irrational rage. "Fine," I'd say. She'd wait, and knowing perfectly well she wanted more, even if she couldn't bring herself to ask for it, I'd say, in a flat tone, "I have to go, Amma." Her disappointment saturating the silence that followed. "Already?" "Yes, I've got to study. We've got tests next week." Her voice, growing softer: "Oh. I see. Well, then, goodnight." A click in my ear, the terrible squawk of the dial tone. I'd watch the basketball girls for a while longer, then return to my room.

Instead of going home for the Diwali holidays in November, I made an excuse to my parents, and I went with a group of older students to the coast for the weekend. We lounged under tatty, colorful umbrellas, drinking beer and talking far too loudly. One of them was an MBA student, the son of the owner of the largest toy company in the country. The toy-king's son drove a dark blue Mercedes and had a cell phone, and he was drunker than any of us. He tried to kiss me later that night, but I pushed him away, and he staggered back, wiping his mouth. "Such an ice queen," he laughed. "Why? Your mummy told you to stay away from boys in college?" I shrugged, but his words cut deeper than I wanted to admit. Each time I caught sight of him across campus from then on, he would hug himself and shiver, then nudge his friends and laugh.

But apart from that minor unpleasantness, I was all right. I liked my roommate, Rupa. She almost never spoke, but she loved potato chips, had an obsession with them, and so I'd buy her enormous bags of chips from the college canteen and leave them on her bed, just for the pleasure of seeing her face light up when she found them. I know she liked me, too, and if things had been different, if she had been less shy, perhaps, or if I had been less guarded, we might have become real friends, but we never did. As it was, whenever I felt myself starting to want to confess something, to tell her about my mother's infuriating behavior, for example, I left the room instead, ending up walking alone around campus until I heard the bell for curfew.

It was with a sense of apprehension that I went home for Christmas. I had never been away from my parents this long, and I did not know how I might find my mother. Would it be the sleeping and the coldness? Or would it be the plotting, the glittering eyes? But it was neither. My mother seemed simply tired and glad to see me, and at first, ashamed as I am to admit it now, I was disappointed.

How to explain that? To start with, let me say that it would be disingenuous to pretend that my apprehension in going home had to do only with her, or rather, with how I might find her. Because, for the first time in my life, I was also wondering how she might find me. I wanted her to see my new adult mind, my confidence, the way I'd learned to carry myself in college. I wanted, I'll admit, to impress her. I wanted her to see me as an equal, no longer a child, wanted to outplay her at her own games of wit and derision, and so I was cool to her, made caustic replies whenever she asked me questions (she asked very few), smiled distantly when she spoke to me, bending my head as though I'd risen so far above her that it was difficult to hear her at all. I executed this plan with about as much grace and skill as might be expected of a teenager, and on my third evening home, after I'd said something particularly obnoxious, my mother stood up. Addressing nobody, she said, "The air in here is a bit stuffy, isn't it? Must be all the college education."

She left the room. Seething, I turned to my father. He had seemed preoccupied the past few days, unusually so, even for him, and he barely seemed to notice my mother's exit.

"God, what's wrong with her?" I fumed, wanting him to agree, to become my collaborator, to join with me in condemning her, but he just sat there, drink in hand, while Simon and Garfunkel sang "Mrs. Robinson" in the background. "She thinks the whole world revolves around her," I went on. "Why can't she just be *fucking* normal, like other people?"

At the expletive, my father blinked and looked up, as I had hoped. But when he spoke, it was only to say, "You know I love you, Shalini, and I'm proud of you, but the way you've been behaving to her these past few days, I'm surprised she didn't walk out sooner."

"Why are you shouting at *me*? I didn't do anything."

"I'm not shouting. I'm just saying that you could be a little nicer to her," he added softly.

"Nice?" I stared at him. "After all the things she's said to me over the years? The things she's said to you? You want me to be *nice*?"

I was trembling. I didn't know where the rage had come from, or how long it had been growing in me, but I was incandescent with it. But my father only dropped his shoulders and shook his head, and I knew that he would not fight me. I stormed off and shut myself into my room.

I returned to college early in the new year, carefully nursing the embers of my rage. The same day, I saw the toy-king's son, who went through his usual hug-and-shiver charade, while his moronic friends fell over themselves chuckling. Instead of ignoring him, as I'd learned to do, I let my feet grind to a halt, then made my way straight up to him. He was sitting on the hood of his Mercedes, and he flinched as I approached, as if I might intend to hit him. I wasn't sure myself that I didn't. But all I did was nod my head toward the car and say, "Let's go for a drive." His eyes widened, but he did as I asked, while his friends gawped. We drove in silence to the beach, to the black-and-white lighthouse on the rock, at the base of which, surrounded by the detritus of discarded beer bottles, squashed cigarette butts, and cloudy plastic bags, I let him push my knees into the gritty sand, hating myself, hating her. Exactly as she promised I would.

30

EVEN BEFORE I OPENED my eyes, the morning after the panchayat meeting, I knew something was amiss in the house. I walked up the corridor to the kitchen; Aaqib was sitting there with his grandmother, who was working on the milk churn that stood in the darkest corner. The churn was a long, thin wooden pole that extended all the way down from a hook in the ceiling and disappeared into a pot; wound around it was a length of sturdy rope. The ends of this rope were now wrapped around Riyaz's mother's knuckles. She pulled first one, then the other, and the pole spun in the milk with a high-pitched moaning sound. When she saw me, she nodded toward the fire, where a pot of tea was simmering. Nobody served me anymore, and I took it as a compliment. I moved to sit on the straw mat and ladled myself a cup of tea.

"No school, Aaqib?" I asked.

He shook his head, eyes downcast. Just then Amina entered the kitchen, her face sweating and flushed, a bundle of firewood in her arms. She let it clatter down in a corner, then picked up a few sticks, sitting down across from me and leaning over to place them in the fire. She wouldn't meet my eyes. She leaned back, her fingers interlaced around her knees, rocking back and forth.

"Aren't we going to milk the cow?" I asked her, trying to sound light.

"I milked her myself," she said, not looking at me. "I woke up early. You were still sleeping."

"Oh," I said. Then, after a few seconds had gone by, I asked, "Where's Riyaz?"

Her mouth tightened. "He went down the mountain," she said.

"Oh," I said again. I glanced at Riyaz's mother, who had not stopped her churning. The squeak of the churn sounded forlornly through the kitchen. Aaqib was curled into a miserable little ball, watching his grandmother's hands as they moved back and forth.

"I'm sorry, Amina," I said. "I did try talking to him." But even as I said it, I was aware of my mendacity. Because I had not tried, had I? Not really. Instead, I'd chosen the coward's way, chosen to stand there, letting his eyes seek out my own, imagining that I saw in them a hunger for me, which had turned out, in the end, to be a hunger for something else entirely.

Amina looked up. "I know, Murgi," she said softly. "It's not your fault. I just hope nothing happens to him, that's all."

I thought of all the stories Bashir Ahmed had told us over the years about this place, of chudails that could snare you and leopards no man could kill, and to these I now added the dangers that I had come to discover: militants and soliders, bears and broken legs, nighttime intruders whose goals were unknown. "Nothing will happen," I said with a confidence I did not feel. "You'll see."

The atmosphere in the house stayed tense all day. Amina worked, mostly alone, while Aaqib moped around on the front porch. I tried to entice him out of the house, suggesting a walk to the shop to buy sweets, but he just shook his head. When Riyaz's mother came out of the house with a sickle in her hand, I went up to her on impulse. I pointed at my chest and then at Aaqib and then the sickle. She understood in a second what I was asking, and I could see her hesitate. She glanced at her grandson, and a softer look came into her face. She nodded then slipped on her plastic sandals.

"Coming, Aaqib?" I asked. When he looked reluctant, I added, "Come on. I need you to teach me. Otherwise, I'll cut my hand off." I waggled my hand, then pretended to scream as it was severed from the rest of my body. He finally gave me a smile, tucking his hand into my outstretched one. I caught sight of Amina as we left. She was shading her eyes, watching us, but she said nothing.

We headed downhill from the house, past the cornfield and the pine tree that marked the boundary of their land. The land dropped off steeply here, but the grass grew thick and plentiful. Riyaz's mother stepped off the path, her body almost parallel to the mountain, and began to seize handfuls of grass, cutting them close to the base with the same smooth motion. After a few minutes, she gathered up a great sheaf of green then handed the sickle to me. I grasped it, feeling the wood warm where her fingers had been, her sweat making the handle slick. I made my way cautiously off the path, Aaqib following me, showing me where to cut. I squatted and began to hack away. With a frown that reminded me of Amina, he said, "No, not like that. More smoothly." The grass felt rough in my fingers, but it was a warm, living roughness, like that of a dog's matted fur. In a few hours, I would start to feel the cuts, the hundreds of razor-thin edges making invisible wounds on my wrists and palms, making them sting, but for the moment, I was aware of nothing but the crisp snap of the stalks, the warm green smell that rose from my fingers, Aaqib, no longer morose, but animated, issuing a flood of instructions, the sun hot and welcome on my back and neck; and when we displayed the bundle to Riyaz's mother, I thought I caught on her face the faintest flicker of a smile.

* * *

Sania was waiting for me on the porch, as always. We went together into the room with the tall windows. I had her read from her history textbook; then I asked her questions about what she'd read. She answered with her fist clenched, thumb tucked in. When we were finished, Mohammad Din walked in. He was leaning on a thin wooden cane this evening.

"Salaam alaikum," he said.

"Walaikum salaam," we responded together. "Are you all right?" I asked, when Sania had gone off to make tea.

He set the cane against the wall and lowered himself down. "Oh, I'm fine, I'm fine. Just tired. Usually I try to forget that I am an old man, but on some days, I am forced to remember."

"How was the panchayat meeting?" I asked.

"Very good," he replied, though his enthusiasm seemed less convincing than usual. "It went very well. It could not have been better."

I glanced at him, wondering whether to say anything about our eavesdropping; then I decided he might not take it kindly. "I'm glad to hear it," I said.

"Yes, we made a lot of progress," he declared firmly. "A lot of progress."

"How nice," I said. "You must be pleased."

"I am, I am." He then proceeded to tell me of the results of the meeting, the committee that had been set up, which he referred to as a "peace committee," the daily evening patrols that the men of both villages would carry out until everything was judged to be safe. I don't know what prompted me, but when he fell silent, I asked, "Will Riyaz be on these patrols?"

"Why do you ask that?" he said, frowning.

I shrugged. "He seemed a little upset when he got back from the meeting, that's all."

"Ah," Mohammad Din said. "Well, since you asked, no, I don't think he will be."

"Why not?" I asked.

Mohammad Din's forehead tightened. "Well, it's a little complicated," he said delicately.

I thought of the look on Riyaz's face the previous night as all those men melted away, leaving him in a circle of isolation. "I thought maybe you didn't want him to join because of Bashir Ahmed," I said, adding, "Because of what people say Bashir Ahmed did."

Mohammad Din glanced down. "So Amina finally told you," he said.

I nodded. After a second, he shrugged. "Then there is no reason for me to pretend," he said. "Yes, that is why I think it better that Riyaz does not join the patrol. His presence would cause anger, amongst the Hindu villagers, especially, and that is not what is needed right now."

"Then you think it is true, what they say about Bashir Ahmed?" I asked. "You said the other day that it was foreign militants who killed those Hindus, not Kashmiris."

"It *was* foreign militants," Mohammad Din said quickly. "But it was no secret that Bashir was involved with them." He sighed. "Look, it is very possible that Bashir did nothing at all. But how can I explain to you what it was like, the time of the militancy? It was a very strange time, and one I hope I never have to live through again. It made people turn into the opposite of what they were, made them do all kinds of things they would never have otherwise done. Bashir was the last person I would have expected to do a thing like that, and yet..." He shook his head. "Now you see why I do not like to talk about this. It is a very sad subject for me."

"But," I objected, "even if it was true, why should Riyaz suffer? He's done nothing."

"I know," Mohammad Din said, and this time there was a note of real sadness in his voice. "Believe me, I have done all I can for him. I give him work when nobody else does. I make sure that Khadijah Begum gets her medicines. I've even given them money when they needed extra.

But there are times when I also need to think about the others in my panchayat. I need to consider their feelings, too. It isn't fair to Riyaz, I understand that, but I cannot change the past. All I can do now is make sure the future is peaceful. For *all* our people."

Sania came back in with the tea, and we dropped the subject. We talked about other things for a while, then Mohammad Din set his cup on the floor and clapped his hands. I looked up. His mood had altered completely, the sadness caused by Bashir Ahmed gone. He was suddenly smiling.

"Now," he said, "I did not want to rush you, but my daughter here keeps pestering me, and so I must ask: Have you had a chance to think more about what we discussed the other day? About teaching? Have you decided what you would like to do?"

I don't know what I might have said if I'd had much longer to think, but at that moment, I caught sight of Sania's face. It was pinched with anxiousness, and her lips were pale. And I thought, for the first time in years, about Suneyna. After I had said whatever I'd said to her mother in the corridor, I'd come back into the classroom and continued to help Suneyna build her tower. She pointed politely to a red block or a green one, which she had never done before, and thanked me when I handed them to her. It would have killed me to admit it at the time, but *this* was the thing that prevented me from ever going back to the school. Not shame at my behavior, not the disgusted looks of the other teacher. Simply the idea that she, an eight-year-old girl, was *tolerating* me. Now I watched Sania, whose thumb was tucked into her fist, as was her habit when she was concentrating, whose lips were moving, as if she were mouthing the words she wanted me to say, and I felt a surge of love that was so strong my vision went dark for a second. And it was impossible for me to say then, as it is now, just who that love stretched to encompass.

And I heard myself say, "I want to stay."

There was a second of quiet, and the room seemed to erupt as Sania threw her arms around me in delight, nearly knocking me to the ground and upsetting the teacups, as Mohammad Din laughed and thumped my back and said, over and over, "Well done!" In the middle of the commotion, I closed my eyes and repeated the words in a softer voice, as though some invisible person were listening in the corner. "I want to stay."

I went back to the house in a strange, floating mood, caught somewhere between elation and apprehension. Amina was sitting in the kitchen, and for the first time since I'd arrived in the village, she was doing nothing at all. It was unsettling to see her hands idle, hung loose over her knees like the wet clothes she hung on the line. She was staring into the fire. All the way home, I'd rehearsed the announcement that I would be staying, bracing myself for their various reactions, but the sight of her anxious figure made me forget my excitement. I hurried over to her.

"Amina, is everything okay? What's wrong?"

"Riyaz." Her voice was thick. "He hasn't come back yet."

I glanced outside at the sky, which still held some light. "It isn't that late. The azan hasn't even gone. Don't worry, Amina. He'll be back."

She nodded. I didn't want to leave her alone, so I sat down on the other side of the fire and tried to distract her with bright, inconsequential questions, to which she responded with a shrug or a single word. Aaqib came in silently and sat next to me. As he did so, his foot grazed a plate of flour that was sitting by the fire, and Amina turned harshly on him. "Careful!" she snapped. "Are you blind?" He stared at her, his eyes enormous and full of hurt, and she whirled around, muttering.

Half an hour later, the azan began from the mosque, the singer a supple-voiced man with an extraordinary range that would not have been out of place in any concert hall in the world. When it ended, Amina and I glanced at each other; then, as if by some signal, glanced away. After a while, Riyaz's mother came in and began to heat up dinner. It was impossible to tell what she was thinking, whether she too was worried, although it seemed her hand was a little jerkier than usual when she ladled rice onto our plates. Amina shook her head stubbornly when her plate was offered to her.

It was a dreadful meal. Aaqib pushed the food around on his plate without actually eating a bite; Riyaz's mother ate doggedly, not lifting her eyes even once; and in my throat there was a knot of fear so large I could barely swallow. Amina, for her part, appeared unable to sit still; she stood up every few minutes, went to the kitchen window, then came back and sat down. It made my own nerves jangle; I longed to scream at her to stop moving, but I didn't dare.

"He'll be back soon," was all I said, but the assurance began to sound weak, even idiotic. What if the robbers, whoever they were, had caught Riyaz, or injured him? What if he had run into the soldiers? I thought of the way the subedar's finger had brushed his gun, with such familiarity and lightness, and I could not suppress a shudder. Aaqib seemed to sense something of my thoughts, because he gave a corresponding shudder next to me. Without thinking, I put my arm around him and held him close, and he pressed into the crook of my arm. Then I noticed Amina looking in our direction. Her expression was grave, but she did not say a word.

Riyaz was more than two hours late now. It was well past dark. There were lights all over the mountains, but they only made the empty portions seem darker. And then Amina stood up again. Her face was bloodless, and she seemed to sway slightly on her feet. I thought she was going to faint, but she held up a hand.

"Listen," she said.

In the silence, we heard the dull, faraway clang of mule bells. Aaqib made a little whimpering sound, but he didn't stir. Amina stood arrested, her chin thrown upward. The bells sounded again, closer this time and dolefully quick, as if the animals were being chivvied faster than they were used to. Then Riyaz's voice, forceful: "Get on! Move! Up you go."

Amina's eyes glittered.

Nobody in the kitchen moved for what seemed like hours. Then, at last, Riyaz himself appeared in the doorway. He looked exhausted, his mouth set in a grim line. I looked quickly for any signs of injury, but there were none. He came into the kitchen without a word and sat down a little distance from the fire. His mother handed him a plate, and he began to eat, head down and eyes fixed on his food.

Then Amina, who had been frozen all this time, spoke. "Why are you late?" she asked, her voice deadly quiet. "Where were you?"

He didn't answer her.

"What happened?" she asked again, this time louder. "Was it the soldiers? The robbers?"

He shook his head.

"Then what *was* it?"

For some reason, his eyes went to his mother, and it seemed that she knew what he would say before he said it, for she sat up. Then, to my surprise, he looked straight at me.

"There's trouble," he said. "In Kishtwar."

Riyaz had been waiting that evening for a driver, who was coming in from Kishtwar with some goods for Mohammad Din. The driver had not arrived at the appointed time, and when Riyaz tried calling him, there was no answer. He was tempted to leave, but he knew Mohammad Din would not be happy with him, so he waited. Hours later, the driver himself had called, saying that there were mobs on the street in Kishtwar, and he couldn't leave. "Mobs?" Riyaz had asked. And that was when he found out that over the past few days there had been the same strange incidents in Kishtwar, rumors of black-clad intruders, unsettling stories, rising tension between Hindu and Muslim neighbors.

Apparently, early that morning, some Muslims had caught hold of a man they claimed was one of the intruders. He'd turned out to be a young Hindu, and they'd given him a sound thrashing. Within the hour, there were dozens of Hindus on the street, swearing to set fire to Muslim houses. And by the afternoon, a mob of Muslims had formed. The army had been called in to intervene, but not before two more men had been beaten in clashes between mobs. A curfew was promptly declared; the roads were empty. No Muslim in his right mind, the driver informed Riyaz, would be going anywhere tonight. There were rumors that a Muslim neighborhood, close to the mosque, was already on fire.

I thought of Zoya and Abdul Latief, and tasted fear like iron at the back of my throat. Were they all right? Had they been at home when all this violence broke out? I thought of their door at the top of the green steps, and hoped fervently that it was locked. And then, looking at Riyaz's mother, I remembered with a shock that her entire family lived in Kishtwar. She sat motionless, the firelight playing on her stony features, making the gold in her nose glint.

There was silence after Riyaz had finished speaking. Amina was biting her lip so hard, I saw she'd drawn blood. "Tell me one thing," she said to him quietly. "After what has happened today, after these things you've told us, do you still plan to go down the mountain tomorrow?"

To this day, I believe that if she'd used any tone but that one, he would have said no. But, as it stood, there was a sarcasm in her question that reminded me, oddly enough, of my mother. And as soon as he heard her, a willful, obstinate look came across his face. "Yes," he said.

She stood looking at him. Then she went out of the kitchen, leaving us all staring after her.

I went to my room and pulled my rucksack from the white cupboard where it had sat untouched since I'd arrived. I set it down on the floor and felt about inside. My hand closed on a sheet of paper. I drew it out and unfolded it, looking at the two numbers in Abdul Latief's large, looping handwriting. For the first time since I'd left Bangalore, I wished desperately for a phone. I thought of the small cell phone that Riyaz owned, but Riyaz was shut away in his room, along with Amina, and I dared not disturb them. No sound had issued from behind the door for the last hour, and the silence was worse than any screaming match could have been. I tried to think of Zoya instead. Was she all right? Had she and Abdul Latief managed to barricade themselves at home before the trouble started? Then I thought of Stalin, roving about Kishtwar with his gun in his skinny arms, wearing his ridiculous, too-large helmet, his finger light on the trigger, quivering at the thought of action, of mobs flooding the streets like tides of dark water.

I went back to the kitchen, where Riyaz's mother was unrolling the mattress she shared with Aaqib. Perhaps she was more upset than I'd thought by the news from Kishtwar, or perhaps it was due to our brief camaraderie during the grass-cutting earlier, but instead of staring at me, she nodded to me to come in. I helped her tuck the edges of the sheet under the mattress, then sat on the sackcloth beside the fire and watched as Aaqib fitted himself into the curve of her body, his eyes soon closing. She did not sleep, but lay on her side, her headscarf folded beside the mattress, her head propped up on her hand. I looked at her and wished again for a language we could both speak.

"I made a decision today," I said to her. She looked up at the sound of my voice, then back at the fire. "I'm going to stay here, in the village. Become a teacher. Can you believe that? Me, a teacher? I know you'll probably laugh when you find out." I looked at her face, the gold stud gleaming in her right nostril, the gray hair flattened from being under the headscarf all day. "I love this place," I said quietly, and as soon as I said it, I felt a tremor run through my body and knew it to be true. How had I never admitted it before today? I loved this place, and I loved its people too. I loved this old woman by the fire, whom I could not understand and who could not understand me. I loved the little boy she was cradling, who was trying so valiantly to be brave. I loved the boy's father, whose very presence was confusing to me, and I loved the boy's fiery mother, who was a far better friend than any I deserved. Over time, I told myself, I would try to deserve them all. "You have to make a decision," my father had said one evening in a restaurant, and wasn't that what I had done? I had decided; I had chosen this place, these people, this life, with its secrets and its violence, its hardness and its beauty, and even though I was not yet worthy, even though I would never fully belong, I would not leave. I would stay and try.

Riyaz's mother's eyes had started to close. I remained very still, not wanting to disturb her. Her head slipped off her hand and her eyelids fluttered open for a moment, but she was already asleep, and her eyes registered nothing. Soon I heard her breathing steadily through her mouth, each exhalation a little wheeze. Aaqib's sleeping face was perfect, at peace. I stood up carefully, dusted my hands and turned to make my way toward the door, only to find Amina blocking my path.

"Murgi," she said. "I need to talk to you."

Once in my room, Amina went straight to the window and stood there for a long time, looking down at something. I didn't know what it was until she said, "You can see Kishtwar from here, you know."

"You can?" I moved to stand beside her. "Where?"

She pointed at a cluster of lights, spreading amoeba-like on the distant valley floor.

"I didn't know," I said softly. "I've been watching it this whole time. Every evening."

She squinted sideways at me. "You like watching things, don't you?"

"What do you mean?"

She shrugged. "Just something I've been thinking about. All this time you've lived here with us, you've eaten with us, and I still don't know anything about you. You watch, you ask questions, but you never tell us anything about yourself. That's a little strange, don't you think?"

I laughed, as if she'd made a joke, but her words had disturbed me. Not only because she'd never said anything of the sort to me before, but because it reminded me, almost exactly, of what my father had said to Bashir Ahmed the night of the party. The same hurt cynicism.

"I really don't know what you're talking about, Amina," I said, trying to sound nonchalant. "You don't sound like yourself. Are you not feeling well?"

But she did not respond, and I fell silent. We stood like that, with me watching Amina, and Amina looking out of the window, until she turned away from the view to face me.

"Murgi," she said. "I'm leaving tomorrow."

Of all the things she could have said, this was the last one I expected. It was as if she'd told me she was going to join the circus. I stared at her, unable to find a response.

"I'm taking Aaqib," she added. "We're going back to my family's house for a while."

"Why, Amina?" I managed finally to ask.

She shrugged. "He'll have his cousins, other children to play with. The school there is better than the one here, too."

That wasn't what I'd meant, and she knew it perfectly well. "What about Khadijah Aunty?" I blurted out. "How will she manage without you?"

She shrugged. "I've already talked to her. She understands. We'll be leaving early tomorrow."

"And the soldiers? The robbers? Is it safe for you to go?"

"This is my home," she said simply. "No soldier or robber knows it better than me. Anyway, a few other villagers are going in that direction, so Aaqib and I will go with them."

I still did not dare mention Riyaz. "What about Bashir Ahmed?" I almost pleaded. "He *needs* you, Amina. You *can't* leave."

A shadow of pain crossed her face. "Ma will be here to give him what he needs," she said dispassionately.

Many times over the years, I have wished to have this moment back so I could alter what I said to her next. I would tell her that I was sorry for my part in throwing her life off course. I would sit with her on the mattress, look straight into her face, and say, *Ask me anything you want.* I would tell her about Bashir Ahmed and his stories, about the apartment with the mattresses, about the party and what came after. I would tell her about my mother and how she'd died. I would tell her that I'd no idea how to have a friend, much less be one, but that, if she would let me, I would try.

But what I said was, "Be careful, all right? I don't want anything to happen to you."

She smiled at me, and for a second, her face was lit up, bright with mischief and all her fierce, irreverent joy. "Me?" she asked. "What could ever happen to *me*?"

She turned to leave the room, then stopped as though something had occurred to her.

"Oh, by the way, Murgi," she said, "speaking of Abbaji, I talked to him. It took a while to convince him, but he finally agreed."

For a second, I had no idea what she was talking about. My head was full of fleeting images: Aaqib hanging upside down from the branches of the peach tree, his T-shirt fallen over his stomach. Aaqib asleep against my arm. Amina under the storm of the waterfall, kohl running from her eyes. Amina tossing a handful of grains to the chicken, the sun dredging up the gold in her brown eyes.

"Agreed to what?" I asked.

"To see you, of course." She raised an eyebrow. "Isn't that the reason you came to this place at all? You can see him after lunch tomorrow."

At the door, she turned once more to look at me. I thought—I hoped—she was about to say something else, that she would burst out laughing, tell me it had all been a joke, she and Aaqib were going nowhere, nowhere at all. *Go to sleep, Murgi. Remember, the cow will be waiting.* But she said nothing. She just looked at me, and before I could let out the breath I was holding, I was alone.

They were gone before I woke. They must have left while it was still dark. I imagine mountain paths rolling out under their feet, fog peeling with the heat of their breath. I imagine Aaqib walking ahead of his mother, in his faded *Superstar Happy* T-shirt, hands clasped behind his back, his sturdy little legs carrying him toward an unfathomable future.

I think of that boy all the time. He will be older now, taller, naturally, with his grandmother's firm jaw, and his grandfather's green eyes. Quieter and more solemn than he was when I knew him, which makes sense, given everything that happened shortly after. A dutiful boy with a heart-stopping smile, popular with his peers, adored by adults, but with a door in his heart that sometimes falls open without warning, causing him to suddenly wander away from his friends, from his mother, to seek out a solitude in which he can wrestle with the dark whisperings of his heart.

At least, this is what I imagine. I don't suppose I will ever know.

31

I GOT MY FIRST cell phone for my nineteenth birthday. A package arrived at my college hostel, and inside it were a neat box and a note in my father's handwriting. *For our champion,* it said. There was no mention of the Christmas vacation, my outburst, my rudeness to my mother. By then, I still hadn't fully gotten over my rage, and I did not make my first call to their landline for more than two weeks afterward. My mother picked up. "Hold on," she said, before I could say anything. There was a long pause, during which I could hear nothing but a dull rhythmic thud. Then she came back to the phone. "Yes," she said, sounding breathless, "tell me."

"Amma, what were you doing just now? What was that noise?"

"Oh, that neighbor of ours, you know, the one with the brat of a son? She's been yelling at these poor street kids for playing cricket outside her house. They're *street* kids! Where else are they supposed to play? Each time their ball goes anywhere near her gate, she pounces on it and won't give it back. So I decided if she likes balls that much, I would oblige. I went and bought thirty boxes of tennis balls and threw them one by one into her compound. I hope she has fun picking them up."

She sounded so satisfied I had no choice but to laugh. She began to laugh too, and when she made no mention of my rudeness, I was so relieved that I was especially forthcoming with her; we even had something resembling a pleasant conversation. At the end of it, I said, with a burst of guilt-inspired earnestness, "You know you can call me if you want, right, Amma? I'm always here."

"Of course I know," she said placidly.

After that, things seemed to take on a more optimistic color. I plunged back into my classes with renewed energy. I studiously avoided the toy-king's son, and after a while he grew bored with me, looking right through me whenever we happened to pass each other. Rupa and I went to the movies together, sitting on the seawall afterward, sharing a packet of potato chips, throwing crumbs to birds, and watching the wind scuttle the waves, and all the while, my cell phone was tucked into my pocket or my backpack, ringer turned high, ready to receive my mother's calls.

Except she didn't call.

I went home several times over the next two years, and she always seemed slightly different. Garrulous, goofy, stern, placid—I could never tell from one visit to the next how I'd find her. The final time I went home, I found her standing at the gate looking out at the road one evening. There was nothing to see, just a street dog trotting with its tail raised high, a driver taking a nap in the backseat of his auto, his bare feet sticking out the side.

"Waiting for somebody?" I said, then wished I hadn't.

She turned and smiled. "No, little beast. Just standing here."

"You haven't called me little beast in a long time."

"Well, you haven't been little in a long time."

"But still a beast?" I asked, trying to make her laugh, but she only smiled.

"You should call me, Amma. What else did you give me the cell phone for?"

"I will," she said, still gazing absently out at the street. "I will."

I went back to college, expecting nothing to come of it, as before. But I was wrong. She began to call all the time.

In the middle of classes, my phone would buzz loudly, making everyone jump, and causing the professor to glare at me. "Sorry, sorry," I'd mutter. She'd call at seven in the morning, then at seven forty-five, then again that evening at five. She never had anything to tell me, and though I'd promised myself I wouldn't lose patience, I frequently found myself gnashing my teeth at her protracted silences. She would keep saying, "So what else?" as though I'd called her, instead of the other way around. Sometimes I'd make an excuse, guiltily hanging up. Once, she called just before I was about to drop off to sleep. As a way to get her off the phone, I said, "Why don't you go out tomorrow? Go shopping or something."

"Shopping?" she repeated, sounding a little like her old, mocking self.

"Or visit friends," I added quickly.

"A quaint idea. Except that you seem to forget I've never had any."

"That's not true," I said.

"Oh? Enlighten me then."

I hesitated. "What about Bashir Ahmed?" I ventured. "Wasn't he a friend?"

Silence on her end. Then, "You know, I'd forgotten all about him."

I was supposed to be studying, but I could not concentrate and so I'd gone out to watch the girls play basketball. It was a very warm night, the air heavy with salt, and the combination of heat and humidity had driven me from my room. I stood at the edge of the concrete and watched the girls' shadows knifing across the yellow-lit court. They laughed and grunted and flung casual insults, and I found myself smiling. For once, I had not taken my cell phone with me.

It was the hostel warden who ran to find me, a plump figure bounding into the spotlight. "Your father," she panted. "The hostel phone. He needs to talk to you right now. Go, quick."

This is what my father told me.

He had left for work that morning, as usual, at eight o' clock. My mother had wished him goodbye. Stella had arrived at eleven and done all the housework, watered the plants, cooked. After she left, my mother had gone to the corner shop; the shopkeeper said she'd come around four in the afternoon; he remembered because she was unusually sweet to him and because the only thing she bought was a tall green can of mosquito repellent.

What she did after that can only be guessed.

My father came home at six forty-five, poured himself a drink, and sat in the living room for over an hour, listening to a record. John Coltrane, he told me in a daze. *Live at Birdland.* My mother was nowhere to be found, but he didn't wonder too much about it; he simply assumed she'd gone out to buy something and would be back soon. But when she didn't come home by 8:00 p.m., he wandered about the house, calling her name, in case she'd fallen asleep in one of the other rooms.

Outside the guest bedroom, whose door was closed, he'd caught the sharply astringent odor of a chemical, as though she'd fumigated the room for cockroaches, and he opened the door.

By then, she'd tumbled off the guest bed onto the floor, her head thrown back, her neck stiff and at a sickening angle. He only had to take one look at her, then at the can of repellent on the floor, its spray nozzle pried off, to know exactly what had happened.

He snatched her up, threw her limp body into the car, and rushed her to the hospital, even though he knew she was gone.

V

32

THE RED-AND-WHITE COW ROLLED her watchful eye toward the door as I entered, then, seeing who it was, she relaxed, letting her head drop. I went up to the calf, who was already straining at the rope that kept it from its mother. It jerked hard just as I was trying to undo the expert knot that Amina had tied, and the rope slipped from my hand, burning my palm.

"Shh," I said, "it's just me. You know me."

I finally managed to get the knot loose, and while the calf sucked greedily, I looked around the dimness of the barn. From the other side, the two mules looked back at me with their soft, huge eyes. Riyaz was still here.

I coaxed the calf back to its stake and tied the rope into a knot, willing it to hold fast. Then I squatted by the side of the red-and-white cow and began to work. As I did, unbidden, the image of Amina came to me, as though I'd summoned her back. And without being fully aware of it, I began to imitate her movements, the quick downturn of her wrists at the end of each stroke, her way of spreading her fingers wide to relieve the cramp in her palms, even the angle at which she held her head, and briefly, it seemed to me that we occupied the same space, moved inside the same body, her movements and mine in perfect synchrony. For a moment, I was almost certain I could hear her breathing, deep and measured, only to realize the breathing was my own.

I heard a sound behind me, the crunch of someone stepping onto hay, and turned to see Riyaz at the barn door. He wore his brown kurta, the one he'd worn the day I first met him in Kishtwar. I turned back to the cow and kept working. He said nothing, but I knew he was still there. When I rose, holding the full pot in both hands, he stepped back to allow me out into the cool air.

We looked at each other in silence, but it was not the same silence as when we'd stood at the edge of the porch, watching darkness fall over the valley. This silence was different; it was filled with the sound of Amina's absence. Riyaz was the first to speak.

"You've learned a lot," he said, gesturing down at the pot.

"Amina taught me well," I replied and saw him grimace.

I was about to pass him and go up to the house, when he said, "There was a call this morning for you."

I paused. "A call?"

"Yes," he said. "On my cell phone. It was Saleem."

For a second, the name did not register. Saleem? I knew nobody called Saleem. Then I remembered. Orange hair, poetry, Kishtwar. "How did he get your number?" I asked slowly.

Riyaz shrugged. "Probably from my mother's relatives in Kishtwar."

"What did he say?" I recalled the mobs, the soldiers, the violence that had supposedly broken out the previous night. Was he calling to tell me they were okay? Or—my heart dropped—had something happened to Zoya? "Is everything all right?"

"He said that they're all fine. But he thinks the situation will become worse all across the area. He is worried about you. He thinks you might be frightened up here."

"Me?"

Riyaz's lips, I noticed, were very dry. He had been speaking very fast, but now he fell silent. I waited, knowing that there was something else to come.

"He wants to send a car for you," Riyaz said in a rush. "To take you back to Jammu, so you can get back to Bangalore from there. He says he sent you up here, so he feels responsible for you."

I could not respond, could not think. Saleem wanted to send a car? To take me from here?

"But," I said at last, "you told us last night that all the roads were closed."

"They are closed," Riyaz said, "but he—Saleem—said that this driver of his knows all the back roads, and he can get you to Jammu. The only thing is that you need to leave right away. Tonight," Riyaz added, as if I might not have understood.

I began walking up to the house, holding the pot out stiffly. Riyaz fell into step beside me. As if the uphill movement had freed him to speak, he said, in a low, urgent voice, "So? What should I tell him? Should I tell him to send the car?"

I stopped walking. We were on the porch now. There was a terrible eagerness in his face, and one look was enough to tell me exactly what he wanted. It wasn't hard to recognize, after all, that desire. It was the same desire that had propelled me away from my father, from Bangalore, that had put me on the train to Kishtwar. The desire that had brought me here. The pure, blank promise of escape.

"You want to come with me?" I asked dully, though it wasn't really a question.

He licked his dry lips. "You'll help me, won't you? I won't be able to do it alone. I don't know anybody there except you. You'll help me to find a job, a place to stay. I don't need a lot, you know that, and I'll do anything, whatever you say. I promise. And once I'm settled, I won't trouble you ever again. Just please help me with this one thing."

"Riyaz," I said weakly, "you can't just leave your home."

He drew himself up. "Why not?" he asked. "Didn't you?"

I had no answer to that.

"So what shall I tell Saleem?" Riyaz repeated.

I looked down at the yellow-white surface of the milk in the pot. My hands shook, and a soundless ripple passed across it. Maybe he was right, I thought. Maybe it was time to give up and go home. I would see Bashir Ahmed in a couple of hours, I would talk to him, and then it would all be over, wouldn't it, this little adventure? And maybe it was for the best. Amina was gone, Aaqib was gone, and I didn't know when, if ever, they would come back. And this life I had supposedly *chosen* for myself, this *decision* I had made with such hubris and joy, how much was it really worth? Was it worth the idea that I had somehow destroyed the family I'd come to love? Was it worth the constant feeling that I was an intruder, that no matter how many years I stayed, I would still never fully belong to this place, or it to me? I wavered, on the verge of telling him to call Saleem, but then I imagined climbing into a car, the mountain roads twisting and winding toward Jammu, the highway tea stalls, the green roadside signs, the village falling far behind me, and an instinctive rebellion rose at the back of my mind, a blank white wall of refusal. "No," I said.

He froze.

"I'm not leaving, Riyaz," I said quietly. "I've got an offer. To become a teacher. In the school here. I wanted to tell you before. I'm not going back to Bangalore."

It was as though he didn't understand me. He just stood there, feet planted slightly apart, not a man but the statue of a man. "Riyaz," I said softly. "Did you hear me?"

"I heard you." His voice came through gritted teeth. "I'm not deaf."

"I'm sorry."

He didn't reply, turning instead toward the valley. The spaniel, who had been nosing about one of the flower beds, came up and sniffed his ankles. He took no notice of her, did not bend down to scratch her ears or her belly, but continued to stand there, his eyes darting around, as if searching for something to vent his rage upon. Then he caught sight of the pine tree, pulsing and swaying with the dark shapes of crows, and his eyes narrowed.

"Enough of this," I heard him whisper.

He disappeared inside the house. Not knowing what else to do, I took the pot of milk to the kitchen and handed it to Riyaz's mother, who took it with the barest nod. I was about to sit down when Riyaz stormed out of the house, his face set straight ahead. He had his rifle in his hand.

Riyaz's mother stood, nearly upsetting the pot of milk. We both rushed out to the porch, but Riyaz was no longer there. He was striding down along the side of the barn toward the cornfield, his kurta billowing, the spaniel flying ahead of him. They paused at the edge of the corn, then they plunged in together. We waited, but the silence that followed stretched on, unbroken even by the sawing song of the corn stalks, the sighing of their leaves.

Then the air was ripped open by a single explosion. An enormous black cloud shot up from the pine tree, scattering in all directions, making it seem that the tree itself had come apart. The air was suddenly filled with screeching and cawing, a deafening cacophony.

Riyaz's mother went back inside, but I couldn't move. I stood, unable to take my eyes off the wheeling shapes, so dark against the blue sky. Then a movement in the corn caught my attention. I saw the spaniel dart out, heard her frenetic barking. Right behind her was Riyaz. In one hand he held the gun aloft. In the other, by its legs, he held a spreading black stain, dark and shiny as an oil spill. It was a single large crow. He looked up and after a moment beckoned me to come down.

I ran down past the barn, and it seemed to take ages. When I was finally standing in front of him, Riyaz held out the dead crow, which was larger than I'd previously imagined. "Here," he said. "Hold this."

"Excuse me?"

"I need to get something from the house, and I can't put it down or she'll get it." He nodded toward the spaniel, who was slinking around us, belly low to the ground, her yellow eyes rapt on the bird in his hand. Without thinking, I shook my head.

He laughed softly, nastily. "So," he said. "You want to stay, but you can't even do a small thing like this? How do you expect to survive?"

I knew he was angry and that there was no conviction behind his cruelty. But all the same, it set off something in me, a flare of my mother's obstinacy perhaps, or just plain, old-fashioned defiance. I put my hand out and firmly grasped the dead crow's feet, my hand grazing Riyaz's briefly.

"I'll be back soon," he said curtly, and left me there.

For some reason I'd expected the crow to be cold and heavy and dense, but it wasn't. It was warm and dry and light. The wing tips gently brushed the dirt, the beak was like dark gray rubber, and the chest, unexpectedly muscular, was a glossy purple black. *Look at me!* I cried silently, not wholly sure who I was addressing. Riyaz? My father? My mother? Amina? *Look at me! This is my life now! Do you see?* I shook the bird, as if to make my point to my invisible, silent audience, and it shifted slightly. And that was when I saw what I hadn't noticed before: the bullet wound just beneath the right wing, the feathers there simply vanished, as though rubbed out by an eraser. And the wound itself, bone white at the edges, darkening to a sunken, marbled red in the center, the blue-black feathers around it clotted with blood and still glistening.

I glanced up and saw Riyaz standing at the edge of the porch. He was looking down at me. I raised the bird slightly, like proof of something. But his eyes were in shadow, and I could not tell what he thought. Moments later, he was beside me again, drawing a length of string from his pocket. And though the bird had not felt heavy all this while, my arm ached as soon as I'd relinquished it. Riyaz shinnied up the nearest tree, and with a few nimble motions, trussed the bird by its feet and suspended it from one of the branches. It twirled slowly, darkly festive, like the paper streamers in Bashir Ahmed's room. Riyaz jumped down.

"That will keep the others away," he said. He sounded grim but satisfied.

"It will?"

He shrugged. "For a little while, anyway."

33

All morning, I was restless, the thought of seeing Bashir Ahmed looming over everything like a shadow. I kept going out onto the porch to look at the hanging crow. From there, it merely looked like a blur, the black flag of war or death spread against the tree trunk. The living crows in the pine tree did not seem particularly affected by the loss of their comrade. They still clung to the branches, still circled, though I had to admit they appeared slightly less willing to drop down toward the cornfield. In the meantime, I kept myself busy with the tasks that, until yesterday, had been Amina's responsibilities. I'd watched her do them so many times, my body seemed to move automatically. After washing the breakfast plates and pans at the outdoor tap, I swept the mud porch with the stubby broom, and scattered a handful of grain to the chickens, watching with a conflicted sense of triumph as they came sprinting in from all corners of the porch.

In the early afternoon, Riyaz set off for the mosque, and I went to the kitchen, where Riyaz's mother had lunch ready. We sat quietly until Riyaz came back, and then she laid out three plates, filling them with steaming rice, chicken, and gravy that ran to the edges. I tore at the chicken with my fingers, surprised by my own appetite, my unabashed craving for meat. Riyaz, as soon as the meal was over, took himself out again, muttering something about needing to cut wood for the stove. His mother looked at me. I pointed to the pot of rice on the stove, the bowl of meat sitting on the floor beside it, then toward the back of the house, where Bashir Ahmed's room was.

Without a word, she filled a plate and handed it to me. I poured a steel tumbler of water, then carried both up the corridor. Halfway to Amina and Riyaz's room—now only Riyaz's I reminded myself—I had to stop for a moment, because my legs were trembling so hard.

Pushing open the door of the bedroom, I noticed right away that certain objects were gone. Amina's kurtas, her headscarf that had hung on the handle of the cupboard, and for a moment, I wanted to turn around and leave. Then, steeling myself, I walked up to the colorful curtain and listened for some signal—a cough, a clearing of the throat—but I heard nothing to indicate a person waited on the other side. I took a deep breath, nudged the curtain aside, and went in.

He was sitting up in bed, hands folded primly over the thick pink blanket.

His head turned slowly as I entered, and his eyes, which were already sunken, seemed to recede even farther into their sockets. This time, there was no silent howl of terror, but a flicker of fear crossed his face nonetheless.

"I brought your lunch," I said.

He said nothing, watching as I came forward into the room. When I hesitated, he nodded toward the table beside his bed. I moved his skullcap aside and set the plate and tumbler down then stepped back, not knowing how to begin.

Bashir Ahmed broke the silence first.

"You've grown," he said, and I felt the same thrill at hearing that voice, unchanged.

"That's what happens after eleven years."

"Eleven years," he said slowly. "Has it been eleven years?"

I nodded.

"And after eleven years," he said, "you're here. How did you find us?"

"It was because of your story. The one about Shah Baghdadi. I looked on the internet and found that it had happened in Kishtwar."

"You remember that story?" he said, a note of surprise in his voice, and, I thought, of pride.

"I remember all your stories," I said.

The kerosene lantern in the corner flickered, going dull then bright. I looked around at the room. A tiny plastic-framed mirror hung on the wall above a mud shelf, and few bright bolsters lined the walls. There was a closed wooden chest in the corner, presumably for Bashir Ahmed's clothes. It was a lonely room, but not unwelcoming, and something struck me suddenly.

"Is this the place?" I asked.

He looked up. "What place?"

"Where the militants stayed. When they came."

Bashir Ahmed had stiffened at the word *militants*, but then he nodded. I looked around again, and he did the same, as if he hadn't lived with these things every day for years.

"It's a nice room," I said finally. "I like it."

"Thank you," he said, bending his head. "I hope you are comfortable in your own room."

"I am, thank you."

It was all just an elaborate prelude, of course, these polite inquiries. We were playing for time, circling the real reason I was here, circling the subject of my mother, neither of us wanting to be the first to mention her. Again I had the feeling he was waiting, fearful, for what I would say.

"There's trouble in Kishtwar, you know," I told him. "It started yesterday."

He nodded, though without much interest. "Yes. Amina beti told me."

Hearing her name appended to the endearment *beti,* which had always been mine, was more painful than I could have imagined. "Amina left," I said quietly. "She went back to her own village this morning. She took Aaqib with her."

He remained unsurprised. Of course, I thought, she wouldn't have left without saying goodbye to him. She would have sat by his bedside, teasing him, coaxing a laugh from him, consoling him over her impending absence. Begging him, as a last favor, to let me see him again.

"It was because of me," I blurted out. "She left because of me. It was my fault."

For the first time since I'd entered, I saw a glimmer of his old self in his sunken eyes. The self that had looked at me when my mother was rude or negligent or even cruel, the funny downward tug of his mouth that warned me not to be angry with her. "You shouldn't think that way," he murmured absently.

"Then why did she leave?" I cried, more desperately than I'd intended.

And all of a sudden, we had exchanged roles and I was the one waiting, terrified of what he would tell me, while he sat in silence, lost in his own thoughts. But in the end, he only said, with a touch of tiredness, "For many reasons. A person can leave for many reasons."

As soon as he said it, I saw him at our gate in the dark, my parents asleep in their bedroom above. *Tell her, beti, that I am sorry. For everything.*

But he was speaking again. "We all made it difficult for her," he said. "From the second she came into our house, we made it difficult. She tried hard for many years, but it was too much for her in the end. Don't blame yourself. It is not your fault."

I nodded, but my throat was still tight. Bashir Ahmed leaned back, a grimace crossing his face as his legs shifted under the blanket.

"Does it hurt?" I asked, glancing down at his legs.

He looked at the covered bottom half of his body as if it were someone else's. "Sometimes. When it's cold. But most of the time, I don't think about it."

"You don't?"

"It all happened so long ago," he murmured. "I've almost forgotten . . ."

"How can you forget something like that?" I objected.

He didn't answer right away, and when he did, it was to say, wryly, "I see that you haven't changed. You still like to ask questions."

"I'm sorry."

He gave me a smile that reminded me of Amina. "I'm just teasing you, beti."

He'd called me *beti.* My entire body filled with warmth, and I felt lighter. The strangest part, I realized, of standing there, speaking to him, was how comforting it was. I'd always found his physical presence reassuring, even during the brief spell when I decided that I hated him.

"Isn't there something that can be done?" I asked. "Surgery or—"

He smiled. "Do you know how much surgeries cost?"

"I'll pay," I said impulsively. "Whatever you need, let me help. My father—"

But he shook his head. "Beti, I was not lying to you when I said I was fine. I really don't think of it anymore. And tell me this: even if my legs were all right, where would I go? Back out there?" He pointed to the wall of his room, beyond which lay the yard, the cornfields, the village. "You know what they say about me there. Why would I go back?"

Somewhere at the back of my mind, a doubt had crept in, a sly, insidious doubt, wearing a young soldier's vain little mustache and speaking in a whining voice. *Ask anybody.*

"After you left Bangalore," I said, when a few seconds had passed, "what happened? I mean, what happened with the militants? Did they stop coming?"

He looked away. The stubble on the folds of his slack throat was pure white. "They kept coming," he said at last, speaking very quietly.

"You couldn't stop them?"

"I didn't try to. After I came back from Bangalore, beti, I was angry." He didn't need to say why, and I didn't have to ask. "Most Kashmiris I knew were angry, but I had never fully felt it myself. But when I came back from Bangalore for the last time, I felt it finally. I wanted to help any militant I could find. I wanted freedom, for Muslims, for Kashmir, and I was ready to do anything. It was as though I could suddenly see the world clearly. It was a world in which Kashmiris would keep dying, and everybody else would keep having dinner parties." He paused. He wasn't looking at me, but I blushed all the same. "So," he said, "the militants came and I did not stop them. It went on like that for five more years."

I waited, but there was no more forthcoming. He had gone silent.

"And then?" I asked.

He looked up. "You sounded like your mother when you said that." I held his gaze steadily, and he shrugged. "And then," he said, "it all ended."

He attempted to sit up. I hurried to help him, arranging his pillow so that it supported his back. He settled back and again folded his hands on the pink blanket. It was as ordinary as if he were sitting in our living room. Any minute I would turn and see my mother.

"It was all going bad anyway, beti. In the beginning, there were just two or three militant groups in this area and they all knew and respected each other, but slowly more and more groups started to form. One group would split into two, under different leaders, and they would spend months fighting each other instead of the army. Some groups were willing to talk with the government, others were not. It became so bad that if you heard gunfire at night, you didn't even know who was doing the shooting. And for us ordinary people, nothing changed. The fighting had been going on for more than ten years, but the freedom they promised us never came."

I didn't turn, but I felt, as clearly as anything, my mother sitting on the chest in the corner, leaning back against the mud wall. Now, I thought, we were all here.

"And so it went on like that, with the army coming one day and beating up people for not telling them about the militants, and the militants coming the next day and beating up people for talking to the army." A new, dry note entered Bashir Ahmed's voice. "Sometimes it seemed like they were playing a game with each other, which they were both enjoying a lot, and the rest of us were just a way to keep the score."

My mother's face was very calm.

"Luckily, by then, they had almost stopped coming to our house. Maybe there would be one every few months. The last militant who ever stayed with us was a young fellow. He came in the winter. He liked me, because he said I reminded of him of his uncle. His uncle had died of cancer, I think. Anyway, this boy, he was the one who told me about the plan. He said there was a Hindu village a couple of hours away, which had always supported the army. He and his group were going to kill a few men there. Just to keep them quiet, he said. To make everyone remember who was in charge."

My mother opened her eyes, and for an instant I believe Bashir Ahmed saw her too. He was staring in the direction of the chest, his eyes blank. "He was such a young boy. I felt I had to say something. I tried talking to him, but he didn't listen, so I threatened to go to the army camp and tell them what he had told me. We had a big fight, and in the end he called me a fool and a coward. Then he left and I never saw him again."

I had opened my mouth to ask a question, but Bashir Ahmed held up his hand, and I shut it.

"Let me first say this," he said. "I did not kill those men, but their deaths are still my fault. I made myself believe that nothing would happen, that the boy was just talking. So when I heard those men had been killed one thing became clear to me. That boy was right, beti, and so was your mother. I *am* a coward."

He had mentioned her. I felt the air in the room shimmer.

"But you still didn't kill anyone. So why do people say you did?" I asked.

He shrugged. "I don't know. I have asked myself the same question a thousand times. Maybe the boy said something to somebody, maybe the message got confused. But once the story started, there was nothing I could do. In the end, the word must have reached the soldiers. Maybe someone from this village even gave them my name." He sounded meditative now. "The only thing that still surprises me, after all these years, is that the soldiers hardly touched me. Yes, they broke my legs, but that was quick. Usually, the things they do to the people they catch . . ." His voice was hushed, and I thought briefly of Ishfaaq, Zoya's vanished boy. "It was as if I was being *protected.* Allah was keeping me alive, beti. Allah wanted me alive, so that I would never forget what I was."

We were silent for a long time. My mother was no longer in the room, no longer anywhere.

I said in a whisper, "Please come to the kitchen. Please. I can help you walk."

"No," he said.

I was about to protest, when he held up his hand. "Beti, please. This has nothing to do with you. I have done enough to hurt my family already, and I do not wish to hurt them again even by chance. Please. I understand why you are asking, but I cannot do it."

I looked at his face, and for once in my life, I did not argue. I shut my mouth and nodded. He nodded, too, then his expression changed.

"When I first saw you," he said softly. "That day, when you came in by accident, I thought, just for one second—"

I looked at the ground.

"But now when I look at you, I see your father," he said in a firmer voice.

On some impulse, I said, "I didn't tell my father I was coming here. I lied to him. He doesn't know where I am. He doesn't know I came to find you."

A disapproving frown crossed Bashir Ahmed's face. "You shouldn't have done that, beti. He is still your father."

I dropped my head in shame.

Bashir Ahmed was still watching me, though his eyes were distant. I suddenly wondered what he and my father would think of each other now, if they could meet again as older men.

I had the strange suspicion they would become friends.

But I had no time to dwell on my father, because now the air shimmered again, acquired a tense edge. Bashir Ahmed's hands were creeping toward each other once more, entwining for comfort. I saw a bead of sweat form on his waxy brow.

"Beti, your mother..."

I didn't help him. I was seeing her as she had been on the night of the party. Her eyes so dark, hair brushing her shoulders, bangles glinting. Full of excitement, full of schemes.

"Where did she want to go?" I asked.

Confusion flickered in his face. "What do you mean?"

"The night of the party. She wanted to leave with you, right? Where did she want to go?"

The smallest, saddest smile crossed his face. "She wanted to come here, beti," he said, and made a gesture with his fingers, which took in the entire landscape around us.

I could not believe it. My mother, in this place? It was impossible to imagine. My mother walking these narrow stony paths, sitting crouched beside the fire, sleeping on a thin mattress? My mother sweeping the porch, feeding the chickens, milking the cow?

As if he had read my thoughts, Bashir Ahmed said, "I tried to tell her it wasn't possible, but she wouldn't listen. It was like that joke I used to make with her, about the spectacles. It was as if she couldn't see anything clearly. She said all kinds of things, beti, scary things. She said she would go mad if I didn't bring her; she said she would jump off the roof, but how could I do what she was asking? Your father had been kind to me and you were just a child. So I—"

"So you left," I finished for him. "You left us behind."

The fear was back in his face. "Beti," he said, and his voice cracked. It was a desperate sound, and it jolted me out of the trance I hadn't known I was in.

I looked down on him, one of the few people in the world who had really known my mother, who'd made her laugh, who had been charmed and stupefied and enraged and wounded by her, and I could find no anger in myself, nothing but a desire to give him peace.

"She died," I told him gently. "Three years ago."

His eyes were screwed shut, and he was nodding, though I didn't know whether it was to say that he already knew, for Amina must have told him at some point, or to encourage me, without words, to say the final thing.

I took a deep breath. "It was suicide," I said. I didn't know the word for *suicide* in Urdu or Hindi, so I said it in English, surprised at how easily it slipped out, how meager a word it really was.

I'd seen him cry before, but this was different. There were no muffled sobs, no shaking shoulders. He cried with a quiet, bereaved dignity, tears rolling into his stubble. I felt a stirring of sympathy. How much guilt he carried, this old man. "Is that why you didn't want to see me for all these days?" I asked. "You thought I was angry?"

He nodded, shamefaced as a child.

"Listen to me," I said. "Please, listen very carefully. What my mother did wasn't because of you. Or me. Or anybody. That's not why I came here. I came here"—I paused—"because I wanted to see you. That's all. I missed you when she died, and I wanted to see you again." I paused, then added, "I loved you. We all did."

His hands unclasped, grasping for mine. I sat down with him on his bed, in that hot room with the paper streamers waving slowly above my head. I felt no urge to cry, but I was aware of a great silence suffusing my body, as if my heart were slowing down to a normal human pace, as if a huge racket that had played constantly in the back of my mind had suddenly ceased.

I held Bashir Ahmed's hands for a long time. Then I released them and stood. He looked up, seeming suddenly bereft, his face betraying alarm. "You're going?" he cried.

"Only for a while," I said. "There is something I have to do. But I'll come back, I promise."

I touched him on the shoulder and left.

34

I ARRIVED ON THE porch at the same time as Riyaz, returning from the mosque. He saw me and stiffened, but I didn't give him time to react any further. My mind was working fast, making rapid calculations. Approaching him, I said, in a low voice, "Riyaz, is your cell phone with you?"

He nodded dully.

"All right. I want you to call Saleem and tell him to send the car."

His eyes went wide. "Really?"

"Yes."

A frown of suspicion knitted his brow. "Why? Why did you change your mind?"

"I've thought about it, and you're right," I said lightly, trying to calm my heart. "I can help you find a job in Bangalore. You'd be able to earn a lot more money than you do here. You'd be able to send it back for your parents. For your mother's medical treatment, for Aaqib's school, for everything else. After everything you've done for me, that's the least I can do for you."

The frown had relaxed somewhat but hadn't entirely left his face. "And what about you?"

"Me?" I pretended not to know what he meant.

"What about staying here? Becoming a teacher?"

"Oh, that," I said, trying to sound airy, convincing. "That was just a silly idea I had for a while. To tell you the truth, I don't think it would have even been possible. Can you imagine me, a teacher?" I attempted a laugh, but it came out strained, unconvincing.

Riyaz eyed me. "Are you sure about this?" he asked.

"Of course I'm sure," I said hastily. "Now call Saleem, please. It may already be too late."

He was pulling out his cell phone and scrolling hurriedly through it, when I slipped my feet into my shoes and laced them up. He glanced up from the screen, his expression of panic almost the same as his father's had been a few minutes ago. "Wait a second. Where are you going?"

"To Mohammad Din's house," I said. "I want to say goodbye to him and Sania."

At least, I thought, *that* was the truth. Or nearly.

The whitewashed house on the ridge was as pretty as I'd ever seen it. The rippled tin of the roof looked like silvery water, and the neat cement path leading to the wooden front door was straight from a fairy tale. Sania was sitting on the porch, barefoot, a book open on her lap.

"You came early today, ma'am," she said in English, and I felt a flare of pride.

"I just came to tell you I can't have our usual lesson today, Sania."

"Are you sick?" She was on her feet, looking worried. "Is your health all right?"

"My health is fine. I just have something to do. I'll tell you all about it tomorrow, okay?" I looked over her shoulder into the house. "Is your father at home?"

We went into the room where we had our lessons. Mohammad Din was sitting on the floor, surrounded by papers, but it was clear his mind was elsewhere. He was staring out of the window, but he quickly took off his spectacles when we came in, pressing his fingers to the bridge of his nose and saying, "What a surprise. Come in, come in. Salaam aleikum."

"Walaikum salaam. I'm sorry to disturb you," I said. "I know you have a lot of work to do."

"This?" He waved a hand around at the papers. "None of this is urgent. I'm just trying to take my mind off what is happening in Kishtwar, that is all. I'm always happy to see you."

"Has there been any more news?"

"Nothing, except that there is still a curfew. People are allowed out only two hours a day, to buy the things they need. Inshallah, I pray it doesn't get any worse than that."

I sat down across from him. Sania was hovering anxiously by the door. "May I speak to you for a few minutes?" I said in a low voice. He nodded, turning to his daughter.

"Could you make some tea for your teacher, Sania? We can't leave her thirsty," he said. His tone was jovial, but the command was nonetheless implicit. Sania looked momentarily mutinous but went off to the kitchen. Alone, Mohammad Din looked at me. "What is it you wish to talk about?"

I looked at him, wondering if I could trust him. *The nicest person in the world,* Amina had said.

"I was just thinking," I began casually, "about Riyaz's mother."

"Khadijah Begum? What about her? Has something happened to her?"

"I was just wondering about what would happen if she, I don't know, really fell sick."

He narrowed his eyes. "Is she all right?"

"Yes, but I was just wondering. In case something happened to her."

"I'm sure Riyaz would take care of her."

"And in case Riyaz isn't here to take care of her?" I pressed.

He picked up his spectacles then put them down again. "What's all this about?" he asked, a trace of irritation in his voice. "Naturally he will be here to take care of her. Where would he go? And in case he isn't able to, for some reason, I would of course be there to help. Why do you ask?"

"No reason," I said quickly, but seeing that he wasn't convinced, I added, "It's just that I worry about them sometimes. Because"—I hesitated—"because of Bashir Ahmed, and what happened during the militancy. What people say about him."

His face altered, lines appearing that hadn't been there a second before. "Yes," he said softly, heavily. "We have already talked about it, and, as I told you, I will always try to help Riyaz and his family. It is part of my duty to this village."

I nodded, relieved that the last obstacle to my growing plan had been cleared away. Mohammad Din, meanwhile, seemed distracted again, looking off into the valley.

"It's funny," he said. "With the trouble in Kishtwar, it reminds me of those days again, the worst days of the militancy. There was this same feeling in the air, you know. That time had stopped. When you would just sit and wait for days together for something to happen, not knowing how bad it was going to be." His voice drifted into silence. "Of course," he said, suddenly sounding crisp and businesslike, "things are different now. Those days are over, the days of progress are here. We must forget what happened and try to move on. It is the only choice."

"Some people don't have that choice," I said softly, thinking of Bashir Ahmed in his room.

He looked closely at me, then seemed to soften. "I can see that you really care for their family," he said. "As I told you, what happened with Bashir was a very sad thing, and every single day I wish it had been different." His voice betrayed a dreaminess I hadn't heard from him before. "Bashir's problem," he said, "was that he couldn't decide what he wanted. He tried to have everything at the same time, and it got him killed in the end. One day, he wanted to work outside the village, then the next day, he wanted to come back. One minute, he wanted to help the militants, then the next minute he wanted them gone. He—"

I'd been half listening, thinking of Riyaz waiting for me at home, but now I started. "Wait a second," I said. "You knew that Bashir Ahmed was helping the militants?"

Mohammad Din blinked. "I'm not sure what you mean," he said stiffly. "Everyone knew he was working with them."

"But you said he wanted them gone. That means you knew he stopped wanting to help them."

He was silent for a while, then he said, "Yes. I knew."

"How?"

Mohammad Din shrugged. "Bashir told me."

On a hunch, I said, "Were *you* the one who got him involved?"

His eyes flicked immediately toward the door, but Sania had not yet come back with the tea. He looked back at me, one eyebrow raised, and I thought I read a challenge in his expression.

"Yes," he said casually, as if it were beside the point, "but only because he needed the money and said he wanted to help. I had no idea what it would lead to, that those poor men would die, otherwise I would never have approached him. And all that was many, many years ago. At the time, I was a younger man myself. I believed, as did many others, that militancy was the right path to help our people, but obviously that is no longer the case. Now I know we must fight through political means. That is why this election next month is so important."

It was clear he wanted the subject closed, but I wouldn't let it go. "You told me once that Bashir Ahmed was the last person to do something like that."

"So what?" he said, and there was the beginning of anger in his voice now. "I was clearly wrong. As I've been telling you, with Bashir, you never knew. One minute he was one thing; the next minute he was another." He snorted. "And he was always interfering in things when he shouldn't have been. Telling militants what they should and shouldn't do, trying to argue with them, when he himself had never picked up a gun to fight. Why couldn't he mind his own business and keep out of what he didn't understand?"

But as soon as the words left his mouth, I saw his eyes widen slightly.

"You knew about that?" I asked after a second. "You knew he'd argued with the militants?"

"I don't know what you're talking about," he snapped.

"Yes," I insisted, "you do. You just said you knew that Bashir Ahmed tried to stop working with the militants, that he'd argued with them. So when the Hindus were killed and people started saying he was responsible, why didn't you say something to defend him?"

"What difference would it have made?" he snapped. I'd never seen him anything other than genial and warm and in perfect control of himself. But he was enraged now, there was no doubt about it. His face was dark, the muscles thick and tight across his jaw.

"It *would* have made a difference!" I insisted. "Everyone respects you! They would have believed you. And, who knows, maybe then the soldiers wouldn't have arrested Bashir Ahmed!"

"The idiots weren't *supposed* to arrest him in the first place!" Mohammad Din roared. Then his face went perfectly white. For a second or two, there was silence in the room.

"What did you say?" I said blankly.

He didn't reply for a long time. His face was lowered, and his eyes were closed. It seemed he was gathering himself, putting certain vital pieces back in place.

"What did you say?" I said again. But it was too late, the anger that had propelled this conversation was gone, and I knew he would never betray himself again. When he finally looked up at me, it was with his usual smile: benevolent and patient. A politician's smile, I suddenly thought.

"I'm so sorry," he said. "I didn't mean to be rude. It's been quite a tiring week. I always enjoy talking with you, but I have a lot of work, as you can see." He was speaking graciously, but with a mechanical absence. "Forgive me if I don't come with you to the door."

Shakily, I stood up to go. He took up the nearest sheaf of papers, but didn't look down at them immediately. He said, "Wait."

I stopped.

"Before you go, there's something I wanted to tell you," he said. "I spoke with the headmaster again last night. He says that they have received permission from the education board. You can start teaching next week. Assuming," he added softly, "that is what you still want to do. Assuming you still want my help in this matter."

I stared at him, suddenly unsure of him, of myself, of everything he had told me. He must have guessed some of what I was feeling, for he sat up straighter.

"For the last fifteen years," he said quietly, "I have done nothing but try to help my people. They have been forgotten by everyone, including the government that's supposed to take care of them. They are poor, uneducated, many of them are sick, and none of them know that they should be treated better. I'm the only one fighting to give them a better life. Do you doubt that?"

I shook my head.

"In that case," he said, "this is your choice. You can stay and help me make things better for them. Or you can go back to Bangalore, to your life, and forget about us. Forget about Sania, about Amina, about Aaqib. Forget about this place. It will be easy for you. But me? I cannot forget. I may have made mistakes, but don't forget, I also stayed here to put them right." He leaned back against his bolster. "Now," he said, putting on his spectacles, "it's your turn to decide."

Like a fool, I stood there, unable to speak, unable to do anything but stare.

"You know," he said, apparently apropos of nothing, "Amina came by this morning to say goodbye before she left."

I pressed my lips together.

"A good girl, Amina. Very sweet, very trusting," Mohammad Din mused. "Quite different from you, no? You are a person who, I think, trusts nobody. I noticed that about you right from the beginning. In a way, you are a bit like me."

"I'm *not* like you," I said through gritted teeth. "I haven't harmed anybody."

"Oh?" He tilted his chin up and regarded me with a hint of amusement. "And if you were to say that to Amina, do you think she'd agree?"

I could feel my face heating up.

"Right," he said coolly, fully in control of himself and the situation again. "So let me ask you one last time. Do you wish to stay in this place and see what you can fix? Or do you wish to go back to the place you came from and forget about everything?"

He was looking at me with coldness, as if it could make no difference to him, or to any of them, what I did, whether I stayed or left or disappeared from the earth entirely. And, ashamed as I am to admit it, that was what decided me. The sad fear of being invisible.

Through gritted teeth, I said, "I want to stay."

Mohammad Din nodded. "Then it's settled," he said, crisply. "We will not discuss any of this again. Now if you don't mind, I should finish my work."

I walked blindly to the doorway of the room, then out onto the porch. I put on my shoes and stood staring at the mountains. I was about to walk away, when I heard Sania come up behind me. "Ma'am," she said quietly. Before I could say anything, she had wrapped me in a tight hug. When she stepped back, she seemed suddenly older than sixteen, her moonlike face dimmed.

"Bye, ma'am." She nodded once at me and went indoors.

Back at the house, Riyaz was sitting on the porch. "What took so long?" he said, leaping to his feet as soon as I came up. "I called Saleem. The car will be there for us in two hours, but we need to walk almost as long to get to where it will be. Did something happen?"

"No." I avoided his eyes. There would be time to think of all of that later. Right now, I had to focus, make sure everything would go as I had planned. "Are you ready?"

He pointed to a black backpack that sat beside the door. "It has everything I need," he said, unable to keep his nervousness from his voice.

I nodded. "Then give me five minutes to get ready."

I went to my room, took out my rucksack, and threw all my clothes into it without caring. Pushing my hand into the front zipper, I drew out the white envelope my father had given me the night before I left Bangalore. I slipped this into the pocket of my jeans along with Zoya's phone numbers. I went back to the porch and Riyaz. His mother was hanging up clothes on the line, paying no attention to us.

"She thinks you're coming back?" I asked him. He nodded, and I knew he was close to tears. I went up to the old lady, who did not stop her work as I approached.

I knew whatever I might say was pointless, but it still seemed important to say it.

I said, "I know you never really liked me, Khadijah Aunty. I don't blame you. The worst part is, I'm about to do something that will make you like me even less, and I am very, very sorry for that. Sorrier than you could know. I just hope I'm able to explain all of it to you someday."

She gave me the same look that had taken my full measure the day I'd arrived. Then she went back to hanging clothes.

I stood there, momentarily immobilized by fear and doubt.

Then I shook myself. *Enough of this.* Turning back to Riyaz, I said, "Let's go."

35

We struck out east, on a rocky path across the mountain, not toward the town above the river, Riyaz told me, but toward another village, which had a rough road accessible by trucks and the hardier sorts of car. Riyaz walked in front with my rucksack, relinquishing to me his small black backpack. Preoccupied with thoughts I could only guess at, he did not make much conversation, apart from terse, practical remarks about the route. However, I was grateful for the silence, for I was trying to clear my own thoughts, trying to bring my plan, if it could even be called that, into focus. I had to wait, I decided, until we were nearly at the car, until he was fully committed to the idea of leaving. Any sooner, and I would risk making him lose his nerve.

At one point, Riyaz stopped and said, "Let's go this way, it's a shortcut." He gestured toward a steep lip of rock, below which I could see a trickle of a path used by goatherds. He tossed down my rucksack and took the drop in one leap, while I slid down inelegantly on my backside.

After that we picked our way through tall, dry grass that came up to the backs of our hands, interspersed with weeds, lurid vines, and sharp nettles. Here and there, I spotted piles of burned rubbish—plastic bags with flaky, necrotic fringes, smoky lightbulbs—and, once, the bleached skull of a sheep.

Riyaz hooked it through the jaw with a stick.

"Leopard," was all he said, and he let it fall.

Then we were descending faster, the path all but nonexistent now, scrambling down again and again between patches of terraced land, uncultivated for the moment. I was so wrapped up in this rhythm that I barely noticed that we'd almost lost the sun, until Riyaz said, "Careful," and I saw that the patch of dark earth I was about to step onto was a puddle of muck.

"How much farther?" I asked, keeping my voice lowered, though I didn't know quite why.

"About ten minutes," he murmured back. "The village we want is across that field."

Below us was a large field of corn, sturdy and tall, a month or so away from being ready for harvest. I took a deep breath and glanced up. A half moon slid out from behind a bank of clouds, lopsided. This was as good a place as any.

"Riyaz," I called softly. "Wait. I need to say something to you."

He turned.

I looked deep into his face. "Are you sure about going to Bangalore?" I asked. "I need you to think about it very carefully before you answer. Is that the life you want?"

His eyes darted around uneasily, but he finally nodded.

"Listen to me before you say anything, okay?" I urged. I fumbled in my jeans and drew out the white envelope. "I've thought about this, and I promise you it's going to work. It's going to be fine. In ten minutes, we'll reach the car. When we do, I want you to get in. Without me. I want you to go to Jammu. From there, you can catch a train to Delhi, and then another train to Bangalore. When you get there—no, listen to me—" I said as I saw him draw a breath to protest, "when you get to Bangalore, I want you to call this number." I showed him the front of the white envelope, on which I'd written my father's landline number.

"That's my father, okay? Tell him I sent you. Tell him you're looking for work, for a place to stay. He's a good person; he'll help you. I promise. He'll help you with anything you need."

He was staring at the envelope in my hand, his face eerily composed. It frightened me, his blankness, and I wondered again if I were doing the right thing. Then I recalled Mohammad Din's sneer—*If you were to say that to Amina, do you think she'd agree?*—and I felt myself momentarily weaken. "Do you understand what you need to do?" I asked, trying to sound firm. "There's no reason to be afraid. You're going to be fine. You don't need me. Your father made this trip a hundred times, and there's no reason you can't do the same."

Still, he didn't react. A lock of his hair fell over his forehead and I had the urge to push it back. I resisted it. "Riyaz," I said. "Tell me you understand."

"What about you?" he asked finally, his voice dead.

I shrugged. "I think I'll try being a teacher, after all."

He didn't ask any further questions. He didn't need to. What each of us wanted was clear enough. What each of us wanted was the same thing.

"I can't pay. For the train," he said. "I don't have enough money."

I opened the flap of the white envelope to show him the notes inside. His eyes widened. "That will get you to Bangalore," I said.

"I can't take this," he said, but there was no conviction in his voice. We both knew he would take it. I opened the zipper on his black backpack, which I still carried, and slipped the envelope inside. I swung the pack onto my shoulders again, while he watched me in silence.

When he stepped forward and put his mouth on mine, I wasn't exactly surprised. It would be more accurate to say that I was grimly, fatalistically glad. His lips were dry, his arms were about me, the smell of hide and sweat and smoke was in my nostrils. Before I had a moment to think, my body began to move, to respond, my fingers automatically moving up his back, feeling the ridges of muscle and bone, the roughness of his hair, my mouth pressing greedily to his. I cannot say how long it might have gone on, but then I opened my eyes and caught sight of his expression.

It was the expression of a proud person determined to offer up as compensation the only thing still left in his possession, and it made me feel unimaginably sick. I pushed him away from me, and he stumbled back, his arms falling to his sides.

My heart was pounding. "Riyaz, don't—" I began.

I was going to say, *Don't do this,* but suddenly I noticed he was no longer listening. His head was cocked to the side. He was frowning in the direction of the cornfield, which stretched out like a dark, unparted sea before us.

"What is it?" I whispered.

But he only put his finger on his lips. I tried to listen but could hear nothing apart from the clacking of insects, the plaintive lowing of a cow. Riyaz was moving, light as a cat, toward the field below. Trying to match his footsteps, I followed. At the edge, he paused to let me catch up with him, and, together, we entered the dark, swaying field.

Now we were surrounded by the tall, whispering stalks, the long leaves falling across our paths like swords, barring entry. Riyaz moved with impossible stealth, and I did my best to follow suit, though I knew I was making far more noise. Here and there, sticking up from the ground, were the broken stalks from last year's harvest, a foot long and as sharp as skewers. I was concentrating on avoiding them, and so I did not see that Riyaz had stopped until I bumped into him. He turned, motioning that I should remain where I was. Then he went forward a few feet, very quietly, and looked out between the stalks. I caught sight of a clearing, the shapes of men.

Even from where I was, I could see his back stiffen, the way he went as still as a hunted animal. In an instant, he was back beside me.

"We have to go," he whispered urgently, motioning in the direction from which we'd come. "Right now. Go, go, that way, go."

"Why? What happened? Who is it?" I blabbered, starting to turn.

"Go! Just go!" he hissed and gave me a slight push. I took two faltering steps, then overbalanced, my hand flying out for support. It found a cornstalk, and I leaned with all my weight against it for a second. I recovered my balance immediately, but the stalk groaned; then, almost as an afterthought, it cracked. The sound was as loud as a gunshot.

For a second, the whole world seemed to be immobile, the wind stilled in the corn, the insects cowed into silence. In that otherworldly hush, a voice called out: "Who's there?"

My legs started to tremble. I knew that voice. I glanced at Riyaz. His eyes were closed.

"Whoever you are, it would be better for you if you showed yourself," the voice called. It betrayed no fear or alarm, but a kind of bored annoyance. It was the same voice that had confronted me across the field of lightning-struck trees, the voice that had made me piss myself in fear.

"Riyaz," I hissed urgently.

He opened his eyes, but he seemed unaware of me standing next to him. He was looking at something beyond me, listening to a voice that wasn't mine. Then he snapped back to attention.

"Listen to me," he said. "Whatever happens, don't show yourself. Understand?"

"But—"

The look on his face silenced me. I nodded. And, as soon as I had, a strange peace, almost a lassitude came into his face. He turned back toward the voice and the clearing. When I realized what he meant to do, I grabbed at him, but I was too late and succeeded only in catching the corner of his brown kurta. He shook me off easily, as though I were no more than an irritating fly. The last thing he did before he walked out into the clearing to meet them was to lift his arms like a dancer. Only then did I realize he was still carrying my rucksack.

As quietly as I could, I made my way to the edge of the clearing, trying to stay out of sight. As I expected, twenty or so feet away was the subedar. His men were scattered around him, a few of them with their guns pointed at Riyaz, who was now in clear view, arms lifted.

The subedar's voice floated to me in my hiding place.

"Well, good evening," he said. "Come closer, please, no need to stand so far away."

Riyaz dropped his arms and obeyed. I wished desperately that I could see his face, but he was blocked by my bulging rucksack, which the subedar was eyeing too.

"Such a heavy load," he murmured. "What is your name, friend?"

I waited, but there was no answer from Riyaz.

"Didn't you hear me?" the subedar repeated. His soldiers, apparently having judged that there was no immediate danger, had lowered their guns and were looking on like mildly interested bystanders. "I asked you a simple question. What's your name?"

Still Riyaz didn't answer. The subedar straightened. "You're quite the talkative fellow, aren't you?" A few of his soldiers chuckled.

Say something, for god's sake! I silently pleaded with Riyaz. But even before the thought was complete, I recalled Amina's pinched face, her falsely light voice saying, *Sometimes, Murgi, I think he* wants *them to beat him up.*

"Well," the subedar was saying pleasantly, "if you won't tell us your name, the least you could do is put that heavy bag of yours down and tell us where you're going. We're all bored and we would love to hear that story, wouldn't we?" He glanced around at the soldiers, who nodded and grinned, evidently well rehearsed for their supporting roles in this bizarre and terrifying play.

Riyaz said nothing, but, after a pause, he let the straps of my rucksack slide off his shoulders. It hit the ground with a thud. Now I could see his shoulders and back, the sweat staining his kurta.

"Good," the subedar said. He made a signal to a young, pimpled soldier, who stepped forward. In a single motion, so swift that I could not have told you exactly what happened, he had hooked his leg behind Riyaz's. The next moment, Riyaz was lying on the ground on his chest, his legs splayed out behind him. One of his sandals had flown off and was lying a few feet away. Still he made no sound, not even so much as a grunt when his body hit the dirt. Absurdly, I felt a spark of pride.

"I'm very interested in this bag of yours," the subedar was saying. "Do you care to tell us what important things you're carrying? Maybe some black clothes, hm? Maybe you're one of these robbers everyone is talking about these days. Or maybe"—his eyebrows arched—"maybe you've decided to take a secret little trip over the border? Maybe your militant friends are waiting for you there? Shall we take a look inside and see which one is true?"

This time he didn't even pretend to wait for an answer. Instead, he nodded to the same pimpled soldier who had tripped Riyaz. I suddenly recognized him as the one who had complained about his cell phone signal. "Open it," the subedar ordered.

The soldier swung his rifle onto his shoulder and heaved my rucksack over. Squatting beside it, he drew the zip open, gripped it with both hands, and shook it hard. I watched as all the belongings I'd hastily stuffed inside fell out in full view of the gaping men—my jeans and T-shirts, my underwear, and, last of all, my bras, flopping onto the dirt. The pimpled soldier leapt back with a cry, flinging away my rucksack as if it contained poison, staring around wild-eyed at the others. The subedar's composure was gone: he was obviously rattled.

"What is this?" he demanded of Riyaz, who, honestly this time, had no answer to give.

At that point, there was a snicker from one of the soldiers. It was past twilight now, so I could not tell which one had laughed. The subedar whipped around. I saw him peer searchingly at each of his men, all of whom stood with downcast eyes, and when he looked back at Riyaz, his expression shifted. A cold, remote implacability entered it.

"Pick him up," he ordered.

The pimpled soldier reluctantly stepped forward again. When he seemed to balk at touching Riyaz, the subedar barked, "I said to pick him up! Are you deaf?"

The soldier bent down and cupped his hands under Riyaz's armpits, dragging him onto his feet. The subedar came up and leaned in close to his face. I saw Riyaz raise his head, and I knew he was staring back at him. There was something uncomfortably intimate about such prolonged eye contact, and despite all that I had seen, naïve fool that I was, I really thought, for a mad, hopeful moment, that the subedar was about to let him go.

Instead, he kicked him. Then he put his hands on Riyaz's shoulders and drove his knee deep into his stomach. This time Riyaz did make a sound, a deep, wordless grunt that flew to me in my hiding place, making me shut my eyes. If the other soldier hadn't been holding him up, he would have fallen to the ground again.

"You Kashmiris," the subedar said. His voice rang out clear, full of contempt. "There's something wrong with all of you, I swear." He tapped his temple. "In your heads."

Riyaz's head was gently bobbing, as if in agreement.

"I've been posted here three times in the past ten years," the subedar went on, "and the more I see of you people, the more I think you're all sick. You like wearing ladies' clothes, eh?" He snorted, letting his eyes sweep in disgust over my bras. "Some days I think we should shoot the lot of you, save ourselves the trouble of dealing with your nonsense from now on. I'm telling you, old, young, man, woman, it doesn't matter.

There's something wrong with every single one of you. And the longer I stay here, the crazier you all seem to get. Look at that one over there."

He turned and pointed to a dark shape on the ground a few feet behind him, and when I saw what it was, all the air seemed to go out of the world. All this while, I'd thought it was a large rock or a mound of dirt, but now that the subedar was pointing, I saw, with chilling clarity, that it was a *boy*.

A boy wearing a bulky red sweater, his knees pulled close to his chest in a fetal huddle. A boy of twelve or thirteen, who, as if aware that he was being discussed, raised his head wearily for a few seconds, then dropped it back on his knees.

And when he saw the child, Riyaz said the first and only words he would speak in front of them: "Yah Allah."

"Retarded, that one. Totally mad." The subedar had returned to his conversational tone, as if the two of them were friends sitting across from each other at a table. "We didn't realize until later. He can't talk. Just stares if you try to ask him a question." He eyed Riyaz. "Sort of like you. Want to know what he did this morning? Sat in a tree and threw shit at us. *Shit*." He shook his head. "What kind of child does that? Even after we arrested him, he wouldn't stop giggling. Totally mad, I'm telling you."

There was a moment of stillness, and then—again, it was impossible to tell who moved first, I saw Riyaz wrench one of his arms free of the grip of the soldier who'd been holding him up, I heard the subedar say something sharp, I saw several soldiers step forward at once—and then they were all upon him, with fists, boots, the dull end of rifles. Even if I'd made a sound or stood up then, I don't think anyone would have heard me. They were chillingly methodical about the way they kicked him, using no more energy than necessary. Time seemed to flatten, to elongate, as they closed in on him, and I crouched in the corn, Riyaz's command not to show myself still ringing in my ears.

Riyaz's command.

But it isn't so simple, is it? It cannot be so simple. And if I don't admit it now, then what good is any of this? These crude and terrible details? As I have said, the chance for nobility is past.

So: It was not Riyaz's command that kept me hidden. It was cowardice.

Through the thicket of legs, I caught sight of him. He was pressed into a shape that seemed to me too small for a person. I could not say how long the beating lasted. Sometimes I think it couldn't have been more than ten or twenty seconds. At other times, I think it went on for hours.

And the whole time, I stayed hidden.

Then the subedar, who had been standing off to the side, said crisply, "Stop."

The soldiers stepped back, clearing the space around Riyaz. Now I could see the side of his face. He was still conscious, I noted with craven relief, his fingers curling like an infant's, his legs moving gingerly in the dirt. The subedar was looking at him with a thoughtful expression.

I thought it was over, that they would leave, but then the pimpled soldier, the one who'd emptied my rucksack, stepped forward again. Riyaz covered his face, but the soldier was picking up something from the ground, and my heart sank. It was one of my bras. The black cups dangled from his fingers, twirling like the paper streamers in Bashir Ahmed's room, like the dead crow in its tree. The soldier pulled Riyaz to a sitting position and quickly forced the straps over his shoulders without fastening them. Riyaz's sat there, his chest crossed by a slash of black.

"Doesn't fit," the pimpled soldier remarked. "Needs one size smaller, I think."

The subedar smiled tightly, and, once the rest saw his approval, they laughed.

"Let's go," the subedar said curtly, and then they began to collect their things, backpacks, caps, water bottles. The soldier who'd been holding Riyaz let him go, and he collapsed on his side.

Another soldier tapped the boy, and he glanced up, unaware, it seemed, of everything that was going on. He barely glanced at Riyaz as he got slowly to his feet, his movements like an old man's. The soldiers were forming a ragged line, and he fell into step with them. Four soldiers in front of him, four behind. None of them glanced back.

I waited until I was sure they were gone. Then I hurried to his side.

"Oh god, Riyaz." There was a bruise on his left cheek, and I couldn't bring myself to touch it. It was too intimate and what had just happened had erased any intimacy that might have existed between us. I touched him on the shoulder instead.

He rolled onto his back, and my bra came into view. The straps had slipped down onto his elbows. And then, ridiculously, I remembered Bashir Ahmed, holding a white blouse up to his chest, saying solemnly, *It even looks good on an ugly man like me.* I fought back a sob and eased the straps off his arms, flinging the bra as far into the undergrowth as I could.

He was struggling to sit up, and I helped him. Now I could see his face. Apart from the bruise on his cheek, his right eye was already swelling, there was a deep cut on his lower lip, and the collar of his kurta was torn. His breath came in snatches, and his eyes were closed.

"Riyaz," I whispered again, my voice strangled. "Please say something, please. Tell me if you're okay. Did they break anything?"

He shook his head.

"Are you sure? We have to take you to a hospital. The car is close by. We can—"

"No," he croaked, his eyes still squeezed shut.

"What do you mean, no? Look at what they did to you! You have to go to a hospital."

"No," he said again.

Then he opened his eyes, and it was all I could do not to cry. He looked like a stranger. The burning anticipation of earlier was gone.

The rare, roguish smile was gone. Even the sullen, dissatisfied man I'd first met was gone. The person who looked at me was empty of desire, empty of fear and longing. Only a flicker of obstinacy remained, somewhere far back in his eyes.

"The car will be gone by now," he said.

"That doesn't matter," I said. "We can call Saleem again. We can ask him to send another car, another driver. I—"

"No!" This time he almost shouted it, or would have, except it came out as a wheeze. He was breathing heavily, his nostrils flaring. Then he pushed himself to his feet, in excruciating stages, like a toddler. I hovered, ready to help him if he fell but somehow knowing that he would not welcome my touch. What had taken place seemed to have put years of distance between us.

As soon as he was upright, he stumbled with a cry. I leapt forward, but he waved me away. "My leg," he grimaced. His right ankle had ballooned.

"Sit down," I pleaded, but it was as though he hadn't heard me. He began to hobble around, picking up my clothes, which lay scattered everywhere, some muddied with the imprints of boots. Helpless to argue, I did the same. I shoved them into the rucksack, retrieving the black bra and jamming it at the very bottom. Finally, I zippered the rucksack and turned to him. "Riyaz," I said quietly. "What do you want?"

He was gazing over my shoulder. I knew he would never look at me directly again.

"I want to go home," he said.

The darkness solidified as we made our slow way back to the village. Stars appeared in frozen relief. Riyaz had bound his ankle in one of my T-shirts, and I'd found him a sturdy branch to use as a crutch, but he could not walk for more than ten minutes at a stretch without needing to rest.

At one point, I said, "What will happen to that boy?"

Riyaz, on a rock with his injured leg stretched out, did not reply. I did not ask again.

It was almost dawn by the time we arrived back at the village. There were the familiar markers: the silver glint of a granite wall, a friendly dog loping up to sniff our feet, a rooster shaking sleep from its crown, the whitewashed walls of the mosque.

The only person we met was a very old man, coming downhill. He glanced at me and noted Riyaz's injuries, but all he murmured was, "Salaam alaikum." His aged skin had the clarity of water. We passed on without another word exchanged. Five minutes later, we heard a crackle, a cough, and then his warbling voice on the mosque loudspeaker, singing the first azan of the day.

36

I woke in the room with mud walls. In my room. On my mattress. I did not know how long I'd been asleep, but my first impression was of all of this having happened before. Waking up to this room, the same delirious exhaustion, the sun cutting a powerful angle across the floor. Hadn't I just done this? I struggled to put events in their proper order.

I blinked and turned my head to scan the room, making a half-conscious inventory. The half-painted walls, the white cupboard, the regular wooden beams of the ceiling, my rucksack. Then, in a nauseating rush, I remembered: the soldiers, the boy, Riyaz's ankle, the excruciating walk back to the village, stumbling into the house just before dawn, falling asleep before my head touched the mattress.

I gripped the window ledge and stood up. The view from the window was as it had always been, the pressed mud porch, chickens scratching in the flower beds, clothes swaying on the line, but at the same time, it all seemed somehow altered, as if each object and creature had been turned a few inches in the night to reveal a slightly different aspect of itself.

Wincing at the ache in my muscles, I walked slowly to the door. My rucksack sat upright beside it, demure and dusty, an unsettling reminder of the night's events. I gave it a vicious kick and it toppled meekly on its side. In the corridor, I looked up and down for signs of life. The door to Riyaz's bedroom stood wide open. After a second's hesitation, I peeked in, but the room was empty, with the black backpack tossed carelessly onto his mattress, the sheets twisted and churned. Where had he gone? Could he be with Bashir Ahmed?

As I stood there, I heard voices at the other end of the house, in the kitchen. I began walking toward them, trying to think. I would have to convince Riyaz, I decided, to seek medical treatment. I would have to convince him to call Saleem. I would—

I was still moving toward the kitchen and the front door. Outside, I could see my mud-caked shoes, which I'd flung off on reaching the house. There were Riyaz's mother's thick plastic sandals. And, puzzlingly, beside them were two pairs of tall, muddy, black boots I'd never seen there before. I stared at these for perhaps a quarter of a second, trying to identify them, and then my throat contracted in fear, my brain screamed at me to turn around, but by that time, it was too late. I was already in view of the kitchen, and the people inside were turning to look at me.

I stopped, my heart beating wildly.

Riyaz's mother sat by the fire, dark shadows under her eyes, slowly stirring a simmering pot of tea with a metal ladle. In the center of the room, leaning back in two plastic chairs that had been brought in from the porch, were the subedar and the young pimpled soldier, the one who'd put the bra on Riyaz and snickered, "Needs one size smaller."

Strangely, as soon as they saw me, they scrambled to stand, their heavy dark uniforms incongruous against their bare, exposed feet. But I suddenly ceased to wonder about them, because I'd caught sight of the last person in the kitchen. Standing in the corner, in a furry pink cardigan, with one arm wrapped around her body and the other pinching her lip, was Amina.

"Murgi," she said when I came in. And no more.

I did not know whether to look at her or the two soldiers. The subedar had taken off his cap. It was an odd gesture of respect, but I had no time to wonder about it, because Amina moved forward, smoothly taking charge of the situation.

"I was just about to wake you," she said in an ordinary, cheerful voice, as if we'd seen each other only ten minutes ago. "These men have come for you."

My head spun. Had I heard her right? For *me*? I glanced wildly around at the various faces watching me. Where was Riyaz? Was he all right? Had they seen him?

As if she'd read my thoughts, she said, in that same carefully ordinary voice, "There's no problem, Murgi. They just want to talk to you, that's all." And all the while her brown eyes were looking into my own. She placed no extra emphasis on any of the words, made no unnecessary gesture, but I knew that she was reassuring me, telling me that Riyaz was all right, and was also warning me to say nothing about him. With every ounce of self-control in my possession, I turned to the soldiers. "Yes?" I said.

The subedar coughed into his hand.

"I'm so sorry to disturb you so early, madam," he said apologetically. How could this be the same man who had sneered, *Be careful before you call them your friends*? The man who, just last night, had said to Riyaz, *Some days I think we should shoot the lot of you*. He spoke diffidently, his gaze fixed on the ground. "But we have our orders, madam." He paused. "From Brigadier Reddy."

I glanced at Amina for help, but I could see at a glance that she'd never heard this name either. "Who?" I asked.

"Brigadier Reddy, madam. He has asked us to escort you to the camp in Udhampur." The subedar's tone was hushed, reverential. "He's a very important man, madam, Brigadier Reddy."

"You've made a mistake," I said slowly. "I don't know any Brigadier Reddy. I've never—"

Then I broke off, recalling, like a blow to the belly, the number I'd entered into my phone before leaving Bangalore. My father's friend, the one I'd promised to look up and never did.

My father had finally found me.

The subedar was evidently ill at ease, shifting from one foot to another, but his subordinate, the pimpled young soldier, was gazing around the kitchen with open, undisguised interest. Without warning, my anger overflowed.

"What are you looking at?" I hissed at him. "This isn't your house!"

The pimpled soldier flushed and muttered something to the subedar. "Please forgive him, madam," the subedar said. "He says it reminds him of his mother's kitchen in Bihar."

I looked at the pimpled soldier, trying to remind myself that he was the one who had humiliated Riyaz, but as hard as I tried, I could not connect him to the cowardly, cackling bully of last night. I wondered whether or not his mother in Bihar knew the half of what his job entailed.

Misreading my silence, the subedar hastened to reassure me. "I will deal with him later, madam," he said. "But right now, I am requesting you to accompany us. We must take you to brigadier sir's house by this evening."

And then, as if my head had been underwater all this while, I realized what they were asking. I saw again the forest of their legs closing in around Riyaz, heard the blows, saw the dust fly up, and I felt something splinter at the center of my chest.

"I'm not going *anywhere* with you!" I cried. "Understand! Who do you think you are, you—"

There was no telling what I might have said next if Amina had not stepped in right then. She crossed the kitchen and put her arm around me. To them, it must have looked like a gesture of fondness, of sisterly affection, but her grip was viselike. *Shut up*, it told me, and I did.

"Please excuse us," she said politely to the soldiers. "We will come back in a few minutes." She began to guide me firmly out of the kitchen. *What's happening?* I wanted to ask her, but she gave me no chance, steering me instead up the corridor. As soon as we were in my room, she let her arm fall away from my shoulders. She closed the door and faced me.

"It was them!" I shouted, near tears. "They're the ones from last night!"

She put her finger to her lips and gestured in the direction of the kitchen.

"But how did they find me?" I cried, dropping my voice to a strangled whisper. "The brigadier—Amina, that's my father's friend—so my father must know, but how? Who told him?"

Amina had been quiet this whole time. Now she looked up and said, "I did."

My body went cold. "You?"

She nodded. "I asked Riyaz to contact the people you stayed with in Kishtwar. They're the ones who called your father." She straightened her back. "Murgi," she said firmly. "I'm asking you to go with them. With the soldiers."

I stared at her.

"Go with them," she repeated. "Otherwise they will hold it against us, and they will come back. And if Riyaz is here, then it will be ten times worse for him. For all of us. Please go with them, and don't say anything about Riyaz or what happened last night."

"You know about what happened?" I whispered.

She nodded.

"Where is Riyaz? Is he all right?"

"He will be. He went to the doctor. Mohammad Din is taking care of him, so don't worry."

I looked up sharply, my heart quickening. "Amina," I said. "I have to tell you something."

"Now?" She glanced toward the door. "They're waiting."

"It's important. You need to know."

I tried to think how to begin. How was I to tell her that a person she loved, the person who had been the sole reason for her family's survival these past several years, was the one who had been responsible for destroying it in the first place? Would she even believe me?

She was waiting for me to speak. She looked wrung out and exhausted; it must have been very early in the morning when she started out to make her way back to the village. Unconsciously, her hand went up to tuck a strand of hair behind her head, and she began to chew on her lip.

I said, "I was there, Amina. I saw how the soldiers beat up Riyaz. They didn't see me, but I was there. And I did nothing about it."

She frowned. "That's what you wanted to tell me?"

"Yes," I said.

She was quiet. There was nothing she needed to say, really.

"Amina, I'm very sorry," I said. "About everything."

The words seemed to cause her pain, because she closed her eyes, then quickly opened them. When she spoke again, her voice was perfectly even.

"I think, Murgi," she said, "that it's time for you to go home."

We looked at each other a moment longer; then I nodded.

I looked one last time about the room, and my eyes fell on my dusty, battered rucksack. "They saw it," I said quickly. "Last night. They would recognize it if I carried it out there."

Her eyes narrowed. She picked my rucksack up and crossed the room, shoving it to the back of the cupboard and quickly locking it in.

"What are you going to do with it?" I asked.

She did not hesitate. "Burn it."

We went back to the kitchen. The two soldiers jumped to their feet again as soon as they saw me. Amina slipped away from my side and went over to her mother-in-law. Standing shoulder to shoulder, the two women watched me, as did the soldiers, all of them waiting for me to speak, waiting for me to announce my decision.

"I'll go with you," I said.

The subedar gave an audible sigh of relief. "Thank you, madam," he said.

I followed them outside, where they laced up their boots, while I slipped my feet into my stained, worn shoes. Amina had come to stand on the porch, arms crossed, in her pink cardigan.

Once the soldiers were ready, the subedar glanced at me. "Ready, madam?"

I nodded.

We began to walk away, then I heard Amina call out, "Wait!"

She was hurrying up to me. In one fierce motion, she threw her arms around my shoulders and hugged me tight. Her mouth was at my ear, a warm, breathing presence. Tears came to my eyes, but just as I was about to return her embrace, I felt her moving; she was reaching into the pocket of her cardigan; she was drawing something out and pushing it against my stomach. Mechanically, I grasped it, and my fingers recognized the soft paper, the stack of money.

"You forgot something," she breathed. "I was going to call you Murgi, but that's not your name, is it? I'll have to try to remember that. Bye, Shalini. Have a safe trip home."

She stepped back, a harsh little smile hammered to her lips. I could feel the soldiers watching us curiously. I turned from her and walked past them, up the trail that led to the main path. After a few seconds, I heard the crunch of their boots behind me.

* * *

We walked without speaking, except for the subedar, who asked every ten minutes if I needed to rest. The change in his attitude, now that he knew I had a connection to someone as important as the brigadier, was remarkable. He was solicitous, making sure I was given frequent sips of water from a plastic bottle the young soldier carried for him. At one point, he fell into step beside me, clearly wrestling with something he wanted to say.

"Madam," he burst out finally, "when I met you the other day, while you were going for your walk, when I helped you find your way back to the village—what I said that day, it was a joke, madam. I would not have done anything to you, I swear. It was just a joke."

"Let's see if the brigadier finds it funny," I said flatly.

His face twisted with fear and anger, and he did not try to talk to me again.

I cannot remember the route we took. I walked blindly, aware only that after more than two hours, we came to a rough road hacked into the mountainside, ending abruptly in a jumble of uncleared rock and dirt, the same place, I assumed, where Saleem's driver had waited in vain for me last night. I couldn't help looking around, but there were no cars in sight. Only two army vehicles waited, parked back to back: a jeep and a covered truck.

The subedar jumped down onto the road and thudded his palm on the driver's side door, where a third soldier was asleep behind the wheel. He started, blinking, then quickly saluted. The subedar opened the back door of the jeep and stood aside. This was clearly meant for me, but I ignored him. I was staring instead at the covered truck. Two tarpaulin flaps concealed whatever was within. My heart began to race; I was thinking of the boy in the red sweater.

It would have been so easy. Take two strides forward, rip the flaps open.

"Madam," the subedar said. "Please get in."

Move, I thought. *Just move.* But my legs wouldn't obey. Nothing, surely I would find nothing inside. An empty truck, that's all it was. That's all it was.

"Madam," the subedar said, his tone harder now, "you have a very long way to go before you can rest. Please get into the jeep."

I got into the jeep, head meekly lowered. The subedar slammed the door shut, and the driver brought the engine coughing and sputtering to life. Leaning back, I looked in the side mirror of the jeep, half hoping that I would see some sign of movement against the smooth tarpaulin skin of the truck and half hoping that I wouldn't. But just then the driver reached out a hand to adjust the mirror, turning it slightly inward so that it showed me only my face.

37

By the time we arrived in Udhampur, the mountains seemed to have shrunk to nearly nothing, small and unthreatening and obscured by fog. We entered the cantonment, and right away I could sense the order, the underlying sense of authority. The streets were ruler-straight, lined with neat culverts. Even the trees, planted at regular intervals, seemed to grow at the same angle. I saw a heavily pregnant woman on an evening walk, cell phone pressed to her ear; two boys with cricket bats; a soldier on a bicycle, his knees thrown wide. Another soldier stood before a closed gate. We passed the tank in its grassy circle, its barrel painted in stripes.

The brigadier's house was a tan-colored bungalow with a large garden in front. It had the austere, regimented feel of barracks, despite the unruly spray of lavender bougainvillea that floated down from the terrace. I got out of the car, and the driver sped away. I opened the low gate and walked toward the front door, which was strung with chilies and limes to ward off the evil eye. A wrought-iron table and two chairs had been set up on the lawn, which was blue in the evening light. I could see the remains of a tea service: a silver teapot, a cup and saucer.

The door was opened by a short, slender man, with the smooth, unlined face of someone from the northeast. He wore a civilian's blue shirt tucked into dark trousers, but there could be no doubt he was a soldier. He seemed unsurprised to see me. For a second, I thought he was the brigadier, but then he said, in English, "Brigadier sahib is in his study. Please come in."

He led me to the living room. I sat on the edge of an elaborately carved sofa and looked around. The room was dimly lit by a pair of lamps, and it was filled with objects that had obviously been chosen with care: paisley silk curtains, a royal-blue Kashmiri carpet, a carved rosewood coffee table under a sheet of green glass. Objects occupied every wall and surface: a sleek onyx Buddha, the stone bust of a woman, garishly painted masks, mustard-skinned Rajasthani puppets, mirrored tapestries, and wooden fans. The opulence made me doubly aware of my grimy clothes, the sweat in my armpits, the dust of travel in my hair.

Then the brigadier entered the room, and, this time, there could be no doubt of who he was. He, too, was dressed in civilian clothes, but he carried himself with the quiet confidence of someone who took authority so much as his due that he was not made pompous by it. He was tall and sinewy, his hair was combed neatly to one side, and his dark, broad-cheeked face was clean-shaven and wreathed in a smile. His eyes, which held an eager, boyish light, made his exact age impossible to tell.

"Good evening," he said, in soft, British-inflected English, coming toward me with both hands stretched out, as if I were a visiting dignitary. "I'm so glad that you've finally arrived. How was your journey? I trust everything was comfortable?"

"It was fine," I said, my tone curt.

He raised his eyebrows, but passed smoothly to the next thing. "Has Ramchand brought you something to drink?" he asked. "Ah, there he is. Thank you, Ramchand."

The slender man came back in bearing a tray with a sweating glass of ice-cold orange juice. He set the glass down in front of me and went to stand in the corner of the room.

"After your journey, I can only imagine that you're in need of a little refreshment," the brigadier said in his musical, low-pitched voice. "I'll join you, but I hope you don't object if I opt for something slightly stronger. It's a vice, I know, but I'm perfectly useless without my evening peg." He signaled again to Ramchand but the man was already moving, clearly used to anticipating the brigadier's needs. He opened a dark rosewood cabinet, which turned out to contain several gleaming bottles and a row of glittering cut-crystal glasses. He poured a deep amber liquid into one of the glasses and handed it to the brigadier, immediately retreating to his corner.

"Your father, if I recall correctly, is a devoted rum man," the brigadier said pleasantly.

"Yes," I said. The last thing I wanted to do was make conversation with a soldier, any soldier, but his tone was so courteous, the room so warm and pleasant, that further rudeness seemed like it would be egregious. "I prefer whiskey, though."

The brigadier's face brightened. "Oh, then why didn't you say so? You must try some of this. No, please, I insist. It is wonderful stuff, just wonderful. Ramchand, would you—"

But even before he finished the sentence, the capable Ramchand was already setting a glass of whiskey beside my untouched glass of orange juice. I raised it to my lips. The first smoky sip was like a match being struck inside my mouth. I could not remember the last time I'd had a drink.

"Thank you," I said, a little less grudgingly than before.

"Damned good, isn't it?" The brigadier held his glass up admiringly. "A present from a former Japanese cultural attaché. He brings one every time he visits. Brilliant man, but a bit of an eccentric. An expert puppeteer, of all things. We had him over for dinner once, and he put down his napkin in the middle of the meal, went over and took those two puppets off the wall, and gave us an impromptu show." He pointed to the two Rajasthani puppets on the wall. "It was the first time I'd heard Indian puppets speaking English with a Japanese accent. It was really quite alarming." He smiled. I tried to smile back, but the whiskey was spreading its warm fingers in my chest, and, after my hours of travel, I was too depleted to respond.

The brigadier must have seen this in my face, for he sat up and said, his voice a little sharper, "Of course, this isn't the time for my silly stories, as my wife would no doubt remind me if she were here. You've had a long day. Ramchand has your room ready, doesn't he?" He glanced at Ramchand, who nodded. "If you'd like to follow him, he'll take you there."

In the corridor, Ramchand gave me a quick, assessing glance. "Luggage?" he murmured. I shook my head. He betrayed no reaction.

The room he took me to was decorated with the same sophisticated, well-traveled sensibility as the living room. A tall four-poster bed stood against one wall, covered by a block-print bedspread. Two curved antique swords were mounted above the headboard, along with a round, rusty shield. A series of delicate painted Chinese vases lined the top of the rosewood dresser.

Ramchand pointed to a door. "That is the bathroom," he told me. "The hot water is ready. I will go and bring you some clothes to wear. Then you will have dinner with the brigadier." With a last professional look around the room, he left me alone.

I went into the adjoining bathroom and locked it. It smelled of perfume and soap, honeyed, feminine smells that belonged to another world. I looked at my face in the mirror above the sink. There had been no mirror in the house in the village, and this was the first time in weeks that I had looked at myself. I felt a brief shock of recognition, followed by an obscure disappointment. I was thinner, yes, my hair a bit longer, but other than that, I had not changed at all. But, then, what had I expected? A manic, holy gleam in my eye, as in the eyes of those ragged, hippie

Westerners I sometimes saw around Bangalore, with bare feet and billowy clothes, matted blond dreadlocks, consecrated by their first exposure to yoga and the poor? Prayer beads around my wrist, a curly *Om* tattooed on my shoulder, and a cache of photos in which I smiled next to a pair of gaunt village women, to whom I would later casually refer, at dinner parties or in bed with new lovers I wished to impress? *They have so little, you know, but that just means they're more connected to the things that* really *matter.*

I sat down on the closed toilet lid. I thought of Amina. I thought of Riyaz's mother. I thought of Aaqib and Sania. I thought of Riyaz. And I waited for something to happen, for tears to come, but they did not, so I stood up, took off my clothes, and stepped into the shower.

The water that gushed from the showerhead was nearly scalding, battering the back of my neck, the top of my skull, but I welcomed it. Bottles of shampoo and conditioner had been set out for me, and I liberally used them on my tangled hair, which smelled like woodsmoke. I scrubbed my body three times with the bar of white soap, which shrank to half its size, and then I wrapped myself in the thick blue towel that was hanging on a hook.

When I emerged from the bathroom, I saw that Ramchand had laid out a set of clothes for me on the bed. A kurta, a salwar, and a dupatta, all in pale pink chiffon. I recalled the brigadier's mention of his wife; these must be her clothes. The kurta was a little short in the arms, but the feeling of the clean cloth against my skin nearly undid me. I glanced longingly at the bed, wanting nothing more than to fall into it, but the brigadier was expecting me to join him for dinner.

He was already at the dining table, which was covered in a white cloth, an absurd array of dishes around him—peas and potatoes, a steaming tray of rice, palak paneer, fried okra, two kinds of dal—all of which, I couldn't deny, smelled very good. The brigadier glanced up as I came in. A strange expression crossed his face at the sight of my new clothes, but he said nothing.

"Bit much, isn't it?" he said, seeing my eyes roam the loaded table. "I'm a poor eater, but Ramchand insists on this display every evening. Befits my status or something like that. I don't complain, because he takes all the leftovers to a poor family in Udhampur. As long as he does that, he can make a maharaja's feast every day, as far as I'm concerned."

As we ate, he talked easily, clearly practiced in the delicate art of conversation. Not once did he press me to make more than a perfunctory reply, as though he sensed that I was not overeager to talk. He asked me nothing about where his soldiers had found me, and he showed no curiosity about what I'd been doing there. And despite my initial prickliness, my distrust of him as a soldier, I found myself starting to relax in his presence, listening to his lilting voice telling amusing, inconsequential stories about people he'd known. He ate very little, as he'd said, just two rotis and a tiny cup of dal, but I could not stop eating. Ramchand had left my glass of whiskey by my plate, and I sipped at it between mouthfuls of food, feeling myself sinking lower and lower in my chair.

The brigadier and I were almost done with the meal when Ramchand returned carrying a cordless phone on a tray. He held it out to the brigadier. "Bangalore," he murmured.

The brigadier glanced at me, inviting me to pick up the phone. Unthinkingly, I shook my head. I could not bear the idea of talking to my father, of listening to his anger and hurt relief, of answering his questions. The brigadier appeared taken aback, but quickly recovered. Taking up the phone himself, he said in his pleasant way, "Well, good evening, sir. Yes, it's me, I'm afraid. Always a pleasure to talk to you, as well. Oh, yes, yes, everything's fine. I was just about to call you, in fact." He listened for a few seconds. "Not at all. I perfectly understand. The thing is she dropped off to sleep as soon as she got here. No, no, she's fine, don't worry; she was just tired. Yes. I'll have her call you first thing tomorrow." My father spoke again, and the brigadier listened, his eyes fixed on me. On his lips there was a hint of a smile, youthful and conspiratorial, which suddenly sent a wave of warmth through my body, separate from the warmth of the whiskey. At his shoulder, Ramchand stood like a wax statue, betraying none of what he thought.

"Yes, yes," the brigadier was saying, still watching me. "That's true. No, she is traveling at the moment, but I'll be sure to give her your regards. Yes. Oh, don't mention it. Yes, goodnight."

He set the phone back down on the tray and Ramchand took it away. For a moment, we sat across from each other in perfect silence.

"Thank you for talking to him," I said.

He nodded.

"How did he sound?"

"Worried."

I turned my face away, aware that the brigadier was still watching me. He coughed, and I thought he was finally going to interrogate me, but he did not.

"What I'm about to say," he said, "might sound a little presumptuous. If it is, feel free to tell me to mind my own damn business. I don't know what happened between you and your father, or how, exactly, you ended up in the village where my men found you, and frankly, it's not my place to ask. But I *do* know when someone has been through a hard time, and I can see that you have. So here is what I'd like to propose: if you wish to rest a little before returning to Bangalore, my house is at your disposal." Seeing that I was about to speak, he raised a hand. "This isn't any kind of grand gesture on my part, whatever you may think. I'm away for most of the day, and Ramchand, as you can see, is not a reluctant cook." He smiled. "I have a modest library, there's a TV in my study, and Ramchand will get you anything else you need. You'll have no obligation but to relax."

I stared at him, wanting instinctively to refuse. He was a soldier, no different from the others, and I wanted nothing to do with soldiers ever again. But my eyelids were heavy, and he had been so tactful and gracious, nothing like the others. I thought of the bed waiting for me, then of what he was offering—the promise of suspension, however brief.

"Thank you," I said. "It's a very kind offer. If you really don't mind—"

He smiled, clearly pleased. "I really don't. I'll see that Ramchand provides whatever you need. In the meantime, please think of this place as your own."

We rose from the table. I wished the brigadier goodnight and went back to my room. Lying on my back on the bedspread, I looked up at the two crossed swords, the rusted shield. I expected sleep to elude me, expected to miss my room in the village, but the softness of the bed was devastating after all those weeks on a mattress on the floor, and I was asleep within seconds.

My first thought on waking was that I was late. Amina would be waiting by the barn, impatient to get on with her day. Then, as I slowly took in my surroundings, the muslin curtains blowing at the window, the crossed swords, the comfortable sheets that smelled of laundry detergent, I remembered where I was. There would be no more milking, no more Amina.

The brigadier had already left for his office. Ramchand showed me out to the table on the lawn, then brought out an endless parade of breakfast dishes, tea and eggs, toast and idlis, poori and bhaji. At one point, I stood up and tried to help him, but the look he gave me was pitying and faintly scornful, the look one gives to a person unschooled in the proper codes of behavior, and after that I gave up and let him serve me.

After breakfast, I wandered through the house. One of the doors, which I assumed led to the brigadier's bedroom, was closed. I browsed through his study, where glass-fronted cases held ramparts of books, and a small TV was bolted to the wall. Behind the wide mahogany desk was a framed map of Kashmir from the 1930s, its contours unrecognizable. I sat in the brigadier's leather chair and looked up at it, knowing that I would not find the name of the village I was looking for, but unable to help myself. On the desk were photos: one of the brigadier in uniform, chest dripping with medals and badges, standing next to the smiling, twinkly-eyed Dalai Lama; another of him with a very serious-looking Japanese man in a black suit, perhaps the former cultural attaché he'd told me about. I noticed there were no personal pictures of the brigadier, none of the wife he'd mentioned, nor of any children. As I sat there, the phone on the desk rang loudly. I heard Ramchand answer it from another part of the house. I wondered if it was my father, wanting to talk to me, but Ramchand obviously had instructions that I was to be undisturbed, and I was grateful for it.

The brigadier returned around five thirty in the evening, going straight to his room to wash up. He came into the living room, dressed in dark slacks and a blue shirt, his hair glistening wet and neatly combed. He sank down with a sigh in his armchair and smiled at me.

"How was your day? Feeling a little better?"

I nodded.

Ramchand served our drinks and the brigadier leaned forward. We clinked glasses and the sound hovered in the air for a second like the clear bell tone of a tuning fork.

"You've changed costume, I see," he commented, leaning back, his eyes running up and down me. I was wearing my own clothes again, my jeans and T-shirt, which Ramchand had earlier left on the bed, washed, ironed, and folded. Beneath the odor of detergent, the fabric still held the faint memory of woodsmoke, reminding me of Riyaz's mother. I had remembered too late about the sheet with Zoya's phone number tucked into the pocket of the jeans, and all I'd drawn out was a pebble of white paper, which had refused to unfold. "This suits you much better."

"The kurta I wore yesterday was your wife's?"

"One of her many, yes. She has a weakness for them. A set for every day of the year."

"Where is she?"

"Visiting her relatives," he replied. "In Coimbatore."

He said this with every appearance of frankness, but I noticed his eyes briefly tighten. And he must have realized that I'd noticed, for he sat up in his chair. Changing the subject, he said, "I wanted to say this last night, but I didn't want to be indelicate. I heard about your mother, and I'm very sorry. It is the most insufficient thing a person can say, I'm aware, but I'd like to say it anyway."

I was about to give him the perfunctory thank-you I'd perfected, the one I gave to all strangers who offered condolences about my mother, when he added, completely unexpectedly, "It's a damned thing, I know. My father committed suicide when I was twelve."

I looked up, all of a sudden short of breath. "Your father?"

He nodded. "He was in the navy. Rank of captain. Threw himself off the ship one night, a hundred kilometers off the coast of Myanmar. He was thirty-eight years old."

I could not find an immediate response. He was looking at me, serious but not stern. His eyes, I suddenly noticed, were rimmed by attractively long, feminine lashes.

"My mother was forty-five," was all I could say.

He did not reply, and, strangely, it was his silence, rich with unspoken sympathy, that made me go on. Not to fill the vacuum of speech, I realized with some surprise, but because I *wanted* to.

"She took poison," I said. "It burned her up from the inside. I've never told anyone else."

His eyes did not stray an inch from my face. He did not gasp or feign shock. He did not click his tongue or murmur something inane. He only asked, "Were you close with her?"

"Yes," I said, then hesitated. "Well, at least I thought I was. I thought I knew everything about her, but it turned out I was wrong."

"You can never know everything," he replied gravely.

I raised the glass to my lips, to realize my hand was trembling. "It's funny you should say that," I said. "My mother said the same thing to me once."

"Well," he said, holding my gaze, "your mother was a wise woman."

Right then, Ramchand came to summon us to the table, so we rose and went to the dining room, where another feast had been laid out.

"You know, I had an idea," the brigadier said, after we'd taken our seats across from each other. "I was thinking, if you want, I could take the morning off tomorrow and show you around the cantonment. It doesn't sound terribly exciting, I know, but I thought you might like the change. Only if you want, of course," he added quickly. "I understand if you'd rather be left alone."

I looked at him. Faint blotches of pink had risen in both his cheeks, though he didn't seem aware of it. I found his shyness unexpectedly poignant.

"That sounds nice," I said, and saw his face light up.

"Wonderful," he said. "Just wonderful."

He was at the table on the lawn the next morning, reading a newspaper, which he folded and put aside when I came up. He was wearing his uniform.

"Good morning," he said, smiling. "Ready for the grand tour?"

After breakfast, which was as extravagant as all the other meals had been, I laced up my battered shoes and joined the brigadier on the road.

We walked at a leisurely pace, the brigadier with one hand tucked into his pocket, the other gesturing toward various buildings, whose names and purposes blended together for me, except when he pointed to a high-walled complex and said, offhandedly, "The army pool."

"Pool?" I asked. "You mean a swimming pool?"

"Yes," he said. "Do you swim?"

"Not really," I said, and he asked nothing more.

We walked on, and other soldiers started to appear, younger men with strong bodies, with mustaches and beards trimmed, or clean shaven, each of them stopping in his tracks to salute the brigadier. He spoke with them, his tone distant but pleasant, asking after their health, their families. But once, he frowned and rebuked a soldier about my age on the state of his boots. I watched the soldier's face crumple with terror, watched his hand tremble as he struggled to salute, and for the first time I really understood the absolute power the brigadier possessed over them.

"What?" he said, noticing that I was watching him.

"Nothing," I said

He laughed. "I know that 'nothing.' It means the exact opposite. Come on, spill it."

"What would happen," I asked, "if you found out that your soldiers had done something wrong? If they'd broken a rule?"

"Broken a rule?" He frowned, considering it a while. "Well, I suppose it would depend on the rule, but, in general, we don't look kindly on that sort of thing. Why do you ask?"

"No reason," I said, and he gave me a quick sideways glance.

"Quite the enigma, aren't you?" he murmured, and, for some reason, the words sent a quick, lightning flash of warmth up my spine.

We began walking back to the house, passing more soldiers, all of whom stopped in their tracks and greeted the brigadier with a salute. Merely walking beside him conferred a similar power on my person;

most soldiers did not even dare to look at me, some gazing straight ahead, others glancing away quickly, as if afraid of giving offense. I was still thinking about this when I realized the brigadier was looking at me.

"What?" I asked.

He cleared his throat. "Look, I wasn't totally honest with you earlier. When I told you about my wife, I mean. She's with her relatives in Coimbatore, that much is true, but she's not just visiting. We haven't lived together for over a year. She left me the day after our son went off to college. Ramchand is the only one around here who knows about it. Even my son doesn't realize. He still thinks the only reason his mother isn't living with me is because she doesn't like the winters here."

"Why are you telling me this?" I asked after a pause.

We had now arrived at the gate of his bungalow, but before the brigadier could answer, Ramchand came out. Ignoring me, he began to speak softly to the brigadier, who listened with his head tilted forward. I watched as the expression in his face was arrested, changing to concern, then to frustration and anger. He asked a question of Ramchand, who answered in a low voice. I stood off to the side, not trying particularly to overhear, but then I heard Ramchand speak the word *Kishtwar* and froze.

Before I could do anything, the brigadier himself approached me. "I'm so sorry," he said, still sounding urbane. "Ramchand tells me I'm needed at the office. I'll have to leave you on your own for a while, I'm afraid. Do you mind?"

"Is it Kishtwar?" I asked. "Did something happen?"

He raised his eyebrows.

"I overheard Ramchand mention it," I said quickly. "Please, could you tell me what's happening? I have friends in Kishtwar. I just want to know."

I could see him wavering on the edge of refusal. Then he sighed. "It's a bit of a mess, honestly," he said. "Kishtwar is under curfew, as you probably know, and it all seemed to be under control. But an hour ago, a few Muslims apparently decided it would be a good idea to attack the army camp out there. They tried to climb the walls, with nothing in their hands but stones and sticks. Naturally, they didn't get very far. Nobody was hurt, but one of the boys lost his grip and fell, hitting his head. We've got him in the hospital, but, rumors being what they are around here, all of Kishtwar thinks he's dead. People are out on the streets, and a few houses appear to be on fire." He glanced at me. "Which part of Kishtwar do your friends live in?"

"Near the mosque," I said. "The city center."

I thought of the hundreds of houses and shops that surrounded the mosque and marketplace, all of them packed tight. I thought of the shoe shop next door with its dozens of flammable cardboard boxes. I must have swayed on my feet, because the next thing I felt was the brigadier's warm hand on my back. "Steady there," I heard him say, and his voice sounded strange. Ramchand appeared to have been turned to stone, for all the reaction that he showed, and a second later the brigadier's hand floated away. He coughed. "I'll be back as soon as I can. I promise," he said. As if on cue, a dark car with tinted windows pulled up to the house and the brigadier got into the backseat. The car rolled away, leaving me feeling strangely bereft next to Ramchand, whose bland expression still had not changed.

"Lunch is ready," he told me and went back inside.

I sat numbly before the spread, unable to eat. Ramchand made no comment when I rose, having touched hardly anything, but he began to clear away the dishes. Not knowing what else to do, I went back to the brigadier's study and sat in his chair, noticing for the first time that the worn, cracked leather held the faint smell of the aftershave he used, something citrusy and bracing. I waited until the top of the hour and then I reached for the TV remote and switched on the news.

The newsreader's pink lips moved, talking about the recent spate of farmer suicides; talks between the governments of India and the United States over a civilian nuclear deal; the arrest of an incumbent MP for assaulting a rival candidate in an upcoming election; the final day's results from the Zimbabwe vs. England test series.

There was nothing about Kishtwar.

I switched to another news channel, and then another, but not one of the groomed and polished newsreaders barricaded behind their desks said a word about it. There were no images of screaming, angry crowds; no shots of policemen and soldiers advancing slowly shoulder to shoulder; no bodies sprawled in the street no blazing houses. It was as if it weren't happening at all. I felt a numbness, an unreality, creep slowly over my bones, coating them like oil. Finally, I simply turned the TV off, and then I just sat there, my hands folded in my lap.

A light came on, surprising me. I hadn't realized it had gone dark. It was Ramchand. The digital clock on the wall read *10:49 p.m.*

I started up from my chair. "Is the brigadier back?"

"He is still at the office. Is there anything you require?"

"No." I sank back down. Then I said, "Yes. Yes. The pool."

It stretched on forever, the unbroken surface a perfect, arctic blue. White lights anchored below the water gave it a still, tomblike quality. Beyond it was nothing but endless, dark trees, framed in the distance by mountains, and the night sky deepened its eerie, medical glow.

Ramchand left me at the entrance, after telling the single guard that I was the brigadier's guest and was to be given complete privacy. He did not say when he would be back. Alone, I pulled my T-shirt over my head and slipped out of my jeans, leaving them in a pile on the dew-wet grass. In only my underwear, I stepped to the edge of the concrete, watching the wavering black stripes that marked the swimming lanes.

Then I pushed off with my toes and shattered the perfect surface.

It was not water. It was something else, a material of this world and yet alien. It was sound turned fluid, wind turned liquid, nothingness made into a cool, physical substance, and I let myself fall through it, heavy as a corpse, willing myself never to come up. But my body wouldn't allow such a thing, of course. When I couldn't sink anymore, when my lungs threatened to split, I felt my limbs click to life like machines, felt them drive me up to air and to life, and it was only when the cold air blasted my face, only when I heard myself gasp and felt my chest expand, greedy, felt the sting of chlorine in my eyes, that the water became water again, ordinary and welcome, and I began to swim.

I had not swum in years, and the burn in my muscles began even before I'd finished a single lap, but I ignored it and pushed on. As I swam, I tried to keep thoughts at bay, tried to be nothing but a body, but it was useless; snatches of sound pressed on me, images and sensations crowding in. The clicking of cornstalks and the spaniel's bark. Sania's finger moving along a page, and Amina biting her lip. Aaqib's small hand in mine, and the heat that rose from the flank of the red-and-white cow. A white house built on a ridge, too pretty to be real. Bashir Ahmed's white stubble, and his hands folded on a pink blanket. The distant smell of smoke, and the glint of a rifle. The screeching of crows as they circled and circled, looking for something to eat.

The clouds shifted and the moon came out. I needed to stop; my lungs felt as though they would crack my chest open, my heart floating bloodily away from me, trailing veins and slivers of muscle and white fingers of fat. But I refused to stop. I swam, forcing my aching arms over my head, each stroke bringing another shot of memory: Riyaz holding out a piece of wood on his open palm. Aaqib hanging upside down from the peach tree, T-shirt fallen over his belly.

I swam faster.

Stalin saying, *Will you meet me again tomorrow?* The woman on the train offering me her phone. Abdul Latief changing channels late into the night. The click of Zoya's knitting needles.

My hand slammed against the concrete side of the pool, sending a searing pain up my arm. I scissored around, kicked, and set off again.

Mohammad Din saying, *You are like me.* Amina: *I think it's time for you to go home.*

A town on fire.

In the dark, the swimming pool was as broad as the ocean, rippling like a field of corn. My mother sat in the shade of an umbrella, ankles crossed in the sun. The pine tree swayed at the very end, tall, heavy with its dark, living fruit, the thieving intruders, snatchers of corn and chicks alike. They may have been frightened off for the moment, but they would not be kept away for long. They would delay, patient, clever, biding their time. Soon they would return to consume everything.

I stopped swimming. There was a figure standing at the other end of the pool.

Vapor billowed from the blue surface of the water, making it hard to see. For a second, I thought it was the security guard, spying on me, but from the way the figure stood, confident making no attempt to hide, I knew it was the brigadier. There was something bulky under his arm. He did not call out, did not wave. I could not see his eyes, but I knew he was watching me.

Something grim and purposeful took hold of me. I began swimming toward him. Each time I lifted my head, he was a little closer, another of his features revealed: his chin, the peak of his hair. I swam right up to the edge of the pool and stopped, my fingers pressed to the concrete.

He squatted down and offered his hand. I let him pull me out of the water.

Water slid in runnels down my stomach, my inner thighs, but the brigadier did not look down. His eyes were locked on my face. He handed me the rolled-up towel that was under his arm.

"Ramchand told me you forgot to take one," he said.

I wrapped myself in it, picked up my clothes, and we walked out of the building. The guard was nowhere in sight. The same black car was parked across the road, though without a driver. The brigadier slid behind the wheel. I got in next to him. The interior was spotless and smelled of incense.

He drove very slowly through the sleeping cantonment, hands on the wheel at ten and two, like a learner. He did not look away from the road and he did not speak to me. He had the air-conditioning on but switched it off when he heard my teeth chatter.

He stopped the car in front of the bungalow and we got out. We walked up the front path and into the house. Ramchand was in the living room, untying the drapes, and his eyes followed us as we went past him, past the study, and to the brigadier's bedroom door. He was very close behind me, and I felt his hand brush my towel-wrapped hip as he reached past me to turn the handle.

The brigadier's bedroom was surprisingly plain, given the rest of the house. A simple bed with gray sheets, a Godrej almirah instead of a cupboard, a chair and dressing table with a comb and a pair of nail clippers. Cotton curtains at the window. No clothes in sight, no disorder.

I felt him come up behind me. He did not put his arms about my body, did not touch me, just stood there, his breath at my ear, his chest, with all those medals, an inch away from my back. I realized he was waiting for me to begin, to indicate what I wanted.

I turned to face him. His expression was half-wry, half-suspicious, as if he didn't quite trust that this wasn't somehow a trick. I opened my mouth to speak, but the effort required was too great, so I simply let the towel fall. I unhooked my soaking bra and peeled off my underwear.

Then I slid beneath the sheets, my skin tightening where it came into contact with the clean fabric.

He'd watched all this with close attention, and now he began to undress. First, the medals, which he laid out in a neat row on the dressing table next to the comb and the nail clippers. Then his shoes and socks, which he placed by the chair. Then his belt, which he looped over the handle of the almirah. Next, his shirt and pants, folded and placed on the chair. Standing in only his white vest and briefs, he looked down at me, then he pulled them off. His stomach was just starting to go slack, but there was still the good definition of muscle. His nipples were very light, and by contrast the hair on his chest very dark, though some of it was flecked with white. He smiled.

I moved aside, and then there was no more thought, for he was there, under the sheets, the impossible fact of another human body, with its warmth and odor and breath and movement. The foreignness, the utter otherness, of him. As if I had suddenly been struck blind, it took me a moment to identify whatever I touched. *A mouth,* I thought with pained wonder. *A tongue. A thigh. A foot. Fingers. A knee. A chest.* Feature by feature, I constructed him, I saw that his eyes were open, and in them was the same amusement, as if he knew better than I did why I was here. It irritated me, so I plunged, taking him into my mouth. It worked, his breath snagged. He lightly touched the top of my head with his fingers, a gesture both astonished and cautionary.

But I shook off his hand and went on. He groaned but didn't touch my head again. I closed my eyes to shut out everything else—where I was, where I had been, who I had known. Locked into that deadly rhythm, I felt the rest fall away, felt myself shrinking, shrinking so that I encompassed only one thought, or felt the thought expand to occupy me, felt it multiply itself, so that my mind became a place of mirrors, all surfaces reflecting back to me a single lonely idea: *This is all I am.*

When I came up again, his eyes had changed. All the irony had been shaken out of them. He looked apprehensive, and it caused me a sliver of pleasure. I moved onto my back and guided him so that he was over me. He hovered for a second, searching my face, but I closed my eyes. Then I felt him bring himself low, his forearms resting on either side of my head. I pulled my knees back, felt the pressure of his body, its whole weight, and then, without any warning, we were inside a different rhythm, fast and greedy, trying to grab, it seemed, something that was fleeting.

I sneaked a glance at his face. His eyes were closed now, so I watched. His jaw was slack, but the muscles of his neck were strained and there was a frown on his face that could have been mistaken for one of displeasure. Then his eyes flew open, but there was no recognition in them, it was pure reaction, the need to make some extravagant bodily gesture, and his pace quickened. I felt his body heave hard against mine, go still, then shudder. He did not let out any sort of cry. For another second, he hovered over me; then he carefully let himself down at my side and lay on his back.

Light from a passing car floated across the curtains. I lay still for a moment, then reached for the brigadier's thick hand and placed it between my legs. His eyes, which had been scaly and clouded, snapped back to attention, and his hand followed every stroke, matching my pressure. I lifted my hand away and he continued, propped on his elbow, absorbed in his task. I closed my eyes and focused on the dark churning that had begun, low in my stomach, its tendrils spreading to the rest of my body, down my legs and up across my back, sending out thick, warm ropes that wrapped themselves around every organ, lifting me imperceptibly, inch by inch, above myself. And then an immense surge upward, then a pause, pure silence at the highest point above the black.

Then I was falling, pleasure sparking and shooting into every corner of my body. The black surface rose far above my head. The tendrils loosened their grip and withdrew. The churning diminished, then died, leaving just the occasional pulse, a ripple in the dark.

Then I began to shake. My body was thrashing and I could not stop it.

"What?" I heard the brigadier say. "What happened?"

But the shaking wouldn't stop. I gripped the sheets in both fists until I could control it. The brigadier had his arm around me. He stroked my hair, then my back, then my hair again.

"Please," he murmured. "Whatever the problem is, I wish you'd tell me. I'll help you, I promise. You just have to tell me."

Footsteps passed outside the door. I imagined Ramchand moving about outside, his ears trained not to hear what he could not fail to hear, his mind trained not to know what he knew perfectly well. Loyal, I thought. He's loyal.

I pushed the sheets off and stood, then walked over to the window. Pulling the curtain back an inch, I looked outside. The street was empty, utterly quiet. Slowly, very slowly, the trembling subsided.

Then, from nowhere, a young man appeared. He had his chin thrown up and a smile on his face. His steps were decisive, though not hurried, and I watched as he reached the end of the street and was lost to sight.

"Shalini," the brigadier said softly.

I turned from the window. He was sitting up in bed, the sheets gathered around his waist, folded and rumpled. There was something sad in the way he watched me.

"I saw something," I said.

He smiled. "Just as long as nobody saw you."

"No," I said. "When I was in the village. I saw something there."

"What do you mean?" he asked.

Instead of answering, I asked, "What happened in Kishtwar tonight?"

"Oh, not much in the end," the brigadier answered. "People broke curfew, paraded around for a while, made a little noise, threw a few stones, but then they decided it was better to go back home. It's all under control. That mosque neighborhood, where your friends live, is fine, by the way. I've asked my men to keep an eye on that area for the next few days, just in case."

That surprised me. "Thank you," I said.

He gave me a little bow and a sad smile. "As I keep saying, I'd like to help you, if only you'll tell me what's wrong."

I stared at him. I thought of the way soldiers looked at him, the fear evident in their eyes. Then, suddenly, I made a decision.

"In the village," I said. "I saw a boy. He was with your soldiers. They'd arrested him or abducted him or something. I don't exactly know. But they'd taken him away from his home."

The brigadier remained silent for several seconds. Then he said, "A boy?"

I nodded. "Yes. According to them, he hid in a tree and threw shit at them. But there was something wrong with him, the boy. Mentally, I mean. I don't think he meant to do it." I paused. "It was the same soldiers you sent to get me."

For a long time, he just looked at me. Then he said, his voice all of a sudden brusque and professional, "Tell me exactly what happened."

"I just told you."

"You saw him throw shit at them?"

"No."

"But you did see this child with my soldiers."

I nodded.

"Was he hurt? The boy?"

"No," I said. "He seemed all right."

The brigadier nodded. "And they told you about him? About the shit and the rest of it?"

"Well—" I hesitated. "They didn't tell me exactly."

He looked up. "Then how do you know?"

"I overheard them talking about it to someone else."

"Overheard them?" The brigadier frowned.

"Yes. They were talking about it. I was close by and I heard."

"Did you say anything to them about it?"

"No."

"Why not?"

"I—" I broke off. "Look, you said you'd help if I told you."

The brigadier looked at me thoughtfully, then he slid out from under the sheets and began to dress. Just as methodically as he'd removed his clothes, he began to put them on. Briefs and vest. Pants. Shirt. Belt, socks, shoes. And, last of all, his medals. Fully clothed, he looked at me again.

"I will help you," he said, "but I still think there's something you aren't telling me. Something you're holding back."

And then I couldn't stand it anymore. I thought of all the secrets I had carried as far back into my childhood as I could remember. I felt them pile one on top of another, suffocating me.

I was so tired.

"Shalini," the brigadier murmured.

"I was hiding," I blurted out. "I was with someone. A friend of mine. We were—we were on a walk, and we saw your soldiers. They heard us, and my friend told me to hide. He was the one they told about the child. But I was right there, and I heard every word, I swear to you."

The brigadier was listening intently. "You were with a friend," he murmured. "A man?"

I nodded. "Yes. And your soldiers, they—" I broke off, looking down, breathing hard.

"Yes?" he prompted me.

"They hit him," I said. "They kicked him. I thought they were going to kill him."

"Who? The boy?"

"No. My friend. They beat him for no reason at all." My voice dropped to a whisper. "They broke his ankle, I think. He could barely walk."

The brigadier's lips were pressed tight. "Is your friend all right?" he asked. "Has he seen a doctor? Is he getting treatment?"

"Yes, I think so."

"Good." The brigadier ran his hand over his face. Then he turned to leave the room.

"Wait!" I cried. "Where are you going? Are you going to arrest those soldiers?"

He turned. "I promised that I would do something," he said quietly. "And I will."

He walked to the door. "Ramchand will have dinner ready soon. I hope you'll forgive me if I don't join you. It's been a devil of a day, and I'm a bit tired."

He reached for the door handle then stopped.

"Oh, one more thing," he said. "Your friend, the one with whom you were on that . . . walk. I need to make sure that he's all right. What's his name?"

I hesitated. Then I said, "Riyaz. Riyaz Ahmed Batt."

It was the first time I'd spoken his whole name aloud.

The brigadier nodded. "You really care for this person, don't you?"

"I do," I said softly, but he was already leaving. Left by myself, I realized that I was still naked. I crossed the room and picked up my clothes. I wrapped the towel around myself and slipped out into the corridor. The brigadier was in his study with the door closed, light seeping from underneath it. I went to the kitchen and found Ramchand with the back door open. He was smoking, looking out into the small yard behind the brigadier's house.

"Ramchand," I said. "Would it be possible for me to get a car to Jammu tomorrow?"

He nodded without turning to look at me.

I went back to my room and lay on the bed, staring up at the swords and the shield. I noticed that the shield was damaged, a deep dent over the place where the heart would have been.

VI

38

The baggage carousel at the airport jerked by like a broken movie reel. I stood before it for a long time, even though I knew it would bring me nothing. A stained red gym bag trundled past, its zipper snapped off. All around me, people crowded in, pressing up against the cracked conveyor belt, craning their necks to better see their approaching luggage. When I could no longer bear their jostling, I turned and walked out of the glass doors of the airport and into the Bangalore night.

It took me almost no time to spot my father. It wasn't just the simple elegance of his white shirt with the sleeves rolled up to the elbow, or his gleaming suede shoes, that made him stand out. It was his way of resting his elbow on the metal guardrail, hands clasped lightly. He was set apart by this quietness, marked by it, and the people around him seemed to recognize it, for they granted him a hair's breadth of distance, a tiny bubble of calm in the crowd.

Then he glanced up. For a second our eyes met without recognition, and we saw each other, I think, not as father and daughter, linked inevitably by blood and by history, but as strangers whose ties to each other were accidental a matter of chance. Then the second passed, and he was moving, he was gesturing toward the gap in the guardrail, I was walking toward him, and then he was hugging me, the soft material of his shirt rubbing against my cheek, his smell unchanged, tea and aftershave and shoe polish, and his hands, which were my own hands, circling me, holding me close.

Just as he and my mother had done so many years ago in the train station, he kept his arm tight around me as we walked to the car, as if to protect me from the world, or, it suddenly occurred to me, to keep me from disappearing into it again. He paid the parking fee to a woman in a beige uniform, and then we were out on the road, heading home. The lights from the streetlamps draped themselves like gauzy scarves across our legs, across my father's hands on the steering wheel, across the side of his face that I could see.

Now, finally, he turned.

"I would have understood, you know," he said in a whisper. "Why you went. I would have understood why you felt you had to go. You could have told me. But never mind. I'm not angry. I'm not angry, because you came back." He lifted one hand from the steering wheel and gripped mine. "You went away, but you came back."

Never had I heard him speak in this way. All the lecturing, the hectoring, all the logic, was gone. He was nearly praying.

I did not leave the house for days. I stayed in my room, either sleeping or lying awake in bed, waiting for my father to come home from the factory. We ate dinner together. We sat in the living room, while he chose a record to play. We listened to the music. We did not talk about where I had been. Neither of us was ready to talk about it.

When Stella let herself in on that first morning after my return, I impulsively threw my arms around her. She submitted to my embrace for a grudging second, then stepped back.

"How are your children?" I asked.

She lifted a perfect eyebrow, as though she found the question preposterous. "They are the best children a mother could have."

* * *

My father had, in my absence, sold our old couch, and replaced it with a divan, scattered with half a dozen brightly colored pillows and bolsters. He told me he'd seen the divan in a store, arranged just like this, and had simply bought the whole thing. It was no longer the room in which my mother had slept, in which Bashir Ahmed had told his stories, the room of afternoon shadows. To my own surprise, I found I had no regrets.

One evening, I walked into my bedroom to find a brand-new cell phone, the latest model—still in its box and sealed hermetically in plastic—which my father had bought and left there for me.

Gradually, he and I began to talk. I told him about bathing in the waterfall, about learning to walk on mountain paths, about milking the cow every morning—which made him smile. I told him about the soft-eared mules that lugged up all the necessities of life, bags of rice and flour, sacks of cement. I described the chickens scrabbling greedily for grain, the fields of swaying corn, how I'd gone on a walk and gotten lost. Though I did not do it intentionally, the stories I told him were ones leached of trouble and secrets, the innocuous tales of a naïve, bumbling traveler. I wanted him to laugh, wanted to ease my transition back into this life, wanted him to forgive me, and so I reduced the place I'd loved—the place of hard rock and dry air, the place of dead crows and houses that clung so fiercely to the mountain—to a quaint, provincial backdrop, and I hated the ease with which I did it. But how could I explain all the rest, the things that had mattered? How could I tell him about what it had been like to walk away with Amina watching me? To watch Riyaz hobble through the night, his face a scribble of pain, both from his broken ankle and from the growing comprehension that he would spend the rest of his life in the village, going up and down the mountain with his mules until he died? And what about all the rest—Mohammad Din and his terrible crime, Bashir Ahmed in his self-imposed exile, the nighttime robbers, Kishtwar on fire, Sania with her head bent over a book, Aaqib falling asleep against my arm, the soldiers who stomped through the lives of so many? How could I explain to my father what I myself had no words for? How could I tell him about the person I'd discovered myself to be up there?

Only once did we come close to speaking the truth. My father was sitting on the divan, looking lost amongst the piles of bright cushions, a drink in his hand.

"So," he said casually. "Did you finally find him?"

I looked up. "Who?"

"You know who. Our old Kashmiri friend. Did you find him?"

I hesitated before replying, "I found his family. They're the ones I stayed with."

"Oh," my father said, and I could not tell if he was disappointed or relieved by my answer. "Right. He was married. I'd forgotten."

I waited, but there was no more forthcoming. I probably would have admitted the truth if he'd pressed me, but he didn't. Ours has always been a story of cowardice, of things left unsaid, and neither my father nor I made any reference to Bashir Ahmed again.

On a Sunday evening, a couple of weeks after I came home, my father suggested we go to one of his favorite restaurants for dinner. It was the first time I'd left the house, since my return. We climbed the stairs and were seated by a waiter, who greeted my father by name, and then we went through the rituals. Rum for him, whiskey for me. We ordered. We talked. About the unseasonably hot weather, about the traffic, which was worse every day, or so it seemed. He told me he was in the process of buying four acres of land for a second factory outside the city. Then he cleared his throat.

"Just before you left," he said, "you remember what I told you? About getting married?"

I nodded.

"I think I may have found someone."

Her name was Jaya. She was a doctor, divorced, no children, living in the U.S. Now she was thinking about returning. They'd spoken many times over the phone, exchanged several emails, and she was planning a trip to Bangalore in a few weeks. Nothing was settled, he was quick to assure me, and even if they liked each other, nothing would happen for a long time.

I was quiet after he'd told me. Then I asked, "Do you have a photo of her?"

He laughed, sounding relieved that my reaction was so mild. "A photo? Do I look like a teenager to you? I don't carry one with me." Then his face became serious, and he leaned in toward me. "Are you sure you don't mind?"

"Why would I mind?"

"Because of Amma," he said simply. "You were always her protector. Like a little bulldog."

"Well," I said, looking away, "I didn't do a very good job, did I?"

"It *wasn't* your job, Shalini. If it was anyone's, it was mine."

And then he told me about the doctors. It was why he'd insisted I attend college away from Bangalore, so that I wouldn't find out she'd been seeking treatment. I sat very still, and then I asked, "Why didn't you tell me before?"

He shrugged. "She didn't want me to." Then, unexpectedly, a smile appeared on his lips. "There was one fellow, supposedly this world-famous psychiatrist. I don't know what happened, what he said to her exactly; I was waiting outside. She was in there for barely a minute and then she opened the door and came storming out. In the loudest voice you could possibly imagine, she told him, 'You are the stupidest man I've met. Also the ugliest. I could forgive either fault on its own, but the two together are a bit too much for me.' You should have seen the faces of the people there, Shalini."

I stared at him for a stunned second then burst out laughing. He glanced around guiltily, then started to laugh too. We did not lower our voices, but laughed the way my mother would have. After that, for some reason, it was easier to look at each other.

The waiter brought our bill, and my father laid down his credit card.

"Oh, by the way," he said, taking another card out of his wallet. "I almost forgot about this. Your friend, the photographer, dropped it off."

It took me a moment. "Hari?"

"Right." He laid the card down on the table, and I picked it up. It was an invitation to an exhibit of Hari's photographs at the Alliance Française. The date was the coming Friday.

"I told him you were out of town, but he said I should give it to you anyway," my father said. "He seemed like a nice enough chap. Maybe you should go."

"I don't know." I pressed the corner of the card into my thumb. "We didn't exactly part on the best of terms."

"The only way you'll be able to change that is if you go."

"'Without action, there is only waiting for death,'" I said with a smile.

"I said that? How brilliant of me," he murmured.

That night, I took the card up to my room and set it on the table beside the wooden animal.

The week passed, and then on Friday, as I was flipping through channels in the late afternoon, I suddenly sat up, because there, on the screen, was Kishtwar. First, I saw a sweeping shot of the Chowgan, eerily emptied of its picnickers and cricketers and looking more like a wasteland than anything else. This was followed by a shot of various streets, a few of which I recognized, including the intersection with the pharmacy where I'd first talked to Stalin. Since my return, I'd tried to follow the news about Kishtwar, reading about how the curfew was still in place, but how "normalcy" had returned to the area, as though normalcy were a child that had wandered away and briefly gotten lost. Most of what I'd found had been on the internet; this was the first time I'd seen it covered on TV. The army, the reporter was saying, had lifted the curfew; phone and internet service had been restored. I thought of the brigadier sitting in his living room, satisfied with his work, Ramchand hovering, as usual, at his elbow.

I sat up, relief coursing through me. Suddenly it occurred to me how I could get in touch with Zoya. *I asked Riyaz to contact your people in Kishtwar,* Amina had told me. *They called your father.* With any luck, the call would be recorded on our landline. I picked it up and scrolled through the log of received calls. And there it was, a number with an area code I knew now to be from Jammu and Kashmir. I hastily dialed it on my new cell phone, my heart beating painfully fast in anticipation. Zoya picked up on the second ring. "Hello?"

"Hello!" I hated how forced I sounded. "Hello, it's me, Shalini."

There was a long pause. Then Zoya said, "Hello."

"I'm in Bangalore now, and I just wanted to call and see how you are. How things are, I mean. In Kishtwar. I was just watching the news, and they said that everything is all right. I mean, the curfew—" I broke off my babbling. "Zoya?" I said. "Hello? Are you there?"

"Yes," she replied evenly. "I am here."

"Are things all right over there?"

"Yes," she said. "Things are fine."

I couldn't understand the coldness, the formality, in her voice. Was she annoyed that I had not kept in touch with them after I left Kishtwar? But she knew as well as I did that I had no phone.

"Is something wrong?" I asked.

Instead of a reply, there was a series of muffled noises, the sound, I realized, of the receiver exchanging hands.

"This is Latief" I heard Abdul Latief say after a moment.

"It's so nice to talk to you again!" I cried. "How have you been?"

"Fine, thank you." Again, I noticed the formality in his tone. "I'm sorry, Zoya had to go. Saleem is here with us, and his family also. Can we call you later? This is your number?"

"Yes," I said. "This is my number. Please call anytime. Anytime."

Without another word, he hung up. I stood there, staring at the sleek instrument in my hand, uneasiness at the back of my mind. Don't be silly, I scolded myself. You just caught them at a bad time. They would call back and be themselves again.

I waited all evening, but the call didn't come. Finally, driven to distraction, I grabbed the invitation to Hari's exhibit off my bedside table, sent a message to my father's phone to tell him where I was going, and jumped into my car. My father was right, I thought. Hari had been kind enough to invite me to his exhibit after everything. The least I could do was show up. To fix what little I could. To act.

The Alliance Française was a white building set amongst tall trees in an old and stately part of Bangalore. I parked and climbed a set of wide red steps through the door and into a square courtyard, around which Hari's photographs had been arranged in white frames. People milled around, and a DJ, a pretty young woman with dreadlocks, played music in a corner. I could not spot Hari, so I walked slowly around, looking at the photographs. They were all ones I recognized; I'd stood outside the frame for some of them, the homeless man with the crushed plastic bottles for sandals, the children with their bloated bellies and sandy hair, the toothless old woman beside her dusty vegetables on the pavement. I still could not think of them as good photographs, prettily composed as they were, but I finally saw in them something of Hari's huge and well-meaning heart, which, admittedly, asked none of the difficult questions, but which had once opened itself to me for the same reason.

I was about to turn and look for Hari again when I stopped, because I was looking at a photograph of myself. I knew it was me, even though the figure appeared only in silhouette. The photo was taken from below, and showed me sitting on the ledge with the water tank on Hari's terrace, the sky behind me tangled with clouds. The colors were vivid: the violent blue, the whipped-up white, and my silhouette so black, leaning so far forward any viewer would think I wished to fall. My eyes moved to the white card pasted to the wall beside it. *Safety*, the card read.

"Do you like it?" a voice said behind me, and I turned. It was Hari. He wore a kaffiyeh around his neck, the fringed black-and-white tassels drooping over his *Free Tibet* T-shirt.

"I like it very much," I said. "I had no idea you took it."

"Well, you weren't exactly paying attention to much back then." He came up to stand beside me. "So you're back. Your dad said you had gone on a trip."

"I had," I said. "I only got back recently."

"I was worried, you know. When you disappeared. I couldn't even reach your phone. I tried calling you probably fifty times."

"I'm sorry, Hari. I really am. It was a terrible thing to do."

He didn't reply. His eyes were following the pretty young DJ, who had now left her station and was crossing the room, approaching us.

"Congratulations on the show," I said. "It's very exciting."

"Thanks," he said absently. "So, if I can ask, where'd you go on your mysterious trip?"

"To Kashmir," I said.

He raised an eyebrow. "Kashmir? Were you living on a houseboat?"

"Not exactly."

"I went to Kashmir once when I was a kid. My parents decided one winter they wanted to ski. They were nostalgic for Europe, I guess. All

I remember was this guy at the hotel where we stayed. He was a huge fellow with a beard. He terrified me. Then, of course, the place went to shit, and we never went back."

The dreadlocked DJ was almost upon us, and I saw Hari's face change, saw a light come into it, and I realized that my father had been wrong. There would be no reconciliation with Hari. Here too I had done too much damage.

"Well," Hari said, shrugging, "welcome back, I guess. And enjoy the show."

He walked away toward the DJ, and together they approached a group and began talking. I saw her arm, flashing with a dozen bracelets and bangles, slip around his waist.

I turned away, not knowing what I felt, and at the same moment, my cell phone began to vibrate in my pocket. I drew it out, and my heart leapt at the number. I hurried out into the evening air, taking deep breaths to calm myself. Then I picked up and said, "Hello?"

"Hello," said a soft, musical voice on the other end. "This is Saleem."

I stopped at the top of the red steps. Why was it Saleem who was calling? Where was Zoya?

"Hello," I said. "How are you?"

"Fine, alhamdulillah." And I heard in his voice, too, the new, stiff tone, the forced politeness not so different from Hari's. And suddenly I was afraid.

"Are you with Zoya Aunty? Is she okay?"

"Yes, I am at their house. They are both fine."

"I'm glad. I thought—"

He cleared his throat. "They have asked me," he said, as if reading an official declaration, "to request you not to contact them again."

I sat on the step with a thud, the world going briefly dark around me. "What did you say?"

"I am sorry," he said. "I am simply conveying their request."

"But *why?*" I whispered.

Instead of answering, Saleem asked, "Tell me, do you know someone called Brigadier Sameer Reddy?"

My head came up so fast that a pain shot through the back of my neck. "What?"

"You know this name?"

"Yes, he—" I stopped. "Why? Did something happen?"

More silence. Then Saleem sighed. "Last Friday," he said, "this Brigadier Reddy came with some of his soldiers to the village where you stayed. They came to the home of Riyaz Batt."

I could have screamed. "Please," I begged. "What are you saying? What soldiers?"

But he ignored me. "They made the whole family come into one room. Then this Brigadier Reddy said he'd got a complaint about Riyaz, and they took him away."

"*What* complaint?" I whispered.

"It was all nonsense. Something about a little boy. I couldn't understand it all. They arrested him on the spot. His family has not seen him in a week."

"No!" I screamed it so loudly that the buzz of talk from inside the building was momentarily silenced. "You're lying!"

Saleem was unmoved. "Why would I lie to you about something like that?"

"Where did they take him?" I asked desperately.

A bitter note entered his voice. "If we knew that, do you think we would not go straight there and find him?"

"But you *must* know something," I begged. "You must know—"

"Enough!" Saleem roared. "How can it be that you *still* don't understand? Even after everything Zoya showed you, after you found out about Ishfaaq, how can you *still* be surprised? They can do *anything.* They can take him *anywhere.* He is *gone.*"

Saleem paused, as though collecting himself. Then he continued, "His wife is in Kishtwar to file a case for him. Zoya is helping her. Inshallah, they will be able to locate him."

"Amina? She's there? In Kishtwar?" I whispered.

"Yes," he said. "She is here. She's staying in Zoya's house."

And just like that, I saw Amina sitting with Zoya in the hall, Mohammad Latief next to them, the blue thermos of tea laid out on the ground, along with three teacups. Amina, with her pink cardigan, toying with her scarf. Zoya leaning over to command her to eat; Amina giving her a wan smile. I found I could not breathe, and it was with difficulty I brought myself back to Saleem.

"It is my fault," Saleem was saying. The anger had gone, and he sounded merely sad. "I was the one who suggested you visit their village. If I had not done that, none of this would have happened. That poor man would be at home. So in a way it is all my fault."

"Please," I said. "Please, just let me speak to someone. Let me speak to Zoya . . . or Amina . . . please . . . just for a minute . . ."

He sighed. "I'm afraid it is not possible."

"But I have to *do* something!"

"*We* are doing something," he said coldly. "You have done enough. Now I must go."

The call went dead against my ear.

Behind me, the people at Hari's show were still milling around. Their soft murmurs reached me from what seemed like another universe. I heard the tinkling of music, then the abrupt sound of someone shattering a glass. There was a shocked silence, followed by a gale of laughter.

I tried Zoya's number again, but it simply rang and rang and rang.

At home, my father was bent over his laptop at the dining table, tapping the keys with his index fingers. It was an email, and I wondered dully if it was to the woman, Jaya. How much had he told her about me during my absence? Did she know that I'd run away? Did she know that I was back?

When I walked in he stopped typing and took off his glasses.

"How was it?" he asked, smiling.

"Wonderful," I lied. "Appa, can I ask you something? Do you have the brigadier's number?"

"Sameer? Of course I do, but why? Is there a problem?"

I saw the worry in his face and assumed a cheerful tone. "No, not at all. Actually, I just wanted to thank him. For his hospitality."

My father face cleared. "That's a lovely idea I'm glad you thought of it." He reached for his phone and scrolled through it. "Here," he said. "Use mine."

"Thanks, Appa," I said, and then I impulsively kissed the top of his head.

He blinked. "What was that for?"

"No reason," I said. I went upstairs, closed the door to my room, and locked it. I sat on the edge of the bed and called the number. It rang several times, then I heard Ramchand's soft voice saying, "Hello."

"I want to speak to him," I said through clenched teeth.

"Sorry, who is speaking?"

"Ramchand, you know who this is. Give the phone to the brigadier."

"I'm sorry, brigadier sahib is busy."

"Give it to him!" I screamed, only to hear my father's anxious voice from downstairs. "Everything okay?" he called up.

"Everything's fine," I called back. Then I dropped my voice to a whisper. "Ramchand give him the goddamn phone, otherwise I swear I'll track down his wife and son wherever the fuck they are and tell them everything."

There was a clink, and I thought he'd hung up; then I realized he had only placed the phone on the silver tray. After ten seconds or so, during which my palms began to sweat, I heard the brigadier's languorous, "Good evening, Reddy speaking."

"You're finished," I hissed. "Your fucking career is over. You fucking asshole."

"Goodness," he said, "that's certainly an interesting way to start a conversation."

"You lied to me. You said you would arrest those soldiers. You fucking lied!"

"On the contrary," he said, "all I promised was that I would do something, and I did. The boy you saw, you'll be happy to know, is back at home with his family."

"And what about Riyaz?"

"Riyaz? Oh, yes. Your friend. Well, he hadn't done much harm to the boy, thank goodness."

"He did *nothing* to him! It was your soldiers!"

"I beg your pardon," he said, "but the boy tells it very differently."

I thought of the boy's eyes as I had glimpsed them that night, the blankness, the utter absence of thought. What had they done to the poor child to extract such a confession? They probably hadn't needed to do much.

"I know what you're thinking," the brigadier said, "but I assure you, the boy was very forthcoming in his testimony. He seemed quite happy to talk. And when my chaps searched your friend's house, they found a weapon. That was, as they say, the clinching evidence."

"A weapon?"

"A gun," he said pleasantly.

"*That*?" I could hardly get the words out. "That's for *crows!*"

"For crows? How interesting. I'll have to write that one down. Anyway, be that as it may, my chaps know a threat when they see one. I'm afraid we had no choice but to arrest him."

"You asshole." It was all I could manage. "You asshole."

"As you keep saying."

"I'll go to the media," I said suddenly. "I'll go to the newspapers."

A beat too late, I realized I had said precisely the thing he had been waiting for. The mask of urbanity slipped away, his tone changed, turned icy. "Be my guest, Shalini," he said. "But do you mind if I give you some advice about talking to the press? Make sure you enunciate, because they're not very smart, those journalist bobbies. They tend to get excited and mix things up. They'll want to know about how you ended up with those Kashmiri villagers, who, I might mention, have a long and colorful history of militancy. You'll have to explain your relationship to your friend—what was his name? Riyaz? Late night walks, hiding in the corn, and him with a wife and child . . . they'll love that." His drawl became exaggerated. "And they'll want to know all about you, too, of course, and about your family. Which means, sadly, you'll have to answer questions about your mother and how she died. Can of insect repellent, yes? Wasn't that what I remembered hearing? Nasty business. Oh, and don't forget your father. I'm sure he'd be only *too* delighted to cooperate with the press. He won't mind a dozen cameras flashing in his face when he goes out to get the newspaper, reporters shouting questions about his daughter's links to Kashmiri terrorists. In fact, he'd probably enjoy it a great deal, wouldn't you think?"

He paused, perhaps to let me speak, but I had nothing to say. I was thinking of my father at the table downstairs, his fingers tapping away at the keys, his ear tuned for any sound of distress from upstairs, from me.

"You know," said the brigadier, "it has to be said that your behavior in this whole matter hasn't been exactly aboveboard either. Running away from home without telling anyone, landing up in some godforsaken village in the middle of nowhere. Not the actions of an innocent. But then"—and here he laughed nastily—"one could hardly accuse you of being an innocent, could one?"

I stared at the wooden animal on my bedside table.

"It would seem I've lost you," said the brigadier pleasantly. "What a shame."

For the third time that evening, a call went dead against my ear.

39

I AM THIRTY YEARS old and that is nothing. The world has changed every instant I've been alive. It has been six years since I went looking for Bashir Ahmed, six years since I returned to the city where I was born, a city grown and mutated beyond all recognition, and where I still live. Living, which, in my case, means the work that I do, the few friends that I've made, the weekly dinners I eat across from my father, and all the empty hours that fall in between.

I have thought every day about the people I left in the mountains. I have thought of Riyaz. I have wondered if Zoya helped Amina to find him and what was done to him in the meantime. I have thought about Bashir Ahmed in his room, and about Riyaz's mother, who never trusted me. I've thought about Aaqib and what he will come to think of me in the future, or if he will even remember the time when a woman from Bangalore lived in his house. I have thought about Mohammad Din, who, like me, must live every day with the knowledge of what he has done.

I have thought about them all. I have not tried to do more.

For six years, I have given myself one reason or another for not speaking, for not acting. Most of the reasons in one way or another had to do with sparing my father, but all of them are, in truth, intended to spare myself. Even two summers ago, when a fifteen-year-old boy was shot by the army in Srinagar while coming home from school, and I watched hundreds of enraged men and women spill out onto the streets, risking their lives, I managed to say nothing. But it is enough now. I am aware that I am taking no risks by recounting any of this, that, for people like me, safe and protected, even the greatest risk is, ultimately, an indulgence. I am aware of the likely futility of all that I have told here, and, I am aware, too, of the thousand ways I have tried to excuse myself in the telling of it. All the same, whatever the flaws of this story or confession or whatever it has turned out to be, let it stand.

Six years ago, a few months after that final, awful phone call with the brigadier, I drove myself to the agency. Ritu got up from her desk and hugged me with unfeigned warmth. "Jesus," she said, "look at you. You've lost so much weight. I'm jealous."

"I'd like to come back," I said. "To work."

Her face clouded over "We've got a full staff," she began, but seeing my expression, she quickly added, "but maybe I could find something for you. We couldn't hire you full time, so it would be project-to-project. I realize that's probably not what you . . ."

"That sounds perfect," I said firmly. "Thank you."

And that was how I came to spend the following weeks driving around in my car, checking the pollution levels within a ten-kilometer radius of every school in the city, using a paper map and an outdated handheld meter that beeped stridently before it gave a reading. After that, Ritu found other jobs for me, scraps of work that paid almost nothing, but provided me with a sense of purpose and, strangely enough, protection, for which I was grateful. The work I did for her was conscientious and careful, and, after two years, she took me back full time.

And it was around then that I told my father I wanted to move out of our house and find my own flat. He began to cry but kept saying, "No, I'm happy, I'm happy, I am."

Jaya, the woman my father had been corresponding with, arrived in Bangalore soon after my return. She stayed a week at the Oberoi and she and my father went out to dinner three times. I met her, as well. She was short and no-nonsense, wore glasses and had a big laugh and I liked her right away. At the end of the week, she flew back to San Jose, both she and my father promising to correspond further before making any decisions.

A few days later, she wrote to say that she had given it a lot of thought, and while she had truly liked my father, she had decided to remain in the U.S. She could not leave her practice, she said, the patients with whom she'd built relationships over decades. My father was disappointed, but not, I think, devastated. Some part of him, I suspected, was probably even relieved, for he never again talked about remarrying. He and Jaya continue to correspond, writing long emails back and forth, in which they discuss everything about their lives. These days, in conversation, he refers to her with affection as "my wise doctor friend."

He had a minor heart attack last month. "Not even a tickle," he kept insisting, but I spent five nights with him in St. John's after his bypass surgery, watching his face as he slept, then watching the crucifix on the wall, smiling to myself at the knowledge—no, the certainty—that if my mother had been there, she would have stood up and put it in a drawer.

When they rolled him out of the ICU and into his private room, my father spent hours holding my hand. My father, who, in a few short years had grown older, his features softer, his body losing its definition. He'd fallen asleep like that, and when he woke up, his face betrayed terror until he saw my face, and then he smiled, still under the influence of the anesthesia.

"Thank you, sweetheart," he mumbled.

As if I was the one who saved him.

* * *

I saw him last night for our usual Sunday dinner, a ritual that, I think, gives us both more comfort than we are willing to admit to each other. We had talked about nothing all evening, and then I drove him back home. He went inside, closing the door, leaving me standing on the mat outside.

Instead of walking back to my car, I stayed there a moment in the dark.

I could hear him walking around inside. I imagined him going, before anything else, to his LPs, greeting them like old friends, running his fingers over their well-worn spines. I imagined him taking his time, looking for the right one, the one that would carry within it whatever he was feeling tonight. Soon, I knew, he would find it. Soon he would slide it from its cardboard sleeve, place it on the turntable, and lower the waiting needle.

About the Author

Madhuri Vijay was born and raised in Bangalore. She is the recipient of a Pushcart Prize, and her writing has appeared in *Best American Non-Required Reading*, *Narrative Magazine*, and *Elle* India, among other publications. *The Far Field* is her first book.